Praise for the ...vels

LINDA ROBERTSON

Wicked Circle

"Plenty of layers for readers to slice through. . . . Themes of love run throughout this novel from passionate to familial, keeping everyone guessing as to just what choices will be made."

—*RT Book Reviews*

"A fast-paced urban fantasy with an extended family drama theme."

—*Alternative Worlds*

"The ending of *Wicked Circle* had me immediately wanting more. I love this kind of gritty urban fantasy."

—*My Keeper Shelf*

Arcane Circle

"Took the various aspects of urban fantasy I love, threw them all together, and created a masterpiece of discovery, devotion, and desire."

—*Bitten by Books*

"Urban fantasy at its best, with lovable characters and the perfect mix between action, romance, and magic."

—*Book Lovers Inc.*

"Action filled, sexy, and full of promises for future installments."

—*Scooper Speaks*

Fatal Circle

"Well written, fast moving, and fueled by a mix of romance and paranormal influence. A must read!"

—*Darque Reviews*

"Packed full of action, intrigue, and events that would not let me put this book down. . . . This book was a wild pleasure to read."

—*Fangtastic Reviews*

"I love this series and this book did not disappoint. . . . I'm hooked, baby!"

—*Book Lovers Inc.*

Hallowed Circle

"Robertson brings back the magic and the mayhem. . . . Twists, turns, and narrow escapes keep the pages turning."

—*RT Book Reviews* (4½ stars)

"An instant classic, featuring a refreshingly wise and likeable heroine."

—*Affaire de Coeur* (5 stars)

"Readers will find themselves swept off their feet, without the use of a broomstick, and into a dangerous world that is teetering on the edge of a war between the non-humans. Very entertaining!"

—*Huntress Book Reviews*

"Exciting characters with a good story line that equals . . . pure magic."

—*Fallen Angel Reviews*

"An enthralling supernatural urban fantasy filled with mystery, romance, and intrigue. . . . Loaded with action and a cast who make the paranormal seem normal, so much so that readers will believe that they exist. . . ."

—*Alternative Worlds*

"*Hallowed Circle* is near perfection."

—*Book Lovers Inc.*

"Make sure you don't overlook this series."

—*Mondo Vampire*

Vicious Circle

"A breath of fresh air . . . I read the novel almost straight through."

—*Urban Fantasy Fan*

"Another new entry into the urban fantasy genre—with an interesting twist to it."

—*SFRevu*

"Well-developed supernatural characters, mystery, and a touch of romance add up to an out-of-this-world thriller."

—*RT Book Reviews* (4 stars)

"Refreshing and unusual."

—*Fantasy Literature*

"An adventure filled with strong characters and their tangled human emotions."

—*Darque Reviews*

"All you could look for in an urban fantasy, with witches, werewolves, and vampires mixing it up and each adding their own uniqueness to the story."

—*Romance Junkies*

SHATTERED CIRCLE

LINDA ROBERTSON

POCKET BOOKS

New York   London   Toronto   Sydney   New Delhi

Pocket Books
A Division of Simon & Schuster, Inc.
1230 Avenue of the Americas
New York, NY 10020

This book is a work of fiction. Names, characters, places, and incidents either are products of the author's imagination or are used fictitiously. Any resemblance to actual events or locales or persons, living or dead, is entirely coincidental.

First Juno Books/Pocket Books paperback edition February 2013

JUNO BOOKS and colophon are registered trademarks of Wildside Press LLC used under license by Simon & Schuster, Inc., the publisher of this work.

POCKET and colophon are registered trademarks of
Simon & Schuster, Inc.

For information about special discounts for bulk purchases, please contact Simon & Schuster Special Sales at 1-866-506-1949 or business@simonandschuster.com.

The Simon & Schuster Speakers Bureau can bring authors to your live event. For more information or to book an event contact the Simon & Schuster Speakers Bureau at 1-866-248-3049 or visit our website at www.simonspeakers.com.

Manufactured in the United States of America

10 9 8 7 6 5 4 3 2 1

ISBN 978-1-4516-4893-5
ISBN 978-1-4516-4892-8 (ebook)

For Deb and Steph,

friends long lost and then refound.

When life is bad—and even when it's good—

you make it better.

Also, in fond memory of Heather.

You are missed.

THANK-YOUS

Red-Caped Hero Thanks:

Shannon and Missy
for beta-reading partials on short notice.
And, additionally, Audra, Beth Anne, and Michelle
for carb-a-licious Mock Nights and witty repartee.
It keeps me sane. . . .

Java and Chocolate Thanks:

To the gals—and guy—at
www.word-whores.blogspot.com
for the fun weekly post topics.

Margarita Thanks:

Hagatha's Bluff

Reverent Gratitude:

For the Many-named Muse. Keep rockin'!

CHAPTER ONE

Giovanni Guistini sat rigidly before the fireplace in his private rooms, teeth clenched, seething.

Franciscus Meroveus and the Excelsior had made a damned fool of him.

He squeezed his hands into fists so tight that his fingernails pierced his own flesh.

Yes, I agreed to assume the Quartermaster's duties; I took what glory had belonged to Menessos, just as Menessos once took my throat.

His pride had gotten the best of him; he saw that clearly now.

As an advisor to the Excelsior he was a man of wise counsel, accustomed to rank and privilege. He was not a bureaucratic nanny meant to settle childish quarrels between subordinate vampires who should be able to resolve a land dispute on their own. He was not accustomed to preparing paperwork, writing reports, or dealing with the many petty matters of managing a haven, let alone overseeing the havens in a quarter of the nation. It had become swiftly evident that the Quartermaster's position was one for a businessman, not a warrior.

Giovanni had backed down.

He hated losing. Anything, even death, was preferable to admitting a defeat.

That trait had been with him in life, and remained with him yet.

Presently, drops of blood welled into his palms, but he noticed no pain. Neither did he note the wetness nor the coppery scent.

The Vampire Executive International Network—VEIN—had become weak. *Executives.* The word left a foul taste in his mouth.

The men of the modern world fight with words, with mandates and policies. The vampires have been lured into the paper power play.

VEIN needs warriors. But how can they have warriors when even the Excelsior himself—the "Supreme" vampire—is nothing but a corporate stiff? He plays their game when instead he should cast off his Italian suit and show himself to be the fearsome monster that all the mortal humans assume he is. . . . Then they would cower at his feet, and he could rule the world.

But he lacks the vision. He has no desire for true supremacy. He is guided by plotting diplomats like Meroveus.

I was a leader among men once, and all I needed was a sharp weapon to wield.

That ended in 1453, when Menessos set his fangs into the soft flesh of Giovanni's neck, viciously tore it open . . . and left him to die.

It seemed the great failure of his past life had been reborn in his present. Nothing was happening as he'd hoped. The doom he'd envisioned for his enemy—Menessos condemned to a cell, locked in chains with only the corpse of his traitorous witch as company—had not transpired.

His already clenched teeth ground tighter as he brooded over his recent defeats.

Then a noise drew Giovanni's eyes from the dying embers.

A shadowy figure lurked on his balcony.

He rose from his seat, intrigued.

Because of the lofty position he had held as a man, people often sought to appease him to gain his favorable influence. Even in service to the Excelsior, there were times when a vampire endeavored to befriend him for the sole purpose of leverage. Bitter lessons had calloused his heart, but the emotional disconnect enabled him to rise in rank and power. Suspicion and deception had enabled him to keep it.

Cautiously, he stepped toward the open French doors.

The cloud cover passed and the moon's glow created an outline of quicksilver that highlighted a woman's figure, chest heaving as if she couldn't catch her breath. Giovanni might have thought her an assassin, but she was not even trying to hide her presence, and she was definitely *not* dressed for stealth. As she posed in a half turn, the lunar light created a satiny sheen across her evening gown.

It had been many centuries since a woman coveted him enough to assert herself—but this was clearly no ordinary woman: His balcony was nine floors above the street.

He yearned to be desired, but he well knew how revolting his disfigurement was. The heat of his longing cooled as wariness gripped him. *What woman would come to me for* me?

His doubt tripled as the silver-gray of the gown and the raven-black tresses clicked in his memory to reveal his visitor's identity: Liyliy. The oldest, boldest, and most beautiful of the three shabbubitum.

Daughters of a king, she and her sisters had been

blessed with the power of truth-sight, but a curse had doubled their power and turned them into something more harpy than human. Centuries later, according to the legend, their power tripled when they were Made vampires. Bearing substantial power, the dangerous trio had been bound into stone millennia before Giovanni was even born in mortal life. When the idea of freeing them arose as a means to evaluate the loyalties of Menessos, he had pushed for their release, eager for them to bring destruction to his enemy's door.

For over five hundred years, his rage had boiled, steeping his craving for revenge in bitter spite. He'd come so close . . . and failed. He wanted to wage war upon Menessos and leave everything the vampire had ever built, or ever loved, in ruins.

Now, seeing Liyliy before him, that vindictive need to retaliate reared up as never before. If this potent shabbubitu stood at his side, his vengeance might be possible.

"Come, Liyliy." He opened his hands and gestured toward the open doors, inviting her into his rooms. Only then did he feel the pain in his palms and realize blood was dripping from his self-inflicted wounds.

He squeezed his hands into fists again, trying to hide the blood. When first he'd seen Liyliy's human form, he'd desired her. He even admired her true owlish form for its deadly attributes as a swift-moving, sharp-taloned weapon. Beauty, anger, and power in one . . . she was a tantalizing creature. He did not want to appear foolish in her eyes.

But as she limped into the light of his chamber, he saw she was grievously wounded.

The acrid smell of charred skin and feathers wafted on

the night air. The left side of her face sagged. Her eye was imperceptible under the swollen mass that stretched across her cheek, perhaps missing altogether. Her mouth had been re-formed into a gruesome sickle-curve, and, as if her chin were merely wax, bloody globules of flesh dangled from it.

Her shoulders were no longer flawless and pale. Patches of raw redness ringed blisters the size of his fist. Her left forearm was twice as thick as it should have been, and rows of singed feathers protruded from it. Her ring finger and pinky were elongated and rigidly held in a painful twist.

In shock and disgust, Giovanni's mouth fell open.

Liyliy growled. "Have you not seen your own grotesque countenance?"

His hands jerked to touch the mottled scars that marred his throat, but he stopped himself.

Despite her ruined face, Liyliy's voice remained a sweet alto. Shamefully aware that his own voice was a sickening croak, he replied, "It haunts my every waking minute."

"That is why I've come to *you*." As she spoke, a large blister on her cheek burst. Viscous fluid oozed out and dripped from her chin. She seemed unaware of it.

Giovanni could not keep the revulsion from his features. "Who did this to you?"

"The witch."

She meant Persephone Alcmedi, the court witch who had marked Menessos. She was said to be the fated Lustrata as well. She hadn't seemed like much, but to have mutilated a shabbubitu like this, she was clearly not to be underestimated.

Liyliy eased forward. "I want her dead."

I bet you do. He understood how disfigurement could feed the need for revenge, but he was not a novice at negotiation. "So?" he asked, then remained silent, confident that she would make her offer.

The breath of magic crawled over his skin. He thought to retreat a step, but she clasped his wrists, lifted his hands, and began licking the blood from them. Though still wary she might seek to bespell him, he remained steadfast.

"Relax," she whispered. "Let me clean you up."

As her mouth moved along his skin, he had to shut his eyes so he would not see her ravaged face. He concentrated only on how her warm, soft tongue felt. And it felt good.

As she switched to his other hand, he felt a flare of magic again.

Her injuries were still fresh; she had not had time to adapt to the loss. *That* was the magic he'd felt. She was using her aura to help her see, to guide her movements—the lost eye would leave her otherwise struggling.

With this understanding, he relaxed and he gave in to the sensations created by her mouth, her lips. He shivered when her tongue flicked between his fingers and gasped as she sucked each finger, knuckle to tip.

"I know what you want," she whispered.

Women always said that. They always meant something sexual. They never really knew. "And what is it that you think I want?"

"To see Menessos suffer, to watch him grovel at your feet before he dies."

Giovanni opened his eyes.

"Seeing him in agony in front of his entire haven, torn and bleeding on the floor before his own throne . . . that only scratches the surface of what anguish I wish for him."

"He will feel great pain if the witch dies."

Giovanni lifted his chin, but said nothing.

"We have enemies in common," she said. "Enemies made stronger by their union. So we must forge a powerful alliance of our own."

The possibilities tempted him, but he was well aware he was no match for Menessos's wizardry—not that he would point out his own weakness to another. And—quite clearly—even a shabbubitu was inferior to Menessos's witch.

"You and I cannot do this." He pulled his hands away and let his arms drop to his sides.

"Don't deny me," she said crossly.

"We can't defeat them!"

"Of course not. But there must be others who would rally to our cause. You, with your position, with your hatred for him, you know who they are. You know where they are."

Giovanni considered it. A few ideas sprang up. All of them were complicated at best.

Liyliy must have taken his delay as a precursor to refusal. "Don't you dare hold your tongue. Speak! Tell me who we need to aid us"—her misshapen hand rose toward him—"or I will draw the names from your mind."

He gave her a flat stare. "Threats are no way to begin a partnership."

"We *must* act quickly." Her fingertip stroked his cheek lovingly. "They grow stronger with each passing day."

Giovanni was disgusted by her touch but wanted it to linger all the same. He turned and paced away. "*We* do not."

"We will overcome any current disadvantage by increasing our numbers . . . if you will but give me the names."

He stopped before the fireplace and grabbed the poker to jab irritably at the embers. Holding it made his injured hands ache, but he felt better with something solid in his grip.

Her undamaged hand encircled his arm. "There will never be a better time."

She was right about that. If Menessos was ever to be brought down, it had to be now. It would be sweet to deliver the blow that knocked him from his pedestal. Then Giovanni would follow it by robbing him of what glory and success he sought with the witch and the Domn Lup. That would truly be perfect.

Giovanni faced Liyliy, and even though her wounds were hideous, he saw something very desirable. *All I need is a sharp weapon to wield.* Her need to retaliate had forged her into a shrewd weapon—one with a razor-sharp edge.

"We begin with your sisters," he said.

CHAPTER TWO

Goliath stared into his closet at the plastic and pleather that dominated his wardrobe. The Goth persona suited both his role as Menessos's loyal lieutenant and occasional assassin and his rank as the haven's second-in-command. Also, the clothing enhanced his elongated scarecrow body in an effectively intimidating manner.

But he would not be donning the usual collar-to-ankle shiny black tonight.

His title had been elevated. He was no longer the unsmiling Alter Imperator. Now, he was the Haven Master.

His eyes closed as he shut the closet door, mentally sealing his former status—and antics—in the past. Turning his back on the old him, he faced a new future, and the new attire it required was dangling before him within a zippered garment bag. There was a silver tag on the zipper, and on it was written *With much respect, Risqué and Sil.* Both women were Offerlings here in the haven.

He unzipped the bag.

Within was a trim-cut suit that combined Asian elements with a steampunk/vintage style. It was black, made of leather and velvet. The collar would be snug around his throat and had metallic silver thread stitched into an intricate design mixing regal fleurs-de-lis with laughing skulls. Large silver buttons and strategically placed rectangles of silver chainmail accented the coat without looking blatantly like protection. The cuffs maintained the trim styling, but, again, the silver stitching and oversized button added a majestic flair.

This new style blended what was with what would be, capturing his unique menace, as well as the formality, status, and respect of being a Master.

He had been assured that the dark suit was becoming on his rail-like frame, and that the contrast of his platinum hair and pale skin would lend a fierce, penetrating quality to his so-blue eyes.

As he wrapped his body in his new clothing, he felt the importance of the title he was accepting more than ever.

Fifteen minutes later, he entered the Haven Master's suite—rooms he would soon occupy—with a new confidence in his stride. He passed the stone altar and approached the seating area meant for private conversations with political VIPs. Here, two regal armchairs were placed directly across from each other. In the space on either side, two rounded leather couches completed the circular feel and could each accommodate six onlookers.

The rear wall was composed of stacked stone and a thick wooden mantel. The horizontal lines of it were broken only by a pair of white marble pillars flanking either side of a wooden door with iron studs set into it.

Altogether, it was an elegant room. Since they had moved the haven to Cleveland, this particular room was his favorite. Especially the armchairs.

In days to come, this would be *his* suite.

For the time being, Menessos remained in residence and now lay behind that massive door to the private chamber. Until his Maker dealt with the current problems, Goliath did not intend to press the issue of where he lay during his dead hours.

His feet carried him near the plush seats. He wondered if sitting there would complete the legitimacy of the authority that had suddenly become his. His fingers trailed the back of a chair as he rounded it. He was ready to place himself into it—

—until he noticed Ailo and Talto sitting on the floor in the corner, watching him.

They would not be witness to his first moment in one of the master's chairs.

He passed by the regal armchair and with a toss of his head shook out his white-blond hair. Draping his lanky form across one of the leather couches, he glowered at the shabbubitum.

Their loathing for his master was understandable; thousands of years ago, Menessos *had* bound them and their sister, Liyliy, into stone. Only recently released, they were out of place in a modern environment. He didn't like having them here, but he would not trust them where they could not be monitored, either. *Damned if you do . . .*

The main door opened and Meroveus, Advisor to the Excelsior and currently their esteemed guest, entered the suite. "She is back?" he asked.

"That is what I'm told," Goliath answered. "If you're referring to Ms. Alcmedi, that is."

"I am. Is she here?"

Leaning on one elbow, Goliath reclined. "She required a shower." He wanted to give his nose a quick pinch to indicate she'd reeked of the scummy edges of Lake Erie, but he refrained. He was a Master now; taunting disdain was no longer acceptable.

Mero headed for the iron-studded door.

Goliath cleared his throat.

In mid-reach for the knob, Mero stopped. His hand fell to his side and he turned on his heel. "I have been disrespectful. Forgive me, Haven Master."

His sardonic grin flashed fang. "Does urgency always make you thoughtless?"

"I assumed that Menessos was still lord of these chambers, and that she was with him in the rear chamber."

Goliath sat up, placed his elbows on his knees, and clapped his hands together. "Hear me, Advisor Meroveus, and do not forget my words: The former Haven Master may have extended you many courtesies, but barging into his private chamber—especially if you think Ms. Alcmedi may be attending him—would be particularly dangerous."

Mero glanced at the main door as if he would leave, but there was uncertainty in his expression.

"To be honest," Goliath added as he stood, "I have not yet made claim to these rooms, and, as you have assumed, the former Quarterlord is in the rear chamber. However, *my* Erus Veneficus has her own suite." He used the formal title of the court witch for impact.

Mero blinked.

It seemed to Goliath that the other vampire had not considered that in declaring this the Cleveland haven and Goliath the master of it, Persephone would by default become Goliath's court witch. Her services were now his to command.

"It is urgent that I speak with her," Mero said. "Will you permit this?"

Goliath had not been able to confer with Menessos since he'd returned from retrieving the witch, but he knew that in any given situation buying time would serve him well. As the new master he could always shorten the time frame, but only if he had secured the option of having time at the outset. "She has been through an ordeal and I must insist that she be permitted to rest. Tonight, she will be troubled only for a medical examination. Surely, given the circumstances, you understand and will delay your interrogation until tomorrow evening?"

If Mero was displeased, he kept it from showing in his features. His hesitation, however, made it evident that he was weighing his options.

"As you wish, Haven Master, but may *I* insist that she not be permitted to leave the haven during the day tomorrow? If her condition is such that she requires rest, perhaps guarding against any . . . overexertion . . . would be wise."

Goliath nodded. "I will consider your advice, Meroveus."

At that moment, Menessos emerged from the rear chamber wearing a fresh, clean suit. His clothing had been soaked upon his return. The Offerling named Risqué had attended him initially, and she informed Goliath that Menessos claimed he'd helped the Erus Veneficus out of Lake Erie. Her grateful embrace, he'd explained, had drenched him.

"Much better." Menessos glanced around. "Am I interrupting?"

"Not at all," Goliath said. "The Advisor came to see the Erus Veneficus. I have said she must rest and will not be questioned until tomorrow evening."

Menessos nodded thoughtfully.

"I have other business that concerns both of you," Mero said.

Menessos walked toward the seating and motioned Mero to follow. "Tell us, then, of this other business." His tone was light and he avoided the armchairs, taking a place beside Goliath.

Mero chose to sit on the leather couch opposite them. He breathed deep to fill his lungs, straightened his spine, and said, "The witch must be taken to the Excelsior."

In the corner, the sisters giggled evilly. It made the nape of Goliath's neck prickle.

Menessos scowled at the sisters and gestured at the door. "Out," he said. Without a word they obeyed. When they were gone, Menessos faced Mero and his tone dropped. "No."

"Considering that she has twice—"

"I said no!"

Goliath could not help facing Menessos. He had seen his Maker angry many times, but it was rare that rage claimed him so swiftly. The sharklike glare Menessos aimed at Mero did not wane in its potency as the moment wore on.

Mero squirmed under that gaze and resituated himself on the couch. "And you, Goliath?" Mero asked. "As she is your Erus Veneficus now, what do you say?"

"Presently, I agree with Menessos. I want my witch here."

"Then, gentlemen, you must give me an alternative solution."

Since Menessos had sat beside him, Goliath took that as an indication he wanted to present a united front to Mero where the haven, and all the people included in it, were concerned. That meant Persephone as well. "Solution? Exactly what is the problem that you think requires my witch being taken to the Excelsior?" he asked.

Mero and Menessos shared a look, then Menessos answered. "The Advisor believes that she is a threat to vampires in general, as I am twice marked."

Goliath laughed. "A threat to whom?"

Abruptly, Menessos sat straighter and glanced toward the door. A second later, there came a meek knock. Menessos rose to answer it. As he stepped out, Goliath caught sight of Persephone in a terry cloth robe. *He feels her presence and runs to her beckoning.*

Mero lifted his chin. "The answer to your question, Goliath, is right there. If she can do such to *him,* she might be able to do it to all of us. Therefore, she is a threat to VEIN in general, both on the local Cleveland level, and on a higher political level."

Frowning, Goliath asked, "If that is true, what sense does it make to convey her to the Excelsior? Would that not be inviting her to attempt snarking him?"

"In a controlled environment that could not happen."

Goliath smiled slightly at that. If Mero thought he could control the environment, he was underestimating the Lustrata.

"If she will accept the Excelsior's marks upon her, then his power would trump any she would have over Menessos. It would ensure that she does not use her authority over him against the vampires."

As second-in-command—Alter Imperator—to the Northeastern Quarterlord, Goliath had been told many of the secrets Menessos knew. Some concerned Mero. He knew that Menessos had turned both Mero and, years later, the son Mero fathered in life. That son was now the Excelsior.

Goliath had to wonder if this course of action was meant to ensure no embarrassment befell the Excelsior's reign, or if Mero could be seeking to strengthen his son's position, giving him sway over Persephone because she was the Lustrata.

There were many prophesies concerning the Lustrata. The one that the vampires were most concerned with claimed she was incredibly valuable to them. Because of this, they could not dare to kill her. But they could do much without killing her. The question was: What would interfere with her destiny, and what wouldn't?

Menessos would know the most about it, so Goliath resolved to follow his Maker's lead. "Dabbling in the destiny that Menessos, the witch, and the Domn Lup share is a hazardous pastime, Mero. I strongly suggest you stay the hell out of their way."

Mero opened his mouth to reply but the door opened and Menessos returned. He reclaimed his seat. He was calmer.

"What you suggest," Menessos said, "cannot be, Mero."

"It must be." Mero quoted the prophesy:

"Lustrata walks,
unspoiled into the light.
Sickle in hand,
she stalks through the night
wearing naught but her mark and silver blade.
The moonchild of ruin, she becomes Wolfsbane.

"According to my interpretation," Mero concluded, "she *must* be marked."

Menessos breathed deep. Releasing it, he said, "Your interpretation is bullshit."

Mero's brows rose in surprise.

Goliath struggled to keep a laugh from getting out.

"The Witch Elders Council will not stand for their Lustrata to be marked by the Excelsior," Menessos said. "Would you risk a war?"

Mero shook his head. "The witches are divided on whether or not they believe she is the Lustrata. Surely the intelligence you have gathered has not failed to inform you of this?"

Menessos waved him off. "Regardless, she is not without power and influence. The goddess favors her. That they cannot deny."

"VEIN will not stand for *you* to be twice marked by a witch."

"What does it matter? I have been stripped of all rank."

"You are not without power and influence, either. The fact that one of those marks came at the direct interference of *her* goddess makes it worse."

"She is also *my* goddess."

Goliath had sat silently while they spoke, but when Menessos's fingers began tapping lightly, he recognized it as a sign of his irritation. He hoped Mero recognized it as well.

"Are you saying that Deric is willing to risk *Her* wrath?"

It surprised Goliath that Menessos used the Excelsior's given name and followed it with emphasis on "Her"—meaning the goddess.

Mero said nothing.

"He does not know Her, does he, Mero?" There was accusation in Menessos's tone.

Mero's cheeks reddened. "He knows the tormentor."

"Hecate is not our bane!" Menessos retorted.

"We are not all as fortunate as you. You lived on and escaped the suffering for eons," he replied. "We have not all had the opportunity to ally ourselves with deities that might show us favor."

Menessos stood. "In that you lie! You chose a path bearing the magic of Her ways, yet you have let Deric proceed into the highest rank our kind offers without spiritual guidance. Do not blame me for this and do not say you haven't had the opportunity to know and ally with Her."

He walked out.

The sisters had taken seats in the area outside the Haven Master's suite, but when Menessos exited, Ailo touched Talto's hand and thought to her sister, *Give me a few minutes before you leave here. I will meet you in the media room later.* She stood up. She rolled her shoulders and resettled her gown. Twitching her fingers, she made the magic that created the dove-gray silk remove all wrinkles.

Ailo walked speedily in the direction Menessos had gone. He was also moving fast. She wanted to speak to him privately, where no others would see, and he was on the stairs—catching him between floors was perfect for what she wanted to do.

She stopped suddenly. With all her will and magic

focused, she centered her meditative self into her core and touched the bond she now had to him, feeling of those the threads with ethereal spirit hands. One thread was for Talto. It felt like silk and resonated anger into her palm. One was for the witch, Persephone. It felt like velvet and crackled like static electricity in her hand. The final thread was for Menessos. It felt metallic, like barbed wire.

She stabbed her spirit-hand onto the sharp twist of metal and real physical pain gripped her body. But she felt Menessos stop. Squeezing that wire, she imagined her bleeding hand holding his and thought, *Please wait. I am following you.*

Releasing the barbed wire, she pulled herself out of the semi-meditation and hurried on.

When she arrived at the stairway, Menessos stood at the bottom, waiting.

The hardness of his features expressed only displeasure.

Ailo descended the steps without rushing.

"What do you want?" he asked.

"Mero bound my sister and me to him loosely. But you"—she tapped the chains at her throat—"you are more thorough."

"Indeed. I know you." He turned on his heel. "I trust you less."

"I helped you long ago."

Menessos stopped.

"Even so," she continued, "I bore an equal share in the Fate you designed for us."

"You were all dangerous, Ailo. You remain so now."

"You bound us away then. Will you do so again, at your first chance?"

Slowly he spun toward her. "Yes." He studied her. "I want no part of monitoring you and your sister forever, Ailo. It would doom anyone."

"I may share my sister's treacherous past, but I have always been the more mindful of us three." She paused, then deposited the seed she had come to plant in his mind: "I know when I am beaten."

His eyes narrowed suspiciously, then he said, "Good."

"They may deserve the stone again, but I do not. I aided you before and it was your deceit that put me into the statue. I will aid you again—wait and see, I will. And this time, I hope, you will reconsider my fate."

When he walked away she let him, smiling as she watched him go.

CHAPTER THREE

Ten-year-old Beverley Kordell watched the world passing outside the car window. Her foster mom, Persephone Alcmedi, was out of town, so she was staying with
close friends, Erik and Celia Randolph. Celia brought her
to the bus stop every morning, but this morning they
had come early. They needed to stop at Seph's farmhouse
and pick up some extra clothes for Beverley.

Usually, if Seph had to be away attending to her duties
as court witch of the local vampire haven, Beverley stayed
at the farmhouse and Seph's grandmother, Demeter, took
care of her. But Seph's mom, Eris, had an accident and
lost her arm. Demeter was with her in Pittsburgh helping
Eris for now. Beverley hoped Demeter—Seph called her
Nana—would be back soon. She missed her and the fantastic creatures that lived on the farm, especially a certain
unicorn, Errol.

When they arrived at the farmhouse, Beverley slid out
of the CX-7 and into the misty morning air, smiling up
at the rural salt-box farmhouse before her. Ever since her
mom, Lorrie, had died and her godmother disappeared,
she had lived here with Persephone.

Though Seph wasn't home, Beverley was glad to be
back. She liked hanging out with Celia and Erik well
enough; they played board games and watched mov-
ies with her. But they didn't have anything around their
home that would shimmer and flash when she squinted at

it. At Seph's, almost everything would cast rainbowlike arcs of light if she looked at it long enough. Maybe it was because they were wærewolves and Seph was a witch.

She hadn't noticed the glimmering and gleaming way things could look until she'd stopped wearing the silver necklace with the flint arrowhead and silver four-leaf-clover charms that Demeter had made for her. Seph had told her to always wear it, but the silver had started making her neck itch badly, so, while at Celia's, she had taken it off and left it in her drawer in the guestroom.

"This should only take a few minutes," Celia said as she walked toward the porch and looked through her keys to find the one for Seph's front door. "We have to get you to the bus stop on time so you don't miss school. It's gonna be a short week. Only two days."

Beverley followed her up onto the porch and squinted at the doorknob. The air around it wavered like it was the sun-kissed surface of a creek.

"Anything in particular you want to wear Thursday?"

"To what?" Beverley asked, blinking.

"Thanksgiving dinner." Celia slid the key into the lock, turned. "Haven't you been listening?"

Beverley smiled sheepishly.

"Daydreaming about unicorns again?"

For most little girls, dreaming would have been all there was to unicorns, but at Seph's there were two new barns out back with real unicorns living in one. Errol, a yearling colt, had taken a fancy to her.

Beverley's gaze dropped for an instant to the purple cast on her arm. She'd broken it at school last week, and when Seph had signed it she'd drawn a little unicorn, too. "Can I see Errol?"

"We don't have time this morning, but after school you can, as always."

When the door opened, she asked Celia, "Will you pick something for me to wear? My mom always picked for the holidays."

Celia ran her hand over Beverley's head. "Oh, honey. You're growing up. Just had a birthday. Don't you want to start choosing for yourself?"

Beverley did want to, but what she wanted more was to sneak into Seph's room again before she had to go to school. Besides, all the grown-ups said Celia was "fashionable," that she had "style." She would pick something good.

"Maybe next year." Beverley hurried up the steps and into the bathroom. After shutting the door, she stood behind it listening. When Celia had passed by, Beverley waited for a count of ten, then slowly opened it and peeked out. She made sure Celia was studying the clothes in her bedroom closet before tiptoeing into Seph's room.

Opening the closet there, Beverley dug straight to the back where the item she wanted was stored. Her little hands grasped the cold sides of the rock-board and she pulled. It was heavy and the cast on her arm made the task more difficult. She lost her grip on the slate—the bottom edge dropped onto the top of her foot.

Stifling her yelp of pain, she regained her grasp and silently laid it flat on the floor before shutting the closet door. Crouching between the bed and the wall so she couldn't be seen from the doorway, she studied all the strange symbols painted across the surface.

She'd heard Seph and Celia talking about this. *Great El's slate.*

They'd said that a person could talk to ghosts with this . . . and that Seph had used it to find her mother.

But how does it work?

Beverley ran her hands over the surface. Her fingers traced the lines of a symbol here, there. They tingled like the fine lines of her fingerprint weren't so fine after all.

She studied her index finger, then compared it to her other hand's index finger. *If one tingles . . . what does two do?* She picked two symbols she liked that were side by side and put her fingertips to the slate. Carefully, slowly, she traced both. The tingling began immediately and resonated through her hands and into her wrists.

Suddenly, some force grabbed her hands. She gasped and tried to pull away, but it just squeezed tighter. It dragged her fingers along to one symbol, then on to another. She watched in horror as all her fingers were pulled across the board, each finger moving independently. The more symbols she traced, the more the tingling increased. It became like a fire inside her skin, swelling up through her thin arms, crackling through the broken bone.

It hurt. It hurt *so bad*. She drew a breath to scream—

—and then it felt good.

It wasn't hot, merely warm. It wasn't warmth like summer, though, not something a thermometer would show. This was warmth of another kind. The kind only a heart could feel. She felt so . . .

Loved.

A shimmer flashed across the surface of the board.

She whispered, "Mommy?"

CHAPTER FOUR

Liyliy, a vampire-harpy, had tried to kill me a few hours ago, and the struggle left me exhausted and sore. That was the reason I was still abed at nearly two in the afternoon. When my satellite phone blared the opening riffs of Ozzy Osbourne's "Bark at the Moon," it startled me, instantly reminding me about all the sore muscles I had.

Mid-reach, I stopped. That was Johnny's ringtone.

He had tried to kill me, too.

My hand shook as my finger jabbed the Answer button. "Hello?"

"Red . . . I'm so sorry." Johnny's voice was barely audible.

I sat up and deliberated whether to play deaf and repeat my "hello" as if I hadn't heard him. I considered being a jerk and hanging up. I even contemplated ripping him a new one.

Instead, I remained silent.

Two days before, minutes after I'd performed the forced-change spell on him and his loyal pack mates, Johnny had attacked me. He'd always retained his man-mind while transformed, but that last time he didn't—he'd been pure animal. The only reason I was still among the living was because I'd pumped ley line energy into him like a human Taser.

"Red?"

He'd frightened me to my core. The unshakeable faith I'd had in him had been shattered by an emotional earthquake. Damage was done. My fear felt like betrayal.

But . . .

Could going through the forced-change spell repeatedly have an undesired effect?

No. I was sure the whole terrible incident could be pinned on the fact that my mother, Eris, had revoked the tattooed bindings she'd placed upon Johnny eight years ago. He suddenly had access to all the power and potential she'd locked away from him. That was surely a disorienting, difficult situation.

I'd helped him dig up the clues, helped him achieve that goal. Hell, I'd even been a part of the reversal spell. So some responsibility for the consequences *was* mine to bear.

"Persephone?"

He rarely used my full given name; he usually called me Red, as in Little Red Riding Hood to his Big Bad Wolf. Or Seph like nearly everyone else. I had to respond.

"I'm here."

"Then say something."

Pushing back the covers, I stood and began to pace. "I don't know what to say."

He paused. "Can you forgive me?"

I wasn't sure.

Part of me said I couldn't allow his attack to be a personal issue because of the fateful trio that Johnny, Menessos, and I forged by binding ourselves magically. The other part argued that no matter the circumstances, attempted murder was very damn personal.

It all happened because Johnny had surrendered to his

destiny. His unique ability to transform at will made him the Domn Lup—king of the wærewolves. It was a position with power, prestige, and perks such as a Maserati Quattroporte. Johnny knew his royal place was unavoidable, but he'd fought it and hid from it a long time. He'd finally pushed forward because it was beneficial to our triple union, but kinghood was costing him his dream of being a rock star.

It had been my fear that he'd lose who he was in the course of this alliance of ours. More than ever, it seemed this fear was being borne out.

On the other corner of our triangle was Menessos. He now bore two witches' marks—mine, of course. That made him my servant. When Heldridge, his former right-hand man, learned of my authority over Menessos, he tattled to the highest vampire authority, the Excelsior. To protect us against the personal grudge of the truth-seeing vampire-harpies sent by VEIN to make formal inquiry, Menessos had allied himself at great personal expense with someone dangerous—a "nameless" guy I had aptly dubbed Creepy.

The secrets he'd wanted to hide from VEIN—secrets even I didn't know—were apparently safe, but our little who-marked-whom secret was out. Menessos lost his haven and his status as Northeastern Quarterlord.

Johnny had accepted great power and lost a lifelong dream. Menessos had lost great power and accepted serious personal risk. It didn't seem fair.

And what about me?

In the last several weeks I'd learned that I was the long-prophesied Lustrata, the Witches' Messiah, She Who Walks Between Worlds, She Who Will Bring Balance, blah blah blah. As this news spread throughout the non-human communities, some scoffed and some believed. I was fine with the scoffers; it was the believers who were dangerous. They wanted to know if I truly possessed the power that accompanied those titles. Yeah, I was a magnet for nasties who either a) wanted me dead to be sure I *didn't* have that power, or b) wanted to try to force me to wield power for their gain.

I guess I'd accepted the endless complications of my status and was well on my way to losing all scraps of naïveté.

At that thought, I stopped pacing. As I stared into the nothingness of a darkened corner, it felt like my innocence had slipped from my grasp and I was watching it skitter across the floor, waiting for it to come to a stop so I could reclaim it.

I wasn't sure it was worth the effort to look for it. Or perhaps it would be impossible to find if I made the effort. Maybe it had rolled into some crack, never to be seen again.

I heard Johnny breathing through the phone.

It wasn't Johnny who had rescued me last night. When I defeated Liyliy, Menessos had been there to bring me to the haven. Sure, Menessos had a hand in creating the monster she now was. And it was he who had imprisoned her, creating her need for revenge. But it was me and my marks upon him that had brought her to Cleveland.

When she pursued me from the haven—according to the Offerling I'd spoken to—Menessos had sent everyone out to search for me.

Had Johnny even known I was missing?

It was shitty of me to compare the two men in my life, but I couldn't help myself.

Though Menessos had drunk my blood numerous times, he hadn't tried to kill me.

Yes he did! He nearly killed you not long after you first met.

We were strangers then, I argued with myself. *Now, we know each other well.*

Better, perhaps, than you should. . . .

Defiantly, I ignored my conscience's scolding. *I will not regret what I did last night.* During the predawn hours, reeling from my encounter, I'd kissed Menessos.

Fine, but clearly you were able to forgive him.

That was true. Considering this, I felt hope.

I sighed heavily into the phone. My whispered answer was, "In time."

"There's so much I need to tell you." Johnny's voice was raw, and the rev of an engine punctuated his words.

I wondered where he was going. And I wondered if I should tell him about kissing the vampire.

It hadn't been a peck.

When our lips had touched, I felt the promise and power of a more intimate union. He'd definitely felt it. It wasn't only the power of the marks between us that had been kindled.

"I don't know where to begin," Johnny said.

His voice drew me out from my memory of a passionate moment with another man. Guilt swelled around my heart . . . but not remorse. *What am I going to do?*

"I'll have that figured out by the time I get back to Cleveland," he said.

That's why he didn't come for me! He wasn't even here. "Where have you been?"

"There's so much to explain, I don't want to do it over the phone, Red. Say you'll see me. I'll come to you. Anywhere. We have to talk. Face-to-face."

"What time is good for you tomorrow?"

"No. It's gotta be today."

My gut twisted. This wasn't a conversation to be rushed. "I can't."

"This is important."

He didn't know what had happened to me or he wouldn't push like this. But if I didn't harbor this fear of him now, I wouldn't mind being pushed. "Johnny."

"Let's have an early dinner. Anywhere you want. Someplace fancy like Mallorca, or even a burger joint like Wendy's. I don't care. . . . I just have to talk to you."

It was past two in the afternoon. I'd have some time to prepare. "Okay."

"Let's say four o'clock. Where do you want to meet?"

I decided to stack the deck in my favor. I picked a certain coffee shop near the Rock and Roll Hall of Fame. The place employed a few witches I knew. I hoped at least one of them was working today.

CHAPTER FIVE

Late November in Northeast Ohio can be cool or outright cold. So, after shoving my feet into a pair of comfy boots, I grabbed a blazer and a hoodie from the closet. Adding layers over the jeans and long-sleeved T-shirt was the best option.

Then, though ready to leave, I stood at my heavy haven door procrastinating.

I was deep within the building. Between me and the world outside were the backstage area, the main stage, a greatly modified theater house, a long hallway, then three stories' worth of stairs, followed by a hundred-yard trek to the entrance.

It wasn't the distance that bothered me. What made me hesitate was the fact that there could be a hundred or more Beholders and Offerlings between me and the doors to the world beyond the haven. Liyliy had made sure to announce to them all that I had twice-marked Menessos—to whom they had pledged their loyalty. Mastering their master was a roundabout way to make them all *my* servants, and to many it smacked of deviousness and ill intent.

My name was surely not to be found on the favorite-persons list of anyone in the haven.

But if I was to be successful as the Lustrata, I couldn't cower from Offerlings and Beholders. Regardless of their overwhelming numbers, they were, essentially, mine. Therefore, they wouldn't dare raise a hand to me.

Right?

I closed my eyes and affirmed to myself that the mantle of the Lustrata rested upon my shoulders. With a turn of the knob, I stepped out.

The door to my room was so heavy, it could have served as the entry to a bank vault in a former life, so, with a push on its significant weight, I shut it and descended the steps. My gaze trailed back. The Offerling on duty was playing *Angry Birds* on his phone and he glanced at me, expressionless, then returned to his game. My focus skipped past him to the door directly beneath mine . . . the entry to Menessos's chambers. The vampire was beyond that door, not so far away.

Winding my way through the backstage maze, I found the former theater house was lit only by the sconces on the outer walls. It was enough illumination for me to traverse the room without bumping into tables. The place was, thankfully, empty of people. As I walked, the darkness and silence allowed my mind to revisit my last exit from the haven, fleeing upon my broom.

Near the entrance to the theater I paused to look back, imagining what it must have looked like, me flying out of here, a giant harpy in swift pursuit.

"Going somewhere?" Her heavy Russian accent made the word sound like *suhm-vair*.

I spun around.

In the doorway stood a tall woman with short, spiky black hair. Muscular shoulders rose and fell with a heavy breath, her bulging arms crossed. Her familiar oval face was frowning.

Ivanka.

She'd served as my sentinel until she'd tried to shoot Creepy in the head. He'd broken her forearm like it was a bendy straw.

It didn't surprise me that her cast was covered in a green wrap that had been marked up to resemble camouflage, or that she wore a black tank top and military fatigues. Her combat boots were untied, with the strings tucked down inside. I was glad her handgun was still holstered on her left hip and not in her hand.

"Yes. I have a meeting in"—I checked my watch—"about twenty minutes."

"You must stay."

"Why?"

"It is order of Haven Master. Erus Veneficus is not to leave premises."

"Menessos said I couldn't leave?"

"No." Her eyes narrowed angrily. "Because of you, Menessos is our master no more."

Right. Suspicious, I asked, "And who is?"

"Goliath."

A sudden fear gripped me. If he had made claim to the people of the haven, then maybe they weren't "essentially" mine at all. I thought it through. Goliath belonged to Menessos, so unless they had done some kind of separation, he was mine as well. By default, things should still be kind of the same as I had expected.

I moved to step around her.

She blocked me.

"I have to go, Ivanka. I'll come straight back afterward."

"Return to your quarters."

Setting my stance and unlocking my knees, I said,

"Make me, if you dare." I lifted one hand and wiggled my fingers. "But be warned: I set the Domn Lup of the wærewolves on his ass with my hands. I defeated Liyliy with my hands. You"—I looked her up and down—"don't stand a chance. Not even with a gun."

Her mouth opened, then shut.

"Move aside."

She retreated one step, out of reach, but angled into my path. "I wish to not lose rank."

"You won't." I brushed past her. She wisely didn't try to stop me. As I climbed the steps and headed for the entrance, however, she was right behind me.

"I go with you, to ensure your return."

"Not necessary."

"I go anyway."

I stopped and spun. "No. This is private."

"Menessos would not want you outside of haven unprotected."

I wiggled my fingers at her again. "I'll be okay."

Being assertive like this was a double checkmark in the plus column. One, because it made me feel good about myself. Two, because affirming my power to someone else reinforced it to me.

As I rounded the turn near the old ticket booth across the lobby from the entrance, an older man with a cane rammed through the plywood-covered door.

Beau. His eyes locked on me and he barreled right toward me. This Bindspoken witch was the owner of Wolfsbane and Absinthe, the local pagan supply shop. He wore his trademark plaid flannel with the sleeves rolled up to expose the white thermal underwear beneath. The cigar perched at the corner of his mouth was also typical of him. However, his hurried, irritated gait and the lowered position of his bushy white eyebrows weren't.

He pointed at me. "It's all your fault!"

The anger in his accusation hit me like a slap. "What's my fault?"

He stomped faster in my direction, but was still slow because of his prosthetic leg.

Even so, I had to fight the instinct to back up. "What's wrong?"

He shouted, "William is catatonic!"

William was his son, and also a wærewolf. Somehow, he'd gotten too close to a witch doing magic and it caused him to go into a partial shift. He'd been stuck that way for a long time, housed and cared for in the upper floors of the local pack's den. When I'd done the forced-change spell for Johnny and his men, Beau had asked that William be included.

Since Beau had given me a powerful charm that had saved my life, I owed him a favor. I'd agreed to have William in the spell. Someone from the den had sedated the wild, half-formed creature in order to move him and keep him still during the spell. He'd transformed fully into a wolf like everyone else. The fact that he had been drugged beforehand meant that when he did not regain consciousness after the transformation, I wasn't alarmed.

"I thought that spell was supposed to give them their man-minds," Beau growled, still advancing, "but somehow it took his away!" He wasn't slowing down to just verbally confront me. He was a freight train about to run me over.

Suddenly, Ivanka shot forward, grabbed his arm, and thumped her cast across his chest in restraint. "Keep back."

"The man-mind doesn't come until the next regular cyclical change," I explained. That was how it worked with the others. But then the others hadn't been mindless beasts for years prior to the spell.

Beau struggled with Ivanka and drew his cane up as if to cudgel her. Even with a broken arm, she was dangerous.

Both were distracted.

I made for the front doors and the last thing I heard as I pushed through them was Beau shouting, "You'll pay for this, Persephone Alcmedi!"

My escape revealed, I sprinted away.

Living in a haven is like living in a movie theater; sometimes when you emerge, the brightness of the world is stunning. Sure, it was presently an average afternoon in late November, but the waning light on the buildings opposite pierced my retinas like high beams. I nearly ran over an elderly black woman. Shouting back my apologies, I ran east on Euclid Avenue, squinting and sometimes pushing my way along the sporadically crowded sidewalk.

If the complaints rising from behind me were any indication, Ivanka was pursuing me with more intent than was socially acceptable. So, I jumped in the nearest cab and gave the driver the address of the coffee shop.

Out the back window I saw Ivanka stop on the sidewalk, her cheeks flushed in anger, and she shouted something in Russian I didn't understand.

Settling into my seat, I tried to take in Beau's news.

William is catatonic.

The spell could not have taken his mind, but then it

was after that spell that Johnny had tried to kill me. I thought back, recalling my wording, considering the placement of the candles, the stones. I analyzed every detail but could not identify a misspoken phrase or anything that was obviously out of place. I could look at the charts, compare planetary positions of the first spell to the second, but I doubted that would make this kind of difference.

That was the only plan I had when I arrived at the coffee shop. Since I'd taken a cab instead of walking, I was early and there was time to talk to the girls before Johnny arrived.

Inside, Mandy looked up from the netbook she had behind the counter and grinned. "Hey, Seph! What are you doing downtown?"

"Meeting a friend here. How've you been?"

She flashed her name badge at me.

"Manager? You got promoted!"

"Yeah. Just last week. Like a show, the business must go on."

The witch who formerly owned this shop had abruptly disappeared. I knew more about that situation than I ever wanted anyone to know, so I meekly nodded and said, "Congratulations." Besides working here, Mandy was an apprentice witch who gave some of her free time to Venefica Covenstead as a volunteer secretary. She was a good kid, a college freshman, and she deserved the advancement.

"So what can we get you?"

"Spiced cider." While she rang me up on the register another girl stepped away to make my drink.

Mandy handed me my change.

I leaned in closer. "Can you get astrological charts on-line on your computer?"

"Of course!"

"Could I possibly compare a couple dates?"

"Sure." She started typing. "I'll log into the astrology subscription the Covenstead maintains. What date did you want to look at?"

Goddess, she talked so fast it was easy to think she must have been drinking double shots of espresso. I told her the two dates in question.

She typed and handed over the little netbook before the cider was finished. "You can take this to your seat and check it out. I have to fill out an inventory list anyway. The first tab is the first date, the second tab is the second date. Who are you meeting?" The last question was accompanied by a sly little smile.

"Thanks. Oh, Johnny. He should be here in a bit."

Her eyes widened. "I thought it might be him. Wow! The Domn Lup in my shop? He's *sooo* handsome, you're so lucky, you know that? Oh hey, will he have an entourage? You know, like the president?"

My head spun at the speed of her questions. "I hope not." That hadn't even crossed my mind. *Were his closest people now his secret service, listening in on his conversations with me?*

"Don't make a fuss over him, okay?"

The other girl handed me the cider.

Mandy said, "Oh. Sure. Wærewolf King of the World, local rock star, and boyfriend of the Lustrata. Of course I'll treat him like he's a regular guy."

CHAPTER SIX

At three forty-six in the afternoon, Johnny pulled up to the parking garage of the Cleveland Cold Storage (CCS) building. Before losing cell phone reception he'd texted Red to let her know he'd be ten minutes late. Sunday traffic had been light and he'd made good time returning from upstate New York, but he still had a few things to do before he saw her. Getting a shower was on the top of that list.

The huge old building, formerly an ice house, now served as the den of the Cleveland-area wærewolves. He had a parking spot near the elevator, but with the sense of urgency he currently felt, he steered the Maserati right in front of the lift and threw it into park.

He retrieved his gym bag from the trunk and got on the elevator to the ninth floor, where an apartment for esteemed guests was located. He could clean up there before heading to the coffee shop.

With a quiet *ding,* the lift halted and the doors rolled back. He stepped into the hallway, but the sound of footfalls in the stairwell made him hesitate. Someone was hurrying up the steps. Someone wearing heels.

In seconds, Aurelia's gorgeous and leggy self burst into view. Having managed the climb in inappropriate shoes, she was surprisingly not out of breath. However, her short skirt had ridden up and Johnny couldn't help noting the muscular flex of her thighs. As he forced his gaze upward, over her low V-neck blouse and onto the perfection of her face, she flicked her long blond hair behind her shoulder and smiled, altering her walk to a more seductive gait. "That must have been some drive," she said sweetly. "You couldn't even answer your phone." She'd been calling him every fifteen minutes for the last several hours.

"You could have left a message."

She drew close. "You and I were supposed to celebrate." The way she articulated the last word left no doubt that she meant a celebration of the naked and sweaty kind.

He said nothing, but repeated silently, *Remember, you're on your way to talk to Red.*

"Were you even going to stop in your office, sire?"

"No. I have to—"

"Are you avoiding me?"

"I have to get a shower and—"

"Oh." Her smile broadened. "Would you like someone to scrub your back?"

You're in a hurry to see Red. "I'll manage."

She pouted. It was entirely, adorably sexual. "Are you sure?"

Johnny turned on his heel. *Cold shower. Cold, cold, cold shower.*

Behind him he heard a frustrated sigh. "So . . . where have you been?" Her tone was on the verge of demanding.

Let her be pissed. What she wants she can't have. He kept walking and gave her a flat-toned answer. "Away."

"Yes, we all noticed the newly announced Domn Lup drove an old woman home and didn't come back." Her scornful sarcasm was not hidden. When he didn't respond she instructed, "Bathe fast. The *diviza* will be here in twenty minutes."

In pack hierarchy, the *dirija* was a pack leader, the *adevar* was an area bean counter who kept tabs on the *dirijas*, and a *diviza* was the region's next step up, serving a function that was part outreach, part campaign manager, part lawyer, and part CEO. They had an incredible amount of authority where local packs and politics were concerned.

Johnny spun back. "The *diviza*?"

Aurelia nodded.

After negotiations went south between the pack and the Ohio Department of Transportation, or ODOT, who wanted to buy and tear down the den building for their new I-90 project, a dossier had been sent to the *diviza* requesting intervention.

Johnny had opted out of the recent meetings, leaving the dilemma to Todd, who would become the pack's *dirija* after Johnny's coronation. They had all believed the issue would be resolved after the new year. "I thought he wasn't coming until January?"

"ODOT and the mayor are very serious about their new compensation package." She advanced on him again. "They demanded mediation to obtain an immediate decision, and demanded it directly of the *diviza,* leaving us out of the loop."

"Bastards. Did the *diviza*'s office contact us?"

"*I* only learned of this a few hours ago." She crossed her arms, enhancing the bulge of her cleavage. "Seems they didn't want to overwhelm you prior to or during your official announcement. According to them, the mediation was scheduled for next week, but ODOT called them with the change at one thirty. The *diviza* immediately chartered a plane, which . . ." Her words trailed off as she checked her watch. ". . . should have landed by now."

Johnny turned back toward the apartment. "Get Todd in here. He has to handle it."

"You're the Domn Lup."

Stopping, Johnny squared his shoulders before facing her again. "And I have another meeting scheduled—one I don't intend to miss. Besides, this will be Todd's pack in a few weeks, so let him handle it how he wants."

"The *diviza* expects you."

Of course he did. The Domn Lup was a power title. Johnny knew that his attendance at the meeting would give the wæres more credibility, more leverage.

This was part of the reason why he didn't want to be Domn Lup. It wasn't solely about grown-up choices and people looking to him for answers he wasn't sure he had. This song and dance was about politics and etiquette. Every meeting would be tainted with a false spotlight meant to illuminate the idea that those involved were important, and that important people made decisions that were good for all. However, the agreements politicians reached were never brought to bear by the politicians themselves. Not getting their hands dirty with the real work meant the ruling class was out of touch with the reality of the decrees they made. Johnny wanted to change that. He wanted to shake things up and bring some rock-and-roll irreverence into play.

"Fuck him," he said, and walked away. Talking about a problem didn't fix it, work did. They would get his presence and full support when they were ready to *work*.

He was three steps from the door when Aurelia's voice sliced down the hall like a razor. "This is how you intend to lead? Ignoring one of the six U.S. *divizas* when he's come to negotiate for your pack's den?"

Again, he stopped, but this time he didn't turn. All he wanted to do was go and make things right with Red and tell her about Evan. But that was his heart talking. His mind knew he couldn't abandon the pack like this. It was their *den*. If they lost it because he'd skipped out on them . . .

Fuck.

"Everyone is watching you, John."

He said nothing, but he hung his head and tried to figure out the perfect wording for the text he'd send Seph to cancel.

Aurelia turned and retreated into the stairwell.

Red will understand. I know she will.

Aurelia had seen to it that a dry-cleaned suit, tie, and dress shoes had been brought to the apartment while Johnny showered. All were black except for the gray shirt. Seeing the spiffy duds, he'd rolled his eyes but put them on, grumbling. Now his still-wet hair was dripping slightly on the tailored jacket shoulders as he stood in the parking garage with Gregor on one side and his self-appointed fashion director on the other.

Todd had parked and was approaching them when a metallic-gray Cadillac Escalade limousine pulled in and rolled right up to them. When the driver hopped out and opened the door, the *diviza* slid out.

He was an older man, his hair a rendition of Einstein's, and his equally frizzy beard at least twelve inches long.

His face was tanned dark, with deep lines across his forehead. Any wrinkles at the corners of his eyes were hidden by his dark sunglasses.

He cocked his head as he surveyed them. He was so scrawny that, with all the bristling hair about his head, his skull seemed oversized for his body. Johnny felt like he was being sized up by a starving elderly caveman dressed for a hip cocktail party.

The old man's gaze settled on him.

"*Diviza,* I'm John Newman," he said. "This is Todd McCloud. He will soon replace me as *dirija* of this pack. This is Aurelia Romochka, my assistant, and Gregor Radulescu, Omori captain."

The older man pulled his sunglasses down an inch, revealing an azure-blue eye on the left, while the pupil of the right eye was bright, reflective silver. It had a startling effect, but then, in a crisp Cajun accent, the *diviza* said, "Delighted to meet you all. I am Jacques Lippencot Plympton and we are late. If you would join me . . ." He disappeared into the limo.

Once settled inside the luxurious interior, Johnny asked, "Where is this meeting?" It was early evening on a Sunday, after all. Government offices were closed.

Jacques's cheeks bulged round in a smirk. "Not far. Not far at all." The last came out more like *ah-tall*. He then spent the entire five-minute ride facing Johnny with that crooked smile stuck in place.

This must be what it feels like to be on display at a freak show.

CHAPTER SEVEN

After school, Beverley rode the bus to her normal stop. When she climbed into Celia's CX-7, as usual, Celia asked about her day. Beverley told her that her best friend, Lily, was absent because she'd gotten to fly on an airplane to Florida, about the experiment they did for science, and about the picture of a unicorn that Bobby drew for her. She still had a crush on Bobby even after he pushed the merry-go-round so fast she fell off and broke her arm.

But Beverley didn't tell Celia everything.

She didn't tell Celia that she had barely been able to pay attention all day because she couldn't wait to get back to the farmhouse.

She held on to the car's door handle the entire distance of the driveway, her feet dancing on the floor mat, ready to jump out before the car even stopped.

"You're sure in a hurry to see Errol today," Celia remarked as she put the car in park.

Beverley usually ran from the car all the way to the barns, but today she wanted to go inside the house. "Can I have some milk first?" she asked as she scurried from the car.

"Of course." Celia cut the engine. "Check the date on the carton, though. Seph's been gone."

"I'll have a juice, then." Beverley knew Celia would be doing paperwork for her house-selling job. It was what she always did after school to give Beverley time to go see the unicorn. So she rushed into the kitchen and selected a juice box from the refrigerator, then, as Celia situated herself at the table and began pulling folders from her briefcase, Beverley returned to the front door. She opened it, closed it, slipped off her shoes, and carried them as she tiptoed up the steps, being careful to avoid the ones that she knew squeaked.

In Seph's bedroom, she stood before the dresser and studied the black obelisk. She wondered why her mom had told her to lift it off its base, but she did as she had been instructed. The instant her fingers touched it, an electric jolt made her fingers squeeze around it. She gasped in pain, but the ache had already faded. She sat the obelisk on its side next to the base piece.

Crossing the room, she dropped gently to her knees and slid the slate out from under the bed where she'd left it this morning. She smiled mischievously as she gathered the slate into her arms, placed her shoes on top, and snuck back down the steps. She peeked down the hall and noted that Celia was sitting with her back toward the barns.

Being as quiet as possible, she opened the door again, slipped out, and shut it silently behind her. On the front porch she paused long enough to put on her shoes, then she walked the long way around the house so Celia couldn't see her through the window. She jogged across the backyard to the cornfield and toward the barns . . . then she slipped into the rows of stalks.

Following the other directions that had been given to her that morning, she walked until she arrived at the trees. She pushed through the bare branches and into the leaf-strewn open center of the grove. She turned in a complete circle, deciding which of the inner trees was the best.

One in particular caught her eye. It was a thick tree, tall and strong-looking. Its roots were bumpy, but spread out wide and high almost like the arms of a chair. Beverley sat, leaning against this tree, her legs stretched before her, slightly bent. She propped the slate on her angled lap.

With her hands poised over the letters, she whispered, "Are you still there, Mommy?" and touched the surface.

CHAPTER EIGHT

Johnny was surprised when the limousine slowed and stopped at a small parking area at the corner of Detroit Avenue and West 25th Street. Jacques exited the vehicle and walked directly toward the big brown door beside the old plaque declaring it the subway entrance. They were going to the underside of the Detroit-Superior Bridge.

Of course they were meeting on a *bridge*. They were dealing with ODOT. People from the Department of Transportation would know this structure inside and out. The lower level was only opened on special occasions, and apparently a negotiation with wærewolves qualified as special.

The dry scent of cold concrete mingled with the dank stench of the Cuyahoga River, which snaked under them. *This bridge connects the West Side with the East Side, and today the stink of both are collecting here.*

Inside, the transportation department reps had taken a position with their backs to the route that the subway cars once traveled. Anything could be hidden in the depths of that darkness behind them.

Breathing deep to sort through all the scents as nonchalantly as possible, Johnny detected more humans than were visible, and a lot of gunpowder and gun oil. Johnny glanced around. This would have to be a position ODOT felt they could defend, one that gave them an advantage. Question was, what advantage did it give them and how could the wæres overcome it if necessary? He shot a glance at Gregor, who nodded.

"*Diviza* Plympton . . ." Gregor whispered.

"I smell them, all right, boy," he whispered back.

"Mediation usually doesn't include bullying tactics like coming in with an arsenal," Aurelia said softly.

Plympton chittered a laugh. "We a-walked in with more strength and power in our veins than they will ever know. They have merely made an attempt to even the odds, Mizz Romochka."

That made Johnny think back to being a new wære, when he first joined this pack. He'd been taught many things, including how to respond when mundane humans became aggressive.

"*The general population thinks guns will protect them from us. When they make a show of force, it is because they fear us and are trying to keep us at bay. We should be flattered that they go to such effort,*" he recalled the former pack leader Ignatius telling him. A father figure to Johnny, Ig had bestowed him with wisdom he hadn't had much use for until recently. "*It makes them feel powerful to have that steel in their hands. But you, John, you have something far more potent inside of you.*"

Ahead, there were five men, front and center. They stood like mob bosses in a police lineup: shoulder to shoulder, hands clasped before them, wearing nice black suits. Scattered around in flanking positions were over a dozen men in fatigues, grouped in threes. Posed for intimidation, these men wore their guns unhidden and their hands were poised, ready to draw.

"These are not the same guys that have been at the other meetings," Todd said quietly.

Something had changed drastically for ODOT to be taking it this far. They didn't intend to lose this negotiation.

The *diviza* continued. "Let's walk, people. Walk like we own the place. Don't hold back. Let their human senses feel what we are, what we can do. Domn Lup, now would be a good time to let some of your sovereignty shine through." He started forward.

The wærewolves crossed the distance, letting that "other" about them radiate forth like the cool breeze before a bad storm.

Being outnumbered four to one against a mostly hidden, well-armed enemy, Johnny's initial reaction was to get angry and offended, but he knew that was surely part of what they wanted. He let that emotion flow into his aura and dared to reach inward and stroke his beast, just one brief, light touch. . . .

The instant he did, it lurched within him like a vicious junkyard dog leaping to the end of its chain.

He felt a wave of heat explode out from him. It drew low growls from those walking with him, and as it hit the humans, they were noticeably affected, responding with either a quick step backward or a head-to-toe shiver.

Johnny focused on maintaining his stride, not faltering in step, and on controlling the wolf inside him.

Off to his left was another man, but this tan-suited fellow was not trying for intimidation. Stout, with thin gray hair, he would not have been able to be convincing as a tough guy anyway. He had already mopped his sweaty forehead a dozen times with a handkerchief, shifted his weight frequently, and twice had switched the briefcase from one hand to the other. "What in Hell was that?" he muttered softly.

While the four male wærewolves formed a line of their own with Johnny and the *diviza* in the middle, Aurelia stepped to the forefront. "Hello, gentlemen. I'm Aurelia, assistant to the Domn Lup. May I introduce the *diviza,* Mr. Plympton." She gestured toward the bearded man, who nodded once. "And you are?" she asked sweetly.

"Our names aren't important," the man in the center said. He wore a bright blue tie.

Johnny took that as a bad sign. They might be legitimate representatives of ODOT, or they might be, literally, hired guns.

"Very well. Are you the mediator?" she asked the nervous man with the briefcase.

"I am." He inched forward.

She closed the distance to him and shook his hand. "Aurelia."

"Baker," he said, soaking in her beauty and kindness. "Scott Baker."

"Nice to meet you, Scott," she said warmly. "Usually this kind of thing takes place in an office, around a table. Since we have neither of those here, how do *you* want to proceed?"

Johnny knew she was charming the man to put him at ease and gain some of his favor for their side. But Scott was obviously not a fool. Caught between wærewolves and armed "government officials" in a last-minute meeting at a secret locale, he recognized the danger he was in. Johnny wondered if ODOT had bribed him.

"As I understand it," Scott said, pointing at ODOT's line of suits, "ODOT wants the Cleveland Cold Storage building and has made an offer which has been declined. You're here to make a new offer."

"Correct," Blue Tie said.

"And you," Scott gestured at Johnny, "simply want to keep the building."

"The location in question," Mr. Plympton said in his lilting Cajun accent, "is a mostly windowless structure that is perfect for the specific needs of our people." His hands flitted this way and that as he spoke. "We've modified the interior extensively over the years and to move the den to any other building would require starting over on those modifications. The purchase price ODOT has previously offered does not come close to allowing us to purchase a new structure in the area and then modify it similarly in order to ensure the safety of our people . . . and yours."

"There are other areas," Blue Tie said softly.

Aha. They want us out of their downtown.

A few tense seconds passed, then Scott asked Plympton, "You are open to considering the new offer they have prepared, though, right?"

"Of course we will consider the new offer."

Scott faced the ODOT reps. "You have the paperwork?"

The man to Blue Tie's right opened his jacket. From an inside pocket he removed a mass of papers stapled together and folded once lengthwise. He handed it to Scott, who in turn handed it to Plympton.

Plympton perused the document, not bothering to remove his sunglasses. "There's nothing new in this offer. In fact, these pages are identical to the last offer."

"That's correct," Blue Tie said.

Johnny let his internal struggle for dominance deepen his voice as he asked, "If you're not offering anything new, why are we here?"

"Oh, we're offering something new." Blue Tie nodded

to the man on his left and he pulled out more papers from the opposite side of his jacket. "It's something that is . . . out of the public eye, for now."

When these papers were handed to him, Plympton quickly scanned through the pages.

Johnny tried to see what was written on them, but the smugness in Blue Tie's voice made him look up.

"You see, we've had reports coming in about this pack," Blue Tie said. "It seems some dubious activities are going on in Cleveland, activities that—according to our investigation—lead back to this den. As the paperwork trail you're now looking at shows, this includes burglary, grand theft auto, receiving stolen goods, trafficking, money laundering, racketeering, tax evasion, embezzlement . . ."

"*That's not true,*" Todd growled.

Blue Tie hesitated only briefly at the outburst. ". . . We even have evidence of insurance fraud, where the widow of one Ignatius Tierney is concerned."

Johnny's hands clenched. They'd made this up. All of it. They'd falsified documents to blackmail them. He could not let them mess with the pack, and *would not* let them harass Moira. His beast slavered and snarled, feasting on his hate. Fur sprouted on the backs of his hands—

Calmly, Plympton reached out and touched Johnny's wrist.

Soothing coolness swirled around his skin. The wolf within him howled in pain and retreated.

"We're prepared," Blue Tie continued, "to deliver all of this documentation to our local and national news organizations. I'm sure they will be happy to write headlines about the new Domn Lup and his pack being sordid criminals. If you don't want to start his rule with an uphill battle to overcome those kinds of black marks—which we *will* put front and center for the world to see—then you really should agree to our terms now."

Plympton laughed. It started out small and quiet, but it grew. As it lifted in volume, the tone became menacing.

"You think this is funny?" Blue Tie asked.

Plympton kept laughing. Johnny joined in, then Gregor, then Todd. They all laughed together as if there was some fantastic joke when they were in fact simply following the lead of the *diviza*. It was not so different from a pack lifting their voices in unison because their alpha howled.

"What?" Blue Tie asked again. The men around him shifted, uncomfortable with the evil, echoing sound. "*What!*"

Only when Blue Tie had clearly shown his anger did Plympton let his mirth fade. "All right, boy. If you want your road so bad, we will give you the Cleveland Cold Storage . . . in exchange for Grays Armory." His voice continued to convey humor.

Blue Tie's suspicion was evident. "No deal."

Plympton shrugged. "You are forcing us out. If we have no den to kennel in, it is your public that is at risk. You don't want us telling the media you're willing to endanger your citizens for your road. Do you?"

"The Armory is a public historical icon and a museum."

"Wærewolves require a fortified structure to keep the beasts inside. Our team has already appraised every building in the city. No other building will protect your city's inhabitants from us like the Grays Armory will."

"Go somewhere else."

"Not happening," Johnny growled.

"We don't have the authority to give you—"

"Then get it." Plympton waved the papers at him. "With your obvious skill for fraud, I'm sure you can come up with something that will appease the people."

"Mr. Plympton—" Blue Tie began.

"To you, this has always been about the building, but not to us. It's about having a secure location for our people and safety for all. You're clearly desperate to get your big road built, so you can have the building."

He pulled his sunglasses off, revealing the wrongness on his silvered eye. The ODOT reps reacted as Johnny had.

"Trade us the Armory and the Zvonul will forget you tried to blackmail us. Don't and . . . well, we'll make sure the first casualties stemming from us not having a safe place to kennel will be those nearest and dearest to you." He pointed at the reps individually, calling them each by name. They shifted uncomfortably. "Shall I name the men hidden in the darkness as well?"

Blue Tie swallowed hard.

"We'll be ready to start our move this weekend, boys. You'd better be, too." Plympton turned and walked away, giggling like a Cajun fool.

CHAPTER NINE

S undown was fast approaching when the cab for which I was paying an immense fare neared my farmhouse. I spied Celia's CX-7 in the driveway and smiled. It would be good to see her and Beverley.

I glanced into the backyard, hoping to see the girl riding around on a prancing Errol, but instead I saw Celia, hands in her hair like she was extremely frustrated. She turned and saw the cab. She started running toward the front.

Something's wrong.

It took long seconds before the cabbie made the turn. "Stop, stop," I cried, threw money at him, and I jumped out to run up the driveway.

"What's wrong?" I called, seeing Celia round the back corner.

"It's Beverley."

"What?" We stopped before each other, both of us panting. I heard voices yelling the kiddo's name in the distance.

"I was working on contracts and she came out to see Errol." Her eyes were red and she started tearing up. "I heard the door open and close as she went out. Then, ten minutes ago, Mountain comes by and asks where Beverley is, since he didn't see her outside. Errol's in his stall, Seph. She never got to the barn."

My stomach felt like it dropped into my feet.

"We don't know where she is. We can't find her. Mountain and Zhan set out in opposite directions around the cornfield."

Mountain was a Beholder and Zhan an Offerling; both served Menessos. They were both very capable, but I couldn't stand idly by. I hurried past Celia. After a few steps, I was jogging, then sprinting. I raced into the first barn where the unicorns and griffons were housed. "Thunderbird!"

From the back, I heard hay rustling and then the majestic tiger-raven stepped into view, his head turned slightly, his one eye squarely on me. He'd lost the other in battle.

"Beverley's missing. Take to the air and find her!"

He loped past me. Five other griffons swiftly trailed him, some eagle and puma, some hawk and panther. I returned to the edge of the barn as they all took flight. In contrast to the dire moment, watching them gave me a sense of awe. They were beautiful creatures, these griffons. They fell into a pattern, crisscrossing the property from above.

Behind me, clip-clopping sounded as the unicorns backed from their stalls and walked out of the barn around me. They lifted their heads to watch the griffons circling. Except for one. Errol nickered low and touched my arm with the side of his mouth as if to ask, "Is she okay?"

Facing him, I'd have sworn he looked worried.

I was. The day was fading fast and thinking of Beverley lost was awful, but thinking of her lost *and* alone in the cold dark was so much worse.

My only consolation lay in the fact my property had

wards to keep the nasties out. If something was able to cross the ley line—empowered barrier, a psychic alarm would alert me, even if I wasn't home. I'd felt no such warning of a breach.

Reaching out with a sliver of power, I tried to detect the flow of energy from the obelisk-shaped piece of jet that Xerxadrea had given me. It rested in my bedroom and was keyed to empower the iron spikes at each corner of my property. I fed it from the ley line, but I hadn't exactly been home to monitor it lately.

Nothing. I felt *nothing* from the ward.

My breath caught. Had I let the power fade from my ward? If something snuck in and—

One of the griffons cried out.

It was the one Mountain called Eagle Eye, a lion-and-eagle male. He gave his cry again and angled his wings to circle back. Errol burst forward and galloped away into the cornfield. Celia and I shared a look and charged after him. I was a dozen steps into the cornfield when true sunset occurred.

I felt Menessos awaken.

His screaming torment ripped through me and my steps faltered.

I fell hard to the ground. It knocked the wind out of me, then Celia stumbled, trying not to step on me.

"Seph, are you okay?"

I wasn't. I could barely breathe and it hurt like hell. I nodded at her.

"Seph?"

She wasn't looking at me, but at her foot. Her shoe had come off, and she was assessing a broken ankle strap.

The low heels she was wearing certainly weren't meant for dashing through a cornfield.

"It's Menessos," I croaked. "Go on. I'll catch up in a minute."

"You sure?"

"Yes. Go." Beverley needed a person to get to her. If she was hurt, neither the unicorn nor the griffon could do much.

Celia turned and, with her one shoe flopping, hurried off in the direction the unicorn had gone. It would have been laughable if the circumstances had been different.

I worked conscientiously on making each breath a little deeper than the last, which should have been much easier than it was. This had been happening at every sundown since I'd staked him. I wasn't certain what it all meant, but I knew Menessos. It was getting worse each night.

An upward glance revealed that all the griffons had gathered in the air and were circling at different altitudes. It was an awesome sight—until I realized they were circling the grove.

Where the ley lines that crossed my property intersected.

Oh no.

Even before I really recovered, my feet were under me and I stumbled forward, gasping and choking for breath.

As I cleared the field, Errol was cantering toward me. He turned and trotted away, then spun and trotted back, only to hurry away again. His terribly nervous behavior struck a cold nerve within me. Then I saw Celia back-pedaling from the tree branches, staring downward with her hands covering the lower half of her face.

No.

I sprinted forward. "Celia!"

"I can't go in!" Her voice cracked. "I can't!"

Of course not. She was a wærewolf and the grove was a small ley line hub. The power there was a no-no for her kind. I should have thought of that.

"There." She pointed.

I plowed into the branches. They scratched at me and pulled my hair as if they would hold me back. But my urgency would not be denied. I struggled forward, thrashing and flailing, snapping the thin wooden arms around me.

As I emerged in the inner circle, part of my brain wanted me not to look, but my rebellious eyes followed the direction Celia indicated anyway.

There, at the base of the biggest tree in the grove, sat Great El's slate, like a teeter-totter perfectly balanced over a high root. Beverley's shoes lay to the side, one upright, the other on its side.

Beyond the grove, Celia's hands fell to her sides. "What does it mean?"

The slate hadn't come out here on its own.

Beverley had brought it—but where was she now?

Easing forward, I crouched and studied the base of the tree. The way some of the fallen leaves were scrunched, I could assume a kid had sat there, but I was no tracker. Even the part of me that could discern differences in energy was rather useless here. The whole place was power laden, and trying to get a feel for Beverley was like looking for footprints in sand after the tide has come in and washed everything away.

I reached out, my fingers rubbing along the edge of the slate—and instantly recoiled.

"Damn!" It was searing hot. I jerked so hard my crouching balance was lost. I fell onto my backside.

"What?" Celia demanded.

"Yes, what?" Zhan asked as she burst from the field and approached the grove.

"You could fry an egg on that slate," I said.

"What is that?" Zhan asked as she bent down and crawled under the branches and through the foliage to get to the inner section of the grove.

"It's my Great El's slate."

Zhan stood and brushed off her hands and knees. Studying the board, she asked, "Is it some kind of Ouija board?"

"Yeah. A spirit board."

"What is it doing out here?" Zhan asked.

I had barely kept that question from forming in my own mind. But there it was. It had been spoken. My stomach suddenly had more knots than a Persian rug.

My gaze lifted and met Celia's through the branches. "She heard us talking about it," I said.

Beverley had been in the kitchen when Celia asked me how I'd found my mother. I remembered Celia saying something about talking to ghosts on it, and though that wasn't exactly accurate, I hadn't corrected her.

Oh, Beverley, were you looking for your mother?

"What does it mean that it's so hot to the touch?" Celia asked.

I didn't want to answer that question. I felt sick. My hand moved to my stomach as I rose to my feet.

"Where is this thing *supposed* to be?" Zhan asked.

That one was much easier to speak the answer to. "Hidden in the back of my closet."

"Oh my God. Seph, I didn't know she was even in your room."

I looked at Celia again. I didn't want to make her feel guilty. But I didn't have to. She was doing that all by herself.

"What's it mean that it's hot?" she asked again.

Staring down at the slate, my stomach cramped with grief and anger and helplessness. "The heat means it's been used. In a very bad way."

I pulled out my satellite phone. If there was any hope of fixing this, I knew I couldn't do it alone.

Zhan stepped closer and gripped my arm. "Where is she?"

"She could be anywhere, or nowhere. She went into the ley line."

CHAPTER TEN

Naked in the dark, Goliath awakened to life with a scream.

He wasn't alone; he could detect the heat of a fully alive body in the room with him. His own body was cold, having lain dead and uncovered for hours. As his heart shuddered into rhythm the thick blood pumped through his veins, thinning more with each beat.

"Light," he groaned.

A lighter clicked and the flame flickered over candlewick. An amber glow filled the modest chamber.

The Offerling waiting to feed him was a transplant from the previous Cleveland haven that had belonged to Heldridge. She was beautiful, with perfectly proportioned features and skin so black she was nearly lost to the dark. Her eyes were a bright, pale brown and her lips had a hint of pink.

"Sil," he said. Heldridge had called her Silhouette, but she'd said she liked the shortened name better.

Sil had caught his eye during the reclaiming ceremony with Menessos. He would have to perform that same ritual on every member of the haven. Marking them and bonding with them would make him stronger, but it would be exhausting initially.

Hunger clenched his stomach and he put aside all other thoughts. Rising from his bed, he reached out and put his hand to her cheek, marveling at the contrast of his ghostly pale skin against the inky darkness of hers. He indicated with his touch that he wanted her to come to him.

She rose. She was unclothed and he pulled her close, breathing the smell of juniper deep into his lungs.

It was a familiar scent.

Lorrie.

At the thought of her name, memories flooded back. The wærewolf had been timid but eager in his bed. She'd feared the strength her beast afforded her, but he'd reassured her and won her over. He'd even been good to her daughter, Beverley. Lorrie had once said she found in him a man she couldn't hurt. He'd found a woman who understood pain and loss, who carried doubt and fear, but kept going regardless. He'd found a woman who saw his flaws and loved him in spite of them.

He'd bought her perfumes, lotions, and soaps made with juniper.

Hunger mixed with desire. He knew he could not have again what they had, but he wanted to mingle blood and feeding and sex again.

Taking Sil by the arms, he practically threw her onto the bed, following her down. Atop her, he kissed her neck and ran his hands all over her body. Her ebony skin was smooth under his hands, under his lips, and when he pierced the vein, she whispered, "Yes."

Her flavor was rich and fine. She tasted like strength.

With a firm grip, he opened her legs. She did not resist. He continued sucking at her neck, flicking his tongue over the openings his teeth had made, and letting his fingers explore other openings. She arched her back as he touched her inside, and she moaned wantonly, welcomingly.

Goliath pushed his torso up and pressed his erection against her. A drop of her blood ran down his chin. Sil reached up and caught it with her finger, then wiped it across her lips. He bent down and licked her lips as he pushed his cock into her.

Remembering Lorrie, grieving for her, and letting her go, Goliath made love to Sil furiously. She had to put her hands against the headboard to keep his thrusts from shoving her across the mattress.

When he was spent and she was thrice satisfied, Goliath lay wrapped in and around Silhouette as if they were yin and yang.

Ailo awoke gently, sweetly, from her daytime death.

Then she sat up with a start, clutching at her chest while the sheet fell away.

As a vampire, as one of the living dead, her heart began to beat again and blood began to flow through her body, allowing her mind to race.

She remembered.

There had been no reason to scream as she woke tonight. There had been no torture. No tormentor. But the dark-haired man had whispered ideas into her ear like he had last night.

Twisted ideas. Wonderful ideas.

Beside her, Talto whimpered. She cried out as her eyelids fluttered and the impossible life of their cursed kind resumed in her body.

No tender awakening for you, my sister? Ailo's lips curved. *I have found favor.*

It was an opportunity she would not squander.

• • •

Goliath showered. The next order of business for the evening was to deal with the issue concerning the court witch. He wanted Ailo and Talto to be left out of it, so he headed to the haven's business office. In addition to the new wardrobe, personal guards came with his new status, so, when he left his own chambers the pair on duty flanked him.

Menessos was pacing outside the office. He turned as they approached. "If you have a moment, I require an audience with you."

"Of course." Goliath preceded him into the office. It was a gentleman's room, with cherry paneling and museum cases filled with weaponry artifacts—Menessos owned all these things. The guards remained outside; one of them shut the door.

The two of them sat, taking seats that were opposite from their usual. Fighting the awkwardness of the situation, Goliath sat behind the desk in the leather-upholstered chair and noted the work waiting for him in the short stack of papers. "What is it?" he asked.

"I must leave immediately. I've received a call from Persephone—"

"She isn't here?"

In a guarded tone, Menessos answered, "No."

"I left orders that she was not to be permitted to leave." He was going to have to question those he left in charge for the day and find out exactly when she left, and who let her get by.

"I am aware of this. Do not worry, she has not fled, but I *must* go."

If she was waiting on Menessos, she would remain wherever she was; if they decided to forcibly retrieve her they would not have to locate her. Goliath shook his head. "Let her wait. We must call Mero to join us and decide what is to be done with her."

Menessos stood, put his hands on the desk, and leaned over it threateningly. "With all due respect, Haven Master, I am not here as your subject to ask your permission to leave. I am here as your Maker to tell you I am going. This cannot wait." He turned for the door.

Goliath stood. "I grow concerned, Menessos." Using his name instead of the usual honorifics stopped his Maker in his tracks. "You are not yourself. As I think back, you have not been since she entered your life."

Menessos was as still as death.

"She beckons and you race to her side."

Over his shoulder, Menessos said, "I never said I was going *to* her."

"Still, you are going because she bade you to go! For her, you have thrown away your status as Quarterlord. For her, you have lost the power base of your haven . . . and she won't even fuck you."

Menessos slowly turned. His eyes had gone dark and sharklike.

Goliath felt a stirring in his core. All sounds were suddenly muffled until his own breathing was loudest in his ears. All color in the room drained until only Menessos remained vivid.

He felt the need to move from behind the desk, and his feet carried him around it.

He felt the need to approach Menessos, and his feet carried him across the room.

He felt the need to kneel before his Maker, his Master, and his knees bent.

Like a bursting soap bubble, everything returned to normal. Goliath scrambled onto his feet again and glowered down at the other vampire.

"You know what obeisance can be forced upon one who wears the marks of another," Menessos snapped.

"This is why you run to her?" Goliath had studied the policies of the witches. Forcing someone to do something against their will was a direct violation of their major tenets. The idea of dragging her to the Excelsior was gaining his favor.

Gravely, Menessos said, "I swear to you: she has *never* used such power on me, though she could have. I go to her because it is necessary. My path and hers are weaving together in this matter and there is much more at stake here than you yet know."

"Enlighten me."

"I cannot, my friend. Not yet. I must get to a ley line before it is too late."

"Why?" Goliath demanded.

Exasperated, Menessos said, "I had hoped to not reveal this to you, but Beverley is missing."

Goliath felt his resolve disappear. If Lorrie's child was in danger, he couldn't stand in the way of Menessos helping. He nodded once to indicate he would not interfere.

"Don't let Ailo or Talto give you any trouble while I am out," Menessos said as he turned to leave.

When his Maker reached the door Goliath called, "Menessos."

The elder vampire turned back.

Goliath hesitated. What he wanted to say, what he wanted to ask for, was very nearly unheard of. But the situation was growing dangerous. He had to have it. He firmed his resolve. "I have asked you for very little since you Made me."

"What do you desire, Goliath?"

Chin level, shoulders square, and voice flowing with confidence he said, "Our bond must be broken."

Menessos regarded him for a heartbeat. One corner of his lips twisted up. "Yes. Indeed, the time has come. You have earned it. I *will* give you that freedom."

CHAPTER ELEVEN

Regardless of Gregor's protest, Johnny Newman made certain he was the last one into the back of the big Escalade. He slammed the door before the driver could do his job.

"Grays Armory?" he snarled.

"Yes. As I said, according to our reports, it is the best choice for the needs of this pack." Plympton had left his dark glasses off and he faced Johnny squarely, giving him a good view of the silvered eye.

Since wærewolves could heal afflictions and diseases that occurred before they were infected with the wære virus, Johnny wondered why the man's injury hadn't healed in his monthly transformations. But then, Ig had suffered from strokes in the months before his death; while the transformation and reversion to human form initially healed him, the strokes recurred earlier and earlier each cycle. Apparently for some there were factors that didn't hold true to the norm.

Johnny decided he didn't want to know the nature of Plympton's wound. "Whose reports?" He had questions about what Plympton had done back there, how he had made Johnny's beast yelp and retreat, but those questions were not to be asked in front of an audience. "Who did the appraisal?"

"Our kind, John. I had the Zvonul send a group out when I learned of the situation. The Armory may be over

185 years old, but the structure was meant to protect those inside. Besides, the castle-like architecture is as bold and imposing as it is beautiful. Very fitting for wærewolves. The pack should be proud to have it."

"And if the locals don't like it?"

Plympton grinned. "Tough titties."

Johnny shot a frown at Todd. They both knew Clevelanders. This would not go over well with the locals.

"The Zvonul made arrangements to get CCS in the first place," Plympton added. "This is no different."

"The hell it isn't!" Johnny argued. "The Armory isn't some run-down building that's out of commission, used only for billboards, and so close to the Flats that no one cares if wærewolves are in it. The Armory is downtown! It's a Cleveland landmark, the oldest building in the city."

"Yes," Plympton said. "That is another part of the reason it is perfect. It has also been the host of many historic events and important social functions. Now it will host this pack."

"But—" Todd interjected.

"No buts!" Plympton shouted, facing Todd. "The pack will cordially allow the local veterans to continue holding festivities there, some touring exhibits. Some halls will continue to be rentable for parties, weddings, proms, et cetera. It will be a great outreach opportunity."

Somehow, the man's bad eye seemed to continue focusing on Johnny independently of where the other eye looked. It was unsettling, but even so Johnny said, "You don't know Clevelanders, Jacques. This is bullshit."

With that, he sat back and pulled out his phone, which he'd switched to silent for the meeting. There were multiple missed calls from Red, and one voicemail.

Aware of the excellent hearing of his companions, he decided not to listen to the message in the limo. He knew she was upset; the meeting had interfered, but it hadn't taken *that* long. He texted her: Just out of meeting. @ den in 5. On my way to you then.

By the time they arrived at the den, she had not responded. That was unusual for her, and it fed his urgency to listen to her message privately. He was the first one out of the limo, not waiting for the driver to open the door for him.

Aurelia exited on his heels. "John. Wait."

"No time. Prior commitment." She was not going to stall him this time. He pulled his keys from his pocket and remotely unlocked the Maserati's doors as he neared the driver's side.

Aurelia rushed forward and threw her body against the door. "John! We have to talk."

He stepped in close, growling low. "Don't you *ever* do that again."

"Don't do what?" she asked. "Something drastic to get your attention?" The sass in her tone infuriated him.

"No. Don't ever touch my car." He forcibly moved her away from the driver's door.

"You need to learn how to be a king, John. The Zvonul are not going to be happy with me if I don't teach you some etiquette, and I can't do that if you don't give me a chance."

"Etiquette? Sounds like you're trying to puss-ify the Domn Lup."

"Hardly. You are a king. Therefore, you don't open your own doors. Not to houses, buildings, or limos. You have someone to do that for you because you are Sovereign."

Irritated, he turned from her and reached for his car door.

"You also need to move," she added. "I've heard about this farmhouse, where you've been rooming in the *attic*. That is simply unacceptable. You need to live downtown, close to the den, in an exclusive high-rise type of place with some prestige. Now, I've got a couple of places in mind already—"

But Johnny didn't hear the rest. He was already squealing tires out of the parking garage and headed into the ever-darkening night.

"I'm going in alone," Liyliy said. "Watch for me. I *will* bring my sisters out."

She let her magical senses guide her flawlessly as she reached for the rear door handle of the unmarked white van that had brought her and Giovanni to Cleveland. They had agreed that chartering a private flight would not go unreported to those at the local haven, while a vehicle could travel between states anonymously, and could arrive perfectly timed to make the best use of the night.

"Wait," Giovanni said. "Take these." He handed her three small objects.

Having used her ability to read a few people of this time period who were savvy with technology, she knew what these items were and how to use them, but . . .

"Why?" she asked.

"Mero and Menessos are both intelligent. While they may have imprisoned your sisters, I doubt that would be all they have done to secure them."

Liyliy was angrily resistant at first—she'd break them out if she had to—but as seconds ticked by, she realized he was right. Her enemies were not to be underestimated.

"Even if they are not contained," he added, "perhaps having spies within might be to our tactical advantage."

"Spies?" Liyliy questioned.

With a sordid grin, Giovanni nodded.

"You said we cannot do this alone, and yet you ask me to make my sisters stay within that vile haven?"

"Increasing our numbers is the priority, but the opportunity to have eyes and ears in the home of our foe could be an invaluable asset. Surely you comprehend this?"

"You want me to let *my sisters* remain where they may be tortured or worse even if I can bring them out?"

"You have suffered greatly, Liyliy. I do not think your sisters will be treated as you have been, but I *do* think that while they may suffer somewhat, leaving them within this haven could make the difference that lets us win the day."

She stared at him coldly. "They are not as strong as I am. They need me. We are stronger together." That was, after all, her whole motive for getting them out.

"Consider it for a moment. We must all sacrifice for this war. Even your sisters."

Without them to help her heal from this hideous disfigurement, she would be trapped as an ugly monster. *I have given enough already*. But Liyliy thought through the possibility of her sisters staying in the vampire's homestead as spies while also being able to contact her with news. Giovanni was right. She could obtain information and guide them, control them, use them to their advantage.

Concentrating, she tapped into her quicksilver magic and caused a portion of her skirting to shrink and liquefy, sliding over her body until it had changed into a hidden pocket that would hold the phones. After she dropped them inside, she again reached for the door and exited the van. It quickly drove away.

Missing an eye affected her two ways: her field of vision was decreased, and judging distances was difficult. Darkness only intensified the impairment.

The evening was young. As she turned her head back and forth in a few quick sweeps to gauge her surroundings, she noted individuals and small groups milling around, some traversing the sidewalks. Seeing her, several people on the sidewalk gasped and their steps stalled until she had passed. Then they hurried on, whispering. She hobbled toward the haven, the contents of the hidden pocket bouncing against her hip, emphasizing her labored movement.

She smugly judged the doors she had smashed through when she'd left this horrid place. They were boarded up, unsightly. The destructive impact she'd had was wonderful. She would make everything ugly if she could.

Then *she* would not be so repulsive.

Goliath had summoned Mero to his office as soon as Menessos left. As the Excelsior's advisor entered, he spoke a greeting and lowered himself into one of the comfortable seats across from the Haven Master's large desk. "I assume the Erus Veneficus is on her way?"

It galled Goliath that his first direct order to his haven had been met with failure. Worse was having to admit as much to this high-ranking vampire. But it *was* Persephone Alcmedi that had gotten away. Goliath mentally kicked himself. *I should have known better.*

"The witch is not in the haven."

Mero rose to his feet. "Where is she?"

Goliath wasn't about to tell him they didn't know, not yet. So he kept his expression one of poise and authority. "Please sit down, Meroveus."

A moment passed, then the advisor sank stiffly onto the chair again. The questions he could have asked and the accusations he could have made all went unspoken, but his rigid mannerisms screamed of anger.

Goliath considered how he might stall for time, hoping that Menessos would bring the witch back. If he was able to achieve such a sham, he would avoid being seen as incapable by the Excelsior's advisor. If caught, however, he would be doubly discredited. He haggled with himself, only to decide that—being a new Haven Master—in this instance guile would not serve him as well as directness and honesty.

"I am not certain where she is at this time, but I am prepared to ask those involved and aware of her departure today to meet us here immediately if you are interested in being present for the inquiry as to why my commands were not followed—"

The pager on the desk phone buzzed. Goliath pressed it. "Yes?"

"The missing shabbubitum just came through the front entrance," the voice on the other end of the line said quickly.

Both Goliath and Mero were instantly on their feet. They headed for the door.

"I must create a binding for her," Mero said. "Please do not allow her to leave."

"I'll do my best," Goliath snapped.

"I was not rebuking you." Mero stopped with his palms out toward Goliath. "Both females, I'm sure, are equally difficult to contain."

Goliath acquiesced with a single nod. "How much time do you need?"

"This will have to be powerful . . . as much as you can give me."

From the darkness inside the haven, a voice that Liyliy recognized as Goliath's addressed her. "You've returned."

It was a simple statement. The slimmest possible acknowledgment. It asked nothing, yet it was full of inquiry. "Was I not supposed to?" She laughed. "Did the witch tell you I was dead?"

"No."

Which question was he answering? she wondered snidely and started forward, not bothering to disguise her limp. "I must see my sisters."

She searched the darkness, and forced her one remaining eye to make the owlish transformation. Like this, the depth perception remained inferior, but the larger pupil could open wide and allow her to function better in the dark. They were clustered in small groups, fifteen vampires in all, scattered across the entry.

For an instant, she felt sick. She felt like crumbling, succumbing to the fear that had been eating at her ever since she glimpsed her new, hideous face. *Attack. Give them cause to slaughter me and end this disgusting existence.*

But that notion passed.

She wanted to see her sisters and repair this damage. She wanted to extract a gruesome revenge upon the witch. She wanted to see all that Menessos had built and cherished burnt to ash.

"I am injured." She clung to a thread of hope that perhaps, with her sisters, the three of them together could reverse some of the damage.

Still Goliath did not answer. By his thoughtful pose it seemed he was considering her request, but the fact that he did not answer gnawed at her impatience.

"I have come back. My actions must speak for themselves. Let me see my sisters, that we might try to heal my disfigurement." She held her breath. It was a risk coming here, but she was betting that they had not anticipated the action, and therefore had not created an alternate means of restraining her. She needed to not linger and give them time to do so. She needed to get to her sisters, heal herself, deliver the phones in secret, and get back out.

She ground her teeth slightly, then she added, "Please. I beg you. I've lost an eye, my arm will not completely change, my leg is twisted—"

"Very well," Goliath said. "I will allow you to see your sisters and endeavor a healing. Then we have to discuss the terms of your remaining here. Am I clear?"

"Yes." She did not believe he would let her remain here unbound, but she followed him to the elevator as quickly as she was able. She didn't know if he avoided the stairs out of consideration for her condition, but she was grateful whatever his motive. Upon reaching the lower floor, she was escorted along the hall to a conference room with a large cherry table and dark brown décor. It was mostly leather and wood, with a few accents of deep hunter green.

She recognized the room. When she had clasped Giovanni's wrists and licked away the blood from his hands, she had read him. Not a full mind scan like she did with the aid of her sisters, but a gentle search into the recent past. After she'd departed the haven in pursuit of the witch, he'd interrogated her sisters here.

Moments later, her sisters scurried in and rushed toward her. "I knew you would not forsake us!" Talto cried even as her eyes widened upon seeing her sister's condition. But it did not stop her or Ailo. Both threw their arms about Liyliy.

Liyliy also took in their appearances with some grief. Both of them wore iron about their necks like slaves. Giovanni was right; her sisters had been bound.

Together they cooed and cried, shushed and sniffled as their reunion carried on for a long minute. They clasped hands and Ailo and Talto pushed images into her mind. They told her that in her absence Menessos had bound them to him and had the iron put round their throats. If they tried to transform, it would kill them. They were so angry, so resentful of him . . . but she had returned. She would save them, they were certain. All would be well.

In return, Liyliy showed them the pocket at her hip, the phones inside. She told them what they were for. "Heal me and take them," she whispered.

Embracing tightly, they each drew upon the magic that allowed them to clothe themselves with quicksilver and silk. Fabric flowed around them, between them, entwining and twirling like lovers wrapped in sheets. Liyliy's sisters began chanting and the fabric liquefied, spilling at impossible angles like gentle silver waterfalls onto Liyliy's skin.

All the magical fabric they possessed had flooded around her, leaving them both naked. It flowed outward to create a circle of liquid that encompassed her, then it filled in, growing deeper until it was ten inches of fluid, hovering unbelievably in the air. Her arms lifted and her hair fanned out as if she were floating in an upright pool of mercury.

Her sisters' chant became a song.

As the song continued, the liquid hardened like a gigantic mirror, sealing Liyliy in place. For a moment she seemed dead, frozen, caught in this strange magic. Then her sisters slammed their fists against the glass, pushing through, slicing their own flesh on the shards, and spilling their blood into the spell they were crafting.

The mirror cracked and shattered in slow motion, each broken piece cascading into sparkling dust, stretching into threads, and weaving into silken bandages that wound Liyliy like a mummy. When she was enveloped, her sisters stood and lowered her vertical body until it lay supine in midair. They each held one of her cloth-covered hands and clasped their free hands together. Still singing, harmonizing in a crescendo rising to angelic soprano notes, they forced the magic to permeate Liyliy. Her body began to glow under the wrapping, shining brighter and brighter until the room was filled with silvery illumination so blinding it seemed the moon had been stolen from the sky and placed in the hands of the shabbubitum.

All at once, that dazzling brilliance winked out.

The sisters' melody dropped into something less divine, something made of deep tones and fast staccato notes. Liyliy's body began to spin between them, the fabric unwinding and splitting in two, part sliding around Talto, part around Ailo.

When Liyliy was unwrapped, she stood.

The almost sentient material had reclothed each of them, with the phones hidden within the folds of their new silken gowns. With tears shimmering in her eyes, Talto held up her hand. The sleeve of her dress formed a hydrous mirror along her palm so Liyliy could view herself.

Her skin was no longer blistered, the globules on her chin were gone, and her face had resumed a human shape. Her eye had re-formed beneath a scarred lid. Lashes bristled this way and that in a drooping line across it.

Liyliy swallowed down bile.

Talto's tears fell.

Lifting her arm so she could view it, Liyliy learned it was no longer mottled with feathers, and her fingers, though still twisted, were the proper length. Her leg felt regenerated. She clasped her youngest sister into her arms. "Do not cry, Talto. It is better than it was."

"Do not leave us here," Talto whispered.

Liyliy pulled Ailo into their hug and by touch told them she had to do just that.

You have a binding upon you. If I free you, Menessos will follow.

Talto began sobbing.

Liyliy shushed her. *Do not fear, little one. Listen to me. I must leave before they put a binding upon me and doom us all.*

Ailo told her Menessos was not there. *I saw him leave in a hurry earlier. To my knowledge he has not returned.*

Liyliy asked why he had left. Ailo told her she had not been able to find out.

Still, Mero may be working on a means to bind me this very second, so I dare not linger. I will remain in contact via the phones, which you must keep secret. I will get you out, but I need you to be my eyes and ears inside the haven for now. We must tear them apart, weaken them as they have sought to weaken us. You understand this, yes?

"Yes," Talto whispered.

"Ailo?"

"Yes. And I have an idea."

Liyliy and Talto let her grasp their hands. She shut her eyes, and power flowed around her. Liyliy felt the energy reaching out, striving to touch something that was both deep within and far away . . . the binding. Liyliy listened inwardly and Ailo's silent plea echoed into her mind.

She was searching for Menessos, reaching back along the bond imposed on her, stretching. She sought him out, eager to report to Liyliy what he was doing.

Ailo found him . . . but he was not alone.

He was performing magic—a heady, dynamic magic— and it felt familiar, like an ancient memory.

Recognition burst into their minds as one.

By the gods, he's doing it again, Liyliy thought. *We must use this.*

CHAPTER TWELVE

It was barely six thirty and the day's light had almost entirely faded as I slid my satellite phone into my pocket. After I'd finished my call to Menessos, Johnny's text arrived—I was grateful for the distraction. He'd simply said he was on his way. Then my Great Dane, Ares, burst from the field and raced toward me in the grove. He was still pushing through the branches when Mountain emerged from the same spot the dog had. "Did you find her?" he asked.

"No," Zhan answered for me. "She's gone into the ley."

Mountain scratched his head. "Is that a good thing or a bad thing?"

Everyone faced me, waiting for the answer. Looking at her empty little shoes made my legs weak and rubbery, but I was trying to reason this all through. "Bad," I said. "I think."

"Explain."

"Witches use sorcery to tap into a line. It's dangerous and painful . . . and, truly, we have to be very careful to not get sucked in."

"So she was sucked in," Celia said through her tears.

There were horror stories about such things. Witches of "ye olde times" who disappeared were often thought to have been dabbling in sorcery and fallen into the ley. Especially if items left on their altars could support such theories. But I had always regarded those tales as exaggerations meant to steer curious young witches back to their craft studies, much like tales of the bogeyman warned children not to venture from their beds at night.

"Explain how you use this board to tap the ley line," Zhan said.

"I'm not sure. When I tap it, I do it directly, without an ancillary device."

"Is the board significant, then?" She began pacing. "Is there a clue in it? Did that make it easier or harder to get sucked in? And does it hold an option for us—or rather, *you*—to bring her back out through it?"

My mouth opened but nothing came out.

All these rapid-fire questions bordered on an understandable panic, feeding my fears, but I couldn't think clearly like this. I had to push the emotion away and concentrate.

My eyes locked on Great El's slate. The symbols painted on it were eerily bright in the darkness as I considered it.

Tapping a ley line directly was certainly more dangerous, and potent, than using a device to filter it. Direct access left nothing to keep a witch from falling into the ley except the barriers inherent in a physical being touching a nonphysical world. I thought of it as an oil-and-water kind of thing. *But* . . . the inherent risk lay in the fact that the ley's intense energy has the potential to transform tangible matter into intangible.

"The slate does not actually create the boundary between life as we know it and the other side," I said. "But it should have acted like an additional buffer."

"What do you mean by *the other side?*" Zhan asked.

"Think of a spirit board like those huge gates in *King Kong*. It stands between you and a world of wonderful and strange things. The fencing is so high and thick that you can't see over it or through it. There are other gateways, but this particular door has a neon sign above it that tells you this door is a unique spot, one where notes can be slipped back and forth underneath. You go there sometimes to ask those inside what it is like there."

With tears brimming her eyes, Celia asked, "Do you mean heaven . . . an afterlife? Is she dead?"

The only answer I had was lame. "I honestly don't know."

Silence fell around us. Another thought occurred to me. I'd focused on the slate because it was right there in front of me and so terribly out of place, but there was something else here that was magical. The grove was all around me.

"Wait." Mountain joined the conversation. "You said that the Ouija-board thingy should have been an extra buffer. When you say 'should have been' are you implying that it wasn't an extra buffer, or that it acted as more of a secret side door?"

I fixed him with my gaze. The big, gentle man was smarter than most people gave him credit for. "Beverley couldn't accidentally open a line and fall in, not with a spirit board, not even here in the grove."

"Not even if she's a witch?" Mountain asked.

"No. First of all," I said, "lines do not randomly open when someone gets near them like the sliding doors at the supermarket. There is a process to opening them, you have to make your own keys. Witches do that, but it takes time and skill."

Zhan crossed her arms. "You said not *accidentally*."

I nodded. "Something took her in." I didn't want to think that meant she was gone. I couldn't believe that. I wouldn't. "Whatever navigated her into the ley must have had a reason, and for that, it *will* be shielding her."

I said it like a command and I saw hope flicker in Celia's eyes.

My satellite phone rang, the number blocked. "Hello?"

A smooth female voice said, "The precious thing you are seeking will be found beside the ley line at Mill Stream Run Reservation, but only if you hurry, witch." The caller hung up.

I held the phone before me, wide-eyed. *Ley line?*

Zhan asked, "What is it?"

My broom would have been ideal, but I hadn't seen it since Liyliy and I fought at Cedar Point. Zhan's lead foot was the next best option. I grabbed her arm. "We gotta go."

Without enlightening the others, I hurried toward the trailer where Zhan had parked her Audi. Once inside the vehicle, I told her we needed to get to the reservation and asked if she knew the way. "Absolutely," was her reply.

She had us on I-71 in minutes, and, as expected, she cast caution to the wind and ignored the speed limit. "Why Mill Stream Run?"

I told her what the caller had said.

"This might be a setup," she countered, slowing down.

"How? She dialed my phone and called me 'witch.' She knew I was looking for something *precious,* and knew it had to do with the ley line."

"Exactly. Who was the caller? What if the kid was played by someone?"

I thought about my wards not being active. I hadn't been able to check them directly to see if I'd let the power run down or if something else had brought them down. "Either way, I have to find out."

"But you don't have to run in there blind."

"That's why you're with me."

"You called Menessos, right?"

"Yes."

"What was he doing about it?"

"He said he'd tap into the line near the haven and see what he could find out. He'd let me know if he found something."

"But it wasn't him that called?"

"No, it was a woman."

Zhan took the Royalton Road exit and turned right. "All right. Where's this line of yours?"

I took a moment to reach out and feel for the line. It ran north-northeast to south-southwest. I pointed to the south.

Zhan turned right onto Valley Parkway. Shortly within the park, the road curved to the east and a paved trail for walking or biking ran along the left side of the road. Ahead was a bridge to our right; the sign said it was Royalview Lane. Zhan slowed down. "Stay on Valley or turn?"

"Stay on Valley."

"How far?" she asked.

"I'm not sure. Go slow."

The trees were all bare. That dim inkling of civil twilight had expired and the full dark of night had settled in like a thick blanket. It was hard to see, and I scanned all around while keeping my focus on the ley line. I noticed the stream to the left beyond the trail.

It occurred to me that the headlights would give us away. I saw a spot to the right where a car could pull off the road. I said, "Stop here. Kill the lights."

The temperature had dropped since we left my home. I shut my door softly, afraid of the echoing sound it would make. I crossed the road and jogged along the empty trail. It ran right beside the road, but not far ahead the path snaked through the woodland a few yards from the road. I heard Zhan behind me but didn't argue about her following. Sensing the ley was well within the tree line, I had the urge to plow into the woods, but the leaves and twigs that would crunch underfoot would also give me away.

After about five hundred yards, I guess, my eyes detected the light of a bonfire ahead.

I hurried onward, ignoring Zhan's whispered protests for me to slow down. I kept jogging along the trail as it curved back toward the road then arced deeper into the woods toward the blaze, which had been built near a large fallen tree.

A hooded figure sat before that blaze and I could hear the singsong chant of a male voice. The smell of burning sage filled the air.

Creepy?

Pissed off, I stepped off the trail then, glancing back and forth between the ground and the fire, trying to make my approach as unnoticeable as possible. If it was him, I was going to need the element of surprise. *Please let that fire crackle and pop and the hood dampen other sounds from his ears.*

Then I saw Beverley. She lay as if sleeping upon the ground before the figure.

He raised his hands high. A green glow claimed the fire, and bolts like laser beams jumped into the air and circled a few feet over the flames. A purple swirl spiraled up from underneath the fire—from the ley line—and slithered into the fire, rising through it like a serpent, snapping onto the ends of the green bolts and swallowing them down. All the colors glinting and sparkling were mesmerizingly beautiful.

He lowered his hands over Beverley.

My hesitation evaporated. I plunged forward, heedless of the noise I made.

Abruptly, the figure turned, hood falling back.

Menessos!

His eyes widened and his head shook back and forth. His voice filled the woodland around me, shouting, "Don't break the circle!"

CHAPTER THIRTEEN

Johnny pulled into the driveway and saw Celia's CX-7. Though several lights were on in Mountain's trailer out by the barns, none were on at the house. Using his key, he let himself in and stood in the darkened hall with the open door at his back and sniffed.

Red wasn't here.

He detected nothing to indicate that she had been there recently, either. She still hadn't replied to his text. *Did she make it home?*

He jerked on his loosened tie, removing it altogether.

He breathed in the smells again. The kiddo. Celia. Mountain. That was it.

Moving closer to the stairway, he draped the tie over the handrail as he stared up at the unlit second floor. Aurelia said he needed to move, to live somewhere else. After what he'd done, Red might not let the Big Bad Wolf back in her home. He couldn't blame her if she asked him to leave, but he wasn't about to go up and preemptively pack his stuff, either.

Returning to the door, he put his hand on the knob and scanned the darkened house once more over his shoulder. He walked out and shut and locked the door behind him, heading for the trailer. His dress shoes were slick in the dew-damp grass.

Through the window, he saw Mountain open his refrigerator and remove something. As he approached the door, he saw the large man hand Celia a can of 7UP. He figured Celia and the kiddo must've been visiting the unicorns again.

At the same moment, Celia and Mountain turned. The wærewolf and the Beholder had both detected him; he hadn't been trying for stealth. Mountain approached to open the door. He didn't look happy.

"Johnny."

"Where's Red?" Johnny asked, glancing around as he entered.

Mountain said, "She and Zhan left a few minutes ago."

She's avoiding me. Guess I deserve it after what I did and then standing her up at the coffee shop.

"He doesn't know." Celia sounded miserable as she dropped into one of the kitchen's folding chairs with much less grace than was usual for her.

"I don't know what?"

"Beverley found and used Great El's slate," she said, pointing toward the woods outside the trailer. "She used it in the grove. Now she's . . . well, according to Seph, she's *in* the line."

Johnny tipped his head, squinting slightly. "You mean Beverley is *inside* of a ley line?"

When Celia's chin dropped to her chest, Johnny's gaze shifted to Mountain, who answered with a nod.

"The lines are just energy, right? How is that possible?"

Mountain shrugged. Celia began to cry.

Mountain headed into one of the trailer's back rooms.

Johnny knelt. "Celia?"

"I was supposed to be watching her," she said. "She

was supposed to have come out here to see Errol. I didn't even know she'd gone upstairs and taken the slate."

"Don't beat yourself up over it. Kids can be sneaky." He had the urge to put his hand on her knee to comfort her, but she was the wife of his former best friend, Erik. He folded his fingers together over his own bent knee.

"But a kid shouldn't be able to sneak like that around a wærewolf." She wiped her eyes. "I guess it's for the best that I'm not a mother."

"Celia." His hand slipped onto her knee then. He felt the spark of energy that flared up whenever he touched a female wærewolf. Their eyes met for an instant and her mouth opened. Before she could speak, Mountain returned with an unopened box of Kleenex and offered it to her. "Did Red say where they were going?"

"No," Mountain answered. "Her phone rang, she answered it, and two seconds later, she told Zhan they had to go."

Johnny took out his phone and hit the speed dial for Persephone's satellite phone. It rang and rang, but she didn't answer. When it clicked over to voicemail, he swore. Loudly.

Johnny paced. *She has to come back here. Unless it was Menessos that called. Then she'd end up at the haven.* He didn't know if he should stay or go. Lifting his phone before him again, he stopped walking and texted Kirk: Inform whoever we have watching the haven that he or she is to report to you immediately if Red is seen there. You notify me at once.

When he hit Send, the pacing resumed. Moments later, when Kirk acknowledged the text, he didn't even break stride.

Mountain walked into the kitchen, then returned with a short glass. "Here," Mountain said, pushing the glass at Johnny, who gave him a questioning look. "Captain and Coke. You need it." He put it into Johnny's hand. "I'll go see that all the animals are inside."

Johnny watched the vampire's Beholder go, aware that he was making an excuse to give the wærewolves time to talk privately. His gaze fell and he stared down into the short glass, watching the ice cubes slowly spin but not drinking.

"At least you stopped pacing," Celia said softly.

He tore his eyes from the glass to meet her gaze.

"What else is wrong?" she asked. "You're wrapped in tension like a field of static."

Not wanting to answer her, he drank.

Celia rose from her seat and drew close. "Erik misses you," she said. A gentle smile claimed her lips. "He'd never admit it but I know. He feels guilty about taking the money."

Under order of the old Rege, the Omori—the Zvonul's version of the Secret Service—had bribed the two other members of Johnny's band with twenty-five grand each. They had told Erik and Feral they were "no longer in Lycanthropia with Johnny." The band was officially dead, and the cash was their severance pay. The former Rege meant to undermine Johnny in every way he could.

"He shouldn't," Johnny said. "When the Omori show up at your door, you comply." He'd said those words before, but he hadn't been the Domn Lup then. Now he wondered what else the old Rege might have had the Omori do. . . .

Celia started to put her hand on his forearm, then stopped. "Johnny, he's not even playing his drums. He needs to. It . . . it gets the aggression out. He's bottling it up and it's feeding that guilt. You guys have to get together and play, if not for shows, then for the fun it was for all of you."

He wondered if she'd felt that flare of energy as well, and if that was why she refrained from touching him.

"You don't have to give up the music," she said. "You can still play as a band."

"The hell he can!"

They spun as one toward the trailer door. Aurelia jerked the door open wide, straining the hinges with her ferocity. "You don't have time for this girlfriend drama, John. In the coming weeks you will be crowned the Domn Lup." She stomped right up to them and glared into his eyes. "You are about to become the single most powerful wærewolf in the world. You don't know the standard security protocols for your own transport, let alone the codes to the mainframe of our intelligence data and personnel files. How can you even *hope* to lead if you don't know these things?" The angry accusations rose in volume until she was shouting, "How will you learn them if you keep running off to be with the damned witch?"

She'd been pushing him since she arrived, working to control him one way or another. The viciousness of her voice and the dominance conveyed in her low tone stoked a rage that threatened to consume him. He'd had enough; he gave in to the fury.

In one hyper-fast fluid motion, Johnny grabbed Aurelia by the shoulders. Fur sprouted on his hands as he backed her across the room and rammed her into the wall beside the door. The trailer shook with the force of the impact. Something glass in the kitchen fell and shattered.

He growled, "Beverley is missing!"

Aurelia dug her fingers around his now furry and clawed hands, struggling to loosen his grip. "Is the girl more important than your own son?"

With a furious howl he threw her to the floor, revealing cracks in the paneling of the wall.

"How do you know about him?" Johnny shouted.

Aurelia must have been dazed and didn't answer. But Celia whispered, "You have a son?"

CHAPTER FOURTEEN

I pulled up short, throwing myself backward and down onto the leaves. I was breathless, panicked, my mind racing.

Menessos had Beverley.

She was out of the line.

"What are you doing?"

"You must stay back until I'm done!"

I had a terrible thought that maybe her body was out, but not her mind. "What are you doing?" I asked again, hating the sound of fear in my voice.

"Her gift isn't complete!"

He turned back to his work and began chanting again.

Gift? Gift? Where have I heard this before?

Without taking my eyes off of them, I crab-walked backward, then Zhan was tugging at my arm to help me stand. Hanging on every syllable, I tried to decipher his chant, but these strange words sounded like nothing I'd ever heard before. They must have been in his original language, Akkadian.

I could see now that he'd drawn a very large circle and used mounds of ash to mark it. My skidding steps had stopped not three inches from breaking this powdery power enclosure. There was another circle within the first ash-drawn circle, marked by nine pegs in the ground and burning smudge sticks in white saucers between the pegs, the source of the sage smell. In ritual it was meant for purifying the space and repelling negative energies. Closer now, I detected some dragon's blood in the mix.

Inside the middle circle was a third ash-drawn one.

A triple circle was cast as a means of ensuring protection, keeping in what's inside, and keeping out what's outside. These precautions indicated to me that he'd taken intense measures.

It hit me: He was doing to her what he'd done to Liyliy, Ailo, and Talto so long ago.

He was drawing a gift into Beverley, bestowing her with a specific power. But according to Menessos's tale, the sisters had possessed a latent power within them, and the blood of a fey grandmother ran through their veins. He'd said it didn't often work on magic-bearing humans.

I jerked out of Zhan's grasp and stalked around the circle. Even through my shoes I could detect the thrum of the line beneath my feet, far below. Some lines are electric, meaning they stimulate energy. Some are magnetic, meaning they attract energy. Some, electromagnetic ones, do both. This portion of the line was clearly electromagnetic.

Inside the circle, the bonfire was positioned right on top of the ley. As I stared at him across the fire, Menessos's eyes closed. His head slowly fell back.

The purple serpent writhed in the fire. It had finished eating the green bolts he had made for it. Now it was searching for more.

Menessos drew smaller bolts from the fire and brought them to circle Beverley's head. He set them at a swifter pace. His hand hovered above her forehead, and the bolts swirled between him and Beverley.

I ground my teeth. He'd baited the line.

As that serpentine extension of the ley partook of the energy it had attracted here, it hovered above the child, sensing those smaller bolts, waiting to ascertain the new pattern before attacking.

As it dove in, Menessos slapped his hand down on Beverley's forehead and screamed words I did not understand. Her mouth opened. The green bolts dropped into her throat, and the purple serpent followed them down. Instantly, parts of her body began to glow purple. Her head was first, then her neck. The glow eased down her arms, and then, though that light was dimmed by her shirt and jeans, it moved down her torso and her legs. When the radiance beamed out from her bare toes, Menessos slid his hand at her brow to the top of her head, and the other smacked her under the chin, shutting her mouth roughly.

The part of the line that was reaching into her was severed by his action. It flopped wildly as it recoiled into the line. Her body began to shake as if an epileptic fit had overcome her.

Menessos kept his hands on her little head, kept her mouth shut, and murmured over her until the fire sputtered and sparked before him. It died down low.

He watched the fire intently, and kept murmuring.

The moment lingered on. She was shaking badly. I was about to shout—

"Now!" he cried.

The flames burst upward with a shimmer of white sparks that rained down upon the child, avoiding contact with him.

As the sparks hit her, they seeped through her skin,

through her clothes, and, little by little, her trembling abated.

When she was still, Menessos removed his hands from her hesitantly, then grinned at me.

I sighed. My shoulders relaxed, but I knew a hot and lengthy shower was the only thing that would truly ease the tension out of me.

He drew a breath—I thought for another sigh—but instead he again began speaking words that were unknown to me.

This wasn't over yet.

Suddenly, I could feel the line's energy thrumming along my skin. It felt like I was sitting astride Johnny's Night Train, feeling the deep vibration that rumbled out from the engine and through the pipes to reverberate through my whole body.

Menessos was drawing the line up to the surface.

What in Hell is he thinking?

Drawing a line to the surface was like putting kinks in a garden hose—magic being the water and the witch being the hose. Depending on the witch, the flow of magic would be controlled, or the hose would bubble and burst.

The vibration resonated into my bones and my whole body buzzed from the inside out. It made me feel dizzy. The temperature where I stood was rising fast. It must have increased fifty degrees in the few seconds I deliberated before leaping away and falling face-first into a pile of dew-damp leaves. As I picked myself up and stood farther away from the warmth, the leaves within the circle—leaves that had dried from the heat contained within the circle—fluttered and danced, pushed aside as the ground bucked underneath the bonfire.

The logs bounced. One rolled right toward Beverley.

Then the ground under the bonfire split open and the logs tumbled into the hole. The rolling one reversed its direction and fell in as well.

I would have felt relieved if Beverley wasn't right on the edge of the opening.

My first instinct was to reach out, dive in, and pull her back from that edge, but I couldn't break the circle. If Menessos didn't draw me a door to let me in, I couldn't help. Instead, I backpedaled and ran frantic hands through my hair. His eyes were closed. Maybe he didn't know she was about to fall in. Distracting him might be a bad thing.

Beverley's body slid an inch toward the crevice.

I took the risk. "Menessos!"

My cry was lost as light exploded up from underground in a beam. It split the night like the megawatt finger of some gigantic god. It knocked me down, but I kept my eyes fixed on the girl.

Beverley's body slid another inch, then another, and I scrambled up—

Some gentle force lifted her, hovering, into that light. Air tossed her dark hair about. Her arms spread outward as if she were floating peacefully in a pool.

It was beautiful, ethereal, and angelic. My mouth fell open.

Something began floating up in the beam; it looked like pieces of ash rising from a campfire, blackened fragments with edges glowing red-orange. These pieces swirled and fluttered around the child, gathering around her hands, bulking up until it covered her arms like extra-long oven mitts.

There was a pulsing to the ash-like substance and the fiery glow grew brighter and brighter. *Hotter.*

"Menessos . . ."

The ash condensed, tightening down on her. Her back arched and her high, piercing scream engulfed my world. Heedless of the circle, I shot forward.

Time slowed down.

Hands held me back. "No!" I screamed.

Zhan put her knee into the back of mine, throwing me down a few feet from the ashen circle. With her weight centered on my spine, she pinned me to the ground. Still, I struggled to move onward, reaching, clawing at the grass, straining for purchase in the earth.

Heat warmed my hands and blew across my cheeks. A few feet away, I'd been on soggy land, but here the heat of the circle was rapidly drying the nearby vegetation. The temperature kept rising until it felt like I was trying to reach into a blazing hearth. Beside me, outside of the circle, dried leaves began to smolder and burn from the heat.

It couldn't be as hot within the circle—both of them would be blistering by now.

Menessos had to be displacing that heat magically.

Inside the circle, he rose to his feet. His hands remained arched, and his features were lined with the effort of containing the power of the ley, transferring the heat, and sustaining the spell. Earth fell away around the crevice edges. The light was expanding. He had to step back to keep from falling in.

He couldn't hold it.

I stopped struggling. Head down, concentrating hard, I tried to send energy to him through the magical bond we shared, but his shields were clamped tightly with all that he was trying to accomplish.

I could help him if—

Something dark cast shadows in the beam from below. Black mist rose, followed by a huge opaque black hand. The fingers caressed Beverley's spine. It was a tentative touch, the way someone strokes an animal when they are uncertain if it is tame. The next touch was braver, longer. Then the fingers slithered around her and clasped her tight. It was like watching King Kong grab Fay Wray.

"No!" I shouted. My voice was not nearly as loud as I hoped, as my lungs were compressed by Zhan's weight on my back.

The giant hand tried to pull Beverley down into the opening in the earth. Judging by Menessos's hand gestures, he was fighting against letting that happen.

Remembering how I'd used the elements to aid me against Liyliy, I called the mantle around me. I could link the elements readily when it was glowing soft around me.

Zhan gasped and wisely got off of me.

With Menessos having taken the time to triple-cast the circle I was willing to bet he had called the elements to guard his circle. I could use my power to manipulate the elements inside the barrier of the circle.

What I needed mastery of right now was earth. With it I could close that crevice—but that was the *one* element that hadn't yet tested me. Fire, water, and air— those I could command.

Air.

Rising to my feet I pointed my index fingers heavenward.

"Hurricane force and twister speed,
Air gust forth and lift her free.
With whirlwind strength but zephyr soft
Hold the child Beverley aloft!
Windstorm fly her straight to me."

I couldn't bring her out of the circle, but I wanted it to bring her to this edge and away from the hole in the world.

But it wasn't to be that easy.

Whatever held her did not want to let go.

Menessos continued fighting from within the circle. He cried out, "Water!"

"Water?" I questioned.

Zhan shouted, "The stream!"

I dropped to my knees and shoved my two little fingers into the ground.

"Water, water, heed my demand,
Flow over your banks and across the land.
With the fury of rapids and a waterfall's might
Reroute this stream right now, tonight,
Filling the torn earth as I command!"

Water came.

"It's going to wash away your circle!"

Even as I called out, Menessos flicked a hand in my direction. His lips moved. Though my ears could not pick up the sound of his voice, I knew he was drawing a door on the circles. But that moment of refocusing his willpower cost him. The giant hand pulled Beverley down. I could barely see her; she was slightly below the level of the ground.

Like rushing whitewater, the liquid poured across the earth, picking up leaves and crashing noisily in on itself. I guided it through the open doorway Menessos had drawn. Fearing Beverley might drown, I mentally pushed the water so it rounded that crevice and spiraled down into it staying mostly to the edge. But not all.

As it splashed about, the fluid splattered across the hand. Where it fell, it sizzled. Blisters swelled up instantly.

A deep subterranean squeal shuddered up through that fissure. The hand threw her upward and jerked out of sight. Seeing Beverley falling, I had an instant to readjust the water and move it from the edges to pool across the opening and catch her.

It did—then she sank.

I fought to whirlpool the water, to make a current that would push her to the top, but I could not feel where she was, and I wasn't sure if my efforts were keeping her down. I couldn't tell how deep the water in my control was.

Zhan, who had been around magic enough to know a cut doorway meant people could move in and out of the circle, raced through—and dove into the water.

I was dumbfounded by her bravery.

For an endless few seconds I debated what I should do. I wondered if they had both fallen from the bottom of the fluid and were now dropping to their deaths. I could be covering up their screams with this whirlpool. If I released the water and they weren't already plummeting, they certainly would then. I couldn't let it go, but I couldn't keep this liquid spinning if it was what was keeping them down, either.

I looked to Menessos, but he was trying to put the ley line back where it belonged, well below the surface.

Zhan's head broke the surface with a gasp. She was carried around the opening twice before she could get a grip on the edge and hold her position. "I have her!"

I slowed the flow of the water, but that allowed the level to drop. I knew if I pulled my fingers free of the earth, my control on the water would end.

But what choice did I have? Beverley's head was still under. If Zhan could have lifted her up, she would have. If I didn't let the water go and get in there to help, Beverley was surely going to drown.

"Hold on!" Rising, I sped through the doorway.

As expected, as soon as my hands were free of the earth the water was freed. It splashed away, crashing down in the hole. I dove toward the edge, reaching for Zhan's hand. She'd caught a thick root, and had her foot wedged on a rock. "Take the girl."

Her other arm was wrapped around Beverley's torso. I reached lower and Zhan used every ounce of her Offerling strength to lift Beverley high enough so that I could get my hands under the girl's arms. I was able to bend my arms and lift her closer to me, but I had no leverage.

Zhan crawled out of the fissure and spun around on her knees. "Don't let go," she said. She straddled me and half lifted, half dragged me away from the edge. All I had to do was maintain my grip and Beverley was hoisted out with me.

When I could, I hauled her away from the hole.

Menessos had sealed up the door he cut and was shutting down the circle, so that by the time Zhan and I had reached a safe distance, the crevice was backfilling.

Ignoring his ending of the spell, I pulled Beverley closer. She wasn't breathing. I began CPR. The third time I breathed into her mouth, her body jerked. I pulled away and she vomited up water. She didn't regain consciousness, but she was breathing deeply and her pulse felt strong to me. A quick examination of her hands and arms proved they were warm to the touch, but un-burnt. I noticed her flint arrowhead necklace was gone; Menessos likely had to remove it before his spell would work. Cradling her, I faced him. Not caring about the exhaustion in his expression or the slump of his shoulders, I demanded, "Why in Hell did you do that?"

He said plainly, "I had to."

The anger in my expression made him look away. He stood, rolled his shoulders, straightened his clothes, and paced a few unsteady steps away. I knew the longer he had to think about it, the prettier and more innocent he could make his explanation sound. "I know it was similar to what you did to Liyliy and her sisters, so start talking." What he'd done had turned out badly for them, and knowing that made the worry I felt now for Beverley clench up tight in my gut.

He turned and there was a hint of surprise in his eyes. "I had to get her out of the line. That was my sole purpose, I swear. But as I brought her out, I realized why she was in there in the first place." Sadness filled his expression. "Had I been less focused on you, I would have caught it . . . but as it is, what power I detected I simply wrote off as yours."

Power? Somewhere between nine and twelve, a witch's power begins to show. But Beverley's mother was not a witch.

"She possesses a power that was not wakeful when Goliath was dating her mother. She had a birthday recently, yes?"

I nodded. She'd turned ten . . . ten days ago. "Why did you pull a gift into her?"

"Persephone, she wasn't just *in* the ley line. She was *riding* it. You know what that means."

His words struck me. The truth had been there all along and I'd danced around it at every turn. I looked down into her sweet face. I ran my fingers around her neck, where the necklace would have been. I moved her hair away. And there was a faint redness where the silver would have been, redness like a fading rash. With her recent birthday and the onset of power with the coming of age, it all made sense now.

"She has fey blood."

CHAPTER FIFTEEN

Johnny turned to Celia. Her eyes were wide and glassy. The shock in her expression cut through his rage and he realized he was roughing up a woman. Though he tried to console himself that Aurelia was a wærewolf and could tolerate it, guilt flashed through him.

"You . . . you have a child?" Celia stammered.

She had heard Aurelia. He knew how badly Celia wanted a child. The fact that wærewolves couldn't breed was her greatest pain in life. Because he and Erik had been best friends up until a week or so ago, he also knew that Celia struggled with a secret resentment over Seph getting custody of Beverley.

Now a child had fallen into his life as well.

"Yes," Aurelia answered, her voice raspy. "The Domn Lup has a human son, a child born out of wedlock to his high school sweetheart, conceived in all likelihood a matter of days before he was made wærewolf." She slowly climbed to her feet. "If you acknowledge him, John, if you bring him into your world, he will forever be in danger."

Johnny turned back to Aurelia. "How do you know about him?"

She straightened her outfit. "We'll discuss that later."

"No." He shook his head. "You will fucking answer me right now."

"How isn't important."

Johnny pointed at the indentation in the paneling. "If you don't answer me, we're gonna find out what it takes to put you all the way through."

She sneered at him. "You wouldn't dare."

He didn't even hesitate.

He grabbed her, lifted her, and the first thrust broke through the paneling and cracked the structure's framing beneath. The second sent Aurelia and various bits of wood, insulation, and siding across the yard.

Johnny exited by the door. As he stepped onto the grass, Aurelia began to laugh. She slowly picked herself up. "The Rege did far worse to me for lesser reasons. It'll take more than throwing me through walls to make me talk." The wind tossed her hair about and she tore off her jacket and threw it down as if ready for a fight. She held her long hair out of her face. "C'mon, John. Put your hands on me again."

The copper-sweet tang of blood filled Johnny's nostrils. A quick scan revealed a gash on her forearm. She seemed unaware of it. Still, his mouth watered. "I'm not the Rege." He'd heard the sadistic bastard had tormented her in many ways; she'd risen through the ranks because she was not only worthy, but she didn't break under the damage he dished out.

"You're not so different. I could always feel his beast. I could feel it rouse, feel it yearning for things. I felt your beast as I got close to the trailer." She laughed softly again. "You're on the edge." She wiped her hand over the wound, covering it with blood. Then she rubbed her hands together and waved them in the air between them. "Lust. Anger. Violence. And now . . . blood."

Fresh and warm, the blood glistened wet on her

fingers. The building breeze wrapped the scent around him, swathing him in heaviness that weakened his knees. Penetrating that scent was another: the heady aroma of her arousal. That perfume of her sex reached through the blood-scent cloaking him and, like a silken lining, slid cool and smooth against his flesh.

Its touch was light, but far from subtle. It breached his skin like a sigh passing through a screen. Once underneath, it warmed as it passed over each sinew, each muscle, stroking and saturating his body with a savage craving previously unknown to him.

Aurelia's pouty lips curved as she stepped out of her dress shoes. "Touch me, John. If you can." She turned and ran.

Unable to resist chasing her, wanting that scent, that sensation, to remain, he kicked off his slick-soled shoes and followed.

She ran into the cornfield, avoiding the grove. It wasn't long before her bare feet were bloodied, and he could smell each drop as the air lifted the fragrance to his nostrils.

The transformation stirred within him, fiercer with each step. He'd been outpacing her, but as he threw off his clothing, pausing desperate seconds here and there for the removal of each article, she increased the distance between them. When he was fully naked, he let the change claim him. In fact, he welcomed it—certain that he could cover the ground quicker on four legs.

With a howl that split the night, he was complete and raced into the dark.

His nose was more efficient like this. All the smells that had enticed him mingled into a mesmerizing medley. His pricked ears were also better. The sound of vegetation crunching under Aurelia's hurried steps and her panting breaths thrilled him, urged him on.

His paw touched fabric instead of earth. *Her skirt.*

Seconds later, something thinner. His nails punctured it. *Her blouse.*

She's naked.

The animal's yearning redoubled, and with a rumbling growl, so did his speed.

Gaining with each leaping stride, he was soon right behind her, so close that he licked the bloody sole of her foot in the millisecond it was revealed in her step. She gasped and stumbled.

The flavor of her blood rocked him. It hit his tongue and many things happened at once.

He saw her fall and leapt, thinking to catch her.

His transformation began reverting.

And he wondered if Persephone's blood tasted this good to Menessos.

He sprang forward, and when his body was parallel to hers, he reached human arms down and encircled her waist, twisting so it was his back that crashed to the ground and not her front.

The air was knocked from his lungs by the impact, and again when her body collided atop his.

Aurelia sat up, straddling him.

The erotic sensation of touching a female wære ran through him, interfering with his recovery. He reached out, tried to sit up. "No. Stay flat." She took his hands in her own and lowered them to her thighs. "Just breathe. A little deeper with each breath."

Under a starry sky that was slowly being shrouded by

the cloud cover steered in by the wind, he struggled to make his lungs work normally. With each inhalation, it seemed, he could bring the oxygen in a little deeper. He found a rhythm in it. The breaths were so shallow it was a quick rhythm, but a rhythm nonetheless.

Aurelia danced seductively to his rhythm. With each of his inhalations, her thighs flexed under his hands and her buttocks lifted off him as she tilted her hips to rub herself along his cock. It made her lean slightly, but the speed made her breasts sway enticingly. As he exhaled she reversed the motion.

As he picked up on the pattern, he reclaimed control of his body. Well, part of it. She—and the tickling arousal—were working in conjunction and having a definite influence he could not resist. He purposely made his next exhale as long and slow as he could manage, reveling in the fantastic feeling of her sex sliding along his growing erection.

Breathing in the mélange of fragrances, staring into her wanton eyes, and feeling the strength of her thighs, he tightened his fingers on her slightly. She had timed his deep breath perfectly and positioned herself at the tip of him, ready to take what she wanted as he exhaled.

But the scent of blood again filled his nostrils . . . and his thought of Persephone and Menessos recurred.

So he held his breath.

She giggled, waiting. Her eyes sparkled.

"No," he whispered. Johnny bent his knees, bumping her slightly forward and effectively keeping her off his cock.

"What?" The glint in her eyes darkened.

She pitched forward, hands punching down onto the ground on either side of his head. She arched her back, and let her breasts sway close to his mouth. "Don't fight me anymore." Her hips gyrated as she pleaded.

"How do you know about my son?"

She stilled for an instant, then she shifted her weight and sat up, running her hands—tacky with drying blood—over his chest.

"There's a bug in your key fob."

His thoughts swirled as he thought back over the past few days, over what conversations he'd had concerning Evan. He realized his entire trip as he drove Toni back to upstate New York had been overheard. Then another thought occurred to him. "Who else can hear the feed from it?"

"Only me."

"So who else knows?"

"No one."

He wondered if he believed any of that. "Get off me." When she didn't immediately move, he added, "Don't make me tell you twice."

She unstraddled him and sat on her haunches to the side, but reached to fondle his cock. He rolled away from her and stood. "John."

He started walking back the way they had come.

"John." Her tone was pitiful.

He stopped. Over his shoulder he said, "No, Aurelia. I know you've fought for rank. I know you've groomed yourself to be on the arm of a powerful wære. But it won't be mine." He transformed again and loped swiftly away.

He collected his clothes, reversed the transformation, and returned to the trailer. Ignoring Celia and Mountain, who were nailing a piece of plywood over the hole in the trailer, Johnny wordlessly started dismantling his key fob under the kitchen lights.

CHAPTER SIXTEEN

Giovanni turned his cell phone over and over in his hand, thinking about what he had heard. The phones he had given to Liyliy were all linked to his own. She might understand the devices of this modern age that she had been suddenly thrust into, but he was counting on her not understanding how they could be manipulated. Or bugged.

He couldn't trust her completely; she had the ability to use magic and he did not. He had knowledge and connections that she needed. He was a tool.

These phones, however, would allow him to hear what she and her sisters discussed and what news they delivered. What Liyliy shared with him would then tell him much about whether or not he should put any trust in her at all.

He had not exactly anticipated that they would call *others* on these phones. They had read the minds of several people by now and had learned phone numbers.

He had heard Ailo say, "What you seek will be found beside the ley line at Mill Stream Run Reservation, but only if you hurry."

Mill Stream Run Reservation.

With his smartphone he'd checked the whereabouts of this location; it was too far for Adam, his driver, to get them there swiftly. He'd have the man check it out tomorrow during the day. Giovanni had to hope the sisters would call each other and discuss this in more detail. He

wondered who they had sent to this place; he had not recognized the woman's voice by her single word: "Hello."

Following the method Menessos had used in binding
the sisters, Mero decided he must empower a choker
with which to bind Liyliy. As he prepared, he'd demanded that a guard contact any woman in the haven
who owned a choker and have her bring the jewelry to
him for inspection.

Only one woman had come: Risqué.

She dropped a leather bondage-style choker on the
altar before him. There was a small lock on the front clo-
sure of it, which was presently open. "Don't ask." She
put the key into his hand, turned on her heel, and left.

He grinned. It was perfect.

But.

This would be a feat similar to a mouse belling a cat.

He didn't actually want to get close to Liyliy. If she
touched him, she could invoke a reading of him. Not
only could she immobilize him—or worse, slay him—by
such means, but she might learn that his connection to
the Excelsior ran deeper than their formal titles. He had
many secrets he wished to keep from her, but that one
was the most dangerous for Deric.

Liyliy left her sisters in the room and entered the hall,
faking the limp she'd had before. There were two
guards outside the door and, as she walked away from
them, one called, "Allow us to escort you."

She turned and waited for them to join her. When they
neared, she grabbed each man's arm and, pulling recent
memories from their minds, had them on their knees. The

memories were of generic haven-living experiences, but in reading the two of them at once the thoughts and images had melded together. They slammed painfully into her mind as a strange mix of déjà vu and double vision. She jerked her hands free and stepped back even as she gripped them by the hair and knocked their skulls together.

Confident they would not be following, she hurried from the hall—remembering to limp at the last. Too impatient to wait for the elevator, she awkwardly climbed up the staircase. Moving was much easier with her sisters' healing, but letting those here think her handicapped gave her the option of surprising them with quick action. Being underestimated might be her only means to rescue.

The hallway on the ground level was empty. She hesitated, holding the banister. In case anyone was watching, she panted as if out of breath.

It's too easy.

With extreme control, she progressed toward the main entry with a shambling gait. When she rounded the old ticket booth and had a clear view ahead, she detected a man's outline against the boards that covered the doors.

"Where is the necklace?"

It was Mero's voice.

She laughed but limped onward, keeping the wariness she felt from showing.

"Liyliy."

"You will never find it," she hissed. Ten feet from him she stopped and put her hands on her hips. "What have you come to try to replace it with?"

"Stay here, Liyliy. Let us work together to heal those scars."

Through gritted teeth she said, "They suit me."

"No, Liyliy. Your beauty suited you. It can be re-gained." He extended his hand toward her.

Tempted for an instant, she searched his eyes. Not counting all the centuries she had been encased in stone, she had never been able to trust what she saw in anyone's expression. She never trusted their words, only what she saw when she read someone was real, because she knew only *that* was true.

Even her sisters, who had always been honest with her, she could not believe unless she confirmed it with a reading touch.

But there was pity in Mero's eyes and she knew it was not fraudulent. He eased a step toward her.

Fool! That is what you want *to see!*

He was your downfall. You wanted to see him, to feel his arms around your body . . . you snuck away, certain that your beauty would win him over.

But your sisters followed you. All three of you were lured to your doom because you wanted him.

And all he felt for you was fear—fear so deep he let his Maker bind you into stone. Your sisters warned you. Everyone saw that truth but you. You hadn't touched him.

You'd forgotten how to read people with your own eyes.

Your sisters hadn't; they knew what was happening. They knew your heart was warming for someone . . . someone oblivious to your fixation on him. They knew it would break your trio apart.

Menessos had mastered the art of reading people. He knew what you were feeling for Mero. He used it against you.

"Did you send your messenger boy to fetch me?"

Mero's hand dropped down. Confusion, distraction marred his features. "What?"

"The night my sisters and I were bound in stone. Your messenger came to me."

He shook his head. "Liyliy. I never had a messenger boy."

With a shout of rage that was steeped in the pain of time, she used her aura as a guide and swung her fist at him. Anger and anguish filled her as she struck him. He backpedaled. Her arms lengthened, sprouted feathers, and she kept delivering blow after blow.

He blocked her. He slammed energy bolts into her.

Feathers flew into the air. She screamed at his resistance, but she felt no injury through the agony of her betrayal.

When the leather collar appeared in his hand, she grabbed his wrist.

She took him back centuries upon centuries.

She put him on his knees, searching for the truth.

On her knees with him, tears pouring from one eye, she learned he was honest. She learned he had been with Menessos that evening; Menessos, who was gathering the last of the supplies for the spell, rehearsing the lines. He had no messenger. He sent no one. He was unaware of her desire for him.

Liyliy released Mero and remained before him, weeping.

Only when the collar was shoved toward her neck did she realize minutes had passed and he had recovered.

She forced a full transformation. The collar would never fit her owlish neck. She snapped at him with her beak and menaced him with her talons, but she did not draw blood. As an owl, her aura was altered, affecting her aim. It took a few swings to master it, then she swatted him hard, knocking him backward into the air. She pulled the transformation back into her human form, and she pushed through the doors with tatters of gray silk trying to cover her.

CHAPTER SEVENTEEN

S imply because she has fey blood doesn't mean you have to gift her."

Though Beverley remained unconscious, the memory of her scream was still echoing in my mind and my tone was clipped as I scolded Menessos.

Several paces away from me, the vampire spread his arms, palms out, assuming the typical innocence-pleading pose. "Being in the line *supercharged* her," he argued. "I couldn't bring her out with that power uncontrolled and leaking everywhere. I had to funnel it onto one focus . . . for her sake and for ours. We can't put her or others in danger, Persephone. What if she were to have a paroxysmal episode?"

He had a point. Any magic-using person in the throes of a violent fit was hazardous to be around, more so if they were untrained. My criticism ratcheted down a notch. "Didn't you say that gifting didn't work on magic-bearing humans?"

"I said it doesn't often work on them. As with Liyliy and her sisters, the presence of fey blood was more important than the ability to tap into universal energies."

I smoothed Beverley's hair. "What gift did she get?"

He didn't answer. Instead, he turned and wandered a few steps away.

As silent seconds ticked away, my unease grew until I couldn't stand it. "Menessos."

The vampire's head dropped slightly and his shoulders rounded.

"I'm not going to like this answer. I get it. Out with it already."

He still didn't move.

Zhan stepped up beside me. Our eyes met and it was obvious we were both suspicious of his hesitancy. Instead of making another verbal plea, I reached through the bond he and I shared. It drew his attention like walking up behind him and stroking his arm.

He spun around as if startled from deep thoughts. His gaze took us in, all of us, but settled on the child in my arms. There was despair in his voice as he said, "She'll never be safe."

Through the bond, my gentle touch turned into a squeezing demand.

"She is a ward-breaker, Persephone."

I blinked, struggling to wrap my head around what this meant. It explained why my defensive protections at home failed. Wards differed from out-and-out spells in that they were purely protective. A spell required a divine and blessed circle in which words were spoken, elements summoned, and, often, gemstones or herbs used as a focus. A ward required only the use, direction, and sealing of energy. It was sorcery.

My stomach flipped at my thoughts of this poor child tapping a line accidentally, feeling the awful stinging pain initially involved with that action. She probably panicked. Somehow, that led to her being taken.

I held her tighter. She had the capacity to interrupt or break a flow of energy meant to protect that which it surrounded; any magical barrier set to keep dangerous things out. Softly, I said, "Most wards nowadays are meant to keep the 'nonsters' out."

"Nonsters" was a media term coined to lump wære-wolves, vampires, witches, and fey together in one non-human group. It was inaccurate, as witches were definitely still human, but the term had caught on anyway.

"She must come with me," he said.

I opened my mouth to protest, but before the words could form I realized that, until she understood how to restrain this power, I could not protect her. She would destroy any defensive ward I attempted to use to shield her. She was also a danger to wæres . . . and I could not protect them *from* her, either.

Unlike vampires, who were down during the day and recognizable on sight, wærewolves could blend into society. Wæres could be working at her school. Her bus might pass some in traffic. We might walk the grocery store aisles with wæres and never know it.

Tears burned my eyes.

In a vampire haven, she would be safe, and so would others.

"Goliath and I will tutor her." He added reassuringly, "When she learns control she can return to you. Everything will be fine. You'll see."

I winced. "You're implying that I won't be at the haven."

He squared his shoulders as if his next words required some great amount of resolve. "You know why you must stay away."

"Mero." He wanted to present me to the Excelsior so I could be marked by him. "I don't want to leave Beverley. When she wakes, she'll need me. She'll be confused and scared. You can—"

"I am no longer Quarterlord. I have no one to command."

"Goliath—"

"—must not tarnish his new position with the blemish of such a choice."

I bit my tongue. I couldn't go to the den or the haven. The witches were torn over the issue of me being the Lustrata, so the Covenstead was also a risk. I had only my own home to run to and it had broken wards. The elementals would protect me, but they had all been through so much already. Inviting trouble to follow me there was selfish.

"Persephone."

When he spoke my name a wave of warmth flowed over me like I'd stepped naked into strong sunlight. It was meant to reassure me, but instead it only pissed me off.

"Menessos—"

"Mero will not be turned from this course of action. You must go to the Witch Elders Council."

"WEC is divided between those who believe the Lustrata means good things for them and those who feel she brings bad things. I don't even know who's on which side of the argument." I needed to find out. *In all my spare time?* I shook my head. "No."

Undeterred by my anger, Menessos crouched before me. He slid his hands into mine without altering the way my arms held Beverley. "My master, you cannot accept the marks of the Excelsior."

Many thoughts flooded my mind. What would Beverley think of this? How would she react? What if she didn't want to be at the haven? What about school? There were no children at the haven— *Stop.*

Menessos was being too nice and too calm about all of this.

I blinked the moisture from my eyes and searched his face. *Why?*

He had quickly evaluated the situation, then skillfully devised a conversation that kept me focused on Beverley and the solution to this new problem.

What was his verbal maneuvering trying to hide?

I sat straighter. "What in Hell had a hold of her?"

He blinked as if to make a denial, saw my expression harden, then sighed. His hands slipped from mine and he stood. "If I had to guess, I would wager it was Nyx."

My embrace tightened protectively around Beverley.

"Nyx?" I asked. "You mean Nyx as in the *deified personification of night?*"

Menessos hesitated, then said matter-of-factly, "Yes."

Zhan turned on her heel and walked away.

"Why?"

"That is what we must figure out."

"And how do we do that?"

The corner of Menessos's mouth crooked up. "Perhaps there is an Eldrenne or two that could aid you. Their reference library is one of the finest in the world. You could research—"

"I'm not going to hide behind the Council's skirts."

He was undeterred. "Two birds with one stone, my master."

"No."

"Then you doom Beverley."

"Don't pull this shit. Not now."

"That is such an odd phrase. Why would anyone 'pull shit'?"

I smirked at him. "I guess it has something to do with getting your hands dirty in a stupid and pointless way."

"I am not needlessly dirtying my hands by trying to protect you while you figure out why Nyx would want a ward-breaker."

I frowned, but before I could speak, a car horn honked. Zhan had brought the car as close as she could to us. As I shifted Beverley so I could stand, Menessos deftly removed her from my arms. I asked him, "How did you get here anyway?"

"After your call I had Risqué gather supplies while I informed Goliath I was leaving. My driver dropped me off."

I stood. "I never realized a ley line ran through here."

"This area is secluded. If I lost control, the isolation would minimize the wild magic's impact on others." He began walking toward the Audi. "I sent my driver some distance away for his own safety. If Zhan can drive us all, I'll let him know he may head for the haven."

He glanced back. "I trust that I will be permitted to ride along?"

CHAPTER EIGHTEEN

When Zhan pulled into my driveway I saw Johnny's Maserati parked behind Celia's CX-7. While seeing the Maserati made my stomach do a little flip—I'd have to confront Johnny now, no getting out of it—something else worried me more. My house sat unlit in the night and another car had pulled off to the side of my seldom-trafficked road. It seemed to be abandoned, but other than my place, there was nowhere close by to walk to or visit. I had a hard time believing anyone had parked there by coincidence.

I realized that Zhan had not cut the engine. *Of course not. Menessos won't drive himself to the haven.* I glanced back at Beverley, wishing she had awakened so I could talk to her and explain. But that wasn't meant to be. Without a word, I slid across the seat, kissed Beverley's forehead, and exited the vehicle.

The wind was picking up and helped me slam the car door before I stalked around the other vehicles to my porch.

Inside, I removed my dew-damp boots, sat them aside, and stood there with my back to the open main door, listening, as Zhan drove away. This big farmhouse felt so empty suddenly. One step, then two. I was the only thing alive in here, the only thing making a sound, and I knew where to step to not squeak the old floorboards.

A tie hung across the handrail of the stairs.

Johnny's. He had a key.

I listened hard. There were no sounds from upstairs, only the roaring of the wind outside.

My touching the silky smoothness of the fabric raised his scent. I pulled my fingers away, leaving the tie there.

I glanced into the living room, where my slipcovered couch and framed John William Waterhouse poster prints were hung. The moonlight was dim, but my eyes had adjusted to the dark. Above the fireplace was a genuine Waterhouse painting, but the fancy art light above it was switched off. The slow flash of a tiny red LED seemed more like an eerie blinking eye than the indicator of a security system for that very valuable gift from Menessos.

Walking toward the kitchen, even my sock-footed steps seemed loud in my ears. My gaze focused on the floor.

A memory flashed. Of Creepy—the otherwise nameless benefactor Menessos had secured an unsettling union with—here, in my kitchen. I had run away from him, leaving him behind me at the door, but he had impossibly materialized himself in front of me.

And, he'd materialized in the cargo hold of the ship Liyliy had held me captive in.

How had he done that?

Outside the wind roared. It caught the screen door and pulled it open enough that when it snapped shut it startled me. I spun around to see leaves skitter across the porch. And I noted the rip in my screen door. Another memory of Creepy.

I turned back toward the kitchen. Johnny wasn't here, and that meant he was probably hanging out at

Mountain's trailer. I walked to the windows to peek outside. The lights were on, and it looked like something had happened to Mountain's trailer near his front door. I wondered if one of the animals had damaged it.

At the thought of damage-causing animals, my thoughts pounced on Johnny. He wanted to talk, to try to work it out. It would not be a short conversation. I was feeling drained and unsure if I could make up with him. *Don't let exhaustion make decisions.*

I took a deep breath and closed my eyes for a moment, recalling the good things with Johnny. Our awkward first kiss. Our funny score-keeping. We hadn't kept tally in such a long time. Larger concerns had seeped in all around us. Maybe if we could bring the fun back . . .

Maybe then I could forgive him.

The wind pulled the screen door and slammed it shut again.

The bang knocked me out of my thoughts. I turned on my heel and headed for the front. I should go to the trailer and let Johnny know I was home.

Before I reached my boots I noticed something on the floor, like leaves scattered all over the entryway.

Moving closer, I was four steps away when, even in that dim light, I could tell the spots weren't leaves but small puddles. *Wet and dark.*

Bloody footprints.

The attack came from behind.

Something hit my neck and jerked me backward and off balance. I grappled at the restraint—the necktie, by the silken feel of it—but could not get my fingers between it and my flesh. I struggled to no avail. I let the fullness of my weight sag against my attacker, but whoever had me had no problem holding me up. I tried to think of something I could grab and bash against my assailant's head, but this section of the hall was clear. Not even a picture on the wall to tear down.

My ears were buzzing. I couldn't breathe.

The mantle.

I shut my eyes, concentrated on my thumbs, and called on fire.

Even as I detected the mantle's change in light with my lids closed, I heard a female voice say, "What the fuck?"

I reached over my shoulders to grab at her hands. Pressing my thumbs into her wrists I let the heat flash out of me and into her.

She screamed, but held on.

On her arm, blisters rose under my pinky—the finger that represented water—and under my thumb. Her scream turned into a growl and she squeezed the tie tighter.

I saw stars . . . needed air . . .

I squeezed harder. The blisters broke. The damaged skin in my grasp slid over the raw tissue beneath. I stomped my heel down on the top of her left foot. Without my boots on, I might not have broken bones, but she still yelped at the damage to her bare foot and the silky ligature around my neck loosened a bit. I used that instant to pull her arms forward with all my might, sucked in a breath, and ground my heel in harder.

She growled again and, in spite of the pain of burns, she forced my weight off her injured foot and managed to jerk the tie tight around my throat again.

But this time I had the fingers of one hand curled around it.

With the mantle still shining, I used my thumbs to burn through the silk.

This, of course, meant I burned my neck as well. My pain-filled scream was stifled by the pressure around my throat, but when the singed fabric tore apart from the pressure, it sent her reeling backward, and my choked cry surged out full force. Gasping, I turned to see a stunningly beautiful blond woman wearing only her underwear, cursing as her damaged foot became her literal downfall. She fell on her ass in my hall.

I didn't stand around trying to catch my breath.

Panting, I leapt at her. She was trying to get up, and my only thought was to keep her down. I shifted sideways and I curled up somewhat so I slammed onto her torso with my entire body. I felt the breath *whoosh* out of her flattened body.

I rolled and straddled her with my knees on her arms to keep her from fighting me. Then I dug my fingers into her hair and cracked the back of her head on my hardwood floor four times.

I would have kept going had it not been for someone calling my name.

Spinning to look over my shoulder, I saw Johnny in the doorway, mouth agape.

"What are you doing?"

My voice was raspy as I said, "She tried to kill me!" *And came closer to succeeding than you did.*

"What?" Johnny rushed toward me. His gaze fell past me to her. "Aurelia?"

She didn't answer. I'd knocked her out.

"You know her?" I stood, rather gracelessly.

Johnny took my arm to steady me. "Yup."

I blinked repeatedly. My question was obvious.

"The Zvonul sent her to be my assistant." He paused and, as a glare took over my face, his tone dropped to a justifying one. "She's very . . . qualified."

I jerked out of his grasp. "Qualified to kill me." As I glowered down at the gorgeous unconscious woman, I asked, "Why is she in her underwear?" It looked like someone had dragged it through the cornfield as pieces of dried and broken cornstalks were stuck to it in various places.

Johnny stepped away. "She's after power," he said. "She's been trying to get close to me since she showed up."

While I was away in Pennsylvania with my mother.

I looked Johnny up and down. His clothing was disheveled, to say the least. There were flecks of grass and shards of cornstalk on him.

Riiiiight. Everything clicked into place suddenly and I knew what his urgent need to talk to me had been about. "Let me guess. She got close, didn't she?"

CHAPTER NINETEEN

Johnny's mind was racing. He was stunned to learn that Aurelia had tried to kill Red, but Red's coarse voice and the splotches on her neck were proof enough, even without the burn right in front. The wærewolf had come close to achieving her aim.

"This is what you had to tell me," Red said when he didn't answer. "She's why we had to talk face-to-face so urgently."

The reproach in Seph's glare was a physical slap. The hard note in her words, even over the gruff tone, was an accusation.

"No. She wasn't." He opened his mouth and shut it. He wanted to apologize again for losing it and attacking her before. He wanted to smooth that situation over before telling her about Evan. But with his assistant having tried to kill her, and Persephone's obvious jealousy, he knew he had to back up and fix this before he could straighten the other mess out.

He knew what he had to do. He took out his cell phone and dialed. The Omori needed to come now.

"Yes, sire?" Gregor's deep voice answered.

"I need you to come to Red's farmhouse ASAP."

"I'm on my way."

"Bring the Omori with you."

"Sire? Is there a problem?"

Johnny looked down at the unconscious woman and said, "Aurelia must be taken into custody."

At that, Aurelia stirred and sat up, eyes wide in disbelief. Red retreated a few steps farther from the woman, then disappeared into the living room.

Gregor asked, "For?"

"Attempted murder."

"Who'd she try to kill?"

"Red." Johnny hung up. He heard Seph passing through the dining area to the kitchen. She appeared again, dragging a dinette chair and holding a rope.

"You can't be serious." Aurelia's droll tone indicated that she'd recovered herself. "The witch is a liability to your rule."

Johnny shook his head. "You're wrong."

Aurelia laughed, a single condescending note. "Of course you can't see it. You've barely lived your life with the pack. Every den is bound by the common denominators of being wolf and fearing the threats of those who are not, but this pack has something more charmingly homey about it. I'll give Ignatius the credit. That's the legacy he built. A pack that was more than pack . . . by aspiring to be family." The tone she used would have been more suitable as a response to learning her house was infested with bedbugs.

"That's not a bad thing," Johnny said.

Aurelia rubbed at the back of her head and climbed to her feet, keeping her left on the heel only. It was obviously injured. "It is for you."

"How so?"

"You kept this family at arm's length, and they were the good ones. What's out there"—she gestured vaguely beyond the house—"is not the same. The higher the rank, the less familiar it gets. In the Zvonul, they're barely more than rabid pack animals. When they see threats, they eliminate them. As you should well know."

Johnny knew. He had met the Rege.

Aurelia swung her arm to point at Red. "If you keep screwing around with the witch, they *will* off you and take your son."

Beyond her, he saw Red's eyes widen at the word "son."

"You said no one knew."

"The information is secured," she said coolly. "If anything happens to me, if I don't check in, locks will be opened."

He glared.

"Also, if I go into custody," she added in a snide singsong voice, "locks will be opened. And you know what will happen then." She paused. "Anticipating that Evan will be able to transform at will like you, they'll turn him."

Johnny felt his heartbeat in his ears. He felt his blood pressure rising. His fists clenched.

"They will raise him to be what they *want* in a Domn Lup." The room remained silent for a long moment, then Aurelia added, "I'm sure their values and ideals would not be in keeping with how you would want him raised."

With that, Aurelia spun and, though she advanced awkwardly using only the heel of her left foot, she rushed at Seph, who swung the chair up to defend herself. Aurelia grabbed the legs smoothly and used her momentum to push the chair at Seph, twisting it so the back of it cracked her in the side of the head. She went down.

Aurelia leapt over her, landing on her right foot and her hands, but she was immediately up and rushing to the door that led to the garage.

Johnny was already in motion, following her swift move, but he fell on one knee, crouching over Seph. "Red? Are you okay?"

"I'm fine," she snarled. "Get *her*."

Johnny ran into the garage and leapt the railing of the steps. Aurelia had escaped out the door to the rear and as he lunged through it, the flat of a shovel whacked against his head.

His knees buckled and hit the ground. Dazed, it took him a second to recover. He saw Aurelia hobbling across the yard toward the road. Even injured, she was fast. *Her car is that way. Mine's closer.*

Pushing himself up, he ran in the other direction around the house, skidded up to the door of the Maserati, and jerked the now fobless key ring from his pocket. In seconds he was throwing gravel as he reversed up the driveway and squealed the tires on the road. Remarkably, Aurelia had made it to her car already.

Catching a glimpse of taillights, he shifted gears and floored the gas pedal.

CHAPTER TWENTY

Goliath stood in the main chamber of the Haven Master's suite. His elbow was propped on the back of the master's chair and he let the full force of his most threatening glare crash over Ivanka.

She was well aware of his displeasure. She had barely made it through the door before lowering herself to one knee before him. Her eyes were kept downcast, her chin low with shame.

As the moment wore on, Mero, beside Goliath, shifted his weight impatiently.

Goliath had not wanted Liyliy to escape, but the fact that she had escaped Mero *personally* meant the advisor couldn't begrudge Goliath the escape of Persephone Alcmedi while the vampires lay dead for the day.

"My orders were for the Erus Veneficus to remain on site." Goliath's tone was sharp.

"I try to keep her here," Ivanka said. Regardless of her stilted English and thick Russian accent, Goliath understood her well; he'd trained her as security personnel when she joined this haven. "Old man come in. He angry."

"What old man?"

"Own shop. Volfsbane and Absinthe."

Mero shot Goliath a questioning look so he explained, "It is a nearby witch supply shop."

"I protect Erus Veneficus when he use cane as weapon," Ivanka added.

"You mean you fought a *mortal* man when he attacked the Erus Veneficus?" Mero asked.

The pointed and accusing nature of his comment wasn't lost on either Goliath or Ivanka. Goliath knew Ivanka's abilities as a sentinel were among the best in the haven; she'd taken his instruction flawlessly. He also knew that *she* knew she was among the best.

She looked up from the floor for the first time since entering and her brows were knit together tight. "Yes," she snapped at Mero. "He is mortal. As per standing haven orders, I did not harm him, just subdue. Not so easy as beating him black and blue. And zis"—she lifted her casted arm—"make even more difficult."

"Did he use magic against you?" Mero asked.

"Beauregard was Bindspoken years back," Goliath said. "He cannot use magic."

"Why would he attack the witch?"

Goliath shrugged.

"He say his son is cad . . . cad . . ." Ivanka paused, snorted a self-critical breath as she tried to remember. "Catatonic. He blame vitch for zis." She added, "While we fight, she sneak out. I try to follow, but she get to cab," Ivanka added.

Mero shifted his weight again. "Did she happen to mention why she was leaving or where she was going?"

"Say she haf meeting, but not vhair." Ivanka's gaze shifted to Goliath. "If she said, I already go there and bring vitch back."

Goliath nodded. "You may leave."

Ivanka rose and turned to the door. Before opening it she said, "She say she come back."

"Of course she did." Mero didn't sound convinced.

"Thank you," Goliath said and gestured her out. When Ivanka had gone, he faced Mero. The bruising Liyliy had caused around the vampire's eye was finally diminishing. "If my E.V. said she'd be back, that's what she'll do," Goliath assured him.

Mero met his gaze squarely. "I have not seen Menessos around the haven tonight."

Goliath remained calm. "I sent him on an errand."

"If he has gone to her and told her what we are deliberating about, she *will* flee. He could have told her that last night when she made her brief visit here. He could have told her to escape while we were yet under the sway of the death. She might have planned the escape with the old man."

"You make valid points." He broke his pose and strolled away with his hands clasped behind his back, thinking.

This was the unavoidable moment where he had to let Mero know where he stood. He'd bought time with his diplomacy yesterday, but that time had run out.

Goliath thought of his confrontation with Menessos earlier and what his Maker had said about the witch. Menessos had made no secret about his opposition to her being taken to the Excelsior when the three of them spoke yesterday evening. The question was, as Haven Master, should he support Menessos? His Maker was starting down a path at odds with the hierarchy of their kind. It was not completely unlike him, but it was rash.

Menessos had been acting more and more rashly since he'd met Persephone . . . conceivably since she'd marked him.

"She could have lured him out of this room," he said. "She could have used her influence to make him reveal any threats. She could have started planning to abscond right then. She could have lost all the integrity I've come to know she possesses due to the desperation of the moment." He turned back. "But I've seen her in desperate moments. She paused to save my life in a desperate moment."

Mero lifted his chin and squared his shoulders. "Do you feel you owe her loyalty for that?"

It seemed Mero was preparing himself for a confrontation, in case Goliath felt it necessary to subdue him.

"We all have to make our own choices, Mero. Yours is evident." Goliath smiled. "My Maker Made you. That makes us brothers of a sort. Out of respect for you, I will not try to stop you, but out of respect for our Maker, I will not help you, either."

Mero said nothing, but he did not move to leave.

Goliath said, "I can see that you are now considering whether or not you should use your rank and authority against me. Commandeering my haven and claiming my people to use them to aid you as you try to seize the Lustrata is a wise—even shrewd—move. Although you certainly should not underestimate her. Still"—he strode around the master's chair and lowered himself into it with all the regal poise he possessed—"I promise you, brother, if you try to take what is mine, I will give you a war."

She will destroy us. Does he not see that? Mero wondered as he left the Haven Master's chambers. He glanced up the stairs at the doorway to the Erus Veneficus's chambers, irritated that they were empty. She'd slipped through his grasp.

Goliath was young, but Menessos had trained him well. The diplomacy he offered was smart. It let him stand his own ground among all sides, yet clearly revealed which side he'd choose tonight if forced to.

Mero knew what he needed to do. He'd started toward the stage when a cacophony of excited sounds arose in the theater house beyond. Proceeding cautiously, he peered around the backstage wall and saw Menessos carrying a child. He was accompanied by a pair of women as different as night and day.

Seven, with her willowy figure and long, straight black hair worn in a ponytail, was on his right. Though a high-ranking vampire in this court, she wore jeans and work boots with her turquoise tank top; her primary job was overseeing the construction and renovation of the bar upstairs called Haven.

On his left was the red-eyed half-demon Risqué, her blond ringlets bouncing. At any given time her curvaceous body was barely covered. Since Mero had arrived he'd seen several different colors of ruffled panties on her. And clear platform heels. The ringlets usually covered her breasts, but when she was on the move, like now, her nipples peeked through.

Seven had gone into interrogation mode. "How long has she been unconscious?"

"About an hour and a half," Menessos answered.

"How long will she continue to be out?"

"I do not know. She may sleep through the night, as it is her custom."

"She will have to be watched around the clock."

Mero wondered what had happened to the girl.

"Indeed." Menessos was coming up the ramp to the stage. "That is why I brought her."

"You do not intend for her to stay in your chambers, do you?"

"No. The child will stay in Persephone's rooms."

"Alone?"

Menessos paused to face her. They both turned to Risqué.

She glanced back and forth between them. "No." Her pouty lips were pursed and her hands were planted on her hips. "No, no, no. I am not hanging out with a . . . child."

Menessos and Seven were not fazed. He said, "You are not dead for the day and you are magically proficient. You can keep her under control."

Under control? Mero's curiosity was piqued.

Menessos continued walking. "Besides, I think she'll like you."

Risqué's shoulders slumped. "But I hate wearing shirts," she whined.

Mero passed through the doorway as the others neared it. "Pardon us," Menessos said and continued on without offering an explanation. Mero hesitated for an instant, then was on his way across the theater. He made his way to the common area one floor up where he had earlier seen Talto and Ailo.

It was an open space with a beige and scarlet color scheme, creating a comfortable living room. The elegant atmosphere was marred, however, by the small group of Beholders playing cards in the far corner. They clustered around an elaborately carved and red felted poker table, but the beer cans, cigarette smoke, overflowing ashtrays, and colorful cheap chips drained all the sophistication from the room.

Those he sought were sitting closer to the room's entry, on a leather couch in front of the large-screen television. They were watching a news channel and soundly ignoring him.

He approached. "Ladies."

Only Ailo acknowledged him, and that was a simple sidelong shift in her eyes. Before she looked away, he said, "Did you learn anything about a young girl when you read Menessos?"

"The former court witch is the foster parent of a girl with dark hair."

"Aha. Thank you." Mero smiled. This was good news. Perhaps Goliath was correct. If her foster child was here, surely Persephone would come back. "The E.V. will likely be returning soon, then, as the child was brought in moments ago."

"I doubt it," Ailo murmured, looking back at the screen and smiling like she knew a secret.

Mero took that to mean that Liyliy was on her way to the witch. *Probably to kill her.* They needed her, alive, and marked by the Excelsior.

He stepped in front of the television. "Where is she?"

Ailo and Talto both kept staring at the screen as if he was not in the way at all. He turned, frustrated, and when he couldn't find the television's power button, he jerked the cord from the wall. "Where, Ailo?"

Both shabbubitum glared up at him. Ailo zoned out for a moment. When she blinked, she said, "She's at home."

CHAPTER TWENTY-ONE

I stood up faster than was wise. My head spun and I stumbled to the wall.

Propped against the wall, I touched my head and felt warm wetness and a lump. *Great.*

I walked to the sink, pulled a clean rag from the drawer, wet it, and held it to the bleeding goose egg on the side of my head as I leaned against the counter.

That bitch said Johnny had a son.

He hadn't denied it.

A son. How old is he? My mother and Nana had teased me that maybe since Johnny is the Domn Lup he was somehow immune to the nonprocreating rule. I didn't buy that idea at all. Because Johnny's memory was blank except for the last eight years, the kid would have to have been conceived eight years ago or more.

My stomach did a flip when I worked my way around to wondering who his mother was.

He has a family somewhere.

I filled a glass with water, added ice from the fridge, and drank it down. Swallowing hurt, but the cool liquid eased my throat. I dumped the ice from the empty glass into the rag and alternated holding it to my head and throat.

I'm a liability to Johnny.

I'd already proven what a burden I was for Menessos. He'd lost his haven because of me. It hurt to know what I'd cost him, but even though the power Johnny was attaining was changing so much about him and our relationship, I didn't want to cause him problems. More than that, I didn't want to be the reason he—or his son—were in danger.

That meant I was alone.

That shouldn't have bothered me. I'd lived by myself for years before all this Lustrata business crashed into my life and took over.

I'd been so worried about Johnny's new title and responsibility changing him, but this destiny of mine was certainly changing me, too.

Not only had I been forced to expand my skills as a witch—skills that included sorcery and the manipulation of dangerous ley line energies—but I'd reconnected with Eris, the mother who had abandoned me. It hadn't ended like a sappy and uplifting Lifetime movie, either. It turned out she was the artist who had tattooed Johnny—her magical artwork locked up all his power and subdued his beast. He'd also been left with no memories. We more or less bullied her into undoing the bindings. Certain complications in wære politics resulted in her losing her right arm.

Sure, it was the bullets the Rege fired that did the damage, but he was there because he was after Johnny, and Johnny was there because my witchery had discovered who'd inked him in the first place. Essentially, I brought danger and misfortune into Eris's home.

I'd also learned I had a half-brother—Lance—who now hated me. Nana was with Eris and Lance now, cleaning up my mess and mending family ties.

I'm a magnet for destruction.

It was probably for the best that Nana stay far away from me.

Hell, everyone should avoid me.

Maybe Johnny should *be with someone else.*

I grabbed the chair from the floor, righted it, and shoved it into its place at the dinette wishing it was that easy to put the pieces of my life in their proper places. I sank onto the bench seat at the table.

Torrid nights with Johnny had made me feel deeply attached and desired in a way that I had never felt before. As far as Menessos was concerned, after bonding magically with him and discovering I'd flipped his mark back onto him, I'd given him my own mark atop it, and now I felt him awaken every night.

In truth, I was anything but isolated.

With Johnny, the moments of seeing groupies fawning over him, of finding them kenneling with him, had hurt me badly, but I believed we could survive the rough patches. Then his beast got the best of him. I wasn't sure I could ever forgive an attack like that, but here, earlier in my kitchen, for a fleeting moment, I'd believed I could.

Before Aurelia arrived.

Not now. Now I knew the Zvonul had given him Ms. Hot-Body McMistress as an assistant. It was an altogether new kind of hurt. Like all those who Johnny was destined to lead had conspired against me and left me no hope of "us" surmounting their will for him.

With Menessos, I'd felt twinges of jealousy knowing Eva was in his bed. I'd been more than angry with him for working the *in signum amoris* spell over Johnny and me without permission, and for being manipulative in general. Even though he'd pulled Beverley from the ley line and surely saved her life, he'd also taken her away and basically forbidden my coming to the haven while telling me I had no choice but to run to the Witch Elders Council.

Wouldn't it be best if I kept them both out of my heart and at arm's length emotionally?

In spite of our triangle—no, *because* of the corollary effects of it—I didn't just feel alone, I *was* alone.

Alone in this big empty house.

Alone in facing this big empty feeling.

Alone with my "what am I gonna do" decision.

My decision.

Mine.

Who are all these other people, these wærewolves and vampires, to think they can make decisions for the Lustrata? The thought came in the voice of Amenemhab, my totem animal.

What could I do to keep the Excelsior at bay while not needing Johnny to hide me or running to the Witch Elders?

Considering what I knew about vampires, I remembered something that could be useful.

It was dangerous. And I'd need Menessos to help. . . .

After punching the buttons to call him, a "this phone is shut off" message played.

I stared at the phone in my hand. That had to be wrong. I redialed. Same thing.

Menessos wouldn't turn his phone *off*. It must have been damaged in the flooding water at the park. I glanced at the clock. Zhan might have been able to drive to the haven by now, but it would be close.

I stood.

I paced.

My gaze slid to the rag in my hand. There in the middle of my darkened kitchen, I held the rag out and squeezed drops of water from the melting ice cubes while turning slowly to create a circle of water around me.

I sat cross-legged and flipped that mental switch for my meditation state to "on."

When I opened my eyes, however, I was not on the shore I was accustomed to.

In fact, I'd never meditated myself into such a dirty place before.

It was a human-made structure around me, not natural, and this place was a wreck . . . crumbling and blackened as if it had burned long ago. Standing, the creak in the floorboards under me put me ill at ease. I brushed myself off and spun slowly. I slid one foot to shift my stance for better balance, and realized my socked feet were a mistake. I should have put shoes on before I meditated.

Somehow this place seemed familiar. If it had not been in such a tragic state, or if there were more light, maybe I could have placed it. As it was, I wanted to get away from the depressing atmosphere.

I took a cautious step. The floor creaked again under my weight and I retreated. Keeping one foot planted, I tested all around, and each place I tried, the boards threatened to shatter like glass.

I'd brought tangible items out of the meditation with me before, and I was certain that if I was injured in this world it would transfer to my physical body. Though danger was not typically an issue, it was part of the risk of coming here.

And it hit me: I hadn't said the rhyme. I hadn't asked for a sacred space. I'd slipped into meditation without the proper safeguards in place. A foolish mistake, and even the attack and attempted murder—perhaps a concussion—were not good excuses for me to be so careless.

I had arrived somewhere that was not *my* meditation space. I'd been pulled into someone else's. I had to get out of here before they figured out I was trespassing.

My knees bent and I tried to sit, but something held me upright.

Oh no.

"You are quite trapped." The whisper was spoken from right behind me.

I felt his body materialize even as the last word formed.

Creepy.

CHAPTER TWENTY-TWO

A head, the taillights gleamed like eyes glowing red in the night.

Johnny pressed the accelerator and felt the Quattroporte's engine respond. He was gaining.

Aurelia accelerated, too. She had probably never been a shrinking violet in her life.

Johnny had admired her BMW 650i coupe in the garage at the den. In many ways her two-door was comparable to his four-door. She could go from zero to sixty in 4.3 seconds—a whole second faster than his Maserati—because her car weighed a little less. But that was only useful in straightaways. Here in the rural areas around Red's house, roads ran straight along the farmed fields for considerable distance, but then abruptly ended or made ninety-degree turns.

He put his windows down halfway, listening as her engine churned. Even over the rushing air he could tell the 650i's engine note was a low, sultry growl compared to the wildcat scream of the Maserati. The manual transmission was slowing her down. She was good but not adept enough at shifting; it was costing her seconds.

Out here, there was no traffic, no side streets for her to hide in. Not that a sleek red BMW would ever "hide" in this rural area. He kept up easily.

But keeping up wasn't enough.

He had to stop her. Aurelia had tried to murder Red.

She had to be held accountable for that—but his stomach twisted at the thought. No matter how this played out, Evan would never be safe. If he let Aurelia go, she would hold this information over his head forever. If he took her in, the fail-safes she'd set up would reveal the secret. The only way to combat it was to stop being afraid of it and put it out there in the open—his way.

The brake lights ahead brightened, and the 650i squealed into a turn. The Quattroporte made the same turn with much more finesse. The BMW should have been able to corner better. Johnny chalked it up to Aurelia's unfamiliarity with the area.

Worse, this particular road, he knew, dog-legged. Another sharp turn was coming up fast, and a farmer had knocked down the warning-arrow sign with his tractor.

Oh shit.

Johnny took his foot off the pedal. If he backed off, maybe she'd slow down. Maybe she'd see the turn—

Aurelia was going too fast. She missed it.

There was no ditch—the farmer's access to his field was right there. The 650i shot straight onto the dirt roadway of the field and bounced along the tractor path. Against his better judgment, Johnny took the Maserati after her.

According to the sound, she was pushing the BMW hard. It wasn't meant for this kind of terrain, and more important, she needed to downshift. The peals of the engine voiced her desperation.

What if this tractor path merged onto another road?

He gripped the wheel and closed the distance between them. Suddenly the 650i lurched to the right, bobbing and dipping, throwing chunks of dirt as it wobbled hastily onto a paved road. The entrance to the road on this end was fine for a tractor, but hell for luxury cars. Once on the road, the engine revved high and Johnny knew she'd double-clutched it for speed.

Trying to make up precious seconds, he slowed as he neared the dangerous spot and made his reentry to the road as smooth as possible.

He could see her taillights in the distance and gave the Maserati all he could. Surely she was thinking this was her shot at escaping and he needed to catch up pronto.

That was when he saw the eyeshine.

Their reckless driving through the field had stirred up the deer. A group of five—at least—were on the move. He saw them closing in on the road and held his breath.

When they bounded into Aurelia's path, her brake lights flashed. The car lurched to the left, then right. One deer rolled up the hood and, legs flailing at broken angles, flew over the roof to skid along the road, while a second deer broke through the now-cracked windshield. The car slid from the road, hit the ditch, and began to roll.

Johnny left his vehicle on the road, hazard lights flashing, and raced toward the 650i. It must have rolled eight or nine times; it was deep in the darkened field—the car's headlamps had shattered. He passed the dead deer; it had been tossed off the windshield as the car spun. He hurried onward, scenting the air, searching for the tang of human blood. All he picked up was damp foliage, metal, and motor oil.

Luckily the car had come to rest right side up, but it was crushed and crumpled. Even as he neared, the motor sputtered and died. His last few steps stalled.

What if she's dead?

What if she isn't?

She lay very still inside, her head drooped forward. He could not tell if she was breathing.

His fingers tried to curl around the door handle. It had compressed almost flat from the impact. He hurried to the other side. Smashed, but not as much.

Concentrating, he stretched his index finger into a thin claw. This fit under the handle. He lifted and pulled. The door didn't want to open. Using both hands on the now-raised handle, he yanked with all his might.

When finally the metal screeched and the door scraped open, the dome light flickered on. The scent of blood was suddenly strong. Instantly his beast roared within him and his mouth began to water.

No.

"Aurelia." He sank into the passenger seat. He looked her over and she seemed to be in one piece, nothing obviously broken. Her purse had fallen to cover her feet. Tentatively he touched her arm. "Aurelia."

Nothing. He knew better than to move her, but he reached up and pushed her hair from her face. Her nose was bloodied. More of the red fluid trickled down the left side of her neck and he could not tell if it was from her scalp or her ear. He touched her cheek, letting the heel of his hand rest under her nose lightly. He could feel the warmth of a shallow breath on his skin.

She was alive. For now.

Implications bounced around his mind. She was alive, but if injured as badly as she apparently was, would she be able to check in and keep the information about Evan from leaking out? He wondered how much time he had to reveal this news the way he wanted to.

He jerked his phone from his pocket, opened it, and searched through the numbers for Doc Lincoln, the veterinarian who treated wæres. Before he could queue it up, Aurelia moaned. The sound grew into a cry of agony as she tried to lift her head.

"Aurelia, don't move. Stay very still. I'm calling for help."

"For help? You . . . you . . . bastard." Her voice grew louder with each new word.

"What?"

Her head had shaken with her earlier effort but now she was still. "Look what you've done!"

"Stay calm. Help will be coming." *I can't call 911. If they recognized me they'd know immediately she's wære. They'd let her die.*

He pushed the button for Doc Lincoln's private number.

"Calm? Calm! You want me to be calm?"

"Yes."

"You're calling for help. I don't trust you or your help."

The phone began ringing. "You're delirious."

"You wish. Why don't you just kill me now and be done with it."

"I'm not calling for help as a ruse, Aurelia. He's a real . . . doctor." *Of sorts.*

She growled. "Spare me the games. No one would suspect a broken neck wasn't part of the crash, John. You better do it before they get here."

Doc Lincoln's message system picked up. At this hour, he wasn't surprised. "Doc, it's John Newman. There's been an accident." He left the details as to where. "Please come ASAP." He shut his phone. "Aurelia, he can help you."

"Riiiight." She tried to laugh but it turned into a strangled cough and blood sprayed from her mouth.

The smell was richer than usual, and there was un-usual warmth to it. His beast rolled its shoulders and wallowed in that scent. He guessed it was arterial blood. He squeezed the phone in his hand. *C'mon, Doc.*

It bothered him that she didn't even try to wipe the blood from her face, but he had told her not to move.

When she'd recovered from the small fit, she said, "I promise you. I will make your life miserable."

"Aurelia."

"Even from behind bars, John. I know everyone," she snarled. "They all owe me favors."

Her threats were irritating but he kept his voice even. "Seriously, you need to stay calm and keep your heart rate down."

"Every day, you'll wonder who around you is spying for me."

The words stung because they were true. "This isn't helping you."

"Every night, you'll wonder who I've asked to assas-sinate you."

"Stop it!"

"Every fucking moment, you'll wonder what I'm plotting."

"Stop!"

"You'll wonder if it's you who's gonna die or your precious witch."

He ground his teeth.

"And every goddamned waking minute, you *will* worry about your son's safety. Little accidents at first. Not life threatening but painful. *Soooo* painful. A broken arm here. A leg there. And then . . ." She laughed a throaty and malicious little laugh. "I can promise you . . . he won't be safe *anywhere.*"

CHAPTER TWENTY-THREE

Within the Haven Master's suite, Goliath was still pondering Mero's reaction when he heard a clamoring on the steps outside and rose from his seat to investigate.

"Has the witch returned?" he asked the guard.

"No. Seven and Risqué were escorting Menessos. He was carrying an unconscious child into the E.V.'s quarters."

Goliath started moving when the guard said "Menessos," but the "unconscious" part sent him up the steps three at a time. He stopped in the doorway and took in the scene before him. Menessos was laying Beverley on the bed in the back of the room while Risqué looked through the closet. She was pushing hangers to the side, saying, "No, no, no . . . God, who bought her these awful clothes?"

Seven, who was starting a fire in the hearth, said, "Pick a shirt and put it on."

Pouting, Risqué jerked a black tank top from its hanger and shoved it over her head.

"Is she all right?" Goliath asked.

The women faced him but said nothing. Menessos had one hand on the girl's forehead. He looked up and said, "I believe so." He paused. "I suspect that she will sleep through the night."

Goliath lowered his tense shoulders, but he did not feel relief. "What happened? Why did you have to get to a ley line?"

Menessos eased down to sit on the edge of the bed. "She discovered a spirit board that has been in Persephone's family many years."

"She used it alone? Unprotected?" Goliath stomped a few paces into the suite.

Menessos raised his hand and stopped Goliath's advance. "No one even knew that she was aware of the item, much less that she would endeavor to remove it from the house by stealth and use it." Menessos explained what they believed had happened.

"You mean she was in the ley?" *Resourceful. She is her mother's daughter.* Goliath had heard tales of sorcerers lost to the ley. Retrieval was nothing short of miraculous the few times it had been accomplished. Like magical brain surgery, precision was everything. Goliath asked, "How did you get her out?"

"I had to gift her."

Goliath's eyes widened and he rushed forward. He needed no explanation to understand what his Maker had done, but still he repeated the words, *"Gift* her?"

He stood at the bedside looking down at her small form. Even with her visage relaxed and peaceful in sleep, her brows rested a fraction low and the ends of her lips were turned slightly downward as if there was pain in her body, or a bad dream was playing out before her closed eyes. Her cherubic innocence was missing.

Menessos said, "I had to fill her with power. It was the only way to separate her body from the ley line and bring her out. Gifting her was the only way to keep her from dying after the dividing."

Separate. Divide. The words held so much meaning.

Only Menessos could have achieved it.

Only Menessos would have dared undertake it.

Goliath was grateful that his Master was powerful and skilled, and willing to risk his own safety. He was thankful the girl was alive and safe.

But.

Beverley would have to live with the consequences of being gifted.

Goliath touched her feet. Her toes were cold. Rather than disturb her to pull the bedding down, he told Risqué to fetch the throw blanket from the couch. When she handed it to him, he covered the girl up, remembering how she'd often fallen asleep on the couch when he was visiting her mother. He'd covered her up many times.

"What gift did she receive?"

Menessos hesitated. "She had already shown promise. Persephone and I missed the power signature, unaware that the girl had fey blood. But she must have. That is the only rationalization for how she could have gotten into the ley in the first place."

Goliath considered this news, but knew his Maker was trying to steer the topic elsewhere. "What gift?" he pressed as he tucked the blanket around her feet.

Menessos lingered over the question.

Goliath faced his Maker, rage darkening his own eyes and resonating in every fiber of his being. "Tell me." His whisper was a heated demand.

Menessos looked up slowly and met Goliath's angry

gaze with a mixture of sorrow and grave intensity. "She has become a ward-breaker."

Goliath stared at him, straightened up abruptly, then turned on his heel, and stared into the flames Seven had built.

Lorrie's child was a danger to them all.

Here, there were barriers meant to keep wærewolves away from havens; it was nothing more than a simple spill of magical energy that gave wæres a sense of foreboding, but it warned them that magic may be in use in the area and kept them out. It was as much for the wæres' own safety as it was for the vampires' security. Those barriers could be nullified simply by Beverley's will. Once she was trained, that is.

He could not suggest that she be left untrained.

Until she learned to control the gift, her presence and unconscious intentions could impact the magical seals. Moreover, having established contact to so much power, if she lost control it would all rush forth, consuming her and everything around her. It would tear the May Company building apart, haven and all. She might even lay waste to the whole of Public Square.

She had to learn to control what she had become.

But after she'd been taught to contain and command her abilities, she would be sought after. Vampires, witches, sorcerers, wæres—even nefarious humans— would see in her an object to use, a tool to open everything from bicycle locks to bank vaults . . . and more.

He glanced at Seven. He could tell by her expression she understood what danger they were all in with the child here. He turned to Risqué, who had donned the tank top. She fussed with the fit of the tight fabric.

It was obviously Menessos's plan that the half-demon stay with the girl for the day.

Goliath was not certain he approved, but he had no alternative. If she was going to stay, she wasn't going to be half-naked while taking care of the child. "Pants, too." His tone did not invite argument.

She clenched her teeth but turned back to the closet.

She did not seem to comprehend how hazardous the situation was with the child there. "You haven't briefed her?" Goliath asked Menessos.

"Not yet."

Goliath nodded toward the half-demon. "Make her understand."

"Risqué, Beverley must stay in the suite," Menessos began calmly. "She will need to eat—see that she gets whatever she wants, but not to the point that she makes herself ill. You must keep her happy and entertained. If you play a game, let her win—but not obviously so. Her mood must remain cheerful. It is the best way to avoid incidents."

Risqué turned from the closet with a pair of flannel sleep pants in hand. She cocked her head. "What exactly would constitute an 'incident'?"

"If she gets upset, things are going to happen that will alarm her and worsen the situation. It is a cycle she must not start."

"What things will happen?"

"You will know," he said sternly.

"You're going to have to train her, right?" Risqué asked as she stepped into the sleep pants.

Menessos nodded. "Yes."

"She needs to sleep all day and be ready for you come

nightfall, so"—she shrugged and had to tug her shirt back down—"why don't I dose her with something when she eats?"

"No," Goliath snapped. "She will not be drugged."

Risqué crossed her arms. "What if there's an incident and I have no other option?"

Goliath eased close to her and mimicked her pose. "I believe you were told it is your job to keep that from happening." Glowering down his nose, he reminded her, "As your Haven Master, I expect you to do what you are told."

Her eyes widened slightly. She recovered herself, set her jaw, and gave him a curt nod. "Of course. I forgot my place, Master, and spoke too freely."

"Don't forget again."

She bowed her head.

Goliath walked away. At the door to the suite he turned back. "Menessos . . . you and I have to finish what we discussed earlier." He did not want to say "You promised to break our bonds" in front of the others. Also, he was not satisfied that Menessos had made Risqué understand the scope of the situation, but he did not want to correct the former Haven Master in front of those he used to rule. It seemed distasteful and disrespectful, so he held his tongue—for now.

Menessos nodded. "Once everything is in order here, I will come to your suite."

Hoping that getting things "in order here" meant Menessos was going to elaborate on the danger for Risqué, Goliath shut the heavy door behind him. As he descended the steps, Silhouette walked through the doorway that led to the stage and smiled at him.

The tension in his shoulders finally diminished.

• • •

Mero hurried up the stairwell to the ground level. With Liyliy's exit, all had returned to normal here, with guards posted on duty. He approached the ranking guard. "I require a car."

Once supplied with a vehicle, he drove, and he worried. So much so that he was speeding. As a general rule, he was not averse to taking his chances at being ticketed if the situation warranted the risk.

This situation doubtlessly did.

Persephone Alcmedi must not be slain.

Although the Excelsior had once given him orders to eliminate her if she was not the Lustrata, he had come to believe that she was in fact the destined witch. That being the case, his orders were to bring her to the Excelsior. He knew what would become of her then.

The Excelsior would give her his marks. He would make her his servant, securing her loyalty through the bond of being mastered and the control it offered, if necessary. She would also be guaranteed a prestigious position as Erus Veneficus of the Excelsior. Having the fated Lustrata under his power and protection would benefit them both, not to mention the boost she would give the Excelsior's status.

And the issue of her spirituality will be a platform from which I can reintroduce Deric to the goddess.

Mero accelerated.

When Mero had left the room, Talto faced Ailo. "He said the child was here. Why would they bring a child into the haven?"

Ailo was staring at the doorway, mind racing over the

same question. "I do not know but I intend to find out." She sat forward and started to rise. Talto's hand on her arm stopped her.

"Our sister told us to tear them apart," Talto whispered. "We can use this information to supplement what plan we devise, right?"

"Yes." Ailo smiled at her sister. "And I have come up with a plan. We must make Menessos believe we are loyal to him."

Talto rolled her eyes. "He will not ever trust us."

"That is why we must decide which of us will act to show loyalty and cozy up to him, and which will be true to herself."

Crossing her arms, Talto declared, "I will not be the one cozying up to him."

"If that is your choice, Talto, I will agree to it. But think, sweet baby sister. If we succeed, and one of us gains his favor, she may have sway over his actions someday. She may even be able to have the other imprisoned—doing so may be the only way to secure his belief in the ruse. It may even come to a discussion of the unfavored being slain—"

Talto gasped.

"I would never allow it, but the discussion may have to be had, do you understand?"

Wide-eyed, Talto's mouth opened and shut, opened again. "We have always stood side by side, Sister. No matter what we faced."

"I know. But Liyliy is not here. We must accomplish this on our own." Ailo knew her sibling was struggling. "I am willing to listen if you have a better idea."

For a long moment, Talto blinked and thought hard.

Ailo waited. Finally, Talto shook her head. "No. I have nothing better to suggest."

Ailo had known Talto would not. She was hateful, vindictive, and vicious, but she lacked the patience to craft a cunning plan. "Then we will stick with my plan, to convince him that we are not unified. One of us will gain his confidence, and one will strike against him. The one who remains true to her nature will have to implicitly trust the one who gets close to him."

Motionless, Talto didn't even breathe.

"Do you trust me this much?" Ailo asked.

There was hesitation, but Talto answered, "You have given me no reason to distrust you, Sister, but as I said, I do not believe he will ever trust us."

"We must give him proof."

Talto's eyes narrowed. "How?"

"If you are to be true to your nature, then you must do something bad. I will reveal this to him so you can be punished. It will gain me a measure of his faith."

"It sounds as if the one who remains true is getting all the ills of this scheme."

"Indeed. But for a good cause. And, assuming that will be you, know that I would beg him to be merciful."

Ailo savored the unease her sister was having over this idea. Talto had always been the weakest of them. "You have been the most vocal about your displeasure with our new predicament, baby sister. You will be most believable in the role of yourself, whereas I have presented myself with more thoughtful silence. It is that obvious ability to discern when I am beaten that will benefit me most as I try to convince Menessos of my loyalty."

With her arms still crossed, Talto stood and paced

away. She shook her head. "No matter how ruthless a game we play with him, no matter how much torture I would bear for this cause, I cannot fathom that he would believe either of us is willing to serve *him*."

"We do not need him to believe I am willing to serve him, we only need him to doubt my loyalty to you."

After a space of nearly a full minute, Talto nodded. "Let me call Liyliy."

"Wait. Let me see what more I can learn. While I am gone, you study the stock exchange information at the bottom of the screen, then convince one of those morons behind us to show you where the computers are kept." She touched Talto's hand and mentally conveyed the idea. "You know what to do?"

Talto nodded.

Ailo rose from the couch and strode to the door. Mero had had plenty of time to reach the ground floor and be out of sight. She strolled into the hall and made her way to the grand stairwell. She was headed down to the court level; a female Offerling was coming up the stairs. The woman was black and wore a sleeveless blouse made of thin, emerald-green material with feminine frills around the collar.

Plan forming, Ailo shifted her apparel slightly to allow the heels of her shoes to rise. "Excuse me," she called in a friendly tone.

The woman looked up with a smile, but it faded when she saw Ailo's iron collar. She stopped. "Yes?"

Everyone in the haven knew who and what she and Talto were. By the change in expression, Ailo knew this woman had a low, suspicious opinion of her. It was not unexpected. She had doubted the woman would be easily lured into giving up information anyway. So, when she was about two steps away, as she said, "I just wanted to say I love your blouse," Ailo stumbled purposely, falling into the Offerling and rolling gracelessly down the steps with one hand wrapped around the woman's bare arm.

Feigning shock, Ailo apologized profusely and indicated her shoes. "We didn't have high heels in the era I am from. They are gorgeous, and I am trying to adapt, but they are still awkward. Even with vampire reflexes, stilettos require some getting used to."

The woman scowled at her, noted a rip in her own blouse, and stalked up the steps muttering that she would have to change.

Ailo smiled down at her palm.

The Offerling she had chosen was more perfect than she could have hoped for. Her name was Silhouette. She was currently Goliath's lover and had wanted to spend some time with him . . . but he'd told her that he had to prepare. He and Menessos were going to be busy for a while this evening.

Mero's out of the haven. Goliath and Menessos will be busy.

That means Talto and I are free to push our plan forward . . . well, my *plan, that is.*

CHAPTER TWENTY-FOUR

What in Hell are you doing interrupting my meditation?"
I hadn't moved and Creepy kept his body pressed tight against my backside. With the floor fracturing around me, I was afraid to step away. The way he was breathing in my ear, I figured facing him would create a new set of worries.

"Questions, questions," he whispered. "With you it is always questions." He spoke without rushing, each syllable a loitering sound, emerging from his lips flavored with both virtue and venom. His hands rested on my shoulders, light but warm. "Always so curious." His hands slid downward with agonizing slowness. "And so beautiful."

I repeated, "Why are you in my meditation?"

"Am I? Or has my dream come true and you're in mine?"

"What?" I asked sharply over my shoulder.

He nuzzled against my cheek, chuckling with an easy finesse that sounded classy and sensual at the same time. It distracted me enough that I didn't notice his hands were on the move until they had wrapped around my waist.

"You entered your meditation in search of aid, did you not?"

"Advice," I clarified.

"Ask *me,* my curious girl." He swayed, pulling me with him as if we were slow dancing. "The questions are free."

The implications made my heart thud in my chest. "And the answers?"

"Ah, now those . . . those have a price."

When I once questioned Menessos about Creepy he had told me as much. I pushed at the hands restraining me. "I am not playing games with you."

He did not let go.

I kept pushing at his grip. My arms lacked the strength to force him to release me. "Let me go."

"Go? Where will you go? Back to your empty farmhouse? Back to your confusion and doubt? Back to a wearying world of multiplying responsibilities? Back to a challenging life that with each passing day promises only greater risks and deeper losses? Is that truly where you want to be?"

My throat was tight as I swallowed down a sudden discontentment. "Now who's asking questions?" I made it an accusation.

He threw his head back and laughed out loud. His voice filled the decaying space, echoing back from the roof high over our heads and bringing flaky, ashen debris with it. When his laughter faded, he rubbed his cheek against my hair and brought his mouth to my ear again. "Do you really want to go?" His voice was low, his breath warm.

"Yes."

"But you've not even asked your question yet."

"Your price is too high."

"I cannot determine my price until I hear the question."

True. I snorted. "Still. I can tell."

"You want something for nothing." His embrace ended. "Go. Return to your privation and ambiguity." He pushed me forward.

"No!" I cried. Time slowed even as I teetered headlong,

afraid to step, knowing that I'd fall through the floor. Twisting, hoping he wouldn't let me plummet, I reached for him.

His hand caught mine.

I fell another few inches before our arms snapped taut. My weight and momentum didn't affect his stance or balance at all, as if I were no more than a feather.

With a sigh of relief, I dangled before him like we'd just finished a dance. For the first time since his arrival, I was able to really see him. He was imperious in a black suit with black shirt and black tie. His dark eyes, straight, shoulder-length black hair, and trim beard made him look austere. The only splash of color was a slim line of crimson, a silk hanky in his breast pocket. When my gaze saw the color, my heartbeat increased.

With an easy tug he hauled me up and into his arms. "No? You do not wish to leave me?"

"Not like that." The breathlessness of my words made me sound inordinately enthusiastic.

A complacent smile curved his lips. "What kind of departure would suit you, then? A simple one? An *easy* one that costs you nothing?"

I squinted, uncertain if I believed what I was hearing. Leaving a meditation didn't have a price . . . but I usually did have an exchange with my totem animal. During those exchanges I guess I did concede information or at least admit to being troubled, and then I received advice. That was how totems worked. Creepy was different; definitely not a totem. He existed in the real world—or he had when he visited my house. That corporality, I reasoned, meant an exchange with him *could* cost me something of physical substance.

I hadn't come here to him purposely. However, my meditation world had a way of taking me to where the answers I needed could be found. My error in forgetting the protective rhyme kept me suspicious. "I thought you made a deal with Menessos to help protect me."

"I am protecting you. Who knows where else you might have ended up . . . and I excel at giving advice and answers as well."

According to the unspoken vibe Menessos had emitted about this guy, he was not trustworthy. I clamped my mouth shut.

He leaned to my ear and, after inhaling deeply, whispered, "You were nearly murdered tonight. The sweet perfume of death lingers around you."

"I wasn't that close," I countered, but couldn't help sniffing the air. I detected a heady white floral scent. It was tenacious in an exotic way, sexy, but there was a dirty undernote. Something earthy and almost cigarish.

"You've been seconds from death many times lately. The redolence that remains beckons me." He stood straight and smoothed my hair. "And here we are. Together. You linger when you could have gone."

"Sure, if I wanted to fall through the floor and awaken in my kitchen with broken legs."

His thumb rubbed my cheek lovingly. "Then ask what you would of me, beautiful Persephone."

There was no other way out. I had to ask something. Then he'd name his price for the answer. Doubtlessly, I wouldn't like his price, but I had to come up with a question specifically for him.

Suddenly I understood why I was here.

I knew how I wanted to deal with the Excelsior's

interest in me, and I knew exactly what I needed to accomplish that. Creepy was uniquely capable of performing the most dangerous part of the process—and likely with a minimum of repercussions, if any at all.

As the question formed in my mind, a lump formed in my throat. It kept the words from tumbling into spoken reality. Swallowing down the fear, I asked something else. "First of all, asking doesn't obligate me to pay your price, does it? I mean, we discuss that after I ask, right?"

His eyes sparkled. In a tone that conveyed sinister confidence, he said, "We will negotiate, Persephone. I promise you."

A chill tickled up my spine, as if racing to the spot on my neck where Creepy's touch lingered.

It took three deep cleansing breaths for me to find my voice.

"Would you be willing to materialize in the private chambers of the Excelsior?"

Amusement danced in his eyes. "You would have me kill the Excelsior for you?"

"No, I would have you bring me a spoonful of the earth from his dirt bag." Vampires did keep small pouches of their home ground in their pillows.

"Ahhh." His touch drifted along my collarbone. "What spell are you casting, witch?"

My mouth clamped shut again. The less he knew the better. Besides, that could be something I needed in the *negotiations*.

"If you will not tell me, I will have to guess."

I lowered my chin, and then stared up at him resolutely. Even making a solid endeavor to remain blank, my seriousness was probably like a billboard in bold type.

He was silent for a long minute, scrutinizing my expression. Then his index finger traced a line downward and his eyes followed it. I felt as if he was staring into me. His hand pressed above my heart. I could not blink, could not breathe, and another chill swept over me. I shuddered as he spoke.

"Despite all the weightless mercy in your heart, a shadow of guilt burdens you. You seek to do no harm, to be a good witch, a light-bringer and ringer of bells, but your path is treacherous. Sometimes steep, sometimes a struggling bare-handed climb. But your noble motivation is only to protect yourself so that you may continue defending those you love."

His hand rose away from my heart and I could breathe again.

His touch was fever warm as he lifted my chin. That warmth spread reassurance through me. "You can create a stake to deter the Excelsior like the one Vivian created to repel Menessos, but it will not stop the Supreme Vampire."

It was my turn to stare.

"I can help you create this weapon if that is what you truly want, but I could do much more to aid you by other means."

Of course he could. This was the nature of Creepy's game. This was the reason that even Menessos—who had mastered the nuances of manipulation—was wary of this guy. Creepy's version of the game was played with exponentially raised stakes.

"Like?"

His lips crooked up on one side.

CHAPTER TWENTY-FIVE

Johnny's hands shot out, reaching for Aurelia's neck. His beast slavered, anxious for a kill—but he stopped himself before he touched her. *No. I will not end her life.*

He pulled himself back.

"Do it!" she cried.

"No. I won't be a murderer."

"You already are! You killed Ignatius Tierney!"

Johnny snorted as if she'd kicked him in the gut. "That was different." Ig had been having strokes and while his cyclical changes corrected the defects, the strokes were recurring earlier and earlier in each cycle. Ig was pitiful. He was going to die anyway. Johnny's taking his throat had given him the release he wanted as well as the knowledge that Johnny would ascend to Domn Lup. It was what Ig wanted. "It wasn't murder."

"Because it was a release from his torment?" Aurelia demanded.

"Yes," Johnny answered softly, his hands coming to rest in his lap. "Yes."

"John . . . you have to kill me."

He stared at the side of her head in the harsh dome light. She still hadn't moved. A bitter thought chilled his stomach.

"Please. I can't feel my legs. I can't move my arms." Her voice cracked. "Don't leave me like *this*."

She'd figured it out already and had been baiting him,

taunting him into finishing her off. But he couldn't kill her in cold blood. He wouldn't.

He wasn't sure what Doc Lincoln could do for her like this. Surely an animal in this condition would simply be put down.

Put down. People who love their pets do that. They do what's best for the pet. And they stay with them while they die.

He looked at his hands.

No. Johnny slid out of the seat.

Inside the wreckage, Aurelia began sobbing. "I can't live like this! Not as an invalid."

He backed away from the car. *I can't do it under these circumstances, either.*

She coughed again and it sounded like blood came up. He turned away. He'd made two steps before he heard, "John. Please. Wait."

He stopped.

She was breathing fast, so pale. Yet there was sweat on her brow. "You have to go to my hotel. The Renaissance Cleveland. Get my purse. Take my room key. It's the Presidential Suite." She coughed again, spat. "In my suitcase, wedged in the bottom left corner, is a key to a public locker at the Greyhound station on Chester Avenue. It's not even a mile from the hotel."

He knew downtown well enough that she didn't have to tell him this, but he refrained from interrupting her.

"Take the key. Get the stuff inside it . . . in the next twenty-four hours." Another cough. "Do it before he gets it. Do it and your son will be safe."

Johnny stepped back to the car. "'He' who?"

She swallowed, spat. "Take it," she whispered. "Get the key."

Johnny sat and reached for her purse, which lay on her feet. As he pulled it away his stomach turned over inside him. Beneath the purse, her right foot was twisted to the side and an inch of leg bone protruded from it. Blood was dripping fast, pooling on the tan floor.

If he had doubted the truth of her claim to not feeling anything, that sealed it. He brought the purse up onto the console between them and unzipped the top.

"Who?" he asked again.

Abruptly, Aurelia screamed. "My feet. Oh my God, my feet! John, do you see that!"

Brusquely, he said, "I saw it."

"I . . . I can't feel any of that. God, please, don't leave me like this."

Johnny's fingers closed around the hotel key card. He zipped the purse up and replaced it gently, hoping she would calm down once she couldn't see her feet again.

"Help me," she begged.

Not trusting his voice to not break, he whispered, "I cannot kill you."

Shallow jerky breaths overcame her and she sobbed again.

Lights flashed down the road. Four sets. Johnny got out of the car.

When the vehicles neared he recognized the three black Chevrolet Tahoes that the Omori had been using, and the last he recognized as Doc Lincoln's pickup truck. They parked behind his car on the road and started unloading.

Johnny headed directly for Gregor. "Let the doc in first," he ordered, pointing at the truck and the plain man who climbed out of it with a large medical bag in hand. Once Doc Lincoln approached Aurelia's car, Johnny pulled Gregor to the side. "I need you to go to Saranac Lake, New York."

Gregor nodded. "What may I do for you there?"

"Get my son and bring him to Cleveland."

The Omori captain blinked twice, showing more surprise than Johnny had expected he would. "Would you repeat that, sire?"

Johnny sat in his car and called Antonia Brown. "I'm sorry, Toni. I know it's late—"

"What's wrong?" she asked.

"I'm sending a man to Saranac Lake."

"What for?"

"I've learned that someone bugged the key fob to my car. They know about Evan. They know I have a son."

"'They' who?"

Johnny's free hand scratched through his hair. He flashed a look at the car in the field. The Omori had taken one of the Chevys into the field. It sat running with the high beams shining into the BMW while Doc Lincoln was checking Aurelia. "I don't know exactly."

"John."

The question in her voice was clear. "I trust the man I'm sending."

"He'll protect us?"

"Yes. He is to bring you and Evan here. Pack only what you need, we'll send for the rest or replace it."

"You don't seriously think it's that simple to uproot our lives, do you?" she snapped.

Johnny wasn't sure how to delicately say what he wanted to say. "Don't you have your affairs in order?"

When she'd tracked Johnny down, she'd told him she was dying. She had about six months.

Toni sighed resignedly. "What if I want to die in my home?"

"I will do everything you ask of me, Toni, but I want Evan with me. I want him here with guards I trust around him. I would not ask this of you unless I was convinced Evan's life depended on it." He respected her resilience and tenacity. She had struggled on when her husband died suddenly. She had struggled on when her teen daughter, Frankie, wound up pregnant by a boy who disappeared before she could even tell him about the child. She had struggled on when Frankie was killed by a drunk driver. She had raised Evan alone for five years. She'd done what needed to be done, her way. He wanted her to be able to die her way, but he had to protect his son. "You will have every bit of medical care that you want. No more, no less."

Silence.

"Toni?"

"I will hold you to that."

"I expect nothing else from you." Another moment passed. "I'm going to send a picture to your phone of the man I'm sending. His name is Gregor."

"Okay."

Movement outside caught his attention. "I need to go now, Toni. Call me if you need anything." He ended the call as he exited the vehicle.

Dr. Geoffrey Lincoln had left the BMW and was coming back toward his truck. What bothered Johnny was the doc wasn't hurrying.

"Doc?"

He stopped in his tracks. He removed his glasses and began cleaning them on the tail of his shirt.

Johnny's pace increased. "Doc?"

"I'm sorry, John."

Johnny's heartbeat was loud in his ears as he pulled up short in front of Geoffrey, not wanting to believe what he knew was true.

CHAPTER TWENTY-SIX

Creepy gazed into my eyes with the kind of adoring sincerity that was meant to make women swoon. I fought against the sensation of free-falling.

"Are you saying you want my increased assistance?" Creepy asked.

"No," I replied, "I'm saying I want to know by what means it is that you think you can aid me more, so I can consider whether I want that extra assistance or not."

His voice dropped to a low whisper. "There's a price for that information."

I crossed my arms and snorted, frustrated with both the predicament and the sensuality brimming in his voice—which had sunk into a captivating tone, melodic and soothing.

"It is a simple thing I ask for," he said, "but very valuable."

"Are you able to tell me what that is, or does knowing what that price is have a price?"

My sarcasm sobered him. His smile faded into an expression of deadly seriousness. His hand pushed my hair away from my shoulder, then rounded the side of my neck. "Let my lips touch yours for one kiss and I will tell you what I can do for you." He made it sound entirely sexual—which was quite a contrast to the placement of his hand, which only served to remind me how fragile and vulnerable the human neck was.

Additionally, bartering to break down the barriers of intimacy always irritated me.

Heedless of both warning signs, I contemplated kissing him.

He gave my earlobe an affectionate little tug, then his gaze traveled over my face, coming to rest adoringly on my eyes. "I have what you need, Persephone."

I believed he did.

To find out what he could do that trumped the plan I had in mind, all I had to do was kiss this mysterious being who wasn't a man, a vampire, or a wærewolf. He wasn't anything I could yet identify. He could work sorcery without pulling on a ley line so he was internally powerful, enough so that he could teleport himself. That wasn't normal.

Maybe the taste of him would give some hint.

I scolded myself soundly. It wasn't like I'd know. Until a few weeks ago I'd never kissed anyone but a human. I was sure Johnny tasted like Johnny, not like some default wærewolf flavor, and I doubted all vampires tasted like cinnamon. So Creepy would taste like Creepy.

What flavor would he have?

I wondered what his lips—a bit wide for his face; not too thin, not too thick—would feel like on mine. His dark beard was trimmed short, but it looked soft. It was a very masculine mouth, as if he could command legions with ease. But the sum total of that impression was created by a combination of things.

Like his eyes.

His stance.

He conveyed confidence and authority.

Knowing how out of control my life was becoming,

being close to someone with his level of self-assurance was aspirational.

Yeah. That's what I want. To be in control of my life, not a victim of it.

Sometimes, in a small corner of my heart, I wished someone else was the Lustrata, wished for my simple life back. I didn't want to be a target anymore.

The wærewolves in particular seemed to have it in for me. Some in the local pack had personal grudges and resentments. The Rege had tried to kill me, and so had Aurelia. Hell, even Johnny had tried, though he might be the only one who had a legitimate excuse for his actions.

The vampires had made their share of threats, too. Heldridge had it in for me. Eva had tried to poison me. Liyliy had kidnapped me, and when I escaped she decided it was better to shred me with her talons and drown me than to have me unmake that necklace. Mero was determined to deliver me to the Excelsior. That would not be good at all.

They all fear me.

They see me as a danger to them.

How do I become something that those who oppose me would not dare to strike against . . . and yet maintain my "self"?

I'd hesitated longer than I should have. I'd taken a tangent along a side path, meandering in my own thoughts, and hadn't answered him. Like a little girl lost in the woods, when I came back to myself and realized my mistake, it was too late. The predator was closing in.

My eyes closed. I held my breath.

Creepy's lips brushed mine.

With his hand at the back of my neck I could not

have pulled away, but I didn't resist. The chaste exploration surprised me. It was just his mouth making contact with mine, barely, then sliding to the left, then the right. It wasn't even a kiss, really. He was feeling me, caressing me in a way that I'd never been touched before. It was infinitely intimate. It took my breath away.

Literally. What I'd held in my lungs escaped all at once in a quavering sigh.

I felt him smile.

Then his lips pressed against mine.

It was a moment of utter sweetness. I yielded. I kissed him back.

His grip tightened. His mouth pressed harder on mine, so hard it hurt. I *mmmm*-ed a protest and tried to pull away but his hand held me firm. His beard was rough now, scraping over my skin. I tried to say no, but his tongue filled my mouth—he tasted of raspberry and orange. No, he tasted like a blood orange.

As the seconds ticked away, he grew rougher. Gripping turned into squeezing, fondling into groping. When I heard the seam of my shirt tear, I thrust my hands under his chin and pushed as I turned away. "Stop it!"

He roared in anger and, clutching the back of my neck, spun me around like a dancer. My knees gave and the next thing I knew I was crouched before him on all fours, looking out at the decaying hall around us. His fingers gripped my shoulders but he wasn't pulling me away from this danger; he was holding me to it. Threads of light sprang from his fingertips and wound down my arms, forcing them to stay straight.

In a raw whisper Creepy said, "I can remove all the

uncertainty, Persephone. I can remove the danger and replace it with serenity so deep you'll wonder how you ever survived without it. Imagine your life without threats, without doubts. You want that, don't you?"

Breathing hard, feeling the floor cracking under my palms, I saw fine fissures appear under my hands and spread. I fought to keep all my weight on my knees. "How can you do that?"

"How matters not, if that is what you desire of me." His voice shook with an intensity that traveled down his arms into my shoulders, vibrating out to my palms. The cracks widened.

"How matters to me!" I shouted, trying desperately to hold the force he was exerting in my legs and back. My muscles trembled with the effort.

"What would you object to?" he growled.

"I object to being coerced by threats."

"Indecision makes me impatient. This method brings answers. Now, what would you object to?"

"Harming others."

"The world must balance. If I give to you, I must take from another."

"Then, do it my way."

He leaned down to my ear. "But your way takes from the Excelsior. It takes his home earth to make a stake such as that. It counters his free will, prohibiting him from coming near you while the stake is in your possession!"

"I need only a little dirt and the stake won't bother him if he doesn't seek to harm me, so I'll accept that risk."

He barked a single laugh. "The stake will not defend you from his human minions."

My jaws clenched. I was the Lustrata, bearer of the mantle. I could tap a ley line and call on energies many witches would not dare to touch. "I can do quite a bit to protect myself."

"Yes, my beauty, you are strong—thrice tested—and your potency is waxing, but you are not yet full as the moon."

Johnny and Menessos would help me. Certain witches would. And the elementals. "I have other defenses."

"Do you dare to underestimate who you trifle with, witch? He is the Supreme Vampire for a reason. His minions will employ others not bound by him, others who will not be held back by your weapon. They will lay waste to all the people who would stand to shield you. They will destroy the flimsy weapon you create. The blood of all those you hold dear will run thick upon the open ground, and they will throw you before the Excelsior anyway. All will have been for naught."

I said nothing and simply tried to breathe normally to quell the fear that rose up when those I cared for most were endangered, and to evaporate the tears burning at the backs of my eyes.

"I have what you need," he said again.

Through clenched teeth I asked, "How would you accomplish it?"

He snorted. "So stubborn!"

"I have to know! I have to think it through to decide."

"Then think, sweet, sweet Persephone. Think long and hard. Call for me when you've decided how you want to proceed." He shoved on my shoulders.

The floor shattered and I fell headfirst into darkness.

CHAPTER TWENTY-SEVEN

Johnny straightened. He squinted at the doc. The man's actions were calm, tending his glasses as he always did. *Did she talk him into killing her?* It was a normal thing for the doc to do. *For him, normal includes putting dying animals down gently.*

"Her internal injuries were not survivable."

Johnny stared with the intention of intimidation.

When the doc placed his glasses back on his nose, he saw it. "Unless someone does an autopsy, you won't know for sure what the cause of death was precisely. My guess is massive internal bleeding from a gastrointestinal wound. She was in hypovolemic shock when I arrived, John."

"Sire, a word?" Gregor interrupted.

Johnny nodded and Doc Lincoln walked away.

"I have programmed the address you gave me into the GPS on my phone. I'm leaving shortly."

He listened to Gregor without looking at him. Instead his focus had remained on the veterinarian, who retrieved something from his truck and returned toward the crash site with it. Johnny had the distinct feeling it was a veterinarian's version of a body bag.

"Sire?"

When Johnny heard that word, he realized Gregor had repeated it a few times. He tore his attention from the wreckage. "I need you to keep her death a secret for as long as possible."

"Absolutely. May I ask why?" Gregor repeated.

"The longer this news is unknown, the safer my son is."

Gregor nodded. "I've put Brian in charge. He's made arrangements for a tow truck to come and is confirming whose land this is so that we may offer financial compensation for the damage."

"And the body?"

"Will go into the back of one of our vehicles for transport. We will see that Ms. Romochka's final arrangements are in keeping with her wishes."

The phrase "final arrangements" were like knives twisting in his gut. *If I hadn't pursued her, she would still be alive. But if she hadn't tried to kill Red, I wouldn't have chased her.*

His hands raked through his hair.

"The Omori can handle this. Perhaps you should return to Ms. Alcmedi's house? I will tell Brian he can find you there if necessary."

"No. I'll stay here until—"

Gregor gripped Johnny's arm. "It would be best if the Domn Lup were not on the scene when the others arrive."

His ascension and subsequent press conference had made worldwide news a few days ago; his distinctive tattoos ensured that anonymity was unlikely. Without a word Johnny turned and walked to his car.

Red's saltbox farmhouse was only a few minutes away, but those minutes passed slowly. His thoughts raced, circling around what Aurelia had told him of the key in her suitcase. He agonized over going to Red's as Gregor had suggested, or rushing into Cleveland to ransack Aurelia's room at the Renaissance Cleveland Hotel.

No. *Aurelia had tried to kill Red.* He had to check on her first.

She'd been through so much lately. Damn near all of it was his fault.

But she subdued Aurelia. He had to admit, that was impressive. Aurelia was—had been—a scheming woman who'd endured much to gain a high rank in the governing body of the wærewolves.

He pulled into the driveway and saw a car that hadn't been there when he left. It was an Audi like the one Zhan drove, but this one was white. The license plate was FANG 12. It was from the fleet of cars Menessos's haven owned.

Perfect. That's exactly what I want to deal with now. Vamps.

He got out and headed toward the front door, but then slowed his steps. The main door was open. The screen door would let the cold air in. He'd left it open when he'd entered, but surely she would have closed it by now. It was pretty cold.

He eased up onto the porch.

From there he could see down the long hall. Red was sitting Indian style on the kitchen floor and her eyes were shut. If she was back, that must mean they found the kiddo. She seemed in a trance, though. He hoped she was doing some witchy thing of calming and thanks.

Then a man stepped into view, circling her with an expression of suspicion. His arms were folded across his chest, then one hand rose thoughtfully to his lips. He had not noticed Johnny on the porch.

Recalling that Ivanka told him it had been a strange

man at Red's house who had broken her arm, he wondered if this was the man.

By the scent, this guy was definitely a vamp, not an Offerling or Beholder.

Since Ivanka was an Offerling, he wasn't sure that she'd have called a vamp a "strange man" or if she would have been wounded by one, but he didn't know the details of what had happened and she hadn't given a description of the man.

This guy was not quite as tall as Johnny, and he wore a tailored black suit that would have garnered the instant approval of both Aurelia and Risqué. His hair was a mass of thick black curls that hung to his waist, secured back in a ponytail. He removed his jacket, and laid it on the counter. The shirt underneath was white. He crouched before Red, studying her.

"Who the fuck are you?"

The vamp twisted around as he rose, quickly scanning Johnny as he entered the house. He gave a respectful nod of his head. "Domn Lup. My name is Franciscus Meroveus."

"So tell me, Francis—"

"Please. Domn Lup, call me Mero."

Johnny stopped on the threshold of the kitchen. "Who invited you in, *vamp*?"

Mero did not answer, but his smug smile showed a hint of fang.

Mountain, Johnny figured. The Beholder was the only one on the premises under the control of vampires. "What do you want?"

The vamp sucked in a deep breath, relaxed his knees, and squared his shoulders first. "I came for the witch."

Johnny recognized the warning signs and mirrored the intruder's pose. Being out of Red's life for a few days dealing with his own issues had put him at a disadvantage. He had no idea what was going on, only that he didn't like it. "You need to leave. Now."

With an expression of annoyance, Mero checked his manicure and said, "Make me."

Johnny had expected the vamp would accept the challenge rather than bow out. He leapt forward.

A bolt of energy slammed into his chest with enough force to knock him backward onto his rump and send him sliding down the hall.

Johnny groaned. *I will not let Red down again.*

Not all vamps could use magic. He'd fought Menessos before and it hadn't been pretty. But he was stronger now. Smarter now. And he knew vamps like this one were very confident. It should be easy to lead him into being *over*confident.

Mero rubbed his fingers over his thumb. "I bet that hurt."

Johnny shook his head as if shaking off something more than he truly felt. He rose up slowly. "She is mine."

"She must come with me." He pulled his fingers away from his thumb and a string of white light emerged and stretched. As his hand rotated around this string it swelled like a balloon, becoming a brilliant ball of blue lightning arcs and flares of pale purple. He tilted his head slightly. "Are you going to insist on making this difficult?"

Johnny had no intention of letting this vampire take Red anywhere. He staggered one step and set his stance. With his hands at his sides, he called his beast. He blinked like he could not see clearly, and waited while the animal slid under his skin.

It was not unlike the way Seph's half-grown Great Dane, Ares, would push his head into Johnny's palm begging to be petted, but this was from the inside. And it wasn't a domesticated canine.

This was wolf.

Long slumbering, after Eris had unlocked the bindings in his tattoos the beast had awakened feral and violent. He had clashed with his inner wolf and won its respect—his strength of will was mightier than the beast's. He controlled it now, but that control had a price—the beast's physical strength was not his own.

He commanded it, *Come*.

All at once, he raced forward and the beast burst forth.

His hands darkened and his fingers grew claws. His torso broadened with expanding muscles. His face transformed and his snout pushed partway out as his teeth grew long.

Mero released the orb.

Johnny slammed it linebacker style with his shoulder and kept going.

Mero's eyes widened and, too late, his hand lifted for another blast.

Having taken the hall in four strides, Johnny leapt as his lower half changed form. He crashed into the vamp and both toppled over, sliding into the dinette set at the rear of the kitchen. Their momentum broke the table legs and sent the bench and one chair tumbling. The tabletop slammed down on them and while Mero struggled against the weight pinning him down, Johnny thrashed, kicking his shoes away, throwing off his jeans, ripping his shirt. A one-armed rearward thrust threw the tabletop against the wall with the landline phone. He heard the crack and crumble of molded plastic. The speaker on the receiver immediately began droning.

A sudden burning pain seized him in the side as the vamp shoved a fiery ball against his flesh. Howling, Johnny rolled away, but his retreat was blocked by the chair now shoved against the wall. Mero had not released the scalding magic so the movement had dragged the blistering ache across his stomach.

Reaching up, Johnny jerked the chair up and out of the way, twisting it and bringing it down on the vamp's shoulders and head. It splintered into pieces. Johnny's paws scraped along the floor, slipping on wood shards, until he'd knocked them away and found purchase on the linoleum. Just as he was fully up, Mero was getting his legs under him.

Johnny lunged, bringing his jaws down on the vamp's arm. He tried to bite through it; he worried at it, trying to tear it off, but Meroveus's arm was like steel. Then something solid and heavy smacked against his head. Stumbling backward, he released Mero. Dazed, Johnny saw that the vamp's other arm, now holding the thick wooden leg that used to be attached to the table, was swinging downward with the follow-through from the blow that had connected with his head. He reared up and thrust in again, aiming for Mero's neck. Mero side-stepped and swung the table leg for an upper-cut strike.

Johnny saw nothing but white for an instant.

Then his body felt heavy, boneless and unmov-able. Pain seared over every inch of him. His eyes were squeezed shut against the scorching energy the vamp was discharging, but he forced his weighty lids open. Ahead, between the flickers of blue and purple light spiking over him, Red sat as she had since before he entered into the house. She was as silent and still as if she was sleeping sitting up.

He must have done that to her, to make it easy to get away with her.

He wouldn't let this vamp take her.

Come, beast. Come, wolf.

Claim me.

His eyes flashed with an inner glow, giving everything a tint of golden brown then draining to palest yellow, like he was looking out from a new-risen autumn moon. He blinked again and the color faded from his vision.

This was more than wolf. This was Domn Lup.

He lifted his muzzle from the floor.

CHAPTER TWENTY-EIGHT

Ailo peered around the doorframe as Silhouette strode up to the guard. Talto snuck a look as well. She touched her sister's shoulder and thought, *This isn't going to work.*

Of course it will, Ailo thought back. In truth, she was tired—she had bespelled Sil and given her a task, then they had found Ivanka and done the same to her. Now, they were going to work magic on the guard posted outside the Haven Master's suite.

The guard looked up from the game he was playing on his phone as Sil approached. "Hey, Sil. Goliath said he was not to be disturbed. Said he'd let me know when he could accept visitors."

"So he's busy?" Sil asked.

"Yeah." He turned back to his game.

Sil started unbuttoning her blouse.

He looked up. "What are you—" the guard began.

"Shhhh." She opened the shirt, revealing her bare breasts. Slipping out of the sleeves, she dropped the garment to the floor and eased forward, lifting her flowing skirts as she advanced. With a sexy smile and a few lithe movements, she was straddling him in his chair. When she kissed him the phone fell from his grip—but Sil caught it before it landed. She gave it back to him and her hands worked at the buttons of his shirt. He did not resist.

But he did close his eyes when he kissed Sil back.

Ailo and Talto slipped into the room. They slinked up behind him and when Sil broke the passionate lip-lock, the sisters clasped hands and each put one palm on the guard's temples. "Don't see us," they whispered, pouring magic into his mind. When they were certain the energy they sent had gotten where it needed to go, they added, "Play your game."

The guard lifted the phone and began to play.

The sisters released him. "Put your shirt on, Silhou-ette," Ailo said. "Now it is Risqué's turn." She pointed up the steps. "Tell her Ivanka is in the business office and wanted to ask her something. You will stay with the girl until she returns."

Sil nodded. The sisters returned to the stage area and hurried to the far side, hand in hand. There they waited, hidden at the edge of the scrim curtains.

Risqué crossed the stage to the walkway that would lead her up and out, then stopped. She stood in place for a moment, cocked her head, and turned toward the spot where the sisters waited in the dark.

Promptly, she stalked over to them and threw the curtain back. "What are you two doing here?"

"Skulking," Talto snapped. "What are you doing?"

Risqué snorted and whipped the curtain back over them. She crossed the stage, took the ramp down into the house, and ascended the steps on the far side. Ailo released Talto's hand and snuck behind the curtain to the doorway. Talto hurried behind her and at the last caught her arm. "I will watch for her. I'll let you know when she is returning." Ailo nodded.

Ailo crossed in front of the guard, who did not respond.

She climbed the stairs to the upper suite with silent steps and knocked softly. Silhouette opened the door.

Goliath stood facing Menessos. They were in the private bedchambers of the Haven Master's suite. All was dark except for the faint light cast by the black candles on the altar table they had relocated into this room. Between the candles sat a black-handled dagger with a stubby blade. He watched as Menessos grasped the dagger and examined it. He stuck one flat side of the blade in the candle flame, holding it there until that side had blackened. Then, after checking it, he flipped it and did the same to the other flat side using the second candle.

When the blade was fully darkened, Menessos sat it once more in position. "This is no small undertaking."

"I am aware of this."

The breaking of the bonds between a Maker and his vampiric offspring was not so dissimilar from the actual Making of a vampire. Instead of severing ties to mortal life, they would be severing their ties to each other. Goliath had seen firsthand that—like the old adage that a woman giving birth comes very close to death herself— no vampire was Made without his Maker risking his own existence. Not all vampires could even Make another. For all that he had seen in service to the Quarterlord, he had never witnessed *this* ceremony before.

It was rare that a vampire's Maker would deign to release him, even when the younger gained substantial rank. But Menessos had agreed. That made this a monumental moment in Goliath's preternatural existence.

So he was nervous.

The fact that Goliath had borne some doubts concerning his master's actions of late added to Goliath's anxiety. "I regret only that harsh words brought us to this moment, Father."

Menessos put his hand on the other vampire's shoulder. "I am proud of you, Goliath. You will be a great Master, and you will keep your haven strong."

Goliath had not liked the sentimental note in his own voice, much less the one mirroring it in Menessos's tone. It was something like the sound of doubt. His expression hardened. His Maker had already been taxed this night. Whatever he had done—and whatever it had been had taken great strength—had saved Beverley. "Should this wait until another night?"

Menessos considered it. "No. I can do this. You have earned it." He breathed in a purposeful pattern.

Ground and center. Goliath did the same.

From the altar Menessos took a handful of sea salt and circled Goliath, murmuring in Akkadian and letting the granules cascade from his hand and create a barrier around them.

> *"Hecate, hear me and give us a sacred space.*
> *Let nothing interfere with this task we face.*
> *Give me strength to honor Goliath's request*
> *And provide him freedom for a rule that is blessed."*

When the circle set, Goliath's ears felt a slight *pop* like when being in an airplane that was about to land.

"Are you ready?" Menessos asked.

Goliath nodded once.

Menessos put one hand over Goliath's mouth. The

nails of the other grew into claws and he gripped the flesh of Goliath's abdomen.

"What hunger I awoke in you, I partook from as your Master. I now grant you the full of that hunger and the sating of it."

Where Menessos touched him, his skin prickled. The electric charge was building.

"It is yours to own," Menessos said. "Yours to keep. Yours to feed. I no longer derive any sustenance from it."

Goliath felt the energy flow like a static libation flooding down his throat. Resonance gripped his gut. Cold and heat passed through him in waves, raising gooseflesh then searing him like desert winds. He jerked with each shift, the sharp difference jolting him harder, longer . . . then tapering until he felt only one even temperature.

Menessos released him, panting hard. His hand reverted to normal.

Goliath said, "I accept that hunger."

When his breathing had normalized, Menessos put Goliath's hands together as if in prayer. Squeezing the clasped hands in his right and placing his left to cover Goliath's brow, Menessos said, "What power I awoke in you, I held tethered to me as your Master. I now give you the full of that power and draw on you no more."

Again his skin prickled as the words were said.

"It is yours to own. Yours to keep. Yours to tend. I no longer hold any authority over you."

Energy sliced into Goliath like searing hot scalpels stabbing deep into his mind and melting there, liquefying into something mystical and molten. It burned into his bones and became one with every molecule of his being.

Menessos released him again, but this time he staggered a step backward.

"I accept that power."

The child slept on a bed in the darkened back half of the room. She was small, petite but pretty. Dark-haired. Ailo stroked the silky strands, and jerked a few free. She jabbed her fang into the flesh of her own hand, where her middle finger joined with the palm. As the blood rose, she wrapped the hairs around the wound like a brunette bandage. Holding the hair there with her teeth, she put her free hand on Beverley's forehead, fingers scratching along the girl's scalp.

"Tell me your secrets," Ailo said through clenched teeth, holding her tongue against the mingling of her blood and the child's hair.

Information trickled into her mind slowly, forming indistinct shapes and muddy colors. She could feel the knowledge was close by, but something was holding it back like an oiled cloth, letting it through only in drips.

Ailo reached up, reached out to that barrier and found one of the leaks . . . and widened it. A flash of birthday cake. A homework paper. The merry-go-round, a laughing little boy. Falling. Pain.

The physical pain linked back to emotional pain. Ailo saw snapshots of a woman in a photo album. She could smell juniper and feel the texture of a certain sweater in her hands.

Talto's voice invaded the visions. "Get out, Ailo! Risqué is coming!"

Ailo didn't have the information yet. She pushed the rift wider.

She saw a unicorn with purple ribbons tied in its mane. Heard the sound of a singing mother's voice . . . then it dropped low and dark. She felt the rip of the ley line consuming her.

The data gushed at Ailo and she gasped, stumbling backward.

The connection was lost.

But she understood what she had seen.

The door burst open behind her and Talto's desperate whisper crossed the room. "Ailo!"

Goliath watched as Menessos reached to the altar and lifted the unsheathed dagger as he said, "My son, you deserve to be your own Master." Menessos pulled the blade across his own palm. The cut was deep. His whole hand trembled as the syrupy fluid welled up.

"Thank you," Goliath said as he pulled his shirt open.

Menessos's bleeding hand shook and his nails again became claws.

The two vampires shared a grave look in silence, then Menessos slammed his hand against Goliath's chest at his heart, curved claws sinking through skin, through muscle, to slide against newly empowered bone.

"What blood we exchanged, I empowered as your Master. I now reverse the exchange of that blood."

What life force vampires knew was bound in their cursed blood. Goliath felt that force coalesce within him, solidifying, turning his veins into thick burning wires. His heart rebelled, shuddered, and stopped. His knees gave—and so did Menessos's.

Goliath screamed, feeling like his body was ripping apart.

"It is yours to own," Menessos rasped. His eyes had gone black. "Yours to keep." Through gritted teeth he said, "Yours to bleed." His voice was breaking. He sucked air as if he were drowning, but it seemed he could not bring any into his body.

Whispered, soundless, the words passed into the air. "I . . . am no longer . . . your Master."

Goliath could not breathe either. He had to say his part or both would be destroyed.

Shaking and struggling, one word at a time, he said, "I accept that blood."

CHAPTER TWENTY-NINE

I landed on ground that might have been soft if not for all the small rocks.

Groaning, I dug my fingers into muddy sand. I forced my eyes open and saw willow branches and a starry night overhead. The smell of water made me realize I was hearing the lapping of a lake at my back. Slowly, and with effort, I sat up. The willow fronds draped around my shoulders like the tree would embrace me. Guess I needed a hug, because I reached up and held the leafy tip like it was someone's reassuring hand.

As I scanned around, I realized I knew this place. It was the land I usually visited when I meditated. Encouraged by this, I shifted into a cross-legged position and prepared myself to leave. I was sooo ready to go home and crawl into my bed. I was going to sleep until I forgot this had ever happened.

Deep breath. In and out. Count backward from ten and awake in my kitchen as I left it. Ten. Nine. Eight. Something was wrong. I usually felt the grip of this world loosen. *Seven. Six. Five.* I should be able to smell the scents of my home. *Four. Three. Two. One.*

When I opened my eyes I remained on the lake shore.

I tried again. And failed again.

"You cannot leave."

I twisted toward Amenemhab's voice. The jackal, my totem animal, strode closer out of the dark. He stood on slightly higher ground and watched for my reaction. I tried to keep the anger and worry from my features, but hiding my emotions wouldn't do me any good with him. "Why not?"

"You arrived through his doorway. You must return through it."

I stood and brushed myself off. "Who is he anyway?"

The jackal sat. "He is who he is."

"What's his *name*?"

"It is not for me to say."

"Riiiight." I should have known. "What are my options?"

"You have only one. Decide how to proceed."

My shoulders slumped. I turned back to the lake and stared at the long and choppy reflection of the moon. I wished I'd had my shoes on when I sat down to meditate. If I'd been wearing them there, I'd be wearing them here and I could kick a rock into the water. I was sure it would make me feel a little bit better.

After a few minutes of silence, Amenemhab asked, "Is the choice so difficult?"

"Well, I can pick very bad, or very, very bad."

"Ahhh. I see. Tell me more."

I glanced back at him. He'd lain down. His getting comfortable meant he was willing to hear me out. All the way out. *Damn it.* I bent over and picked up a handful of stones. I threw the first of them at the water. And the second. Frustrated, I dropped the rest and stomped away from the shore, flopping down to sit beside the jackal.

"Why did you stop?"

"I can't see where they land."

"So?"

I pulled my knees up and wrapped my arms around them. "It's pointless."

"I don't understand."

"I dunno. There's something satisfying about seeing the ripples and in the dark my eyes can't even detect where the rock landed."

His ears pricked forward. "But you know the rock hit the water. You heard the splash. You know the ripples had to occur."

"But I can't see them." I shook my head. "We shouldn't get sidetracked anyway. We need to talk about the choice."

"We are."

I faced him squarely.

He copied the move. "The ripples you're causing on the darkened surface may be lost to your eyes in this dim light, and they may seem insignificant compared to the natural and relentless ebb and flow . . . but you are aiming for the lake and I guarantee you are hitting it."

In my deepest self, the metaphor struck a chord. I scrutinized the surface of the lake. "My dark destiny is flowing and I'm helpless to stop it."

"Of course you are. That's rather inherent in the word 'destiny.' Why would you even try to stop it?"

I ground my teeth. Every word here was telling. Even if I didn't want them to be.

"I told you it would only get harder."

That was true. The last time I'd spoken with him, I'd had a decision to make. His advice then was *Cor aut Mors*. Heart or Death. A choice between the morals and loyalty of the heart, and the insignificance and disgrace of death.

That choice between loyalty and disgrace had been easy to make. This time, however, the choice was not so clear-cut.

Choosing to do things my own way could entangle everyone I cared for and, as Creepy implied, eventually put them in danger. That was what I wanted to avoid. I already carried some hefty guilt; many had died since this whole thing began and it was likely the death toll would continue to rise.

Choosing Creepy's way would doubtless keep my loved ones safe, but I probably wouldn't like his method of securing their safety. It'd turn into something I would feel guilty about.

"You are who you are as well, Persephone. You have the strength you need. And the drive. And the intelligence. Cast away your doubts like the pebbles they are. Let them sink to the bottom; they will never amass into anything that can stop you."

I faced him again.

"A million pebbles will not significantly alter the lake."

"Are you saying my worries about this choice are irrelevant?"

"I am saying that the choice itself is like deciding between two routes to the same destination. One is longer and smoother than the other, but both will get you there."

"Do I have time for the longer, smoother road?"

"The shorter route is more difficult. The time equals out and the choice is more balanced than you know."

"Then, what's the catch?"

"Each road has a separate toll; the imbalance exists in the price that you must pay. Focus not on the choice, but on what it costs you. It is that which you must weigh carefully."

Yeah. Creepy's services weren't going to be free.

"Now, Persephone, let me tell you a little about the art of negotiation. . . ."

CHAPTER THIRTY

With that solid wood table leg—thicker than a base-ball bat and having a square block at the top—Mero had delivered a blow that would have killed a normal man, a blow that should have critically injured any wærewolf.

He could not believe what he was seeing. Before him, the creature gathered itself to stand. Its body re-shifted as it rose, growing broader and taller, exceeding the mass of any wærewolf Mero had ever seen. Only in the woodcut illustrations of ancient texts had he ever seen a creature so menacingly blended. This was part man with every sinew thickened, and part beast, black furred and feral. It stood on two legs, on enormous paws, and the arms ended in hands with thick claws. The head was wider than that of a natural wolf, and dark as pitch except for the pale yellow eyes glowing like coals in a hearth. The long ears were twisted angrily back. Slavering jaws opened. Saliva dripped from black lips that curled to reveal fangs longer and sharper than any vampire's. A guttural snarl filled the room.

Domn Lup.

He had read the legends that said the King of Wolves could take this form. He had never thought to see it with his own eyes.

He held his ground.

She must be taken to the Excelsior. She must become Wolfsbane.

Mero hefted the table leg in his right hand, and readied a white-hot orb in his left.

The wære lunged. Mero swung the wood for another upper-cut impact. The Domn Lup veered left to avoid the strike, then swiped a large paw, hitting the leg hard and giving it more follow-through than Mero was prepared for.

Persephone was not far behind him and he worried that the clublike weapon might strike her. He fought the momentum and held the searing orb out in front, letting arcs of heat whip out to keep the wolf back. He had to get this fight away from her before either of them accidentally broke her circle, or worse, hurt her.

He regained control of the heavy table leg, and, grip firmer, swung it in a downward angle. The beast had to hop back, but leapt forward immediately after. Mero loosed an orb. It hit the wære in the shoulder. As the beast cried out, Mero fled into the hall; the narrow space would be a disadvantage to the big creature.

When he neared the front door and the space widened at the bottom of the staircase, Mero spun around and raised his weapon.

But the creature had not followed behind him.

The attack came from the side, out of the darkened living room.

Johnny barely had to think. The beast's instincts worked faster than his brain could process words, let alone dictate commands preemptively. He avoided the overhead swing of the club and attacked. A ball of lightning heat crashed into his shoulder and he roared in pain.

The prey ran.

Impulsively, the beast moved to follow.

No. Johnny willed the beast to see the other route through the house. It complied.

Leaping from the doorway, he pounced. The vampire faced him at the last second and he knocked him down before the staircase. The beast drew back, teeth bared, ready to kill. He brought his toothy maw down . . . on a scalding orb.

Howling, he jerked back.

The vampire sat up and slammed the club against Johnny's head. Wrapping his claws around the offending object, he tried to wrench it from Mero's grasp. They struggled for several seconds, but as Johnny was atop the vamp, leverage won out. He jerked the table leg free, raised it high, and brought it down toward his prey's head.

A bolt of light slammed into the weapon, knocking it aside at the last moment and jerking it down to embed it into the floor.

Mero hit him with another bolt of energy.

Johnny pulled on the club. He yanked on it—but it was stuck fast.

Mero wriggled in an effort to get away. Johnny stomped a huge paw onto his chest. His prey could not escape, but he pummeled Johnny with blast after blast. He held fiery orbs against his legs. Johnny tore the club free and readied it again.

Another blast diverted it a second time—this time hitting his arms with enough force that he ripped through the oak handrail and spindles of the staircase.

Seeing the destruction he was wreaking on Red's

house, Johnny felt remorse, but the beast saw more weapons. Sharp, wooden weapons. He dropped the club and snapped a broken spindle off at the base. His claws turned the pointy end down.

A stake.

He dropped to his knees, aiming the point at Mero's heart.

The vamp clasped Johnny's forearms, holding him back, but Johnny could feel the trembling in his prey's limbs. He was stronger, heavier, more physically powerful than the vamp. He had only to keep the pressure on. He growled and watched thick saliva drip on his prey's face.

Arcs of energy crawled along his skin, hotter and hotter until the reek of burning hair and skin filled his nostrils. Still, he would not be deterred. This vamp was in Red's house, trying to take her, and she was unresponsive and defenseless. Johnny would not fail her again.

He shoved on the stake and felt the tip rip fabric, felt it pierce skin. Mero gave a desperate scream. The burning redoubled on Johnny's furred arms and then, from behind, someone shouted, "Sire! No!"

CHAPTER THIRTY-ONE

Ailo took a step and nearly fell. Talto rushed toward her. With her sister's arm supporting her, Ailo found walking much easier. They made it to the door. Talto looked back. "You come with us, Sil."

"Why?" Ailo asked. "She needs to—"

"We need time," Talto explained. "Get back to kissing the guard," she added over her shoulder to Silhouette.

The sisters were down the stairs and stumbling toward the entry when they heard the clacking sound of Risqué's heels. Talto spun around, pulling Ailo with her as if to watch the striptease Silhouette had started for the guard.

Risqué traipsed into the room and stopped dead.

"What gives, Sil?"

Both the Offerling and the guard jerked at the sound of her voice. "Why aren't you with the kid?"

Silhouette didn't answer, but she did move away from the guard.

Risqué stomped forward and grabbed the discarded shirt from the floor. "I'll be damned if I'm gonna wear a shirt and let *you* streak around here. What if Goliath saw you?"

Risqué turned back toward the doorway. Seeing Ailo and Talto loitering a few feet within the room, she scowled. "You two can go do your voyeuristic skulking somewhere else." She pointed at the doorway.

Ailo pulled Talto with her and moved for the door.

She felt her sister's thoughts via her grip on Talto's arm and knew the youngest had stuck her tongue out at Risqué. Ailo stopped short of passing through the doorway and watched what happened.

"Seriously, Vinny. Don't let them loiter like that," Risqué said.

He glanced at his phone. "Don't let who loiter?"

Risqué rolled her eyes. To Sil, she said, "Next time an Offerling wants to waste my time, you tell them to kiss off."

Sil's expression dropped into confusion. "She said it was important."

"She was wrong. I assume the kid is still out?"

"She didn't make a sound."

"Like you'd know from down here." Muttering not quite under her breath, Risqué stomped up the steps to the court witches' suite and punched in the code.

Ailo put to memory the pattern that unlocked the door. Only then did she follow Talto across the stage.

"Did you find out what gift the girl received?" Talto asked.

Ailo nodded gravely. "The girl is a ward-breaker."

"Ward-breaker," Talto repeated in a whisper. "Amazing. She's . . . she's . . . invaluable."

"She's a tool," Ailo said sharply. "Nothing more. Menessos did this for a reason."

"We have to call Liyliy," Talto said.

"I'll do that," Ailo said, taking out her phone. "You get to work on the computer aspect of our plan. Find out who runs the funds of this place. Read them. Open a new account. Learn how to make transfers."

Talto nodded and hurried away.

Ailo stepped into the shadows and opened the phone. She did not call Liyliy, however. Instead, she called Persephone Alcmedi and, knowing no one would answer, waited for the voicemail.

"Hello, witch. I know you'll wonder why I'm calling. I just want you to know that your pet vampire is quite busy. You see . . . he placed a spell upon *someone,* an *in signum amoris* spell. It gave him a measure of control and could possibly have been used to salvage his position as Haven Master, but that *someone* reversed the spell to be rid of it." She giggled frighteningly. "He had to find another way to exert leverage over this *someone.* Don't get me wrong—his intentions were pure when he rescued the child. But he's not one to overlook an opportunity when it presents itself." She paused. "Now the child is his guarantee. Should he ever need to exert some control over this *someone*—and you have to admit, bad eventualities do follow *her* around—he'll be able to play this someone like a harp, plucking at her here and there until she's doing exactly as he wishes." Mirthful laughter taunted into the phone. "How does it make you feel, witch, knowing that she belongs to him now? Knowing that because of you she will live among the undead forever?"

Ailo hung up.

Talto walked up the stairs and made her unhurried way to the media room she and Ailo had been sitting in earlier. The Beholders were still there playing cards, so she slinked down the hall to a dark, private corner and took out her phone. Many minutes had passed; enough for Ailo to have called Liyliy. But something felt off to her. She dialed Liyliy.

"Did Ailo just call you?"

"No. Is she not with you?"

Talto's expression darkened. "We are separated at the moment." If Ailo did not do as she said she would now, how could she trust Ailo with the plan they were about to put into action? Worrying over this, Talto realized that Liyliy was panting. "Are you all right? Why are you out of breath?"

"I am hurrying to the place where I am to meet someone."

"You are walking?" Talto remembered how her sister had been limping when she entered. They had healed Liyliy's leg, but still, she had been through much tonight. Talto wished she was there to help Liyliy. She wished she was anywhere but here in this dreadful haven under the control of the one who put them into the stones. Her hand strayed to the chain about her neck. "Why did you not transform and fly?"

"I have tasted blood this night, but a sip only. I struggled with Mero to gain my exit, and now I do not have the means."

Talto sniffled. "I'm sorry we couldn't do more."

"Do not cry, Talto. You did all you could. I'm nearly there. Go on. Tell me what has happened."

"Ailo evaluated the girl."

"And?"

"She's . . ." Talto wondered if there was any reason that Ailo would keep this news from Liyliy. It was good news, valuable news. *It's worth making this a secret only if she is planning on being devious to Liyliy . . . If her loyalty to Liyliy is fading, I've no hope.*

"Talto?"

"The girl is a ward-breaker."

Silence.

"Liyliy?"

"Praise all that is darkly glorious, Talto! This is beyond fortuitous. Truly."

Talto grinned. "And we have a plan for Menessos." She shared the details. "Should we progress with that or do you think we need to change things considering what we know about the child?" She hoped Liyliy would want them to abandon their other plan. Talto was not fond of any plan with the possibility of being tortured by Menessos or abandoned by Ailo.

"You are so brave, little one. You don't know how proud I am of you right now."

"But the plan?"

"Go ahead with it. You will likely create the distraction that allows us to abduct the girl. But do not worry, we will *not* forsake you, little sister. With her in our possession, they cannot keep us from saving you."

Liyliy heard the fear in Talto's voice. She knew the youngest of them would not have come up with such a plan, and she knew Talto was scared, but Liyliy could hardly contain her excitement long enough to reassure her sister.

At the word "ward-breaker" Liyliy's heart leapt. The child could be used to free her sisters from their bondage. And what was more, this little girl could free them all from the influence of the necklace Mero had created to bind them with originally. If her sisters were successful in transferring the cash, and they were able to keep these funds from the authorities, they would have the means to build an army against their enemy. If that was unsuccessful, the girl could be used to get them into bank vaults.

Either way, they would have money, and money would do much to buy the aid of those who also hated Menessos.

I might not need Giovanni much longer.

She saw the van ahead, parked right where they had agreed. She was eager to sit and rest. "I must go now, Talto. We will talk again soon."

Giovanni sat impatiently in the back of the van. The small amount of blood he had sipped from Adam, the driver, had bought time, but it was not enough to sate him.

Liyliy was late and he was hungry.

Then his phone vibrated in his pocket. He pulled it free and connected to the wiretap device on Ailo's phone. He listened as she left a taunting message for the witch and realized it was Persephone Alcmedi that Ailo had called earlier about the park. But he did not understand what she meant about the child living among the undead forever.

Had Menessos Made a child?

The pieces only started falling into place for him when, moment's later, Talto made a call to Liyliy.

The news fascinated him. It stirred a desire for control so deep it swept him back in time for a moment, to the days of his true life, when he'd commanded an army. In his mortal days, when men lived and died at his command, he had known great power. Wielding magic, he imagined, must feel like having that supremacy had felt.

He had no magical ability of his own, but he could make grand use of a ward-breaker.

He'd be unstoppable with her in his control.

He wasn't about to let his enemy possess and direct that kind of limitless resource—but he'd have to strike fast, while Menessos still thought no one knew about the girl's power.

Adam turned in his seat and tapped on the glass that separated them. "Liyliy is coming, sir."

"Start the engine. We must return downtown. To the Blood Culture."

CHAPTER THIRTY-TWO

I stood on the lakeshore alone.

Amenemhab had trotted away after I stroked his back for a while. The previous time we talked he'd said that I'd likely have a new totem soon. I didn't want him to go; I liked him. So, in case this was our last visit, I'd petted him. He was softer than he looked and stroking him was comforting to me. He surely knew I was only delaying what I had to do next, but he let me anyway. He even licked my cheek before he left.

Now, the night sky was star-filled above me. The water remained dark before me. The willow at my back rustled in the breeze.

Inhaling a cleansing breath, I shut my eyes as I grounded and centered myself. Shoulders squared, I visualized Creepy's face in my mind and said, "I'm ready."

The wind picked up and the temperature dropped. The lake began to give off an ever-thickening haze that the air moved around in dancing swirls. In a matter of moments, the world grew shrouded in a gray veil of mist.

He's coming.

The fog shifted and I stared at the lake, trying to make out a shape in it. The moisture in the air seemed to hold all sounds close, amplifying my breathing in my own ears. I could hear the lapping of the waves much louder than before, and a soft splashing as if there were a boat on the water. Behind those sounds, a distant thunder was rumbling closer.

Fearing it might rain here and drench me, I stepped forward, waving my arms as if that would part the gray air. Perhaps if I saw a boat I could get on it and get going before I was soaked. However, my efforts revealed nothing. All I managed to accomplish was to get my socks wetter and muddier and sandier.

I stared at my feet and again wished for my shoes. The thunder was getting louder.

When I looked up I caught a momentary glimpse of a black dragon's head in the mist.

It was gone as quickly as it appeared, but I stepped forward, ankle deep in the lake. "Wait!"

I'd seen dragons here before. They pulled a boat that carried Hecate. She could help me. She was a goddess. She could get me the hell out of here.

I took another step into the water. "Wait!" I called twice more, in case I'd been drowned out by the roaring rumble.

And then it hit me: That rumble was more distinct now . . . like many hooves.

As soon as I thought it, four black steeds thundered out of the mist side by side. Skidding to a stop at the edge of the embankment, they tossed their thick manes and nickered protests. The chariot they pulled was shiny black with a huge screaming skull of silver on the front center.

Creepy stood in the chariot holding the reins with clenched fists. He wore armor that matched the chariot; a crested helmet, bracers, greaves, and a cuirass over his black tunic. Pteruges, feather-like leather strips, hung from the cuirass in black layers, each adorned at the bottom with a silver skull. He raised one finger and gestured. "Come."

I walked to the back of the chariot and, before stepping up onto it, got an eyeful of the backs of his muscular legs. He indicated I should stand beside him at the front. I obeyed, very aware that my muddy socks left tracks on the chariot floor.

"Hold on." He tapped the chariot's upper edge.

I gripped it tight. Good thing; he cracked the reins and the horses leapt into a gallop with enough force they nearly set me on my ass even though I was holding on.

We raced across the field, climbed rolling hills, and delved into shallow valleys. The horses' hooves kept rhythm while small metal decorations on the harnesses—skulls again—tinkled an accenting sound. Add that to the bumpy nighttime ride and somehow, as the minutes wore on and on, I grew so tired that I curled up at Creepy's feet and slept.

"Persephone. Open your eyes."

I roused in the fetal position in the same decaying building I'd started out in.

Creepy stood towering over me. He was in the modern dark suit again. "It is time to decide."

I sat up, scooting away from him, and in doing so discovered that we were on a jagged-edged circular section of floor about four feet across. The rest of the floor was gone. It felt solid and steady, so I doubted it was hovering as much as it was held up by some support beneath. At least the thought that it was something other than Creepy's will keeping us from crashing down made me happier.

I posed, sitting, leaning back on my hands with my legs bent in front of me. This hopefully showed him I was comfortable. *Casual. Be casual.* "I have a question first," I said meekly.

His hands slid into his pockets. "Once again, the questions are free." The words were accommodating, but the tone was tight with irritation.

"I understand that I sought help and ended up with you and am therefore obligated to accept your help. I understand that I can choose to do things my way, or I can accomplish much the same thing another way, one at your discretion."

"None of that contained an inquiry."

"Right. Here's the question." I held his gaze steadily. "What is the cost for your services if I choose my way, and what is the cost if I choose your way?"

His masklike expression didn't change a bit. He gazed unwaveringly down at me for several heartbeats, then his focus slid around my body and returned to my face. "I intend to have you, either way."

My heart sputtered and skipped a beat.

Don't accept the first offer, Amenemhab had said. *It shows weakness. You must negotiate.* He needn't fear. Though Creepy was handsome, I was definitely going to negotiate out of this. Aside from the fact that my moral compass would not let me hop into bed with someone just because I found him attractive, my lips were sore from his *kiss*; sex with him was out of the question. "And if that is not something I am willing to barter?"

"Willing or unwilling is irrelevant. That is part of my price."

I swallowed hard enough to hear it and fought against

the chill tickling my spine. I had to hold some semblance of power here. My totem had mentioned posturing as well. "Submissive" obviously wasn't going to gain me any leniency. In fact, it might have encouraged him.

I stood up. "Part of it? I demand that you tell me what your full price is, with each option. I cannot finalize my decision without knowing." My hands rested on my hips.

He glanced at the ceiling and conveyed thoughtfulness for about half a second. "If I am to proceed according to the design you arrived with, you must allow me to satisfy myself with you in three ways. If I am to aid you in ridding yourself of doubts and avoiding those you love coming to harm as leverage used against you, then you must allow me to satisfy myself with you two different ways."

I scowled. "Satisfy yourself? Geez. Can you make it sound any more smarmy?"

"If that's a request, yes I can."

"Forget I said it." I waved him off. Amenemhab had suggested that I explore his demands, not only to pin him down as to what he meant precisely, but to see if there was information there that I could use to get him to make concessions. "But what do you mean by 'two' and 'three different ways'? Elaborate." I was hoping he meant positions and not that many orifices—then I scolded myself for even hoping he meant positions. This bargain should not be happening at all.

His lips curved. "You want to know how I like to satisfy myself with a woman?" He reached up and rubbed his thumb across my lips. "Remember this?"

They felt slightly swollen, definitely still sore. "That's all it takes to satisfy you? A rough kiss?"

"That was a taste of what I like." He moved in closer.

I crossed my arms defensively.

Ignoring my move, he wrapped his arms around me and whispered into my ear. "I want you naked before me. I want to touch you, to fondle and caress you. I want to grope you until I've found all the spots that make you tremble with desire. I want to bring you to the edge of orgasm. I want to hear you beg me not to stop. But I will."

Maybe I liked his looks, but he'd done things that made me wary of him even before he'd brought me here, gone all weird and gotten physically rough with me. "Listen up," I said forcefully, "I do not *want* to have sex with you."

"I know this." He spun away. "I know you have a skewed image of me in your mind."

He'd gone from aggressive sexual predator to sneeringly rejected date in the blink of an eye. I arched a brow guardedly. "Skewed?"

"Your perception of me was influenced by others." He clasped his hands behind his back. "You will not give me fair consideration so long as you are being swayed by the words of a jealous would-be lover."

Why did he even care about my fair consideration of him? He didn't think . . . *oh hell*. I blinked repeatedly.

"Menessos must have said things about me. Why else would you be so resistant and mistrustful when I am only offering you what you want as you want it, and giving you the option of improving upon that idea?"

"It's not your offers I have issues with, it's your secretiveness about your method on option two and your price for each that are problematic."

He turned back. "You are circumspect only because of his lack of trust—"

"No, I assure you, I'm rather prudent in *all* my decisions."

Ignoring my response, he continued. "—and his actions are rooted in jealousy . . . you *are* beautiful, Persephone." He cupped my cheek adoringly. "He has every right to try to keep you to himself. But he does not have the right to manipulate you so."

My first impulse was to defend Menessos. The second impulse was to put the blame where it should be and remind him that he'd broken Ivanka's arm, poisoned my dragon, and that I had dubbed him Creepy for a reason. But the jackal had warned me that those kinds of actions would only weaken my position. Pointing out his crimes would not inspire him to lower his price. It would only fortify his excuse to dig in and negotiate less.

I had to be cooperative and warm, Amenemhab had said, to find a common ground.

I looked at the man who wouldn't let me leave this meditation until we'd struck up some kind of bargain with sex as his payment, and knew my expression was full of frustrated disdain.

"Cooperative and warm" was not going to be easy.

CHAPTER THIRTY-THREE

The force that hit Johnny was an inferior one, but the blow connected precisely on his knee. He could not keep from falling. As he pitched to the side, something large rolled past him.

Johnny roared and scrabbled onto his inhuman feet, but the large object made the transition much more smoothly.

Brian.

The Omori pulled two pistols from his belt even as he gained his feet. Both pointed at the vampire, who lay unmoving. Then Brian lowered himself to one knee. "Sire. Sire, please. Stand down."

The beast flicked its claws. Rage boiled in his chest.

But Johnny heard.

Seconds ticked by as he struggled with the duality of his desires. *Save Red. Taste enemy blood.* His heart was all for the woman; but his head was filled with fury and his jaws dripped thick saliva. The moment wore painfully on, tension roiling around him like tangible ribbons of hate—then the man surfaced from someplace deep in the waters of his mind and, gasping, fought for control.

One rear paw slid backward. His weight shifted. He brought the other paw in line with this one. Turning his head to maintain his watch on the vampire, he crouched low. Commanding his beast to retreat, he concentrated and held his mental ground as he forced the feral creature inside him to succumb, to shrink and submit.

When the wolf began relenting, his man-form was regained.

His skin felt hot as the cold air of the house swirled around him. Staying down, balanced on his toes, one knee, and the tips of his fingers, Johnny shivered. From head to toe he shook, adrenaline and aggression coursing like whitewater rapids through his veins. He focused on the vampire, but that receding part of him wished the damned thing would twitch once so he could pounce and finish it off. The man knew it was wrong, but the wolf wanted it all the same. If the vamp provoked him, he would be justified. And it would burn up this excess energy.

"Sire."

Johnny's head snapped toward the Omori and a growl slipped out unchecked.

The young man's blue eyes were set, his expression serious. "Sire. Forgive my interference, but you must not kill *that* vampire."

The Omori had put specific emphasis on the word. "Why not?"

"I'm sure you've had some security briefings, sire, but perhaps you don't recognize him. That vamp is one of a dozen or so high-ranking officials included in our OPS training. He's important. Important enough to be on a do-not-kill list."

Aurelia had pestered him about security briefings; he had not made time for them yet. "Who is he?"

"His name is Franciscus Meroveus. He is an advisor to the Excelsior. Killing him would cause friction between wæres and vamps. Hostilities would follow—off the record, underground, and out of the public eye if we were lucky, but it would be ugly nonetheless."

Johnny glowered. He was still breathing hard, but he'd brought it down to rushing breaths through flared nostrils. Control was returning. Gradually. "He did something to Red."

Brian readjusted his grip on the guns, shifted his position, and changed the angle of his aim. The guns looked heavy and fully loaded; even a wærewolf had to amend his pose to avoid muscle fatigue. "Do you want to instigate a war . . . over a woman?"

Johnny fought down a snarl.

"I am at your command, sire." Brian paused. When Johnny didn't answer he added, "If you want a war, this *will* give you one."

Johnny rolled his shoulders to fight off the strain he felt. His body hurt; his arms, his sides.

"Give the word. One way or the other. I trust you to know what you're doing and the ramifications you're bringing on our people." His fingers tightened on the triggers.

Our people. Those two words echoed through Johnny's head. Somewhere along the way they changed into *your son*.

"No." It was more guttural than Johnny wanted the word to come out so he repeated it, making the effort to make it more human. "No."

"Then, let's bind him and tend to your burns, sire."

Ten minutes later, after Johnny had donned his jeans, they had the vampire secured. Meroveus lay on the floor in the space the dinette used to occupy. Johnny had watched Brian loop the rope around the vamp's wrists and ankles in a binding that, should the vamp try to pull free, the rope would just tighten.

"He wields magic. Better gag him," Johnny said.

Brian took care of that also. "Now. Your wounds."

Johnny had examined them. He had tender spots, red and swollen, like third-degree burns that had been healing for a month or so. To have healed this much in one change—and not to have healed fully—meant that they must have been pretty nasty. "I'm fine." He willed his left arm to transform. The fur sprouted and his arm thickened, fingernails thickened into sharp claws . . . then he willed it to revert. This time the burn was still slightly pink. He repeated the partial change on his other arm, then on his torso.

As the fur receded into his chest at the last, he looked at Brian, who wore an expression of awe.

"I didn't doubt you before, sire," said Brian, "but I am honored to witness the very power that makes you our king."

Johnny gazed at Persephone. She still had not moved. "What of Aurelia?"

"The situation is handled. All the details on site and those pertaining to her transport have been attended."

In front of him, Red looked so peaceful and serene. But his gut told him something was terribly wrong. He touched his empty hip pocket. "Did you see my phone?"

Brian started across the kitchen. "Saw it in the debris earlier." He walked down the hall, returned with the phone.

Johnny immediately opened it and flipped through

his contacts until he found DEMETER. He hit Send and glanced at the clock; it was nearly midnight. She was not going to be happy.

The phone rang three times and her familiar voice croaked, "Who's dead?"

"No one," he lied.

"What is it?"

"Demeter . . ."

"Is Persephone all right?"

Johnny let out a slow breath.

"Damn it, John, talk to me!"

"Someone tried to kill her tonight." His gaze flicked over her neck, to the burn, then to the goose egg lump on the side of her head. "She's got a few minor injuries."

"But you don't get an old woman out of bed to tell her that her granddaughter has minor injuries, so spit it out."

"I left to pursue her attacker—"

"You get him?"

"I did."

"Good. Go on."

"When I got back, Red was sitting in the kitchen. Sitting cross-legged with a circle of water on the floor around her."

"She was meditating."

"I figured. But she's still sitting here like that."

Demeter was quiet. "How long?"

"An hour or so. Is that normal?"

"Not exactly." Her coarse voice smoothed nonchalantly. "Have you broken the circle?"

"No."

He heard Demeter sigh in relief.

"I don't know much about magic, but I know that would be bad."

"I'll get Lance up and be on my way."

"No. I'm sending wæres from the Pittsburgh den to pick you up. They will be there in twenty minutes." He hung up with her and made a call to Kirk; he knew it would be handled.

Standing there in the kitchen, staring at Red, he felt helpless.

So he sat down across from her. Her expression had changed. It wasn't exactly serene anymore. It didn't suggest fright or fear or pain, but it wasn't peaceful.

Maybe he was projecting his emotions on her.

He wasn't at peace inside, and it wasn't merely the aches and pains from the recent fight. There was a key in Aurelia's suite that he had to get. For Evan's sake he had to secure the information she had locked away before anyone else did. He considered sending someone to collect the key. Kirk or Hector maybe.

No.

With all the deviousness Aurelia had shown, it wouldn't surprise him to learn the Zvonul had her watched. It wouldn't surprise him if she had enemies who managed some secret surveillance, either.

If anyone was watching her suite, it could mean danger for whoever went to collect the item. He couldn't ask anyone else to take that risk for him. Besides, with him being the Domn Lup anyone who was watching the place would think twice about acting against him.

He glanced away from Red to the clock on the stove. He had time to drive to Cleveland, get the key, and get back before Demeter would arrive. His gaze fell to Mero. He would even have time to deliver that bloodsucker back where he belonged.

Opening his phone again, he called Mountain. The Beholder would keep an eye on Red, and would follow orders to keep from interfering with the magic circle around her.

CHAPTER THIRTY-FOUR

Creepy."

"I accepted that name without complaint, but please . . ." He stood with his palms turned toward me and implored, "Please. Choose another name for me." He dropped his chin. "I regret accepting that name now, as it has only served to reinforce your negative image of me."

I had called him that out of mean-spiritedness. I felt ashamed—

—until I realized he'd given me a bargaining chip.

I had the urge to barter immediately and get the sex issue out of his price. But holding on to the option seemed the shrewder move. Besides, the more he behaved like this, the easier I found the notion of being cooperative. Warm behavior might inspire him to negotiate more.

"Have I not aided you? Have I not acted only to bring your desires to fruition?"

Gently, I said, "I did not intend to come to you for aid in this matter."

"But you are here."

"And I cannot leave without concluding a deal I did not seek to make." I let a hint of blame into my tone.

Sadness dimmed his eyes.

"Sure, my mind was not calm as I sat down to meditate and I forgot to place all the protections, but you intervened of your own will. Your motive is what's *skewed.*"

He conveyed remorse as he said, "I could not help myself. The opportunity was irresistible."

The turnabout in his demeanor was making me suspicious. Perhaps *he* was being "cooperative and warm" to gain concessions from *me*.

"You must admit," he added, "my aid is more ideal to the achievement of your initial goal. My own offering is even more complete than your plan."

I sighed. Back to that. I didn't have any trust in his offer.

"It is the influence of Menessos that has made this decision so difficult for you. You can see that, can't you?"

"Yeah."

"So wipe that slate clean, Persephone. Give me a chance."

"A chance to what?"

"To prove myself to you, that you might find faith in my aid, and in my intentions."

"What do you propose?"

He smiled broadly and offered me his hand.

I gauged him. "Is this going to cost me?"

"Only a little more time."

How much time had passed in the real world? Getting out of this anytime soon wasn't going to happen anyway. I slipped my hand into his.

Immediately, my stomach gave a flip and the decrepit structure *whooshed* into a spin that swirled the darkness with lighter colors. The dizziness hurt and I grabbed Creepy around the waist. When the spin ceased as abruptly as it had begun, all those paler colors grew solid into a new environment.

When the nausea and shock wore off, I released his waist and realized that he'd teleported us to a hill at the edge of a stone ruin. One side of the horizon was inky black, the other was pink and gold with rays stretching mightily; in this place the sun was rising.

"Walk with me," he said. He was still holding my hand as he stepped away. I walked with him but removed my hand. He flashed me a sad look, then noticed my socked feet and led me off the pebbly pathway. We strolled through the grassy yard around the old structure. My feet were wet with dew, but, tender footed as I am, I appreciated the softer place to tread.

"Where are we?"

"Just a place I like."

He guided me to a spot with gigantic boulders rising out of the ground. I turned slowly in a circle to view it all. The ruins were sad in the predawn light.

When I faced him again, he was atop one of the boulders. "The dawn is lovely from up here." He offered me his hand. Begrudgingly, I took it. He hauled me up beside him and slid his arm around my waist to steady me.

My arm didn't slide around his waist in return, but I stood without protesting his touch.

The countryside was misty below. The growing light glistened here and there in the moist air, making it twinkle like a gauzy blanket on which someone had scattered diamonds.

Long minutes pulled the sun higher, until I had to lift a hand as a shield against the glowing brilliance.

"This is a beautiful time," he said in my ear, then pulled back to gaze at me. "The warm light is kind to you. Like summer's caress. But I prefer the night. The moon does not burn the eyes." He smiled and ran his fingers gently over my cheek.

His dark eyes were adoring and kind. A soothing sensation filled me as I peered into them.

"But I have seen how the cold silver light touches you. Your splendor cannot be dimmed by any celestial radiance, only enhanced by it."

Oh my God. What girl doesn't want to hear eloquent praise like that?

However, that encomium was met by my silence. I could not pay him a compliment as kind or as lovely, but I felt compelled to do something that would please him like his words had pleased me.

"I would call you by any name you like if you would tell me what you intend to do if I choose to do things your way."

"I cannot reveal this to you, Persephone."

With a sigh I glanced into the valley below.

"What concerns you so? What is it you fear I will do?"

"You spoke of balance. I do not want you to hurt others or take from innocents in order to secure the safety of my family and friends."

"May I take from the guilty?"

I squinted at him. "I don't like it. This is all on me. Even if it is your action, the blame will rest with me. It's my doing, through you. My karma. And I've learned that two wrongs don't make a right."

"The purity of your purpose is noble and endearing, but you are asking quite a lot, you know this?"

I nodded.

He considered it for a moment. And another. He turned away, paced a few steps along the boulder top, hopped to the next one, took a few more steps, then stopped. His hand tapped thoughtfully at his lips, then gestured as if he was making mental bullet points. Then he strode back.

He snapped his fingers and a stone slate appeared in the air from a shower of black dust. An ornate hammer and chisel appeared hovering above it.

"Do you want me to aid you with this rudimentary idea you have with the stake, or far more thoroughly and safe in my own way?"

I frowned.

"So you want me to help you in this situation with the Excelsior, but only if I can secure the safety of all those you hold dear, without harming others, and without taking anything from others be they innocent or guilty."

After repeating his words silently to myself, my answer was "Yes."

"Then decide: my way or yours. I can only truly guarantee all this if we do things my way."

My frown remained. "If your way can achieve my aim with all the security you have promised, I have to admit it must be a *better* way. But . . ."

He waved his hand and the tools began striking the stone.

My brows flew up and my mouth opened to protest.

"And you agree to my price?"

I clamped my mouth shut.

"I have required less of you by doing things my way."

"True. But."

He put his hand under my chin. "Have an open mind, Persephone. Let me show you who I am. Not who the vampire has told you I am."

I pulled from his grasp. "I just don't do casual sex. There have to be feelings involved for me."

"Why?"

"It's slutty otherwise."

He laughed. "You are a grown woman of above-average intelligence. How can you not recognize that the behavior of adults is always about give and take. You work, you earn money. Give and take. You take the money and purchase things. That's take and give. It's all an exchange. It is only sentimentality that draws the line at sexual relations."

"No. It's morals."

"Yes, that, too."

"You want me to know who you are, but you're asking me to do something against every fiber of who I am."

"But for what you are getting in this instance, I believe it is fair." He gestured and the stone turned in the air to show me what he'd said was written on it.

He stepped close to me and slipped his arms around my waist. He nuzzled his chin against the side of my head and whispered, "Give yourself to me. You cannot leave otherwise. You cannot stay here forever. Your body will die without you, and faster than it would out of want for food and water."

Staring at his chest, I sighed. The trapped feeling was overwhelming. Agreeing to sex with him was the only way out. He could have raped me and been done with it, but that was part of the psychological game he was playing. He was making me choose in spite of the ridiculous connotations it held for me. It was petty. It was part old-world, women-are-property. It was part under-the-table-political-dealing. And a whole lot of it was guerrilla-tactics-forcing-situational-ethics.

It made me mad.

But anger didn't change the fact that I had no options.

His hands moved to the sides of my face and lifted, to make me see him. "Bend your morals for me, Persephone. Let me show you what I can do."

I swallowed hard and told myself, *Here in my meditation world it's not really real.*

Yeah, the situational ethics galled me. It was not who I believed myself to be. It was not who I wanted to be. But there was no other way out. I wanted to kick and scream that I simply would not and that he was a pig for even intervening in my meditation.

But I didn't want to die.

I also didn't want to live with knowing that I'd given in.

Was this what leadership like Johnny was achieving—and like Menessos had lost—was all about?

No wonder Johnny was changing. Compromising one's personal ethics had to have a negative impact. I didn't want to think about exactly how this would change me.

I looked up at him and nodded.

Immediately, Creepy was kissing me again, sucking on my bottom lip—and biting.

I jerked. "Ow!" I tasted blood. "What in Hell do you think you're doing?"

He reached up and wiped blood from my lip. The floating stone drifted close and he wiped the blood across the base. He flashed me a sordid smile. "Sealing the deal."

He jumped down from the boulder, dragging me ungracefully after him with a grip on my upper arm. He pulled me with him as he headed for the ruin. I could barely keep up as he hurried across the grass, across the pebbled walkway, and into the main structure.

My jaw was shut tight to make sure he didn't get the satisfaction of hearing me protest or whine about his speed, his painful hold on my arm, or my poor feet.

He crossed the interior without hesitating, passing the darkened alcoves of the shrine and heading to the rear. There, a stone stairway descended into the dark. He gestured and a light radiated from his other hand. He drew me down the steps, strewn with shards and debris fallen from the arches above. One cut into my foot and I tripped.

As I fell, he tossed the light upward and swung me around somehow. For an instant I wondered if we were teleporting again as everything spun, but the next thing I knew I was draped across his arms like a bride being carried to the honeymoon suite.

The light hovered in the air to brighten our way. Ahead, the pathway had been walled up with mortar and stone.

He glared at it, then blew air through his lips like a silent whistle.

The stone groaned like a deep-voiced specter, then cracked and fell in on itself like so much powder.

It was incredible. There had been no tug on a ley line. No sense of any surge of power from him. Even in this meditation world, when I'd used magic I'd felt the discharge of it.

"Who are you?"

Starting forward through the haze, he said, "Call me Aidon."

My heart sputtered in my chest. My stomach iced over.

With that, I knew who he really was.

CHAPTER THIRTY-FIVE

Johnny drove. He hated the fact that Red had learned about Evan because of Aurelia's mean-spiritedness. He'd hoped that the revelation was not any part of the reason for her current condition. Mentally, he began beating himself up.

Brian had sat silently beside him for miles, then the Omori commented on the Maserati's handling of the country roads and the two of them talked about cars until they neared downtown.

"Dropping off the package first, sire?"

"Yes."

Mero, still bound and gagged, was in the trunk.

The late-night foot traffic in the immediate vicinity of the May Company building was sparse. They pulled up to the curb in front of the haven. Johnny opened his car door and stood, then whistled once.

Out of the shadows, two fierce-looking vampires emerged. One could have modeled for Viking history books and the other could have been a Zulu warrior—except that both were dressed for more modern intimidation in a cold city.

As these outside guards strolled close in nonchalant gaits, Johnny reached into the car and pressed the button to release the trunk lid. "I have something that belongs to you."

Viking peeked into the deep compartment. Zulu

maintained a ready stance and kept watch on Johnny. The Viking stood straight. "We'll take him."

"Keep him out of the suburbs," Johnny said, then slid back into the driver's seat.

The vampires removed Mero from the trunk and shut the lid. Johnny drove away, purposely going in the direction of the den. He stopped at the entrance. After a quiet moment Brian said, "I don't know what you're doing, but I get the feeling you don't want me around."

Johnny nodded.

"I'm down with being your backup."

"Gregor gave you his trust. Any other time, that would be enough for me."

Brian reached for the door handle, but halfway he switched and reached behind him. He offered Johnny his service weapon. "With all you can do, sire, a gun may seem like a rudimentary weapon, but I'd feel better if you took this with you."

Johnny stared at it. His first thought was to wonder if there was a tracer in it.

His second thought was disgust at the idea he'd be living the rest of his life suspicious of everyone. He took the gun.

Brian got out.

Ten minutes later, the Maserati was parked at the RTA Flats East Bank station and Johnny was walking. He had left the gun in the car under the seat. He also had decided to drive well beyond the Renaissance Cleveland Hotel in case there was a tracer in the gun. Hopefully no one would think he'd backtrack.

Zipping up his leather jacket, he turned off West 10th Street onto St. Clair Avenue, passing a few other pedestrians as he walked. At the farmhouse he'd gotten some clothes from his old room that weren't torn or bloody or scorched. He'd chosen black denim jeans, a thick pair of clean socks, and an old pair of Harley-Davidson riding boots. The top shirt in the small dresser he used was one of the shirts they'd had made up for his band, Lycanthropia. This one was faded; he'd proudly worn it as much as he could to advertise the band.

While all of his clothing was comfortable, none of it was particularly warm. The way his heart was pumping, however, he was anything but cold. The coming northeast winter didn't faze him. He had lived in Cleveland a long time. Sure, he'd taken off to Detroit for a stretch. Pittsburgh for a while. But he always returned to Cleveland. He'd often wandered these sidewalks at night. As a wærewolf, in the company of Ig or other pack mates, he had marveled at how prowling the streets as a pack or a pair felt good and right.

Tonight, it didn't feel good or right.

Perhaps it was because he was alone. Ig had always made a lesson of their outings. He never failed to learn something when he walked with the others in the pack.

He tried to figure out the lesson of this walk.

He thought of what Celia had said earlier about Erik. Johnny wanted to resume playing as a band. He wanted to get on stage and rock, to pour out the emotions he was bottling up inside through the song lyrics and power chords, and to sweat out anything that was left underneath the colored lights.

It felt like all that had slipped from his grasp.

He walked a few blocks on St. Clair, then turned on West 6th. He wanted to avoid as much of Public

Square as he could; the vampires kept a tight watch on that area. As he neared Superior, a group of four young men were approaching on the sidewalk ahead. He pulled up the collar of his jacket and huddled into the leather as the wind brought their scents to his nostrils. Sweat. Beer. Pot. Cheeseburgers. They were loud, laughing, and moved like they thought they were tough.

The muscles in his arms tensed, loosened. He was ready.

They passed by, talking among themselves as if he weren't even there.

He sighed, relieved.

What was wrong with him?

His collar had come up because he'd expected them to either recognize him or start something. It didn't bruise his ego that they didn't know him, but it did make him feel like an arrogant ass for fretting about it.

He proceeded across Superior, angling left onto West Prospect. Beyond the parking deck for Terminal City he could see the Renaissance Cleveland Hotel. He didn't want to go in the main entrance, though. He kept walking, passing an alley, then the Tower City Center valet parking service.

When he'd walked with Ig, he was just another face in the crowd, another punk on the city streets. Now, his face had been flashed all over the national news. He'd craved fame via the band, but he had not craved *this*. This was clearly a sporadic kind of recognition, which was okay, but the potential for less fame and more notoriety—if ODOT had their way—made this brand of celebrity even less desirable.

He scolded himself. All this suspiciousness wasn't like

him and it was taking a toll. There were plenty of people he could trust.

Trust.

By the time he was approaching the Higbee Building, he'd figured out that *that* was what was wrong with him. He'd lost his trust for people in general. He'd always had a healthy sense of caution and while he only let a few people get close to him, he'd felt confident that most of the people he had to interact with were open about their motives. Promoters and groupies, guitarists and fellow employees at the music store and the small guitar-making facility—he knew what to expect with all of them. They wanted music from him, in one way or another.

But they had all passed out of his life to be replaced almost entirely with pack.

Aurelia had been right. He'd kept this family at arm's length.

Prospect curved slightly, then he made the turn onto Ontario, his eyes lingering on the blue awnings of the Ragin' Cajun restaurant across the street.

He knew Todd wanted to rule. He knew Cammi— one of the dominant females of the pack—wanted to be on the arm of someone ruling. They had always been that way. While Kirk and Hector had always treated him well, they hadn't gone out of their way to aid him until it was clear what he was. Those in management-supportive positions in the pack were definitely obedient and proficient in his brief experience, but were they always as on the ball for Ig, or were they hoping to make an impression on the Domn Lup? What about the Omori? Gregor had befriended him, but how much of that, truly, could be chalked up to Gregor doing his job?

Everyone he had to deal with lately made demands on him. Not the usual requests like "level these frets" or "change out my DiMarzio pickups for these Bare Knuckle ones" or "which do you like best, Charvel or B.C. Rich?" Those entreaties had clear solutions he was confident he could handle. He missed that certainty.

Out of necessity and the achievement of power, his mind-set was changing and his faith in others—in their honesty, integrity, and sincerity—was dying.

Erik had been his best friend for years. He'd lost that friendship essentially because of his power. From afar, he'd counted on Ig as his father figure. Ig was dead; he'd given the life he was losing anyway to put Johnny into power. Red was new to his life, but he had attacked her because he'd lost control of his beast, then his assistant had tried to murder her because she saw Red as a threat to his power.

Since he'd accepted his fate as Domn Lup, his relationships with the few people he did trust had been shattered.

He was going to have to find a way to fix things with Red and with Erik. He needed to have a few people he could still confide in, who'd give him advice without being affected by the politics of his position. Also, he was going to have to stop the suspicious paranoia, and let his faith return.

He turned off Ontario onto South Roadway and walked past the impressive ionic columns and huge arched windows of Tower City Center. Ahead was the Renaissance Cleveland Hotel.

When he passed through the revolving door and neared the lobby, the opulence stunned him. Vaulted

ceilings with huge chandeliers harkened back to a by-
gone era. He actually stopped and did a full circle to see
it all. Then he noticed that the concierge was watching
him closely. He wondered if the man was simply doing
his job, or if Aurelia had paid him to be her eyes and
ears. Johnny made sure to approach the elevators with
the key card visible in his hand. It would show that he
belonged here. When he stepped into the elevator car he
stared at the floor until the doors had almost shut. At the
last second he shoved his hand between them, forcing
them to reopen.

He expected the concierge to have grabbed the phone
and alerted someone to his arrival . . . but the man had
simply let his gaze trail over to the television where a
rerun of *M*A*S*H* was playing.

Johnny felt foolish. He couldn't be paranoid like this.

He punched the button for the top floor and had to
insert Aurelia's card.

The elevator rose swiftly and deposited him in a
small lobby with a placard indicating the direction of
the various suites. He followed the arrow to the left and
promptly arrived at the proper door. He slid the key into
the lock and saw the little handle light flash green as he
pulled it out.

He turned the knob and pushed the door open on a
darkened room.

Immediately, he knew he wasn't alone.

"Hello, John," Plympton's voice trilled. "I've been ex-
pecting you."

CHAPTER THIRTY-SIX

Hyperventilating was not something I wanted to do, but damn, keeping my breathing even was nearly impossible.

Menessos had not been able to say Creepy's true name to me, but now that I had heard it, his identity was beyond obvious. With all he could do, I should have seen it or guessed who he was.

How did I miss it?

He was carrying me into the darkness, descending deeper and deeper into the tunnel. As the pathway grew more treacherous, the light he'd thrown ahead of us faded into what would have been a tragically unhelpful dimness. Regardless, he proceeded at the same pace, as if he knew his way so well he could have made this journey in the dark.

If he was taking me where I thought he was, he probably could travel it in total darkness.

I didn't want to come with him before, but I really, really didn't want to now.

I weighed my options.

There would be no escaping from him. What I had was the realization of who he was and I could let him know I knew that now, or later. But where we would end up would make it obvious and it might gain me something to not be *that* dense.

"Would you prefer Aidon, Aidoneus, or Hades?"

His only reaction was a sly smile.

"Well?"

"In truth, I quite like Hades."

Ahead, the light stopped before a wide-arched wooden door. When we arrived before it, he put me on my feet. As he stepped closer to the door I realized it had no knob. He stood there whispering words I didn't understand while a 10-watt light glowed like a nimbus around his head. As he spoke the light shifted from white to violet, and the royal-colored illumination edged him with a mystical quality deserving of a god. Then the beguiling imagery faded and the door opened.

"Come."

I hesitated only a second before leaving the darkened tunnel and stepping into a surprise.

It was a familiar, if massive, hall. Turning to glance around me, my eyes took it all in. He gestured and torches lit throughout the hall, illuminating what I was trying to see.

Towering above was the giant stone stairway, each of the thirteen steps rising five feet high and thirty feet across. Yes, even the knobless door tucked into the bottom step was familiar.

I had been here before . . . I'd been on this side of the door in a meditation and when I had passed through it, I'd arrived at Hecate's crossroads—but that was not where Hades and I had come from.

My gaze lingered on that magical door, wondering where else it might lead. I wondered, if I ran through it, could I escape him and the shiny new bargain we'd made?

Not likely.

"This way," Hades said.

Following him across the hall, rounding the various-sized stalagmites, I couldn't resist looking up for the matching stalactites on the ceiling. The skyscraper-tall pillars held the ceiling aloft. It occurred to me that maybe they held up the world I knew.

We walked for twenty minutes before reaching the middle of the room, and Hades wasn't one for small or slow strides. Here in the center there was a wider pathway running side to side, like one whole row of pillars was absent, but the ceiling above was arched and painted with tragic faces. "Where does this lead?"

"You don't want to know," was all he said.

Since I was panting, nearly running, to keep up with him, and the images on the ceiling were so frightening, I didn't press the issue.

When we finally arrived at the far side, a fissure in the rock awaited us. Chilled air swirled through it, blowing my hair about as we passed through. There was dim light ahead, and the air smelled fresher.

About halfway through, the fissure widened into a proper hallway with an arched opening. It was entirely encouraging.

Outside was a small terrace with a short series of steps leading down to a white stone road splitting a forest. To the left and right the land was cluttered with the knobby trunks of thick old black poplar trees and the majestic branches of white willows as they arched over puddles. The road was built up to make significantly higher ground.

We began to walk. After several silent minutes, we passed the trees and the land rose up around us. The road ended abruptly and a field of flowers stretched before us. The breeze was light and the soft scent wafted, familiar and yet new.

"Come," he said.

"They're so pretty. I hate the thought of tromping on delicate flowers."

"Then you will not." He waved his hand as we approached and they moved—literally. They turned their dainty heads down, their lean stems spiraled to make them shorter and their leaves reached into the ground and gathered up their roots like they were little people harvesting tubers.

"What are they?" I whispered, marveling.

"Asphodel."

Hades clasped my hand and brought me to his side and led on. The flowers did not merely part before us, they scurried out of the way—leaving the softest dirt for me to walk upon—then returned to their places and reset their roots, leaving no trace that we had passed through at all.

They had diaphanous white-gray petals so pale and thin they were like dragonfly wings. I glanced at the sky, longing to see those petals glisten in the rays of the sun . . . but the overcast clouds stretched on forever.

I heard laughter and saw movement to my left, yet the flowers did not stir there.

Curious, and a touch wary, my gaze flitted all around the meadow. I discovered many others moving near us. People who were not solid. "Who are they?"

"Lost children. Those wrongly condemned. Suicides."

"Why are they here?"

"They linger for the flowers. This field is soothing to

them. Eventually their mortal aches may wane. If they do, they will find their way beyond the petals."

We walked for more long minutes in a dreamy silence as the breeze picked up little by little and surrounded me with an aroma: sweet like hyacinth and a touch of white lily. The fragrance hovered around me without overpowering my senses. With each breath I felt better and more at ease.

The air blew around us with more intensity and carried a chill that made me aware of how warm his hand was around mine. Even the asphodel shivered as they darted here and there. I scanned ahead and saw a mist engulfing the field.

"Hades?" I asked, my voice breathy and subdued to my own ears. This place was affecting me. That scared me, but I found it difficult to be bothered by that fear. I knew this was wrong, but I couldn't care. "What is that fog?"

"The Vale of Mourning."

"It's cold."

He drew me closer and put his arm around my shoulders. "It is brief; I will keep you warm."

The ground beneath my feet sloped downward. Inside the mist, indistinct figures raced by, or sat near our feet, or lay on the ground screaming and pounding their fists on the earth. Their sorrowful wails were so loud I covered my ears. When the ground eased into a gentle upward incline and the white air thinned, I asked, "Why do they mourn so?"

"They loved unfortunately in life. Here, they come to know what could have been. Until their souls have made peace with that loss, they are ensnared in the Vale."

We were in Tartarus. I knew this, but until that moment it had eluded my consciousness that I was in the land of the dead. *This is only a meditation. I'm not dead.*

We emerged from the Vale where the land leveled off and it was immediately warmer. I pulled away somewhat, but not fully—ahead stood several battalions of ground troops. Considering what alarmingly little knowledge my brain had stored about this place, I was at least able to identify the men ahead. "Those who died in battle?"

"Yes. Fallen warriors of whom the bards sing."

They marched in formations that turned and broke apart as smoothly as a marching band at halftime, each group redividing until they were small units of perhaps a dozen each. Then mock skirmishes broke out. The good-natured taunting they shouted at each other made it clear these men were merely having fun.

Hades led me around the right side of the melee. Those closest took notice of our passage and ceased their scuffle to talk among themselves quietly. One was brave enough to march nearer. "Greetings, Lord Hades."

"Greetings, Patroclus."

"May these men and I escort you and the lady across the Plain of Judgment to the Dividing Road?"

Hades nodded.

Patroclus waved his arm. The men of his group and the one they had sparred with jogged to us and formed ranks around us as we walked. As we passed, circling back to return to the road, the other warriors on the field ceased their tumult and fell into silence.

It was an impressive fanfare, but all in all I felt terribly awkward traipsing alongside a god in my filthy socks.

In the distance were two structures close together. The foremost sat where the road we traveled converged with two others, creating a three-way crossroads, a spot sacred to Hecate. The building was a temple of some kind adjacent to an amphitheater. A crowd had gathered before it.

As we neared, my mouth hung open.

The stage of the amphitheater was sheltered by elaborate awnings. Three thrones sat center stage. It reminded me of the layout on the haven's court stage—and that thought was joined by the realization that Menessos, his second-in-command Goliath, and I, would never hold court in the haven again.

That was both a relief and a disappointment.

But the thought could not remain. In awe of what I was seeing, my mind flitted back to the present. The three thrones ahead were occupied with figures I had not thought to see until my death.

I'm not dead.

I could guess the male on the left dressed in dark robes was Radamanthys. The center seat had to belong to Minos. His scarlet robes were like a splash of blood amongst the otherwise gray tone of the setting. Lastly, Aeacus sat on the right in white robes, holding a scepter and bearing keys upon his belt.

Before them the souls of those waiting to be judged were gathered. As I watched, they performed their duty and the souls were sent to either the left or the right. The left-hand lane was a rutted and muddy path with steep inclines and declines, and all of it was edged with spiked and jutting rocks. The right-hand route was a smooth, flower-lined trail that gently dipped only as it ran under the rearmost structure.

The left-hand path was getting far more foot traffic, but Hades guided us off the road and toward the right, which brought the other structure into full view. It was an imposing black marble palace, surrounded by thick marble walls with rounded towers at each corner sprouting up from the tops of enormous gunmetal-gray skulls. The skulls appeared to be solid steel, with the eyes and nose set with the same marble that made up the exterior of the palace and the defensive walls. The cheekbones of these skulls were so sharp, and the jaws so square, that I would have wagered they were modeled after Hades's own features.

The skyscraping towers were each topped with a dozen black-edged silver banners flapping in the wind. The castle itself was a rectangular, multilevel structure with a crenellated roofline. Long banners like those flying from the tower tops draped either side of the main entry to the palace, and likewise, alongside the main gates of the walls.

A cry of pain resounded across the plain behind me and I turned to see a man who had stumbled in the ruts of the left-hand lane and fallen onto the dreadful rock edge. As I watched he slid onto the road and writhed in pain. No one else on that path seemed to notice him as they passed. No one stopped. "Will anyone help him?"

"He must help himself," Hades said.

"He looks hurt. What if he can't?"

"Then, he will lie there forever."

I frowned. "You could help him, couldn't you?"

"I could," he said. "But why?"

My expression did not change.

"You are compassionate, my beauty. I admire that, but aiding him will not help him. Do you understand?"

I shook my head.

"In this place, he must travel of his own power. He must spend his time in Tartarus. He will find his way to Elysium, eventually." After being silent for several paces, he asked, "Do you think me cruel, Persephone?"

When he said my name many of the men escorting us shot quick looks at me. Some started to whisper, and were signaled into silence by others.

"I don't know what to think."

He squeezed my hand tighter. "Perhaps you are thirsty from our long walk. Patroclus, fetch the lady some water."

"From the well, my lord?"

"No," he said with a nonchalant gesture. "From the eastern river. Its flavor is sweeter."

CHAPTER THIRTY-SEVEN

Giovanni's knee was bouncing impatiently as he sat in the darkened back of the white van. It was parked near Blood Culture—downtown Cleveland's vampire bar.

Neither of them could be sated by Adam every night, let alone two of them. They needed him to drive them, and to watch over them during the day, so they agreed to send him in to buy blood.

It risked exposing that Giovanni was back in town, but Liyliy had already been seen and they hoped the man's purchase would be linked only to her. To reinforce that idea, after Adam had been inside for a few minutes, Giovanni told Liyliy, "Perhaps you should step outside the van and be seen by observers near the club."

"But I am hideous! The people will—"

"You are not hideous, Liyliy. Your sisters did much to heal you." It was true. Though she was far from perfect, she had regained a level of her former looks that, considering how horrifying she had been, he found acceptable. Her body was still feminine and curvy in the right places. Half of her face was normal, but the eye on the other side was sealed shut with grotesque scar tissue. She was fully aware of it and gave him only a profile view of her best side. He could pretend that the other side was undamaged if she kept it turned away.

Wordlessly, she exited the van and paced impatiently

next to it with her arms crossed. The hand with the damaged fingers she kept tucked under.

The hunger was gnawing at him terribly; he imagined it must be worse for her. She'd told him that after she'd delivered the phones to her sisters she had had to fight her way out of the haven.

But she hadn't spoken a word to him about the child.

He hated her for it. And yet he admired her for it as well. *Cunning. Like me.*

His brain was still rushing over the possibilities. If he had the child in his control, no enemy could ever keep him out. He could organize a loyal team and destroy anyone who opposed him.

First, he would seize the girl and use her to bring the Lustrata to his side. Then he'd gather a group of expert thieves and, without ever being on scene for any crime, obtain limitless wealth to fund his goals. He could use his position near the Excelsior to establish his power base while keeping his identity as the architect of all the mayhem a secret. Eventually, he would remove the Excelsior and become King of the Vampires. He would end this peaceful coexistence political game. He'd use the Lustrata—once she'd become Wolfsbane as the legends foretold—to wipe out the wærewolves. He'd burn the witches and enslave the rest of the humans. All that he'd ever dared to imagine was becoming reality . . . all he needed to do was maintain the moment until he could harvest his new, powerful destiny.

Liyliy's phone rang. Giovanni not only heard the ring as she paced outside the van, but he felt the vibration of his own phone in his pocket. He connected.

"Sister?" Talto asked.

"Yes?"

"I've had a concern. What if the child is not trained in magic? Wouldn't that be terribly problematic?"

"As the foster daughter of the Lustrata I doubt she would be untrained," Liyliy replied.

"Still, should we not consider this before I begin my part of the plan? If she *is* untrained, she is a danger to everyone around her, unless Ailo can contain her, should that be necessary. Do you think Ailo is capable of that?"

Liyliy was silent.

Giovanni was watching her out the front window of the van, and noticed that she turned toward the club. Adam must be coming out, he reasoned.

"Only Ailo can say for sure," Liyliy said. "Talk about that between the two of you. I trust you both. I'll talk to you again soon."

When she hung up she returned to the rear interior of the van. Adam opened his door, and once he was situated in the driver's seat, he handed the bottles to her. She accepted one for herself, and passed the other to Giovanni. It was warm in his palm.

"You were on the phone. Did your sisters find anything helpful?" he asked.

She unscrewed the cap to her bottle and drank, bringing the bottle to her lips carefully, as if the motion was unnatural.

He wondered if it was because she did not drink from anything but a living person or if it had something to do with her losing an eye.

After she swallowed, she said, "It was Talto checking in with me. Nothing eventful has happened."

Marveling at the ease of her lie and noting the confidence of her tone, he opened his bottle also. However, Giovanni did not drink. He let the aroma of the blood rise under his nose and he savored the smell. Though nothing would ever be as satisfying as drinking straight from a human, the development of a method to both bottle the fluid and later warm it for vampire consumption had made this manner of feeding less atrocious.

He waited, feeling that pitiless hunger swelling within him and letting it filter throughout his body until it felt like his every molecule was quivering in anticipation. He grew hot. He had to have blood in his mouth, now. Right now.

Only when he could not wait another second did he drink.

Serenity in each swallow, he drained the bottle as he had drained victims in centuries past. As he longed to again. As he would when he ruled.

For his greedy intake, Liyliy stared coldly at him.

Lying bitch. He thought harshly of her duplicitous action, not telling him about the child within the haven.

He wiped his mouth and smiled at her.

He wanted her more than ever.

But he could not have her now.

He could not even dare to touch her. She might read his deception and know that he'd bugged the phones he gave her, and he would not risk that.

CHAPTER THIRTY-EIGHT

What are you doing here?" Johnny asked Jacques Lippencot Plympton.

In the meager light from a slightly opened curtain, the *diviza*'s wrinkles deepened as he squinted. "Because I've heard me a rumor."

"What rumor?"

"That our dear Aurelia has joined the ranks of the dead."

Johnny didn't answer. He didn't even move.

Plympton sat forward and rubbed his hands together. "Betcha you're a-wonderin' who told me."

The moment wore on in silence, then Plympton laughed.

"Well, c'mon in, m'boy. We have oodles to discuss . . . and besides, you're a-lettin' the draft in. I'm not fond of your northern November weather."

Johnny reached for the light switch.

Plympton made a sound, one decidedly disapproving note, that stopped him. "Better to leave the lights off."

"Why?"

"You'll have been seen a-entering the hotel. If these lights come on, that'll only confirm that you've a-come to her room while she's out."

Johnny let the door shut behind him but he stayed near it. "Who's watching this room?" As he spoke he sensed around the room. No one else was here. His eyes had already adjusted to the darkness.

"Maybe several people." Plympton shrugged. "Maybe no one."

"Why would anyone watch her room?"

As the *diviza* sat back in his chair, he was again in the slightly brighter portion of the room. It made his hair seem like a ghostly halo about his head. "Some like to watch lovely women. Some keep an eye on their friends. Some monitor their enemies. Others enjoy a-studying the ways of shit-stirrers like her."

Shifting his weight, Johnny repeated, "Shit-stirrer?"

"She has—had—a knack for trouble. A-finding it. A-making it. A-using it to her gain."

"When I introduced you today I didn't think you knew her."

"I don't—I mean, didn't." Before Johnny could ask he added, "I hear rumors."

The gossip theme wasn't to be missed. "What other hearsay has found its way to your ears?"

"Come on and sit down, John." He gestured to one side, then the other. "Chair there. Couch there."

One put Johnny's back to the window. The other put him in line with other buildings beyond the slightly open curtain. Johnny's most trusted pack mate, Kirk, was a former military sharpshooter. Johnny had learned a thing or three from him about what can and can't be done with such rifles.

Johnny knew he should sack the room, get the locker key Aurelia had told him about, and leave, but Plympton's presence here and his knowledge of her death was enough to make Johnny alter his plan. Though Demeter was on her way and he needed to attend to Red, he had to see what the old man might reveal.

Johnny wrapped his hand around the arm of the offered chair and dragged it to a more neutral position that suited him better. With his back to the wall and no structure to be seen through the gap in the window dressing, he sat.

"You're a-going to do all right, John. That's not flattery. I really believe that."

"Why?"

"Because you're cautious. You think about things. And it's obvious you don't really want it." He cocked his head a little. "It's the men who get all riled up and salivate 'cause they be a-wanting power and clout and influence . . . they're the ones to watch with wary eyes. I have to wonder what it is that they're a-wanting it for."

"You and me both," Johnny muttered. "You have quite a lot of authority. What's in it for you?"

Plympton grinned and flicked the fingers of one hand as if he were dismissing Johnny. "I love me a big flea market, a peppy auction, or even a dingy garage sale. I love to haggle and negotiate. So much so that as a young man I broke into the business of mediation and arbitration. For countless legal situations, I was a neutral middleman a-helping both sides reach an agreement. Then folks found out I was a wærewolf and my phone stopped a-ringing. My business went bankrupt. Apparently, a man cannot be a wærewolf and be trusted to mediate fairly."

There was a hint of old bitterness in his voice, but bitterness that had been dealt with.

"I've been a *diviza* for thirty years." He sat forward

again. "In that time, I've met thousands of wærewolves. Let's just say that the best have tried to fool me, and failed. I can always tell what kind of person I'm a-dealing with."

Johnny waited. "What do you want me to say?"

"Nothing. I can guess what the three of you are a-planning."

Three. Plympton knows about me and Red and Menessos. He almost claimed they weren't planning anything, but that would be a lie. Menessos was always planning something. Overwhelmed with his new roles as the Domn Lup and as a father, Johnny had lost sight of that.

He'd nearly killed Meroveus—a powerful magic-using vamp. He'd thought earlier that with his tattoos unlocked and his full power at his disposal he could defeat Menessos if pushed into a confrontation with him again. Now, he was even more confident of that. Now, he could even tempt an encounter with Menessos to directly ask what the vamp's endgame was.

Besides, he thought, getting back on track with this moment, *Plympton would not believe me if I denied that we had a plan.* So, instead, he asked a question back. "Earlier, at the bridge, their lies enraged me . . . and you did something. What did you do?"

Stretching his feet out before him, Plympton spoke. "Long, long years ago, when there was nary a wrinkle on this old face, I lived in a cabin on the bayou. I ate what I could catch. Fish. Fowl. Squirrel. The occasional 'gator. When you grow up in the bayou, you learn the ways of the swamp. When I was attacked there, I avoided the first pounce. Something chased me, but I used the bog. Had ropes in some of the trees. I made it to one and climbed up, a-wrapping the rope around my arm so it couldn't follow or pull it and bring the branch, and me, down. But it nipped my heel." Plympton paused there for a breath. "I'd heard the stories. I knew what it meant to be bitten. I knew what would be a-happening next. I didn't want it. So . . . I paid a visit to a vodoun priestess."

His voice lowered slightly as he recounted the story. He'd shown her his wounds, and told her his fear. She had examined his injury with distaste and, he thought, disbelief. Then she wiped the stems of some dried blue flowers on his heel. His skin sizzled and burned like fire, leaving the edges blackened. He'd screamed and thrashed in pain, but he'd seen how her eyes widened, he'd seen her backpedal in fear. "What kind of damned flower is that?" he'd asked.

She whispered, "Wolfsbane."

He had begged for her help. She told him to return the following night. Aware that she might try to kill him, he did. "Whether she helped me or whether she killed me, I wouldn't harm or turn others," he'd reasoned. She'd given him a drink and he hoped the poison didn't hurt. But she'd only drugged him.

"The room spun around and everything blurred and stretched. But I didn't black out. I felt it when I hit the floor. I felt the vibrations in the planking as she worked a-hammering spikes into the floor around me. She bound me to those spikes, spread-eagled. When she sat atop me, I knew something terrible was going to be a-happening, but I couldn't do anything about it. Whatever she'd brewed into my drink left my mind a-working fine, but immobilized my body."

"What did she do to you?"

Plympton said, "She had a coarse, ancient version of tattoo needles . . . she drew on my palms with boiling ink and molten silver. It burned in temperature, but the very substance left me feeling like I was being dipped in acid. There was some kind of magic in it; the stuff fused with my skin, into the very cells. Since I had not yet transformed, the beast within me wasn't yet afflicted by the witches' use of that power." He showed Johnny the strange dark symbols in the center of each palm. "She told me to envision myself a-choking the beast, twisting its neck to breaking. Then she told me to see the beast dying and pushed a needle into my eye." He tapped his blind eye. "I've been told that the heated drop cooled under the flesh of my eye and it's lodged in something called the 'aqueous humor.'"

"It didn't keep you from becoming a wærewolf."

"No. Since I'd not yet a-had my first change, I revert to this after each full moon. My body has adjusted to the silver in my flesh. But my beast hasn't. I've had my transformation and kenneling time videotaped. Comparing that with footage of other wæres, the silver clearly makes my transformation a bitch. Every second that I'm a wolf appears to be painful as hell. My pack's caregivers tranquilize me each full moon."

"You knew that touching my arm would have an effect."

Plympton half smiled. "The old Rege could make his hands shift when he was quite angry."

Johnny nodded. He'd seen it up close, but wasn't going to bring that up.

"From time to time, he found reason to be quite angry

with *me*," the old Cajun added, staring into his palms. "That was a-how I learned that with a touch of my silvered palm I can turn away or reverse a transformation . . . at least momentarily." He breathed deep. "Your changing would not have helped us right then."

"I know."

"I'll tell you something else, sire . . . a secret." He tapped his silvered eye and whispered, "I can see the beasts. Even now, I see yours."

Johnny waited, sure the man would go on.

"While I am in human form, I can tell a submissive wolf from a dominant one. They usually match their human counterpart in temperament . . . but not always. Yours is doubtless a king among wolves. To master him, I daresay, is impossible. But to contain him, to coexist with him harmoniously . . . that will be the trick that tries you. Not ruling. You're a man of character, you have ethics and a-see things in black and white. You'll learn to navigate the gray area in between." He snorted a small laugh. "But you already know all that, don't you?"

"What do you want, Jacques?"

"I feel very fortunate to have been able to come here and meet you in person, to handle this building situation with you." Plympton stood. He paced to the left, put his hands in his pockets and jingled change, then paced to the right. "There's a reason you stepped up now and are accepting the position as Domn Lup. These are thorny times . . . with the demise of the Rege—and the dreadful method of it—the upper ranks are all a-dragging around their suspicions of you. There are rumors that you're on the Lustrata's right arm and that the vampire Menessos is on her left. The speculation and curiosity surrounding you has the court a-buzz like never before. When the news of Aurelia's death reaches them, their doubts will go a-doubling."

There was a long pause and Johnny asked his question again.

"Some fear you are a fraud, a creation of the witches' fancy. But I have seen your beast. He's not the product of sorcery." He paused. "There are some who know what I can do. I'll back you up, John. My pledge will be golden. They will assure others."

A third time, Johnny asked, "But *what* do you *want*?"

Plympton pulled his hand from his pocket and held up a small item. It was the key to a paid locker. "I want you to tell me where the locker for this key is located."

CHAPTER THIRTY-NINE

Talto sat in front of a computer. The screen's light was the only illumination in the room. In the darkness beside her was Liam, who in his late thirties was oddly older than most of his Offerling peers. He was good-looking, but not exactly the heart-stopping kind of gorgeous that was required of most of the second-tier vampire servants. She'd discovered he hadn't been given the prestigious role for his looks; he was a haven member due to his IQ alone.

She heard a quiet *splat* and turned to see the drool that was running off his chin had dripped to the tile floor.

Not that his IQ is shining so bright right now.

She frowned in disgust. Probing into people's minds was a nasty thing to do . . . at least the aftermath of it was.

But Liam had been a banker-turned-hacker once. He'd miraculously escaped a police raid on foot, but the hounds were closing in and he literally crossed the path of Menessos, who agreed to save him from a lifetime behind bars in exchange for his services.

In Liam's mind resided many methods of committing crimes electronically. Menessos had required the man to act within the parameters of the law, but that did not mean Liam didn't know how to break those laws.

Talto had taken what she'd needed.

Presently, she had set up a series of new bank accounts in various banks in various countries, and had established a schedule to filter funds from one to another. In a few days, the haven would be reduced to the minimal funding provided by the networks of VEIN, but Menessos's private and very deep financial pockets would be empty.

She opened her phone and typed the word NOW in the body of a text message to Ailo, then hit Send.

Ailo ran across the stage, through the doorway, and crossed the backstage area to pound on the Haven Master's door. The guard dropped his phone, jumped from his seat, and forcibly restrained her even as she tried the knob and discovered it was locked.

"What are you doing?" he demanded.

She twisted in his grip. "I must see the Haven Master immediately! He is still in there, isn't he?"

"He is, but you can't barge in like a madwoman." He noticed her necklace and it seemed he remembered who he was dealing with. He released her immediately, keeping himself between her and the door. "Allow me," he said, and knocked more politely on the door.

Nothing happened.

"I thought you said he was in there," she snapped.

"He is."

"Menessos, too?"

He nodded.

"Is it normal for the door to be locked?"

"They do what they think is fit. Nobody questions them. That includes *you*."

"And what do you do when they think it is fit to not answer their door and a crisis is occurring?"

They glared at each other for another minute with nothing happening.

Ailo needed to get Menessos to catch Talto in the act. She couldn't leave her sister sitting there for hours. "Are you certain they are in there?" she pressed, crossing her arms.

"Yes."

"You get so focused on your stupid phone game, perhaps they have left and you didn't even notice."

"Hey. I focus, but that doesn't mean I'd miss my Haven Master *leaving*."

The door opened slightly. Goliath stood in near darkness within, his gaunt features rather terrifying. "What do you want?"

The guard pointed at Ailo. "She is rather determined to see you."

Goliath's eyes flicked from the guard to Ailo and back. "Get four Beholders in here for feeding. Immediately." To Ailo he said, "When the Beholders leave, you may enter."

"But—"

"Not until."

The door shut.

Her crossed arms fell into fists at her sides.

The guard retrieved his phone and made a call. Seconds later, a quartet of Beholders hurried into the room and entered the Haven Master's suite.

As she waited, paced, and grumbled to herself, Ailo gazed up at the entry to the Erus Veneficus's rooms. Behind that heavy door lay the answer to all her hopes and dreams. Freedom. Splendor. Control of her own destiny. She could live anywhere in the world. She could surround herself with anything and everything she wanted.

She'd have vases of the most beautiful flowers in every room. She'd have colorful birds in cages. She would clothe herself in something other than gray. . . .

Maintaining the safety and happiness of the child would be no easy feat, but she could make the child adore her. Fancy gifts would satisfy any child, and when she grew bored of those, Ailo would buy her more. She would spoil the girl so no one else could satisfy her.

The Beholders finally filed out of the Haven Master's suite, each with gauze pads held compressed to either their necks or their wrists.

Ailo made for the door. The inside remained dark except for a single candle near the door. "Are you here?"

"What do you need, Ailo?"

Menessos's weary voice emitted from the darkened far side of the room.

She sighed angrily. "Unless your delay has allowed her to complete her scheme, my sister is presently stealing the haven's money."

She heard movement instantly. "How?" Goliath demanded.

"She's been talking to me about trying to find out who manages the finances here. She's spent the evening stealing touches off people, looking for this information. I saw her following one of the Offerlings. I'm sure she's mesmerized him, read him."

"Allow me to handle it, Haven Master. They are both bound to me." Menessos arrived at the door looking truly dead. Dark circles ringed his eyes. His cheeks were sunken, and a drop of blood lingered at the corner of his mouth. "Where is she?"

Ailo gasped and retreated a step.

He claimed the ground between them without seeming to move at all. His hands gripped her arms like vises. "Where is she?" His voice was low enough to sound demonic.

In her opinion, Menessos needed to feed from a few more Beholders. "I don't know. I saw her heading up to the first floor with the Offerling. That's all I know."

He brushed past her before she finished. "Vinny, get some of the men up to the accounting offices." He and Goliath were gone in a flash.

With a hidden grin, Ailo followed them.

CHAPTER FORTY

Johnny considered tackling the old man and taking the key by force.

"I'm sure Aurelia a-told you where the locker's located," Plympton said. "I mean, that's why you're here, isn't it? You came to get this key."

Staring, aware that he couldn't play off his presence here or pretend he hadn't known Aurelia was dead, he wondered which of the Omori had leaked details to the *diviza*. Then another thought hit him. "Why did *you* come to get the key?"

Plympton tossed the key up and caught it in his palm, then tucked it back into his pocket and paced to the left again. He scratched thoughtfully at his chin.

Johnny knew he had the ability to kill the old man and take the key, but having the ability to end someone's life didn't mean he had the willingness to follow through. And not just because there'd be *another* body to worry about.

What he knew of Plympton wasn't much: Wærewolf. *Diviza*. Old. Cajun. Enjoyed negotiating. Visited a voodoo priestess who put molten silver inside him. Heard lots of rumors. May never have met Aurelia before today, but she was undoubtedly a source of some rumors he'd heard. She was not, however, his only source.

He asked again, "Why do you care what's in the locker?"

Plympton spread his arms, posing like the Christ the Redeemer statue in Rio de Janeiro. "For thirty years I've haggled *with* wærewolves and *for* wærewolves. I know how they think, how they act and react." His arms dropped. "I've walked the line between our world and the human world so many times that, hell, I know that damn line like the back of my hand."

Johnny squinted at him, thinking.

"I can see you're a-running it all through in your head. I've achieved a fair amount of rank. Aside from my knowledge of certain sensitive information about the Zvonul, my experience alone makes me a valuable resource." Plympton stopped and faced Johnny, that one eye scouring him for a moment, then he resumed his seat and continued. "I don't have a choice now. I have to trust you. I have to believe that when I tell you this, you will live up to your good character . . . and that you will see mine."

The old man's dilemma about trust reminded Johnny of his own current difficulty with it. "Tell me."

"I was approached by a vampire. Over the course of a few months, she repeatedly showed up at various public functions my office was part of . . . then she started showing up at more private functions. Always, there was a hello and a brief, inconsequential chat. Each grew longer, held more questions, offered more details. Then she asked me to provide information about the Zvonul."

"What made her think you were willing to spy on your own kind for her?"

"I advocate for changes, which means I bitch with style."

"Did you agree?"

"This is where it gets difficult, John." He paused. "You see, I contacted the Omori for advice. They wanted me to proceed, pretending to be a traitor. My handler used a voice changer during calls, nothing was done in a manner that was documented. When I tried to record the calls, something about the voice changer scrambled the voice on the recording, so it seems like I'm talking to no one. We never met in person—but I have reason to believe that Aurelia was my handler. Now that she's dead, my reputation may be at stake."

"Surely they'll have a backup plan for situations like this."

Plympton patted his pocket where the key was. "This is the backup plan."

Johnny blinked. The information about his son was supposed to be in the locker. Aurelia didn't mention anything else. "Wait, wait. You think she was your handler, so you've come to her rooms, dug through her things to find a locker key, and now you're certain she's put info about you in a locker somewhere."

"I'm a-telling you, this is how my handler operated. Public lockers. When I was given instructions, they were always in a public locker."

"I thought you said there was no documentation. Written instructions—"

"The paper disintegrated when I touched it. I had to read it in the locker, then touch it to destroy it and leave." He scratched at his chin again. "I may have been set up. I don't know. Hell, I'm not even sure it was a representative of the vampires that approached me."

"You said she was a vamp."

"Yes. Doesn't mean she's on their side."

"Huh?"

"Maybe she's working for SSTIX. You've heard of them?"

"Specialized Squadron for the Tactical Investigation of Xenocrime. Yeah. I've heard of them." He did not tell Plympton about his run-in with Special Agent Damian Brent and Special Agent Clive Napier over the lines of glass on Lake Erie's shore—the only traces of a supernatural battle that he and the wærewolves had taken part in. "You mean there's a vamp out there that you think is not sleeping her day away in a haven?"

"SSTIX is recruiting, John." He let that sink in for a moment. "They're a-looking for haters. If they don't find them, they'll manufacture them, do you a-understand me?"

"You mean they will have the vamp make more vamps? That's not supposed to be easily done. . . ."

"No. I mean they will plant seeds, make their own kind not trust the one they are after until that one is a-ripe for the picking."

Johnny sat in silence as Plympton stood and took the key out again.

"My handler intercepted information that I was being bribed, that I had been giving out classified information to the vamps. Thing is, that information was selected by my handler for the giving. It was modified data. Spies apparently deal not only in information, but in misinformation to make their enemies reveal themselves. When my so-called contacts tried to use the information against me, to make the Zvonul banish me, then I'd have nowhere to go but to them. Do you see? They are going to use our own against us to bring us down from the inside."

"And you believe the information in the locker is what your handler intercepted."

"Yes. I have to get that data. It's the only thing that can maintain my credibility—and you need me to be credible, to vouch for you when Aurelia's death is made public."

Johnny stood. "She told me what was in the locker. She didn't mention anything about any of this. What if you're wrong and she wasn't your handler?"

"I'm certain she was. If she told you there was something in the locker for you, there is. But she meant for us to get it together."

"How do you know that?"

"She directed some veterinarian to call my number; she'd given him a message for me. It was in code, but it meant that I was to come and get the key from her suitcase, and to wait for the monarch. Here you are. She had to have told you where the locker is. That's why I was to wait for you."

Johnny walked across the suite to a dark corner. He pulled out his phone and punched the numbers for Doc Lincoln. That part would be easy to verify.

The doc answered with a voice thick with sleep. Johnny asked, "Did you make a call for Aurelia?"

Silence.

"Doc. Did she give you special instructions before she died?"

"John, it was crazy talk. It made no sense. She said not to tell you."

"Good enough. Get back to sleep." Johnny shut his phone and, shoulders squared, returned to Plympton. "I carry the key."

"I prefer to keep it."

"If we run into trouble, I can protect it better than you."

"If we run into trouble, you're going to change and lose your clothes."

Good point. "But I can change parts of me and keep the pants on."

"Look here, John. If you want to kill me for it, go on and do it, but I am not giving you this key. Show me where it goes, and you can open it with me. There must be something in it for you, you can have that, but I get the documents pertaining to me. That's all I want. Isn't that fair enough?"

The cabbie was literally going out of his way to make his fare larger, and it pissed Johnny off, but he said nothing as the man made another turn.

When they pulled up in front of the blue marquee, Plympton, who had been silent the whole way, got out. Johnny handed the cabbie a twenty, letting his hand go furry as the man reached to accept it. He recoiled with a gasp. "Superior to Thirteenth was the shortest way," Johnny said to the driver, who was cowering against his door. "If you ever drive me again, don't try to cheat me." He hurried to catch up with Plympton, who'd already disappeared inside the silver-steel doors.

Inside, the yellow and white checkerboard floors gleamed in the bright lights. The old man was approaching the lockers, checking numbers against the one on the key. When he found it, he stopped and turned, waiting.

To Johnny's surprise, Plympton offered him the key.

He accepted it, then wondered if the locker might be booby-trapped. Or if Plympton planned to whack him in the head when he was distracted.

Stop it. Still, he angled himself slightly away from the *diviza* as he slid the key into the lock. Gently, he turned the key and heard the mechanism inside click. Delicately, he opened the door a crack. He did not see any wires or smell anything that made him wary. So he pushed it wider. Plympton moved closer.

Inside lay a key fob, with one key and a paper tag secured to it with a green twist tie. Johnny lifted the key and examined the tag. Written on it in Aurelia's scripted cursive was:

AKRON-CANTON AIRPORT. Long-term parking. White Nissan Altima.

A license plate number was printed on the tag.

The two men locked gazes. "Looks like we're a-needin' another cab."

Shortly later, a different driver for the same company dropped them at the RTA Flats East Bank station. This one had wisely taken the most direct route to get them there.

Plympton made a comment about Johnny's "racy-looking vehicle" and grumbled as he climbed into the Maserati's "low" passenger seat, which explained why they had used the Cadillac Escalade limousine earlier.

Johnny knew it was about an hour's drive from here to the Lauby Road airport, and about forty-five minutes from there to Red's, plus the time it took to find and deal with the Altima—it better not send them on to another location. He didn't have the time to run around all night. Demeter was on her way. In fact, she should arrive at the farmhouse in an hour. He texted Kirk: Get an update on the arrival time of the Pittsburgh group for me.

By the time they were on I-77, the reply arrived: ETA 1 hr 23 mins as per their GPS. Took some time 2 reach someone @ Pittsburgh den, have them reply to the request & find 2 wæres 2 take the job, then get them 2 the tattoo parlor 2 pick up the passenger.

Johnny texted back: Good enuf. Thx.

So he had to haul ass on the interstate to be able to get to the farmhouse when Demeter did. He locked in the cruise control at 90 mph.

CHAPTER FORTY-ONE

Ailo followed Goliath and Menessos across the stage and up. Vinny had followed as well. In the hall outside the theater, three more guards joined them. When they climbed the steps to the first floor there were five guards with thick gloves on their hands waiting for them at the top. With a nod from Goliath, they charged down the hall and barged through a door marked ACCOUNTING OFFICE.

The next few minutes were a blur of screaming rage from Talto, gloved guards restraining her, and the call for someone to bring smelling salts to rouse the accountant from his stupor.

Ailo was surprised that Menessos and Goliath didn't immediately jump into questioning the youngest shabbubitu, but their priority was securing the haven's funds. Everyone here was focused on Talto's tantrum. Ailo knew if she could slip away, this might be her best chance to abscond with the child.

But dawn was only a few hours away. She would have to find a place to secure both herself and the child for the day . . . a place the Beholders would not discover.

I could call Liyliy. She must have mortals at her disposal . . . she would aid us, and she would have the resources to get us far from here.

But Ailo wasn't certain she wanted to share the prize with her elder sister.

The guard sent for the medical supplies returned and the accountant was roused. Before he had fully recovered himself, he slid into the seat at the computer, straightened his glasses, and furious typing ensued.

As all this transpired, Talto resisted her captors. She ranted, spewing vile insults, threats, and phrases of hatred at Menessos. "My treachery will never cease, Menessos. I will loathe you for eternity and I will gnaw at you until I taste vengeance!" She jerked loose and launched herself across the room at Ailo. "And you, you bitch!" she cried. "You exposed me! I was only trying to ensure *our* escape!" The guards recovered Talto, but she jerked one arm free. She slapped her sister hard before she was brought under control again.

Menessos must have had enough of her taunts. He walked over, pushed her head to the side, and bit into her neck. She squirmed and screamed—tearing wider the wound his fangs made. He drank and drank. When she slumped in the arms of the guards holding her, Ailo cried, "Master! Please, show mercy to my sister."

Snarling, Menessos spun around. His thin beard was covered in blood. In a flash he was before Ailo, his hand wrapping her throat, pressing her to the wall. "What she sought to steal was mine, and it is my right to exact compensation!"

"Yes, Master. Yes," Ailo pleaded, holding her reddened cheek. "But do not kill her. Please."

Even as she spoke, the blood he drank affected him. The dark circles under his eyes vanished, his cheeks were no longer sunken. She knew he had gifted the child, but she wondered what else he had done this evening that had drained him so.

He was touching her.

Even as her eyes fluttered shut to search for the answers in their physical contact, he jerked away. "No!" he shouted and raised his hand as if to strike her.

She cowered before him and slid down the wall to sit on the floor. "I helped you!" she blubbered pitifully, her hands defensively raised above her head. "I helped you again!"

Menessos held his pose, rigid, breathing hard, then lowered his arm. "That you did."

"I've almost fixed it," the accountant said.

Everyone's attention transferred to him and the computer screen.

With every back turned to her, Ailo eased along the floor and silently exited the room. She headed directly for the suites beyond the theater.

The gloved guards held Talto as she struggled, and their hands flitted about her body in their efforts to keep her contained. She had to be mindful of the fabric of her dress moving and resituating repeatedly to keep the phone from being discovered.

The anger was so easy to show because it was real. The struggle was easy to make because she didn't want to be restrained. It was shouting at Ailo that was hard. But Talto knew when the guard's grip loosened a little that she could break free, that she could fling herself at her sister and scream her condemnation. She knew that would be convincing to the audience at hand.

She did not expect to actually slap Ailo. She thought the guards would pull her back before the attempt succeeded. It hurt her greatly that she was able to get that strike onto her sister's face.

But it hurt her more to read in that brief touch that Ailo's concern was only about fleeing and stealing the powerful child. There was nothing in her sister's thoughts that betrayed a concern for Talto's plight. In fact, there was a measure of pleasure in it for Ailo.

Talto was subdued again, and she felt as if she was the one who'd been struck.

Then Menessos drank of her.

It weakened her as much as it strengthened him. Her world became hazy, her knees weakened. She heard Ailo beg for mercy. She heard Ailo say she'd helped Menessos again.

Though someone held a compress to her neck, darkness swirled at the edges of her vision. She fought to keep her feet under her, then gave up and let her full weight pull her down in their grip. For several minutes, she heard the chatter of the men like the buzzing of bees. She heard the clack of typing, she heard the accountant triumphantly announce he'd corrected all her attempted thievery.

The ambiance of the room shifted from tense and angry to relieved. The guards patted the accountant on the back. Through the forest of legs that were moving about before her eyes, Talto realized they were all wearing pants. No gray silk.

Ailo's gone. She left me. She left me here to die in his wrath. She's taken the girl.

With a scream of anguish she began to sob. "Ailo's gone," she said.

Everyone turned to check the room.

"She made me do this," Talto wept. "She made me

read the accountant. She made me steal from you so there would be a distraction."

Menessos crouched before her. "Why?"

Talto looked up into his eyes. "So she could steal the girl-child."

CHAPTER FORTY-TWO

People say water is crisp and refreshing when they are hot and the liquid is cool. I don't think I've ever been that hot. To me, if a drink has the same adjective as, say, a cracker, something is wrong.

But the water in the goblet Hades gave me hit my tongue like a brittle frost. It was so sweet and so cold at once that it hurt. It seeped through my teeth, infused my tongue. It crackled into my jawbone like magic. And I could feel it moving higher.

"What have you done?"

Hades smiled. "You agreed that I might satisfy myself two ways. You are too suspicious, too *wary* of me, for me to find that satisfaction easily. This"—he indicated the goblet—"will make the transaction smoother for both of us."

My mind raced. The river. He told the man to fetch the water from the river. "Lethe."

He nodded.

"You double-crossing bastard." It was the river of forgetfulness. "This wasn't part of the deal." The magic in the water had risen to my temples. It was reaching its arms—no, its tentacles—of static across my cranium, and fingers of fire curled around my eye sockets. I covered my face with my hands. My knees weakened and buckled.

"Don't take my mind," I cried. "Not my memories."

He crouched beside me and put a reassuring hand on my shoulder. "There's only about a minute left now. It will be all right. I will care for you."

He was erasing from my mind all the people I knew and cared for, wiping away what little I knew about being the Lustrata. "You're stealing who I am!"

"I must be paid, dear Persephone. When I am, I will . . ." He snapped his fingers and the stone of our deal appeared. He read: ". . . secure the safety of all those you hold dear, without harming others, and without taking anything from others be they innocent or guilty." He snapped his fingers and the tablet disappeared. "As promised."

The world swam before me. I felt like I was floating in a river, bobbing on the surface and feeling the current pulling at my feet. I put my hands down to the ground to steady myself. "They'll be safe, you swear?" I choked on the words.

"I swear."

I could tell my torso was leaning this way and that. I was trying to tell which way was up, where my balance was, but I kept overcompensating. I widened my arms and dug my fingers into the ground. "What of my destiny?"

His warm hand cupped my chin. It was stabilizing. I was grateful for it and I loathed him for it all at once. "Who am I to interfere in your grand destiny?"

I held on to his promises as parts of my body numbed. Inside my skull, my brain grew cold. Darkness swirled at the edges of my vision. Consciousness, I knew, was leaving me.

"Hecate," I whispered. *Would I remember Her?*

"Hecate cannot help you," he whispered back. "Our deal is struck." Hades put his lips to mine and I could not fight, could not speak, could not see.

Despair was the last thing I knew as his kiss pushed me under the surface of Lethe's oblivion.

CHAPTER FORTY-THREE

Johnny and Plympton arrived at the Akron-Canton Airport shortly before three in the morning. They followed the overhead signs marked LONG-TERM PARKING, and cruised up and down the long rows of parked cars, searching for a white Nissan Altima. Halfway down the third row, they found it. Stopping the Maserati behind it, Johnny cut his engine. He had time to peer inside the front and back seats of the car before Plympton managed to maneuver out of the "low" seat and join him.

"The interior seems empty," he said.

Plympton patted the trunk. "Check here."

Johnny put the key into the lock and turned it. It clicked and the lid opened slowly. They stood back as it rose by itself. A light inside flashed on.

Inside the trunk sat five plastic cases. Four were black with opaque tops and gray handles, and sized to hold folders and documents. One was red. It sat nearest the bumper and still had stickers on it indicating the price and the case's features.

"My situation with her is newest," Johnny said. "I bet this one is mine." He flipped the latch and opened the top.

Beside him, Plympton pulled one of the black files closer to him and did the same.

Inside the red case were two dozen files with unmarked

tabs. A few in the front sat slightly open and there were pages visible within them. He lifted the front file and glanced through it. It looked like a transcription of his and Toni's conversation on the way to New York.

The fob was bugged. He glanced up at the fob dangling off the key that was still in the lock of the raised trunk lid.

"Yup. This one's mine." He put the file back and pushed the files around inside the case to see if there was anything like a bug or homing device inside there. Finding none, he relatched the top, searched the exterior and bottom of the case, then removed it and sat it in the backseat of the Maserati.

Plympton was standing rigidly at the back of the Altima as Johnny returned. Giving Plympton a little time, he slid the key from the trunk lock and popped the fob apart. He found no microphone inside it. He put it back together. "Is that what you're looking for?"

The *diviza* nodded slowly, engrossed in what he was reading.

"Jacques?"

The old man looked up.

"I have to go now. You'll take this car?"

"Yes." His eyes slid back to the documents in his hands.

Johnny wanted to hurry off, but something kept his feet planted. The old man had been true to his word. He'd let Johnny keep the information that was clearly pertinent to him. "Hey."

"Hmmm?" Plympton didn't stop scanning the paper in hand.

"Diviza."

The use of his title made him break his focus on the newfound data. "Yes, sire?"

"Let's get together tomorrow at the den and see what can be done about your situation."

Plympton shook his head. "Not at the den."

"Wherever you would like, then," Johnny said, extending his hand to shake. "I *will* help you, Jacques."

The *diviza* shook his hand. "And I will give the court my account of your beast."

Johnny pulled into the driveway at the farmhouse at a quarter 'til four, mentally singing praises for the Maserati's speed and handling, and the lack of police on the roadways that night.

Mountain met him at the door. "There's been no change in Persephone," he said.

"Demeter arrive?"

"Not yet."

Johnny strode into the kitchen and stood with his arms crossed. He frowned and he paced. He circled Red. Then he sat before her and mimicked her pose. He couldn't imagine staying positioned like this for hours.

What went wrong?

He wondered if the goose egg on her head had anything to do with it. What if she had a concussion? Doctors tended to want people to stay awake for a while after taking a knock to the head. Did meditation count as sleeping?

The urge to reach out and touch her arm, to shake her gently as if to rouse her from a deep sleep, was overwhelming. But he couldn't do that.

If I hadn't gone after Aurelia, she'd still be alive, I wouldn't have made a deal with Plympton, and Red wouldn't be like this.

From the living room, Mountain said, "There's a car coming up the drive. I don't recognize it."

"Check the plates," Johnny called out.

"Pennsylvania."

"It's someone from the Pittsburgh den bringing Demeter."

He heard Mountain's heavy steps heading for the door.

Johnny stood up, intending to go and greet her, but he stopped when Mountain said, "Look out. The granny looks distressed and she's got a serious move on." He opened the door. "Hello, Demeter."

"Out of the way," she said, pushing through the doorway. She gasped and stopped dead as her gaze took in the hole in the floor near the stairs, the broken handrail, and the splintered spindles. Finally, her eyes locked onto Johnny. "Where is she?" she demanded.

He put his back to the wall and pointed down the hall.

Her bad knees, worry, and the late hour combined to make her wobbly; she barreled past like a wild bowling ball, weaving side to side. Johnny fell into step, albeit on a straighter path, behind her. In the kitchen doorway she stopped again.

He was sure that the broken dinette table and chair, the tabletop against the wall, the bench lying on its back, the pieces of the old phone scattered around, and the set of claw marks torn into the linoleum stunned her. And there sat Red, posed peacefully in the midst of the wreckage that her kitchen now was.

Neither of them spoke.

Breathing heavily, Demeter studied Red. The moment grew interminable for Johnny. When he was about to say something, she finally shuffled one slow step forward.

Then another. With her head cocked, she approached Red. She made two circuits around her granddaughter, and Johnny watched her face for a clue.

"What caused the lump on her head?"

Johnny told her about Red being hit with the chair, but didn't mention that the attacker was a woman or, more specifically, his own wærewolf assistant. "That was after the attack. From the mark on her neck I have to guess her assailant tried to strangle her first."

Demeter looked up from her granddaughter and held his gaze. There was no blame in her eyes, no anger, but the grave trepidation was unmistakable. "This shit isn't going to stop."

He blinked.

"None of you three are safe anymore." Her focus dropped onto Red again and her expression turned infinitely sad. Her hands rose as if to touch the mound of her beehive hairdo—but she'd cut her hair short. She altered the gesture to place her palms on her cheeks. "When we get her out of this . . . things have to change."

Johnny nodded. Demeter didn't even know about Beverley yet. He figured he'd save that for later. The elderly woman had enough on her mind right now. "But you can bring her out, right?"

"Not alone I can't."

"What do you need me to do?"

Demeter sized him up, then glanced at Mountain, who'd come to stand in the doorway from the other room. "Nothing. I need witches."

CHAPTER FORTY-FOUR

Ailo ran through the haven to the theater, across the stage and into the backstage area. No guard had come to replace Vinny. *Good.* She climbed the metal stairs silently, keyed the code on the door, and opened it.

"What the fuck?" Risqué stood up from the sofa. Seeing Ailo, her red eyes flashed and she added, "You can get your conniving ass right the hell out of here."

"Menessos said he needs you to come to the accounting office."

One thin blond brow arched. "Why?"

"Something's gone wrong."

"And that has got what to do with me?"

"He did not elaborate." Ailo was irritated that Risqué wasn't simply complying. "You are an Offerling. He sent for you, and you must go."

Risqué crossed her arms. "I don't know anything about accounting."

"So? Your master sent for you."

"So?" Risqué mimicked her.

Ailo stomped across the room and right up to the one person standing between her and the child. She was taller than Risqué, who must have slipped out of her usual clear high heels to stretch out on the sofa. Looking down her nose at the red-eyed woman, Ailo said, "When he says jump, you ask how high. *That* is how a haven works. Offerlings obey. Period."

Risqué was not to be easily intimidated. Her hands dropped onto her hips. She thrust her nose against Ailo's. "Clearly, you don't know *me* very well."

"Your master said—"

"Honey, Menessos and I have an *understanding*." She pulled away from Ailo and tilted her head. "Besides, he isn't the boss anymore. Goliath rules the haven now, or have you forgotten?" The sweet smile she ended with was as fake as the lie Ailo was trying to use.

Ailo didn't have time for the banter. She had to get the child and get out of there. Balling up her fist, she hit Risqué in the jaw.

The blow knocked Risqué to the sofa with a squeal of surprise and pain. Ailo leapt upon her. Sitting on Risqué's chest, she held her down while repeatedly punching her in the head.

Pinned against the cushion, Risqué's arms were stuck at her sides. She clawed at Ailo's dress, but that was insignificant. Ailo kept punching, right then left, until the Offerling gave up trying to fight back. Surely she would lose consciousness soon.

Then the heel of a clear stiletto pump bit into Ailo's side. She looked down as Risqué drew back for another awkward strike. She hadn't given up trying to fight back; she'd managed to pick up one of her shoes to use as a weapon. This time when it slammed against Ailo's body, it pierced the flesh and sank deep.

Screaming in pain, Ailo instinctively leaned away from the weapon.

Risqué used that moment to flip Ailo onto the floor. She kicked the shabbubitu repeatedly, then clambered onto Ailo's chest and began throttling her about the head. "How do you like it, bitch? How do *you* like it?"

Now Ailo's arms were restrained, but she put her hands against Risqué's thighs and called on her power to read people, urgently probing deep into the other woman's mind. She hissed at the Offerling, ready to give her much agony.

Risqué laughed and punched Ailo in the mouth, splitting her lip on a fang.

Ailo dug her nails in, desperate to force a reading.

Risqué slid her fingers through Ailo's hair, gripped tightly at the sides of her head, and slammed her skull against the floor three times. "You dumbass, I'm the one person in this haven immune to your touchy-feely shit." She twisted to slam her fist against the shoe embedded in Ailo's side.

Screaming, Ailo spat blood from her mouth. She willed a change, wanting to become an owl, but the chains around her neck prevented her from transforming fully. Still, she pushed the change into her legs and feet, feeling talons stretch out from her toes.

Reaching awkwardly up, her talons snatched hold of Risqué's arms and she kicked the woman across the room. Risqué slammed into the stools at the kitchen counter, sending them flying like bowling pins.

Ailo staggered into an upright position as her feet reverted to human. She tore the shoe from her side and started forward. "What are you?" There was no one she couldn't read.

Picking herself up from the floor, Risqué touched her already swollen face, dabbed at one puffy eye. "I'm your worst nightmare."

Ailo called to the magic that clothed her, shifting the

fabric to a short sheath dress, the excess forming silver weapons in her hands, cylinders that fit her grip nicely, with points on either end. "You don't look like more than a mild daydream to me."

"Is this better?" Risqué thrust her hands downward with a jerk and flames swirled across her skin. With a toss of her head, her pale ringlets transmuted into a mass of thin, hissing white serpents.

"Daughter of Hell," Ailo whispered.

Risqué leapt at Ailo.

Diving to the side, Ailo rolled away. Risqué landed on the sofa, knocking it over with her momentum, then setting it aflame with her burning hands. Ailo pounced as she was clambering to her feet, and struck at the half-demon. Risqué threw herself backward, kicking out and knocking the weapon from Ailo's hand. It clanged to the floor and reverted to quicksilver, which pooled and slithered to rejoin with Ailo.

Risqué crouched behind the burning sofa, her every serpentine appendage hissing.

As smoke filled the room, Ailo changed her weapons into daggers and advanced. As she swiped the blades before her, Risqué blocked with fire so hot, it melted the blades as they passed through the flames.

The fire alarm began clanging. With a scream of frustration, Ailo threw a dagger.

Risqué raised her hands to block it but miscalculated the speed, and it sailed through her defenses. She lurched sideways at the last, and the dagger sheared off the heads of three white serpents. Blood dripped from their severed bodies. The weapon clattered to the floor and dissolved into a pool of liquid.

Ailo magicked another dagger from her quicksilver and launched it. The blade thumped into Risqué's torso between her lowest ribs. She fell backward. The dagger pooled on her skin, disappearing inside the wound, only to roll around under her skin, making her scream and writhe, before the liquid slithered out of the wound and returned to Ailo.

A scream from her side drew Ailo's attention.

The child stood holding back the curtain that separated the back half of the room. Her eyes were wide, jumping from the burning couch to Ailo, to Risqué, and back.

Ailo ran to the girl. "I'm here to help you."

She took a step back. "Did Celia send you?"

Ailo started to agree, then she had a better idea. "No. Persephone did. Come with me." When the child took her offered hand, Ailo sent the fabric rushing down her arm, encircling the girl's head, gagging her mouth lest she scream, and wrapping her body in a cocoon of gray satin. It left very little in covering for Ailo, but that was irrelevant. She lifted the girl in her arms and hurried from the room, leaving Risqué gasping for air on the floor.

She heard the sound of many feet rushing across the stage. Leaping from the top of the stairwell, she landed heavily with the extra weight of the girl in her arms. Still, she managed a second long leap, landing behind the door, unseen by those charging in. She slipped into the unlit depths of the backstage and located the service elevator—a minor detail she'd gained from Sil's mind.

CHAPTER FORTY-FIVE

My love, are you recovered?"

I heard the voice in the darkness. A man's voice. It was close to me. Then I realized my so-heavy eyelids were shut. Little by little, I managed to part them and allow some light to hit my retinas.

The man was lying beside me in this soft bed that smelled of sweet white flowers. Indeed, as I moved I noticed the petals strewn about us. *Stephanotis.*

"Love?"

I faced him, and my spine stiffened. He was handsome with his dark hair and eyes, but I didn't recognize him. I chanced to answer. "Yes?"

He smoothed hair from my forehead. "You don't remember me, do you?"

My eyes widened slightly but I said nothing.

"It's all right," he said. "The physician said you might have memory loss for a while."

"Memory loss?" I made a confused face at him. I was sure that any second now all my thoughts would click into place.

He gave me an unconvinced expression. "Tell me my name."

So simple a question. And yet I did not know. "I can't."

"Your name?"

I don't know my own name!

I sat up, heart racing—but his hand on my shoulder was reassuring and warm.

"Stay calm," he said soothingly. "You are safe here. All will be fine."

"How is it going to be fine when I can't remember who I am?" My mind raced, searching for details. I could think in sentences, I knew language, I could identify that we were in a bed, but I could not remember myself.

How the hell do I know those are stephanotis flower petals and I don't know my name?

He leaned in and kissed my forehead. His action was one of familiarity, but it startled me and I flinched. Although he noticed, he didn't seem bothered by it. "Your memory will return. In the meantime, I will tell you everything you want to know. That is what any good husband would do for his wife, don't you agree?"

I winced at his words. The confusion and uncertainty in my mind were disturbing, but the sudden suspicion in my heart made me want to flee. "Yes," I said calmly. "You're my husband?"

He nodded and offered an easy, charming smile. "I am. For many happy years now."

His dark hair was thick and hung to his shoulders. His eyes sparkled with kindness. His bare chest and arms were muscular. He seemed a happy, pleasant man; healthy and robust. His demeanor was calm and non-threatening. Still, I felt misgivings I could not justify. "What *is* your name?"

He hesitated for a heartbeat. "Aidon."

"And mine?"

He kissed my cheek; this time I didn't flinch. "When you remember that, we'll know your memory has returned."

He slid away from me and rose from the bed. He was naked and kept his back turned as he lifted his pants from a seat nearby. "For now, let's walk around our kingdom and see if anything is familiar."

Our kingdom?

He turned and flashed me a smile that could melt hearts. He backed away. "I'll wait for you out here."

After he'd passed through the doorway, I slid from the bed. Unclothed, I looked myself over. No bruises. I felt my head. There was a bit of a knot near my temple. A glance around the room revealed an armoire with one door open, a lovely dress hanging from a hook on the door. It was made of copper- and bronze-colored fabrics. The off-the-shoulder style had a tight, dropped waist. Thin, gauzy layers created bell sleeves, and the matching skirts mimicked them perfectly. I flipped it around and saw the back dipped low except for a single ribbon that, when tied, kept the shoulders in place.

In moments I donned the dress that had obviously been fitted exactly for me—but tying that ribbon was impossible, unless I knotted it, and then it wouldn't be the correct tautness. I was sure he—Aidon—would assist me with that detail. I glanced around for a mirror and discovered one on the armoire door.

My face was . . . unfamiliar.

Then I noticed the red marks and the burns on my neck.

What happened to me?

The sounds of movement beyond this room reminded me that Aidon was waiting for me. I found some slippers in the armoire and hurried out of the room.

His expression lit up when he saw me.

"I need some help with this." I held the dress up in the front with my hands. "There are ribbons in the back that need to be tied."

"I can manage that."

I turned around.

"Forgive me. I should have sent a maid to see if you needed assistance." His fingers were deft with the ribbon and barely touched me, but at the last, as he drew the ribbon into a bow, his fingertips slid across my shoulder blades and made me shiver. "One of them could make a prettier bow, but this will suffice."

"I'm sure it will." Finished, I turned so he could see me. The ends of the satin ribbon tickled.

"My beauty . . . I do adore you in that dress."

I smiled for him, but lost it. "What happened to my neck?"

My question chased the happiness from his expression. Sadness diminished him and he reached out to me, caressing me near the injuries. Seeing the marks must have stirred his anger. His face hardened for an instant, then he covered it.

"It is done, and it will heal. Let us have something to eat, and then we will walk." He offered me his arm.

After a moment's hesitation, I slid my hand into the crook of his arm and began walking with him. "I'm not hungry. Can we just walk? Maybe that will stir up my appetite."

"Whatever you wish, my love."

As we strolled along, the grandeur of this place couldn't be missed. It was merely a hallway, but the carpet was an elaborate wool weave. The curtains were more like tapestries. The walls were crimson and gilded frames held lovely paintings and the occasional mirror. There were sculptures in alabaster, in ebony, and in jade.

My grip slipped from his arm and I roamed closer to a window. Beyond the glass stretched a darkened world of rolling hillsides lit by silvered moonlight and twinkling stars. There was a gentle breeze out there, blowing over the fields and making the plants undulate like the sea.

That silvered light drained the colors, though. I found no recollection in the view.

This vulnerability made me sick inside. This was wrong. Knowing things, but knowing nothing of the people around me, not even knowing where the halls of "my" home would lead me . . . this could drive me mad.

My shoulders slumped and a sigh slipped from my lips.

His fingertips strayed across my skin at my spine, below the ribbon, and traveled downward. It was a gentle touch, affectionate and teasing. My shoulders straightened and my sigh turned from dispirited to desirous.

"Aidon . . ."

"Yes, my love?"

"Show me something I am sure to remember. Something wonderful. Or something terrible. But I must remember!"

He searched my eyes as he considered my request. I waited.

Finally, he said, "This way."

We walked through this incredible palace—*a palace!*—and arrived at a set of huge golden doors set with ivory carvings and iron handles shaped like stephanotis flowers. Twined stems created the handles that curved out in an arch and down to rejoin the iron.

Aidon gestured. "Open them."

I put my hands on the cold iron and pushed the great doors. They swung more easily than I expected, and as they parted a grand hall was revealed. Thick white pillars held up a ceiling so high I grew dizzy looking up. The floor was black marble and, as torches flickered to life, lighting the expanse of the hall, that marble gleamed.

Aidon took my hand and guided me onward. Halfway across the hall, he eased in front of me and took my other hand, dancing me to the right, leading me to the left, then twirling me around. His movements were smooth; mine were awkward. The dancing was strange, and I wondered if this was all a nightmare.

We stopped before an ivory staircase. He coaxed me up the seven steps and knelt between two regal chairs of gold. With his hand palm up, he indicated the seat with more feminine curves and carvings to it.

"This is your throne, my beloved queen."

CHAPTER FORTY-SIX

While Demeter searched her address book and made a call, Johnny asked Mountain if he would watch Red for a while.

Mountain nodded, yawned, and leaned against the counter.

Johnny climbed the steps up to the farmhouse attic. The minute space before him had been his bedroom here. It felt smaller than it ever had before. Not that he was bigger for being the Domn Lup. More like his bright and wide-open world had deflated, constrained by the weight of his responsibilities.

He stared at the simple twin bed he'd slept in. He remembered lying on that bed bleeding after the phoenix had clawed him. Doc Lincoln couldn't stop the blood loss, but Persephone had found a way.

She never let him down.

So much had changed since then. Life had gotten so complicated.

His gaze trailed over to the little amplifier in the corner and the guitar in the stand beside it. Almost without willing himself to move, he suddenly held the guitar in his hands, the strap was over his shoulder, and the amp was plugged in and turned on.

He played, quiet and slow, letting the sad melodies of a minor blues scale ripen and evolve on the fret board. He listened to the notes, but some piece of his mind was thinking about Red. Another piece was thinking of Plympton, and of Aurelia.

The longer his fingers worked at the song and modified it with each repeat of the progression, the more those out-of-control concerns changed from crushing white-water rapids to tranquil little waterfalls, each issue flowing individually over the edge to pool in one placid, peaceful lake. By the time he'd decided that the phrasing of the tune was perfect, his worries had each smoothed into place. He switched the amp off, unplugged the cord, and put the guitar back in the stand. When he turned, Demeter was in the doorway.

"Sounded good. Kind of took me back to my youth. I visited a dance hall or two."

He smiled. "You?"

"It was mostly records on the jukebox, but some musicians would come in from time to time."

"And you danced?"

"Oh yes. I could cut a rug. Jitterbug. All that shit. I was a slip of a girl then—and my knees weren't bad. But that wasn't dancing music you were playing. That was . . . melodious lamentations." She crossed her arms. "There's more going on than my granddaughter being stuck in a meditation."

Johnny thought about denying it, but Demeter was . . . Demeter. He sat on the bed, patted the spot beside him. Her knees were probably killing her after climbing all the steps. She was a spunky old lady, not the type to give up or let things stand in her way. Not even pain. "A lot."

She shuffled over and sat beside him.

"The damage to the house is my fault. There was a vamp here. I thought he might have something to do with her condition. He wanted to take her to the Excelsior."

"Looks like your refusal didn't suit him much."

Johnny shook his head. The broken parts of the house were insignificant compared to the safety of the people he cared about, but he said, "I'll have it all fixed."

"I know. What else?"

He sighed and stared at the floor. "Demeter, something happened with Beverley earlier. She's okay now as far as I know, but she slipped into a ley line. Apparently Menessos pulled her out. I haven't had a chance to follow up on that yet."

"She's fey?"

Johnny looked up sharply. "Huh?"

"She'd have to have fey blood to survive a ride on the line." As she thought that through she rubbed at her knees.

He thought of Toni—another spunky older lady who wasn't letting pain stop her. "Demeter, there's more. Um . . . I recently found out that before I was turned . . . I had a girlfriend and . . ." He stood and paced toward the door. "She gave birth to my son."

"Oh my!"

He turned around.

"Where is she now? Does Persephone know?"

"She knows I have a son, but I didn't get to tell her anything more than that. . . . I wanted to explain but . . ." The fingers of both hands raked through his hair, and he bumped his forearms on the low ceiling. His arms dropped to his sides. "Evan's mother died in a car accident a few years back. His grandmother has been raising him. She recognized me on TV and sought me out. She's dying of some kind of cancer. She only has a few months."

"Oh my," Demeter repeated.

"I'm having them brought to Cleveland."

"To get her treatment?"

He shook his head. "I think her condition is beyond treatment. It's more for their safety. . . . I don't know who to trust anymore." *Sometimes I don't even trust myself.*

Demeter hesitated a moment, snorted, and said, "You ever hear of Aeschylus?"

"No."

"Greek philosopher. Wrote some plays. *Prometheus Bound.*"

"I've heard of that."

Demeter nodded. "Actually, there's some debate over whether or not he truly wrote it, but never mind that. He lived in the city of Eleusis, where the Eleusinian Mysteries were based—that was a cult devoted to the goddess Demeter, you know that, right?"

"No, but go on." Johnny wondered where she was going with all this.

"Well, I'm rather fond of the goddess Demeter for obvious reasons, so this guy is one that I knew a bit about once upon a time, as he was said to have been initiated into that cult. Among other things, he's credited for having said some good things that have stood the test of time."

He thought he knew where she was headed now. "Like?"

"Like: 'In every tyrant's heart there springs in the end this poison, that he cannot trust a friend.'"

Johnny repeated it to himself and let it roll around in his mind.

"If you let all this break you," she said, "if you stop trusting people, you *will* become a tyrant."

He straightened, standing taller. "I trust *some* people. Like you. But there're so many new people that have come into my world all of a sudden. I don't really know them. Because of my rank I don't know if I'll ever know the real them, if I'll see their true motives, y'know? I don't want to simply trust everyone and risk the people I care about getting hurt."

Demeter stood before him with all the ferocity of a lioness in her eyes. "My granddaughter has been nearly killed how many times since she got involved with you and that vampire?"

Johnny's chin dropped shamefully.

"Right now she's stuck in a meditation downstairs. You"—she poked him in the chest—"were here. I bet she saw Menessos tonight, too. *He* resides an hour away." She shuffled a step forward. Johnny eased a step back. "*He* is accustomed to the night, and more than normal stress." She gained another few inches on him, and Johnny retreated again. "*He* can use magic. *He* could probably have fixed this . . . but you called *me. I* had to get my ass out of bed in the middle of the night and come home to fix this."

Johnny could say nothing. She was right.

Demeter put her hands on her hips. "Hate him if you have to, Johnny. Hate him because he wants her and you feel threatened by that. But trust *him,* damn it. You three have to trust each other if any of you hope to survive this."

She brushed past him and headed down the steps.

Johnny followed. "Hey, I didn't mean to piss you off."

"You didn't." On the second floor, she walked into Red's bedroom and lifted a tray off the bed. Demeter had obviously gathered some spell supplies from Red's stock. She must have come up to the attic after listening to him play awhile.

He followed her into the bedroom. "But—"

Demeter turned with the tray in her hands. "I'm not angry with you for calling me or bringing me here. Am I tired? Yes. Cranky? Hell, yes. I want to be here, but you didn't think about who else was at your disposal. Or did you? Did you decide you didn't want him to come to the rescue?"

Johnny admitted, "I didn't even consider him."

Demeter pushed the tray at him. "You carry this. You're steadier than I am."

"Your knees okay? You want me to go first so you can hold my arm?"

"I'm fine," she grumbled and descended the main stairs, gripping the handrail tight. Near the bottom, where the rail was broken, she paused and moved closer to the wall and let her hand slide along it to steady herself.

When she reached the bottom she stepped around the hole in the floor and looked back up at him. "C'mon." She waved. "You better help Mountain get this mess cleaned up before the others get here."

"If they're coming from Cleveland we have an hour."

She snorted again. "You can put the pedal to the metal in that race car of yours all you want, young man, but a broomstick will beat you every time."

CHAPTER FORTY-SEVEN

Goliath directed Vinny and two other guards to remain in the accounting office with Talto, who, despite being alarmingly weakened by Menessos's feeding, had been securely bound to a heavy steel-framed office chair. He'd even insisted the wheels be removed from the chair.

As they descended to the ground level Goliath ordered three guards to rush to the front and check for signs of Ailo's leaving. "If none are found, take positions to contain her. Use the utmost care to see that the child is not harmed," he added. The last three guards were to continue with him and Menessos to the suite of the Erus Veneficus.

He studied Menessos as they ran through the haven. His former master had wiped his face on his sleeve, but smears of Talto's blood still tainted his features. He'd gifted the child *and* relinquished their bond in one night. Either of those feats singularly would have been all any other vampire could hope to accomplish in one night; having achieved both was astounding.

And now this.

Having fed from two Beholders as well as having taken a risky amount of blood from Talto had done much to restore Menessos—but that recuperation was merely physical. By tapping into the ley line, one could empower their magical self like using a highly caffeinated energy drink to fuel the physical body. The line provided a rapid burst, not something that was sustainable as "normal." As with the perks of the beverage, the energy borrowed from the ley line was expended at a faster rate, and in the end, the ley lines tended to take more than they gave, depleting something intangible, exhausting the spirit as well as the body.

Goliath hoped that what Menessos had consumed would prove to be enough to get him through this night. If Ailo was gone, his former master was going to have to work magic again, and utilize that bond created between him and the sisters to find her or bring her back.

Making it worse was the fact that there was little time left before the dawn.

They crossed the house of the theater, seeing several chairs toppled and a table overturned. *She's looking for a weapon,* he thought. The metal furniture would require more time than she had to tear it apart.

They arrived in the backstage area where Vinny had earlier sat on duty. The door to the Erus Veneficus's suite was open. Smoke was pouring out of it. Something was burning inside; golden light flickered within.

Menessos rushed up the steps. Goliath was on his heels.

As they charged across the room, it seemed everything was in flames. The room was destroyed anyway, furniture overturned and broken. Glass and scraps of fabric dotted the floor. The couch was in flames, as were the countertop and stools to the right, the curtains in the back. The stink of all that was burning filled his nostrils, but under it all, he smelled blood.

Beside him, Menessos slowed. A glance revealed

Risqué lying behind the couch. Knowing Menessos would handle it, Goliath pressed on to the back, where Beverley had been sleeping.

The flames had not reached the bed. He threw back the covers and found it empty. He dropped to his knees to check beneath it. He scrambled up and threw back the closet door. He spun to the bathroom and nearly ripped the door from its hinges as he opened it. Not finding her, he rushed back to Menessos.

"She's not here."

The guards ran through the main door, each with a fire extinguisher in hand. They had the flames out in seconds.

"I'll tend to Risqué," Menessos said. "You get Ailo." He called to one of the guards, "Get a doctor in here!" The guard nodded, clanging and clomping down the metal stairs.

Goliath didn't leave. Instead, he grabbed a torn throw pillow, ripped off the rest of the top, and applied pressure to Risqué's side with it.

Menessos cradled her head in his hand and stared into the half-demon's face. "I should have had her slay them. Not bind them to me." His gaze strayed to one of the barstools near the kitchen, to the splintered and jagged edge of the wooden leg that had broken off. "I cannot slay Ailo now that she is bound to me."

"Hindsight," Goliath said. "But you can use that binding to find Ailo or track her, can't you?"

Menessos nodded.

"You find Ailo and let me tend Risqué," Goliath said. "By the time I get her to the infirmary, you'll have the information, and then we will go collect Beverley . . . and do what needs to be done." He was no longer bound to Menessos; he could easily slay Ailo.

Menessos rose to his feet.

Liyliy had known by the exterior of the dingy little hotel that their driver had secured for them—a drab, blue-gray siding above brickwork—that she was not going to be staying in opulent accommodations for the day. She'd glared at Giovanni before entering. He'd said, "They will not search for us here."

Now as she stood staring out the window at a world that was yet sleeping, she tried to think on the news she'd been given this night, but the last few hours before dawn seemed to pass so swiftly. The Death that awaited weighed on her like lead.

"Adam will keep us out of the light and make sure no one enters," Giovanni assured her.

She glanced away from the window to their driver. *Adam.* She hadn't known his name before. He was an older man, plain, trying to dress younger than his years in a solid-colored sweatshirt and jeans. *He'll probably gag us to silence our waking screams as well.*

"I am going for a walk," she said. Her silken gown transformed into gray pants, a warm shirt, and a hooded coat. She worked to make the fabric lose its sheen in favor of a drab, aged dirtiness. Her shoes changed from sandals into full-covering slippers.

"Would you like company?" Giovanni offered.

The gruff sound of his voice grated on her nerves. "No. I will return shortly." She shut the door behind her.

Leaving the parking lot for the sidewalk, she turned left, heading toward a place called Family Dollar. The air was cold, but it felt good inside her lungs. She imagined it freezing all the little emotions in her heart, and when she breathed out, forcefully, she hoped those feelings were expelled with the air.

She could not afford even a small sentimental notion for Meroveus. She would walk until she was certain that he had been purged from her thoughts . . . or she would burn in the rising sun. For if she could not release this mawkishness, she could never achieve her vengeance.

When the darkened store was well behind her, her phone rang.

She thought it would be Giovanni insisting she return . . . but it was Ailo.

"Yes, Sister?"

"Liyliy!" Ailo's voice was strained, hurried and breathless. "I have the girl. I'm outside the haven. I don't know what to do! I don't know where to go."

Her words tumbled out so fast, Liyliy could hardly understand them. When they registered, she stopped in her tracks. "You have the girl and have fled the haven?"

"Yes, yes! Menessos will soon discover my deceit. He'll use his binding to find me or compel me back. The girl roused, but she struggled and I wrapped her up in the *telavivum*. Now she won't wake."

"You wrapped her in your living web?"

"Yes. I had to keep her from screaming."

"Did you read her?"

"No. There's been no time. When I fled she was co-cooned in fabric."

Liyliy's mind was racing. "You haven't killed her, have you? She breathes yet?"

Ailo snapped, "Yes, she is breathing!"

With the power this child allegedly possessed, wrapping her in the strange fabric that clothed them was dangerous . . . no. Magic wrapped in magic. It might be the only thing keeping Ailo safe at the moment. "Have you unwrapped her fully?"

"No. Maybe I should. Maybe then she'd wake—"

"No! Ailo, whatever you do, do *not* unwrap her. In fact, make sure she is covered up as much as possible. Do not touch her bare flesh. Do not read her. Do you understand me? It is very important that you do not touch her or unwrap her."

"But, Sister, if she wakes, she could break this binding from me."

"No, Ailo. Do not risk it."

"I would not have to worry that Menessos would compel my return."

Liyliy hesitated. *"Ailo."* She used the tone that said she was the dominant one.

"I need your help. Please, please. Say you are coming. Say you will keep Menessos from luring me back."

"I am coming, Ailo."

"Promise that together we will make her awaken, so I will be free."

Liyliy realized Ailo had not mentioned their other sister. "What about Talto?"

"She is yet within the haven. We must save her."

She sympathized with Talto's predicament, but now that the child was out of the haven, this was Liyliy's one chance and she had to make it count. "Where are you?"

"I've kept out of sight as much as I could, but carrying the child and having to stay to the shadows is making progress slow. I am walking north-northwest on . . . East Third Street. Do you know this city? Where can I go and meet you?"

Liyliy did not know the city well, but she had seen it well from the sky. North-northwest . . . to the north were a series of parks. "Do you see trees before you? A grassy area?"

"Yes. But bare trees give little cover."

"Go toward the lake, Ailo. There are benches and monuments there. Find somewhere to hide until I arrive."

"Hurry, Sister." Ailo hung up.

Liyliy placed the cell phone into her pocket and called upon the cursed owl within her. The quicksilver retreated into a thick cuff around her left ankle. The phone dangled from a silken pocket attached to the anklet. She screamed and fell to her knees as her body reconfigured itself, grew in size and sprouted feathers. When the form was complete—save the scarring and injuries—she took to the sky, heading back into the city she had moments ago fled.

Though her owl eye saw better in the dark, her field of vision was markedly decreased, and not being able to call on her aura in the same way made judging distances—and landings—tricky.

CHAPTER FORTY-EIGHT

Johnny and Mountain lugged the broken tabletop into the garage, then out the man-door, and leaned it against the back of the garage. It was still very dark and cold outside. The sun wouldn't rise until about seven twenty. "What witches are coming?" Johnny asked as he and Mountain returned to the kitchen.

"I'm not sure," Demeter said. She was standing at the sink watching Red, who sat unmoving as she had been for hours. "I called the High Priestess. I told her to bring at least two witches with her. She will choose wisely."

He grabbed the broom and dustpan and began sweeping up the splinters and wood debris. "What exactly will you do?"

"You ever hear the old witch saying, 'To Know, To Do, and To Be Silent'?"

"Nope," he said.

"It's a good policy."

Johnny kept sweeping. He glanced up when she didn't elaborate. "That 'be silent' part means you're not going to tell me."

"Nope," she mimicked him.

He pulled the dustpan off the broom and handed it to Mountain, then switched and gave the big man the broom. Johnny knew he could crouch to hold the dustpan more easily than either of the two people with him.

When that chore was done, Johnny dumped the pan

into the garbage and Mountain started sweeping the area near the door. Johnny joined him, watching him push the fragments and pieces into a pile. When they were done, there were footsteps on the front porch followed by a brisk knock on the door.

"Demeter," Johnny called as he carried both the broom and dustpan to the kitchen. "They're here."

She passed him in the hall as Mountain answered the door. Johnny dumped the dustpan a second time, then returned to the doorway so he could see what was going on without going too far from Red.

Though Demeter's back was turned to him, he could immediately feel tension radiating off her.

Mountain had plodded into the living room to be out of the way, but the women weren't chattering happy greetings. It could have been the early hour or the situation with Red sobering the moment, but that wouldn't explain the silent hostility at the other end of the hall.

He recognized the pretty witch in front as Hunter Hopewell, the new High Priestess of the Cleveland Covenstead. He knew her because Lycanthropia had played at the Hallowe'en Witches' Ball, her first coven event with her new title. She'd flirted heavily with him at the gig before she'd realized he was with Persephone.

Beside her was a witch with long, straight white hair. Vilna-Daluca—an Elder witch who was far from being a cookie-cutter copy of Oz's Glinda the Good Witch of the South. He'd last seen her when she crossed paths with him and Red at the police station in Valley City. The agents from SSTIX had taken them there to question them about events on the shores of Lake Erie. Though Vilna had gotten Red out of there pronto, she hadn't exactly done so out of friendship. According to what Red had told him, Vilna blamed her for another witch's death. The dead witch—Xerxadrea—was Vilna's cousin or something. And she had left him sitting in the police station.

Last was a witch who wore her white hair in a bun atop her head. This one, however, didn't have a title. She was Lydia, the witch who'd sold this farmhouse to Red a few years back. He remembered her from when the witches put wards up around the property. She and Demeter had some kind of unsavory history.

That explained the rigidity in Demeter's shoulders.

"Ladies . . ." he said, gaining the attention of all of them.

"Hey, I know you," Hunter said. "One day you're in a rock band . . . the next you're the Domn Lup." Her smile was friendly—but not more than that.

"Yeah." He would have preferred she not bring that up, but since she had, and since his status should be respected by these witches, he did not hesitate. "You're all here to help Red, right?" He looked from Demeter to Lydia and back.

"Of course." Hunter nodded. No one else spoke.

He crossed his arms and let each of these women see his defensive concern. "Then, let's get some things straight. According to Red, her last encounter with Vilna didn't exactly reek of friendship." He looked Vilna-Daluca squarely in the eye. "I want her safe, so I'm not sure I want you involved."

Vilna started forward. "Hear me, Wolf King—"

Either the belligerence in her tone or Johnny's

statement must've triggered something in Demeter. She sidestepped into Vilna's path, blocking her.

"The fact is that the Eldrenne is dead because of her! I have my opinions about Persephone and I'm entitled to them, but the High Priestess asked me to come. I am honor bound to do what I can to assist, an' it harm none, and that's exactly what I'll do."

The hall was silent for a moment, as Demeter shot a glance at Johnny that he took to mean she hadn't known about those particular details he'd revealed. She faced Vilna and said, "Make oath to that."

Vilna-Daluca tapped her lip, thinking for a moment. She stepped around Demeter and strode to the kitchen, walking along the counter with her palm hovering above it. She stopped before a drawer, opened it, and removed a knife. After deftly slicing both of her index fingertips and rinsing the blade in the sink, she used the bleeding wounds to draw on her palms with the blood. She made an F shape, with the bars normally horizontal turned downward instead. She held them aloft for all to see.

"Ansuz grant power to my words! Vár, daughter of Asgard, handmaiden of Frigga, goddess of oaths, hear my vow this night! Erinyes, those who punish whosoever swears a false oath, hear my vow this night! Before these mighty witnesses, I say this: I have come to assist and aid Persephone Alcmedi in this predicament. All my actions, all my words, all my thoughts will be focused on that deed until I leave this house. May the Erinyes exact their wrath upon me if I break this oath." Vilna lowered her arms. "Satisfied?"

"Quite," Demeter said.

"And secondly," Johnny cut in before anyone else could speak, "are you"—he pointed at Lydia—"and Demeter going to be able to keep this friendly?"

The two old women eyeballed each other. Neither spoke.

Hunter put her index finger in the air. "From here on out, I vow that if I ever make requests of witches to assist in a situation, I will not base them merely on rank"—she glared at Vilna—"and proximity." She glared at Lydia. "I will, however, ask if there are any conflicts of interest I should know about."

Johnny nodded approval of that vow. "Demeter?"

"It's my granddaughter in need. Of course I'll keep it friendly."

"Lydia?" Hunter asked.

"I wouldn't have come if I didn't intend to help Persephone."

"Good enough for me," Johnny said. "Now, come this way. She's back here."

As they moved from the hall, Lydia caught sight of the damage. Hunter must have been blocking her view of it before. "What on earth happened to this floor? And the stair railing?"

Everyone stopped.

Demeter turned. "I'll explain later. We've already spent enough time talking. Persephone needs our help." She started for the kitchen again.

Johnny stepped out of their way to give them room in the kitchen. Demeter explained that she believed Persephone had been stuck in a meditation—for several hours.

While she spoke, Hunter and Vilna listened and observed Red's position. Lydia, however, strolled around the kitchen with her thin arms crossed, noting the damage to the floor, the walls, the phone. She looked irritated.

"What do you have in mind?" Hunter asked.

"Sorcery," Demeter said.

"Unwise," Lydia countered.

Demeter shot her a nasty look but before anyone could rebuff Lydia's comment, Vilna-Daluca cut in. "What would you suggest, Demeter?"

"If you three can triangulate a ley line flow between you, then you can create a secondary barrier, and I can walk through her meditation barrier."

"Very unwise," Lydia said.

Demeter spun on the old woman. "If you don't want to do anything but cast your negativity around, you can cart your ass back home and I'll put the man inside the circle." She gestured at Johnny.

Lydia looked him up and down. "So it's safe to say you don't have a problem with wærewolves anymore?"

"Lydia," Vilna warned.

Lydia ignored her. "Or is he acceptable because he's your granddaughter's man? Or because he's not bothered by our magic? Maybe it's because he's especially powerful, being the Domn Lup and all."

Demeter's face was vibrantly red as she stepped closer to Lydia. Johnny had seen her worked up before, but not like this. Hunter looked from the older women to Johnny and her expression was clearly asking: *Now what?*

He shrugged. He hadn't known Demeter ever had a problem with wærewolves; she'd always been good to him.

"Ladies." Vilna put a hand on each of their shoulders.

"Leave the past in the past because presently, we have to save Persephone." She squeezed Lydia's shoulder. "Are you capable of utilizing sorcery?"

"I can," she answered defensively.

"Are you willing to use it?"

Lydia hesitated. "Yes."

"Do I need to request an oath of you to keep you focused on the task at hand?"

Lydia pouted. "No."

"Then we proceed with Demeter's plan." Vilna removed her hands from the other woman's shoulders and nodded at Demeter. "Go on."

Demeter stepped away from the Elder and stood before Persephone. For a long minute the room was silent.

"Demeter?" Hunter finally dared.

"She's beginning to fade."

"What?" Johnny asked, pushing closer.

"There are circles forming under her eyes. They weren't there when I arrived."

He crouched to inspect. She was right. "What does this mean?" he asked, voice tight.

"Time is not on our side or hers," Vilna-Daluca said.

"We cannot risk severing the connection that guides her return," Demeter said.

Concern had gripped Johnny's gut, but this was getting worse by the minute. "Her return? She's meditating . . . right?"

Demeter faced him. "It's a meditation, but it's also part astral travel."

Remembering when he and Red had used Great El's slate, and the meditation-like journey she had guided him through, Johnny wondered if they were different.

He'd felt like he'd traveled to the center of his soul, not to some outward place.

"Astral travel. That's projecting your spirit outward, like an out-of-body experience, isn't it?"

"Yes."

"I'm confused. I thought meditation was inward," he said.

She smiled at him. "Meditation often involves self-examination in the serenity you find inside your own soul. But the soul isn't like the physical body, it is mobile in ways that do not involve the gravitational pull of this planet."

He squinted at her. "Still confused."

"There's no up and down in the soul. There's no left or right. No forward and backward. There is only the motion of the will. She doesn't project out from her body. She projects out from her soul, into dimensions that do not exist in the reality we know."

"Seriously?" Vilna-Daluca asked.

Demeter turned back to Seph. "She could do it since she was little. She creates a place and goes there. Totem animals have guided her through many lessons."

"How little?" Vilna asked, incredulous.

"Seven or eight."

"You mean she's *viator*?"

The accent Vilna placed on her last word made Johnny certain it was foreign. Italian or Latin if he had to guess.

Demeter said, *"Virago."* After a pause she turned to Vilna and added, "She's not an average witch. She *is* the Lustrata."

"Someone is spoiling for a fight," Lydia muttered.

"No," Demeter said, not taking her eyes from the Elder. "I know she is, and I know that she wouldn't simply get lost or stuck in a meditation. Some*thing* is keeping her there, keeping her spirit away from her body."

"Do you know anything about her current totem? That could be helpful," Hunter said.

Demeter shrugged and shook her head no. They all turned to Johnny.

He copied Demeter's reaction. "She never talked specifics about her meditations. Would her totem not let her leave?"

"No, no." Hunter clarified, "If she is being kept in a meditation against her will, it wouldn't be her totem's doing. But if we knew the name we could attempt to contact it to learn what was going on. Without a name to call to her exact totem we are not going to find it."

"Good point. If I can touch her forehead," Demeter said, "I can find her totem's name."

"Okay," Hunter said. "So we are going to triangulate a circle of ley line energy around you and Persephone, then you break her circle and we contain it while you learn the totem's name, and then meditate and contact it for advice. When you come out of your meditation, you'll know what to do. Is that the plan?"

"Sounds good to me," Demeter said.

"We might have to hold the ley energy a long time," Lydia said.

"Are you able?" Vilna asked.

To Johnny's eyes, Lydia looked worried, but she nodded. He wasn't comfortable with the notion that, ultimately, he was entrusting Red's safety to the frail-looking old woman's ability to hold a ley line.

CHAPTER FORTY-NINE

I stared at the throne, then at the handsome man kneeling beside it. This was all wrong, but I could not put my finger on why. Drowning in frustration, I could no longer see clearly as my eyes welled with tears. "I do not remember!"

He stood and enfolded me in warm, comforting arms. "Oh, my love, your memory will return. I am confident you will remember me soon."

"But—"

He put a finger to my lips. "Shhhh."

I almost protested, but let that idea go with a sigh.

His finger trailed to my cheek, wiping away my tears. "May I kiss you, my love?"

My feet wanted to retreat, but I held them rooted here. "You didn't ask before," I replied.

"You shied away before."

I bit my lip, but did not offer an apology.

"I understand, love. You do not remember me. But those kisses I gave you earlier were not the type of kiss I want now. So I am asking . . . may I?" His eyes searched mine. Underneath the hope and adoration in his expression, there was a hint of sadness.

Pressing my lips to his was not an unpleasant notion, except for the doubts inexplicably clinging to my heart. Perhaps if I kissed him, the flame of familiarity would ignite and I could remember our love. *Or maybe the unfamiliarity would redouble my misgivings.* I weighed the options. "You may," I said.

Aidon put his mouth to mine. It was a trembling kiss, like a first brush of lips. That he did not immediately take the liberty of a full-on, happily-married-for-many-years lip-lock made me soften to him. He at least understood my perspective.

When the kiss grew bolder, I did not resist. Though my eyes were closed I could feel warmth surging within me like summer sunshine. And yet . . . there was something arid about this warmth, something coarse scouring me like desert sand. Then his voice echoed through my mind, whispering, *You are safe here. All will be fine.* When he broke away, I believed those words and all my worries had faded.

"Too much?" he asked.

"No. Just right."

He smiled. "More?"

All will be fine. I nodded.

This time, his tongue found mine. He tasted of blood oranges. His hands roamed, hot on my arms, teasing under my breast, tingling along my spine.

For an instant his lips left mine and he gestured at the regal furniture behind us. Even as I turned to see what had drawn his attention, the seats slid together, melding into something more like a chaise lounge than a throne. The air around us shimmered and black velvet curtains hung in a circle in midair, providing privacy. A single black marble pillar appeared beside the chaise, and a three-wick amber candle flickered atop it.

I was amazed! "How did you do that?"

"Magic, love. You can do it, but you've forgotten how."
Aidon sat, pulling me down beside him.

I can do such things?

He deposited a series of kisses on my neck, which
were quite arousing, but his warm breath caused a chill
to run down my spine. "I'll teach you everything again if
I have to."

He unfastened the clasps of his vestlike shirt and discarded the garment, then resumed kissing my neck.

My head fell back and my eyes shut as desire trickled
through me. My hands explored the contours of his chest.
Had I known many men? Was this . . . husband . . .
my only lover?

His deft fingers caressed between the ribbons at my
back as he kissed his way down my neck, avoiding the
tender burns. His affection concentrated on the upper
mounds of my breasts.

Heat was rising within me.

"Whatever you wish, my love," Aidon said between
kisses, "by my hand, you shall have it." He stood, lifting
me with him. He closed the distance between us, jerking
me into his arms and wrapping me in his strength. He
kissed my lips again, rough and delicious, and I was locked
in a longing I could not escape, and did not want to.

My hands ran along his back. His body was like
stone, every muscle so hard. I squeezed his backside, and
he bit my lip gently as he growled encouragement.

This moment had all the titillating arousal of the
touch of a stranger, but it was mingled with the security
of a committed relationship and an inherent knowledge
of what pleasure our bodies could create.

He broke the kiss and I instantly yearned for more.

Lust had laid claim to me, but I fought to catch my breath and regain control of my passions.

"Can you feel the storm within you, my love?"

"Yes."

"Can you feel the blaze burning in your soul?"

How did he know? "Yes!"

"Is the flood filling you up?"

"What is happening?"

"You are so close. . . ." He took my thumb into his mouth and sucked on it. *"Malek tsalmaveth."* He switched to the other thumb. *"Basilissa nekros."*

The sensation was strangely wonderful.

"Call your mantle."

"My mantle?"

"Close your eyes. Look inside yourself. There is a light within you, an armor that glows."

My eyes shut obediently. I tried to see within . . . to feel a storm, a blaze or a flood. "I can't find it."

He kissed my palm, my wrist. Working his way up my arm to the inner spot on my elbow, he then moved back to my neck.

"Don't stop," I begged.

"Search deep, my love. Follow the desire deep into this body, then fall into it, fall deep into the sensations rising in your soul. There you will find the light." He squeezed my hands.

And there it was. At the instant I found it, I felt brightness shine out from me.

He gasped. "Yes. There it is, my love. Now hold on to it. Open your eyes."

Silvery light twinkled around us. It was beautiful.

He rubbed his thumbs in circles against mine. "This is how you command fire, love. Right here. In your thumbs."

"I *command* fire?"

"You do. Now choose something to burn. You do not command all the elements yet, so you have to be in contact with something to make it blaze, but since I am here with you, you can push your will through me . . . and burn it without direct contact."

After looking around, I chose the curtains. Focusing on them, I cast my demand down my arms, into my thumb, and passed it to his.

Flames licked over the curtains. The fire gave off heat and light, but did not consume the fabric.

Aidon reviewed my handiwork with an expression of satisfaction. "You are a quick study, my love." He pressed his lips to mine again.

CHAPTER FIFTY

"Wait," Johnny said, facing Demeter. "What if you get stuck in the meditation, too?"

He watched her carefully as she considered the question he had posed like a weapon.

"I don't mean any insult," he added when she hesitated, "but she's the Lustrata and she's stuck. What makes you think you won't get stuck?"

She lifted her chin and set her shoulders. "That won't happen."

"How can you be so sure?" Hunter asked.

"Because. Whatever is interfering with her is doing so because she is the Lustrata. My insignificance means I won't get ensnared."

Johnny shot a glance at Hunter, who passed it to Vilna like a hot potato. Vilna's face twisted into a rather displeased expression, but she nodded. "She has a point."

"Let's do this," Demeter said. She scooted the tray of supplies on the counter closer to her and took up a position near Red.

Hunter sat on the floor and took her shoes off. "So we're clear, Domn Lup: Are you going to be inside the circle or outside of it?"

Johnny shrugged. "Demeter?"

"Doesn't matter, I guess. You can be in if you want to, but I don't foresee there being anything you can do."

"Outside," he said.

"All righty, then." Hunter now had her socks off as well. "You keep your eyes on Persephone and let us know if at any time the magic makes you so uncomfortable you have to leave the area." She cuffed the ends of her pants up. Pulling bracelets adorned with little colored stones from her pockets, she hooked them around her ankles. Then she stood.

"Use this." Demeter lifted a pouch of what looked like petals from the tray and handed it to her.

Hunter sniffed it. "Apricot? Honey? What is this?"

"A mix of agrimony and arbutus petals," Demeter said.

"Ah," Vilna added. "Good choices."

"Why?" Hunter asked. "I use herbs, but I don't recall ever having used agrimony before . . . or arbutus."

"Probably not, dear." Lydia joined their conversation. "Agrimony is best for reversing spells, breaking hexes, and banishing negative entities. Arbutus is used for exorcisms."

"Hold on a minute," Johnny interrupted. "Banish negative entities? Exorcisms? What the fu—fudge is going on?" He changed his expletive at the last, considering who was present.

"Precautions," Demeter answered. "It's helpful, not all-inclusive. We don't know what we're dealing with."

"You said she was stuck in a meditation."

"She is."

"You didn't say the something that was keeping her there might be an evil entity."

"There's no way to know if that's the case until I

speak with the totem, so I'm covering the bases should this be a worst-case scenario. Now step back and let us get on with this."

Begrudgingly, he returned to his spot in the doorway.

With the broom she rode in on, Hunter swept a counterclockwise circle around Red, saying, "With this broom, I sweep all negativity away." The witches moved inside the circle. "Let positive energy flow that our efforts may be pure."

"So mote it be," Demeter said. Vilna-Daluca and Lydia echoed the statement.

Hunter laid her broom on the floor. She took the incense stick Demeter had lit for her in one hand, and the four stones she had gathered in the other. She closed her eyes for a moment and turned in a circle. She stopped and pointed. "North is this way?"

"Yes," Demeter said.

Starting at the north, Hunter walked a clockwise circle this time. She made one slow circuit, letting the smoke waft from the end of the incense. On the beginning of the second go-round, she crouched to place a stone at the eastern point. "Elements of air, of the east, guard this circle and breathe into us the breath of life."

When she rose she did not walk to the next point, she danced to it. He noticed that she moved with the confident balance of a trained dancer. He also noted that she had cute feet; her toenails were painted a dark red, the bracelets were draped at sexy angles, and the stones tinkled when they struck together.

She placed another stone. "Elements of fire, of the south, guard this circle and warm us with the heat of life."

When she rose up, she twirled, then arched her back,

lifting the incense up high. Her hips swiveled and her body swayed. Another spin brought her to the next point and another stone was set upon the floor. "Elements of water, of the west, guard this circle and bathe us in the liquid of life."

When she rose again, she seemed even deeper into the ritual. She had passed him when drawing the circle and he was sure she was no longer aware of his presence. Red and he had talked about magic many times. She'd told him that, for some, the casting of a circle was merely an act of protection. For others, it was like drawing a curtain around the circle, a curtain that transported them out of this world and into the etheric world. If he had to guess, he'd have said Hunter belonged to the latter.

Hunter positioned the last stone. "Elements of earth, of the north, guard this circle and tread with us the terrain of life." She rose and Demeter put a wand into her open hand. "This circle is cast and sealed," she said, making one final ring around with the tip of the wand pointing at the circle she'd swept and danced already. "The elements are present. Lord and Lady, hail! I call to thee. Hear me, Goddess, She who walks alone in the spaces in between, maintain the balance of power we are about to invoke. Aid us to bring your daughter home."

Vilna-Daluca, Lydia, and Demeter stood around Red, each a point of a wide triangle. As Hunter completed this circle casting, Demeter shuffle-stepped closer to Red, not breaking the water circle around her. Hunter took up the position Demeter had vacated.

"Vilna, since you have far more experience than I with ley lines," Hunter said, "I defer to you for the sorcery portion."

With a nod, Vilna accepted the black pillar candle

that Demeter offered. When Hunter and Lydia also held their candles and Demeter had lit each one, Vilna began.

She didn't speak, but she hummed softly. Within seconds, the hair on the nape of Johnny's neck was rising. As she refined the melody, adding a note here and there, she let her voice grow louder. Lifting the candle to eye level, she stared at it intently and sang. Slowly, her right hand rose above her head, fingers curled as if she held a softball. A blue-purple orb of light swirled between her palm and fingers.

To her left, Hunter joined the melody, following it, then accenting it. She lifted her candle, focused on the flame, then raised her hand. When the flickering orb appeared in her hand, an arc-like lightning sprang from Vilna's to connect to Hunter's.

Last, Lydia began to sing. Her addition to the song was bold, fully formed from the first note. She belted her unique tune like it was the chorus of song she'd always known. She copied the position of the other witches and the orb flashed into her hand, followed by the lightning joining hers to Hunter's. A completing arc joined hers to Vilna's.

Blue-purple light filled the space within the circle Hunter had cast, shading the witches with a glow not unlike the black lights Johnny had seen at various clubs his band had played in.

He was listening to the witches' lovely, dark chant, and was rather fond of the strange melody, but he remembered he was to keep his eyes on Red.

God, she's going to hurt when she comes out of this. I'll carry her upstairs to a hot bubble bath, followed by a massage. Anything she wants.

Demeter reached into her pocket and pulled out a four-leaf clover. "Here goes," she said, and placed the clover on her tongue. She reached into her pocket again, and pulled out two stones. One she kept in her right hand, the other she transferred to the left. She slid her foot forward to the edge of the watery circle that protected Red.

With one last glance at him, she breathed deep and pushed her foot through the water.

CHAPTER FIFTY-ONE

Goliath supervised Risqué being moved onto a stretcher, then two Beholders lifted her and kept her level as they carried her down the steps from the court witch's suite.

One of the Beholders asked, "The new infirmary, boss?"

"Yes." When Ivanka had broken her arm, he'd decided it would be to their advantage to have a triage and small infirmary on-site to manage the occasional injuries his people incurred in the line of duty. The space that was formerly used to store stage props was reclaimed for this purpose.

He'd been so busy lately, he had not had time to check the progress. So, he followed the Beholders across the area behind the scrim.

He was only a few yards from the door when a strange smell met his nostrils and he stopped. Glancing around, he sniffed again. It was an oily odor. One present only when the service elevator was in use. "Continue," he ordered the guards.

Running to the gate, he saw the new hydraulic that had been installed; the car had gone up. To his best guess, it remained one level above the ground floor. He pressed the button to bring the car down. Impatient, he paced as the elevator returned, then entered, shut the gate, and pushed the button to lift him up.

When it dinged softly and stopped, he stood stock-still, listening, sniffing.

Ailo had come this way with Beverley.

He opened the gate and searched the area until he found a broken window.

Goliath rode the elevator down. When it stopped, he walked to the infirmary. Voices were coming from a hallway in the rear. He proceeded in that direction and found the hall had four doors. The voices were behind the last one—but lights were on in both of the rearmost rooms.

He peered into the second-to-last room and saw Mero in the bed. Seven stood to one side, watching as their esteemed guest fed from a Beholder's wrist. It was clear, even from a distance, that Mero had been severely beaten.

Goliath raised a brow at Seven; she made an irritated face at him and waved him on.

Looking into the last room, he saw Risqué—still on the stretcher that now rested on an exam table. Ivanka was holding a compress to Risqué's side.

Seeing him, Ivanka said, "I learn field medicine."

"The doctor we've employed is on her way."

"We have a doctor now?" one of the Beholders asked.

"Yes," Goliath answered.

"He give us this hospital," Ivanka said.

The Beholder grinned. "You're gonna make a fine Haven Master." The two Beholders left.

Sil entered seconds after they left. "What is going on?"

He nodded. "Too much to explain just now. You and Ivanka need to stay with Risqué."

Sil nodded and, for a moment, he and Sil stared at each other. Then he wrapped her in his arms and kissed her.

When their lips parted, he left the infirmary. It would take Menessos only a few minutes to locate Ailo and verify her getaway path; Goliath guessed his former master had nearly accomplished this task by now. Still, he had time. . . .

Goliath jogged to his own quarters, pulled off his formal jacket, and tossed it on a chair. Unbuttoning the collar of his shirt, he walked to the table near his bed and lit an incense stick. For a long moment he stood before it, focusing on his intention and breathing the sweet scent of juniper. "I will make sure she's safe, Lorrie. I promise."

A buzzing erupted from within his bedside table. Light seeped out from the edges of the drawer. He frowned. His phone was across the room in his jacket pocket. He pulled open the drawer and saw an old cell phone, folded shut. Persephone Alcmedi had given it to him.

The protrepticus.

His dead brother, Samson, had spoken to the court witch via this magical device.

He reached slowly for it, cautiously picked it up, and then turned it over.

The window on the phone's case face was lit up in a soft green. The caller ID flashing on the screen read: SAMSON.

Opening the phone, he held it to his ear. Tentatively, he said, "Hello?"

"I hope you're ready for all the shit coming your way, Haven Master."

"Samson?"

Silence.

"Samson?" He pulled the phone away from his ear and stared at it, but the screen was now dark.

CHAPTER FIFTY-TWO

Demeter felt her meditative self shift onto another plane.

This was not what usually happened when she sought a quick glimpse of insight by touching someone's head, but she didn't usually do this inside an empowered circle with the intention of delving into another's private realm.

She opened her eyes. *Of course. Nothing's going to go quite as planned.*

Persephone was no longer seated before her; the walls of the kitchen were no longer surrounding her. Instead, she stood before a willow tree at the edge of a lake.

She made a slow but complete revolution, viewing the whole of her new environment. It was a serene setting, green and fertile. The gentle lapping of the water was calming. The smell of wheat was carried on the breeze.

"Hello!" Demeter called.

Startled birds flittered out of branches, their protesting cries echoing back as they fled.

Demeter grumbled and crossed her arms.

Facing the lake once more, she wondered if the totem was a water creature. That would explain the proximity of the lake. She studied the surface, watching for a telltale splash. When no such sound occurred, her gaze was drawn to the island out in the lake.

Seeing Persephone's meditation world was insightful, but she could not shake the guilty feeling that accompanied this intrusive peek into her granddaughter's private space.

"Hello."

Demeter's crossed arms shot out defensively, startled by the voice. Spinning to face the sound, she saw a jackal standing not far away. Her breath caught. "Oh!"

The jackal must have sensed the unease she felt; he sat and pricked his ears forward. He even wagged his tail.

"I'm Demeter Alcmedi." She relaxed her shoulders as she spoke.

"I am glad to meet you, grandmother of the Lustrata. I am Amenemhab."

"Am-men-what?"

"Amenemhab."

"Got it." She nodded once, but wasn't going to try to say it aloud.

"You've come because Persephone is in danger." The wind picked up, cold.

"Yes." Demeter shuffled an urgent step forward. "What do you know of it?"

His head bobbed up and down in an odd canine version of a shrug. His ears lowered, lending him an expression of concern. "I sense the danger, but I know nothing of it. Whatever is happening, it is not happening here."

Wringing her hands, she asked, "Can you not move between planes and find out?"

The jackal's nose pointed at the lake, then the tree.

"This is her plane. I am here until she and I have accomplished all the tasks set before us. I can leave this place only then . . . or when her current physical body dies."

Demeter swallowed the lump in her throat that formed at his ominous words. "What can I do?"

The jackal's snout aimed downward and his paw rubbed his muzzle thoughtfully.

Before he could come to a conclusive thought, a trumpeting roar filled the air. He came to his feet and looked at the lake. The sound had caused Demeter to jump as well, and she turned, too.

Fog was now enveloping the small island and, as they watched, it billowed out across the lake. Clouds roiled in the sky, blocking out the sun. The surface of the lake changed from placid to choppy. The fog crawled over the surface, creeping closer with each moment. Demeter retreated from the water's edge.

A pair of black dragons emerged, yoked to a strange boat.

The next seconds passed in a rapid blur as the dragons emerged partially from the water and a woman wearing a hooded cloak stepped along the plank that stretched between the scaly creatures. A dragon lowered its neck and she descended gracefully to the shore. The woman walked directly up to Demeter. A wrinkled hand appeared from within the cloak and she raised it slowly. Thick, twisted knuckles bent, and cool ancient fingers touched Demeter's chin.

Demeter had been watching the hand, as the woman's face was hidden in the depths of her hood, but as she drew Demeter's chin up, the wind blew the hood back, revealing a kind old face with frightening dark eyes that could see the past, the present, and the future.

"Hecate."

The goddess smiled. "It has been a long time, Demeter Alcmedi."

Demeter's gaze dropped downward.

"Your granddaughter is ever finding herself in the path of danger."

"Because of you."

Hecate laughed. "Your grandmother blamed me for the antics of your youth as well." She sidestepped and began circling Demeter. "But then you, too, were willful, powerful, and stubborn." She paused to whisper, "It is a combination that wrought your bloodline. A combination that tests the soul, invites the notice of darker things, and entices the most tempting desires to your door." Her tone was sharp and cold, as if she spoke icicles instead of words.

"Can you help her?"

"I am helping her." Hecate began circling again. "Do you think I would allow all my plans to be foiled by Hades?"

At that name, Demeter's focus snapped back to the goddess. Her lungs expelled air like she'd been kicked hard. "Hades?"

Hecate stopped in front of Demeter. They locked stares for a few heartbeats. "She went in without the proper precautions. He took advantage of her mistake."

Demeter stood straight. "What are you going to do, Hecate?"

Hecate reached down and snatched Demeter's hands.

She lifted them up and examined each—the back, the palm, the fingers. When she released them she said, "Relax. I seek no bargain with you. I simply want Hades to stay out of my way." She turned away, extending her hand. One of the dragons lowered his head to accept her petting. Finally, she said, "Hades must be taught a lesson."

Hecate wrapped one hand around the horn protruding from the dragon's snout and dug the fingers of her other hand under one of the dragon's cheek scales. With a shout, she yanked it free. The dragon jerked and snorted a complaint with his long fangs bared, but she did not release the enormous creature or shy from its threat. She wiped the loosened scale over the place from which it had been torn, collecting blood on it. Turning her back on the dragon, she faced Demeter again. "Dragon's blood," she said. "The real thing." The liquid gleamed on the lustrous black scale. "Raise your hands. Palms up."

Demeter obeyed.

The goddess held the dragon's scale over each hand in turn, allowing blood to drip onto Demeter's skin. It was dark, dark red, and almost hot enough to burn. "Rub your hands together." She turned and shoved the scale back into place on the dragon's cheek. It grumbled a single note.

Staring at the thick blood smeared all over her hands, Demeter asked, "What is this for?"

"To provide you the strength to hold this." Hecate reached forward and a scythe suddenly appeared in the goddess's hands. She held it out, offering it to Demeter.

• • •

Johnny felt something pop like a bubble, and could see on the women's faces the strain they immediately felt. Seconds ticked away into minutes. Johnny watched the three chanting witches holding the circle, contained within their ley line force field. Lydia was clearly having trouble. Her old hands were shaking as if palsied.

Worried, he remained focused on her. Through three rounds of the chant, her volume lowered. On the fourth time, her voice cracked. Her voice began to rasp, sounding like she badly needed a drink of water.

He willed her to keep going, to have the stamina and the clarity of voice to continue, but on the fifth round, her voice began to falter altogether. Not sure if it would make any difference, he positioned himself behind Lydia and began to sing her part. Vilna looked at him, glanced down at his hands, then at Lydia's shoulders. He let his hands hover over the old woman's frail shoulders. His brows raised, silently asking Vilna if he was doing the right thing.

She nodded.

Johnny's hands lowered slowly, detecting a brittle, heated static before he made contact.

This is going to be bad. He breathed deep. When his hands were completely in contact with her, an electric shock gripped his hands and forearms. He held his breath, fighting to master the pain. Fur sprouted and his claws pushed out. The energy kept pushing higher up his arms, bringing the change with it.

He understood that by his joining their outer circle, the ley line energy was rerouting through him. It was pushing at him from both sides, trying to link. When he wrapped his head around that fact, he was able to release the tension in his muscles and allow the power to meet at his sternum. He itched as fur rose under his shirt, but once the new flow was established, he found he could revert the transformation. Lydia's rigidly held shoulders loosened. She fell silent.

Then Lydia's knees gave way.

CHAPTER FIFTY-THREE

Goliath slid into the backseat of the waiting limo and shut the door.

Beside him, Menessos said, "She is not far." The car pulled away from the curb, tires squealing. "She is hiding in Mall B, near a tree."

"Only four blocks away? Why are we bothering to drive?" Goliath wanted to tell Menessos about the protrepticus, about hearing Samson's voice, but there was no time. "What's the plan?"

"You get out at the corner of the mall, the car will take me closer to where she is hiding, and I confront her directly. The car waits while I try peaceably to get her to return, distracting her while you approach from another direction. You grab Beverley."

"Count on it."

When the car slowed to make the turn, Goliath exited, rolling into the street from a quickly opened and shut door without the car actually stopping. The late hour meant traffic was practically nonexistent. Menessos would be counting on Ailo to detect the car arriving, slowing near her.

It was a good plan.

But.

If he could slay the shabbubitu *and* safely remove Beverley from harm, he would.

Crouched, Goliath hurried in the direction opposite

that of the limousine, circling around to enter Mall B by a pedestrian path.

Malls A, B, and C were large landscaped areas, green oases open to the public. Mall B had the most trees. It also had a medium-height wall to reduce traffic noise from the nearby Shoreway.

In moments, he could hear Menessos's voice. He was pleading with Ailo to return to the haven. Near a tree, Goliath leapt over the wall and landed silently on the grass inside, keeping his body aligned with the tree's trunk.

As he assessed the situation, he noticed Menessos was remaining on the far side of the wall. Ailo was near the wall, with her back against some kind of stone monument shaped like a large square about three feet high and ten feet across. There were stone benches on three sides, and a tree on the other. There was considerable open space between them.

He started forward.

He was fifteen yards away from them when he saw a dark shadow racing ahead of him on the ground. He dived to the side and felt a razor-like talon scrape his ear.

The huge owl screeched and flapped her wings, raising up into the sky.

Goliath had hit the ground and started to roll as he saw Ailo come running into the open, screaming to the sky, "Take us, Liyliy! Don't leave! Take us!"

In her arms, Ailo cradled Beverley, who was mummy-wrapped in gray silk.

A glance at the sky revealed the large bird had circled around and was lining up for another flying dive. Her outstretched talons were open, ready to grab.

There's no fucking way she's going to pick them both up and fly out of here.

Lurching onto his feet, Goliath was racing forward before he was fully upright. From the corner of his eye he saw Menessos leap over the wall and hit the ground running as well.

Ailo turned and lifted one arm out, ready for the owl to grasp her. She had her other arm locked tight around Beverley. When she saw the two vampires advancing on her, a stripe of gray fabric fluttered out and wrapped tight around Beverley's neck. "Stay back or I'll wring her little neck!" Ailo cried.

"Ailo, no!" Menessos shouted.

Goliath sped up.

CHAPTER FIFTY-FOUR

Wide-eyed, Demeter shook her head and took a step back.

"I will send you to the place where they are, Demeter. Strike him with this."

"You want me to attack Hades? A *god*? Are you out of your . . ." Remembering whom she was addressing, Demeter's words trailed off and she ended by clearing her throat.

"If you want her back, his hold on her must be broken. My scythe will accomplish that. She cannot leave his realm otherwise."

Demeter could not move. Not only was the goddess offering up *Her* scythe, She intended for Demeter to wield it.

"Only this will save your granddaughter. Take it."

Demeter mustered her courage and reached shaking hands toward the scythe. Hecate's hands slid from farther down the shaft, allowing Demeter to assume a firmer grip. "Do you have it?"

Demeter nodded.

Hecate released the scythe.

The long blade was unexpectedly heavy. The tip crashed down, embedding in the muddy shore. Demeter maintained her hold, and grasped the shaft more firmly. She bent slightly as she tried to heft the blade from the mud. It shifted but she could not lift it. There was strength in her hands, in the dragon's blood on her skin, but her arms remained weak.

Hecate's hand rested on Demeter's shoulder. *"Falx portare."*

As the words were spoken it seemed to Demeter that she had become the axis point on which the world spun. Dizziness engulfed her. She leaned on the scythe for balance and concentrated on breathing. When the motion stopped, she opened her eyes and found she was standing on the dais of a great throne room.

Before her blazed a ring of fire. Within the circle of flames, a man and a woman lounged, embracing and locked in a passionate kiss. Hades and Persephone.

They didn't seem aware of her presence. The fire must have been blocking her out.

Or maybe the kissing is just that good.

Steeling her resolve, firming her grip, she readied herself to lift the scythe and charge forward. In her mind's eye, she saw herself doing it. She saw the scythe rising, the point taking Hades in the back.

"You are so beautiful, my sweet," she heard Hades say.

Demeter rolled her eyes. Her granddaughter was not going to follow in the footsteps of the goddess for whom she was named. Hades had tricked her, too.

Demeter murmured, "No way in Hell. Or any underworld," raised the scythe, and started forward.

As Lydia fell, Johnny grabbed her arms. Wax splattered across the linoleum as her candle wobbled this way and that. He never stopped chanting as he adjusted his stance so she could lean against him. She managed to lock her knees and maintain her hold on the candle and the lighted orb, but without his strength she wouldn't be holding either aloft. "Not much longer," she whispered.

Suddenly a blinding light emitted from the center of the circle. In its midst, engulfed in brilliance, were two figures. Were they Demeter and Persephone? Johnny had to shut his eyes against its radiance and for a moment he thought Lydia's weakness had broken the circle. Still, the other witches chanted on, so he did, too. The sensation of power and energy did not change. Surely, he hoped, that meant the circle remained strong and intact.

Blinking repeatedly, he willed his eyes to recover but he continued to be blinded by the glare. He heard the rush of wind from within the circle and he discerned Demeter's silhouette, hunched over but slowly standing straight. He squinted to see her better and realized that within the shaft of illumination Demeter was to his right, and Persephone—seated—was to his left.

There was a third figure, Pershephone was with someone. A man. Now Demeter was holding something aloft. Something large, raising it high.

A scythe.

CHAPTER FIFTY-FIVE

Goliath was racing toward Ailo when he saw Liyliy, in her owlish form, turn in the sky. She tucked her wings and rocketed toward them like a missile.

Ailo was backpedaling swiftly, holding Beverley up as if she were an offering to a sky god—but Liyliy's monstrous nature was far more demonic than godly. He could see the strip of cloth tightening around the girl's throat.

There were only seconds to save Beverley . . . save her from death or a fate worse than death with the shabbubitum.

With a few more steps and a leap he could place himself between the owl and the girl, and hope Menessos could use his ancient connection and mastery over her to compel Ailo not to strangle her.

As Goliath planted his foot, ready to propel himself up and into the huge owl's path, he saw Menessos with his shoulders hunched inward, arms down. His face was contorted with concentration, but his fingers were arched, and sparks danced from his palms. His lips were moving in a chant Goliath could not hear until Menessos shouted, "Ailo, fly!"

He's compelling Ailo.

Goliath had a millisecond to react, to decide if he would change his own plan. Or if Menessos, seeing him in action, would change his.

Before this night, Menessos had always been the master. He had always expected Goliath to defer to his will and his choices.

But even though so much had changed, Goliath could not cast away his faith in Menessos now.

The Haven Master slowed his momentum just as Ailo spun around. Her knees bent awkwardly. Her elbows straightened. . . .

Beverley fell from Ailo's arms, landing directly on top of Goliath as Ailo launched herself into the air, soaring over them as she hurled herself up and into Liyliy's path.

Liyliy, in her unnaturally large feathered form, was unable, or unwilling, to alter her trajectory as quickly. Her extended talons slammed into Ailo's body.

The shrill owl voice filled the night. She beat her wings so hard the branches of nearby trees shuttered in the turbulence. Either the unbalanced, unexpected weight of her sister was too much to carry or she was trying unsuccessfully to hover and not land. She forced her legs back and forth, first pushing then pulling, trying to extricate Ailo from her talons—but her long, hooked claws had plunged all the way through her sister's body.

Goliath tore his eyes from the horrific scene to examine Beverley. The silky gray fabric that still swaddled her was surely Ailo's, but it no longer seemed enchanted. The strip that had wrapped the girl's throat had slipped off and now lay dormant and unthreatening on the ground.

Liyliy continued bouncing along the ground, trying to resolve her predicament. More than once, her frantic and deadly movements came too close for comfort. Goliath rolled, placing Beverley behind him, shielding her with his body. He came to his knees and pulled her to him like an infant, then rose to his feet and fled.

Crouched behind the relative safety of a tree trunk, he watched the owl's desperate efforts end as Ailo was torn in half.

The giant owl, screaming miserably, flew into the night sky.

CHAPTER FIFTY-SIX

I pulled away from Aidon's kiss, breathless and content. Well, mostly content. I wanted him to touch me more. I wanted him to take my clothes off and make love to me while this magic fire burned around us. Yet even though my body was all need and desire, my mind . . . or perhaps my heart . . . was clouded with confusion. Being with Aidon felt so good, but, at the same time, there was something not "right" about it.

Out of nowhere, an old woman burst through the flames. She sliced the flaming curtain with a single stroke of a huge sickle and let the momentum of the blade draw her toward us, swinging the blade up for another strike.

Instinctively, I dived off the dais, sliding across the floor and rolling, coming up on my knees. The long, gauzy dress impeded my ability to stand and I stumbled, stepping on the skirt and hearing the fabric rip.

Beside me, Aidon rose to meet the threat. He twisted to the side, and the blade missed his chest by a hair-breadth even as his hands rose to snatch hold of the weapon's long handle.

He laughed at the old woman. "Hecate's scythe in the hands of a mortal?"

The old woman's face was set in determination. "Persephone, come with me now!"

She was looking at *me*. "Who are you?"

Her focus shot back to Aidon. "You cannot have my granddaughter."

He jerked the handle, pulling her forward and off balance. She cried out in pain. Aidon leaned down until his nose was practically pressed against hers.

As he spoke, I saw a man with dark wavy hair and thick markings around his eyes appear behind the old woman. Aidon couldn't have seen him or have known that the man gripped the end of the handle. But the old woman knew.

Aidon growled, "I don't need your blessing, you old hag, and I don't want your consent."

"Or, apparently, Persephone's, you immortal ass."

Squinting into the intense light, Johnny could barely see the action unfolding within it, but was determined to watch every moment, even if it blinded him.

He saw Persephone retreat as Demeter wielded the scythe. He saw the man rise and foil her effort. He saw the older woman, despite her resolve, about to fail. Knowing damn well he was shattering the circle, Johnny maneuvered Lydia away from his body and onto the floor, breaking the conduit of ley energy running through him. He knew this was a bad thing to do, and he hoped the remaining witches could reforge the circle around him—they were a High Priestess and an Elder, after all—but he simply could not risk doing *nothing*.

He shoved the ley energy to either side, ramming it into Hunter and Vilna. The force of it made them both stagger a step.

Free of the circuitous energy, Johnny stepped forward

into the light. In that split second, he bent and grasped the lower end of the scythe. Twisting it to angle the blade into a horizontal position behind the man, he yanked with all his might.

The scythe carved deep into the man's back.

Red screamed. Demeter stumbled and fell to the side. He tried to catch her but couldn't. The man was pitching toward him, across a wide lounge seat.

Behind the man, Red was racing forward, her expression full of confusion and concern. . . .

Concern for the fallen man?

Suddenly, Johnny was suffering the consequences of his actions. Waves of energy coursed through him. Feeling like he had shoved his finger into a light socket, he lurched backward and fell, half in and half out of the lighted core of the circle. All the air was propelled from his lungs by the brusque landing; he fought for the breath to scream, but even as he did, the cry shifted into a howl. Fur sprouted across his body only to retract and sprout again, retract and sprout, until his skin was raw. He writhed and convulsed, unable to escape the clutches of this power riding him.

Stupid thing to do. Stupid. Stupid.

Vilna-Daluca stood over the part of him that was out of the light. She was shouting mightily. Though his vision altered repeatedly from the transformations, he saw Vilna transfer her orb and candle to Demeter, who was sitting on the floor. Pain was evident in Demeter's expression.

Did I fuck everything up? Oh, Red. I'm so sorry.

The next thing he knew Vilna was sitting on his

stomach with one hand on his chest and one raised over her head—the lifted hand flickered and gave off lighted shards like an Independence Day sparkler.

For interminable minutes, she pulled power out of him, discharging it into the circle as Demeter and Hunter channeled it back into the ley. When finally the bright inner circle had faded and only the normal realm of the farmhouse kitchen remained, his transformations ceased. He lay with his eyes shut and listened as the witches shut down the connection to the ley line and took up the circle.

When it was done he lay still panting and not moving. Hunter helped the old witch climb off him and stand. When Vilna had her feet under her, Hunter kept hold of her arm and moved her away from him toward a chair. Vilna paused.

"You okay, Vil?" Hunter asked.

"Yes," the old witch grumbled, then she kicked Johnny in the ribs.

"Ow!"

Hunter dragged Vilna away from him.

"Serves you right," she called back. "You know better than to break a circle! And a circle drawing on the ley, no less. Fool! You could have killed us all!"

Johnny tried to sit up, and decided leaning on one elbow made breathing easier. Vilna settled into a dining room chair where she could still see him.

"You may be the Domn Lup," she grumbled, "but when there's magic being done, you damn well better respect those who are working it! It may seem like a flick of the wrist and a twitch of the wand, but that's the exterior. Calling the power, holding the power, shaping it and releasing it safely, properly, and with the right focus and direction takes skill. Takes energy. And the kind of power that is called up from a ley—hell, boy. You don't want to take the chance on loosing that kind of power."

She paused to breathe deep, and in that moment of silence heard a cough from behind him near the sink. Remembering Lydia and Demeter were both down, he rolled onto his other side.

Lydia lay unconscious to the left.

Demeter was on the right, scooting herself along the floor . . . to where Persephone lay, throwing up.

CHAPTER FIFTY-SEVEN

My throat was raw and the taste in my mouth was beyond vile. Hades's shredded finery had disappeared and, somehow, I was dressed in the jeans, shirts, and socks I'd left home in. I had aches like you wouldn't believe. But I was vertical, sitting at the big dining room table because my kitchen looked like a tornado had been through it. It was a mess—salt, candle wax, goddess knew what else was still strewn about. I didn't care. I was home.

Hunter sat across from me suffering a bad case of the yawns. Vilna was slumped next to her, trying to recover from a bout of sleep deprivation.

Nana sat in another chair, icing her knee. She'd re-aggravated her arthritis. Lydia, looking like she'd come back from the dead herself, leaned against the counter with a bruised hip and a wounded ego.

"What happened to you?" I asked Johnny, who had lifted his shirt to examine his side.

"Vilna kicked me."

After snorting a laugh I popped a couple of ibuprofen tabs into my mouth and washed them down with several swallows of milk. I remembered everything about my nightmarish evening—that was why I chose milk. *I may never drink water again.*

"Deserved it, too," Vilna grumbled.

She'd explained what Johnny had done to rescue me.

Her tone was 100 percent complaint, but somehow she also conveyed a sense of admiration for his "damnably foolish, dangerous" actions.

I was not going to think about any of it right now. There was plenty to ponder from the experience, but I wasn't ready to analyze anything yet—including what my next move as Lustrata would be. I'd already dealt with the devil—or close enough—and suffered for it. As for the deal I'd made with Hades, I had no idea if it still held, but I was far too wobbly right now to think about it—or much of anything else. Other than my bumps and bruises, staying so long in a meditative state had weakened me physically and mentally. And the time I'd spent with Hades seemed much longer than the few hours I'd been "gone" from my physical body. I guess in the underworld human time was irrelevant.

I was just happy to be home, happier still to know the vampires had found Beverley and that she was safe. Goliath's phone call had been brief—maybe too brief to be completely reassuring—but positive. I knew there was more to it, but I was told not to worry about the kiddo, she was in good hands and they'd bring her home soon.

I slugged down the last of my milk. Without a word, Johnny took the glass from my hand and sat it on the countertop. Looking at me with all the hurt and affection I could stand, he lifted me and carried me upstairs.

The entryway to my house was wrecked worse than the kitchen! "What the hell happened to my banister? To my floor?"

"Later. It's all fixable." He carried me up the steps easily.

When he tenderly placed me on my bed, I was more

grateful than I could express. He turned to the door and exited the bedroom. I heard the water running. When he returned to the bedroom, he picked me up again, carried me across the hall to the bathroom, and sat me gently on the edge of the tub. The thick scent of lavender bubble bath enveloped me as Johnny crouched before me and peeled the filthy socks from my feet, massaging as he did. Tartarus had been *hell* on my socks.

It felt so good, I *mmmm*-ed.

"I'll rub the rest of you all night long if that helps."

"The rest of me might be too sore to touch right now."

He nodded. "Stand up?"

I stood. He unfastened the button on my jeans. Reached for the zipper. I put my hands on his and he stopped. He met my gaze with a look I couldn't read, but which evoked my pity.

"I love you," he whispered.

I stared. *He said the "L" word.*

For a moment, the world was quiet and still.

Then Johnny jerked into motion again. "I know you've been through a crap ton of heavy emotional shit in the last few weeks, not to mention physical and mental duress." He worked my jeans down as he spoke. This time I was too stunned to protest or resist. "I don't expect you to say it back, I just . . . I wanted you to know." He'd dropped into a squat and held the ankles of the jeans as I stepped out. Unsteady, I nearly lost my balance, but he rose and caught me before I could put my hand to the wall for support.

Having just demonstrated my inability to do this

alone, he finished undressing me without my resistance. He even deftly twisted my hair up and clipped it before giving me his arm to steady me as I stepped into the hot, bubbly tub. I eased down into the wonderful water, letting its fragrant warmth surround me up to my neck. Glorious. I might never drink it again, but immersion was a different matter.

I lay back and relaxed while he excused himself. He hummed in my bedroom, a sweet melody, and I heard drawers opening, shutting as he gathered my pajamas.

Love.

A half hour later, I exited the tub. After wrapping up in my terry-cloth robe I staggered across the hall to lean in the doorway of my bedroom. Johnny had changed the sheets on my bed, turned the covers down, and fluffed my pillows. He helped me across the room—those ibuprofen had done little more than dull the pain.

I'd just sat down when I heard a knock downstairs on my front door. I heard people moving around, heard voices rise from the quiet tones they had been using.

Then a full-out commotion broke out.

Johnny went to investigate, shutting the door behind him.

I lay down on the bed. *Now what?* There were too many familiar voices talking all at once, and my head hurt too much to try to sort through them. I was so tired.

Johnny will take care of it.

Footsteps were soft on the stairs, then people passed my door. It seemed they went into Beverley's room. *Beverley?* I wanted to rush to my foster daughter's room, but doubted if I was physically capable of even crawling from my room. That's why Johnny had gone.

They brought her back to me. The thought filled my weary heart with encouragement. I smiled to myself knowing I'd see her in the morning.

Long moments later, the footsteps returned to the upper hall and my door opened.

Menessos!

I sat up as he entered. Johnny followed right behind him and shut the door.

"Beverley's here?"

Johnny nodded and came to sit on the edge of the bed. The vampire lingered just a few steps inside my room, however.

"She is here because I am here. When I leave, she must come with me."

I nodded, grateful just for her being in my home. I smiled at Johnny. Something was worrying him. There were tense lines at the corners of his eyes. *He has a son.* There were so many questions in my mind, but now wasn't the time. All I knew was that even though Beverley was not my flesh and blood, I cared for her. I was responsible for her. It put me at ease just knowing she was here.

He must be elated about being a father, yet fearful. A child of the Domn Lup would be in danger, just as Beverley had been because of me.

I vowed to myself that whatever the story was with his son, I would handle it.

Fate had put children into our lives. As I looked into his eyes, I knew that no matter what, we would keep fighting this fight to achieve our destiny. We both had so much to fight *for*.

But what about Menessos? He's lost so much. For thousands of years, he's lost so many loved ones, so much of himself . . .

I patted the other side of the bed. "Come and sit with us."

Menessos obeyed. I reached for his hand, and he scooted nearer on the bed so we could touch. He'd saved Beverley's life tonight. And Johnny had saved mine. I grasped Johnny's hand also.

We three were alone.

The silence was, for once, a comfort and not full of tension.

Menessos and I had been through a great deal tonight that Johnny knew nothing about. And Johnny and I had endured another round of danger that Menessos had not yet been told of. As I spent a moment studying each of them, I was sure they had also suffered situations this night that I was oblivious to.

I understood their weariness. I understood the invisible weight pressing endlessly on their shoulders. I understood the pain in their eyes, pain that had nothing to do with physical aches. I understood because I bore it, too.

We were all here together. We didn't need to speak.

I squeezed their hands.

EPILOGUE

Right after brunch late Thursday morning, Johnny showed up with a baby pterodactyl—he claimed it was just an enormous turkey, but I had my doubts.

Since my predawn soak in the tub yesterday had ended with me so sleepy that I couldn't keep my eyes open, he had tucked me in and snuggled beside me—but he was gone when I awoke. He'd left me a note saying that he was having his son brought to Cleveland and he had to be there when the boy and his grandmother arrived. I understood that, and my heart was a bit relieved that the grandmother and not the mother was coming with the boy. But it meant that we spent a day and a night apart, and we hadn't gotten to talk.

We had so much to talk about.

I could tell by the glint in his eyes that he wanted to talk to me now, but Nana got her granny panties in a twist over that giant bird we had to roast.

She began arguing with him about who was going to cook. I nearly left the room twice, but finally they settled their mock dispute—and then started debating whether or not it was possible to cook a partially frozen turkey. The Internet confirmed it was safe and doable, but would add 50 percent more time to the already interminable five hours the twenty-three pounder would take. Once they had gauged the seven and a half hours and decided they needed to get that thing in the oven pronto, I asked if they were going to stuff it.

Bad move on my part.

Their lighthearted fight turned into some kind of Iron Chef stuffing challenge. When they began disagreeing on whether it was "dressing" or "stuffing," I left.

As I climbed the steps to the second floor, I was confident that no matter what, our Thanksgiving dinner was going to be a scrumptious feast. I showered, then returned to my unmade bed and lay down wrapped in my towel. My whole body remained sore and I was at my limit of ibuprofen tabs. Admittedly, when Mountain had come to patch the hole in the floor yesterday, I shouldn't have insisted on helping. I thought it would help work my muscles out of being tight and achy.

That hadn't been the case.

My body was taxed to its limit by my meditation incident, and by the added strain of all that Menessos had done. When my eyes shut, my thoughts swirled around Beverley. My heart fretted over that "L" word, a boy, and where his mother might be. And my soul worried that Hades wasn't done with me yet.

When everything in the kitchen was under control, Johnny inspected the damage to the house. Mountain had gotten everything patched or repaired except the old rotary phone. Its place on the wall was empty, the cords duct-taped into the hole in the wall.

Demeter dug out a tablecloth and hand washed it in the sink, then threw it in the dryer. While she was waiting on it, Johnny heard her talking to Eris on the phone.

It was clear that Eris was inviting herself and her son—Red's half brother, Lance—to Thanksgiving dinner. Demeter couldn't exactly say no, even when she heard Lance's protests in the background.

When the call ended, Demeter came to Johnny. "I take it your wolf ears heard that?"

"Yup. I'll see what I can do about fixing the dinette table."

"Me, you, and Persephone are three, Eris and Lance make five. Mountain and Zhan make seven. The big dining room set will seat twelve if we pull out all the leaves."

"My son and his grandmother are coming."

"That's nine."

"Gregor is driving them."

"Ten."

"I invited Celia and Erik."

"That's twelve. Four wærewolves. No wonder you brought an ostrich to roast."

"It's just a big turkey. I swear." Johnny sucked in a breath. "I also invited Menessos."

She nodded approval, then abruptly waved him off. "He won't eat."

"He will bring Beverley."

Demeter's face lit up with a grin.

By seven thirty, my world was locked in a blissful moment. I sat at the end of my big dining table and could see into the living room and the kitchen with a turn of my head.

Everyone I cared for most was here, in my home, with full bellies.

Johnny and Erik were laughing it up in the living room with Celia and Gregor close by. Nana and Toni— with Evan sitting close beside her, petting my dog, Ares—were on the couch chatting like old friends. In the kitchen, Menessos had a serious look on his face; he must have been briefing Mountain and Zhan. My mother and half brother were whispering at the far end of the table. Beverley was on my lap and I had my arms wrapped around her.

Her dark hair had been cut into a bob and there was a new necklace around her throat. I had thought, at first, that it was a weave of ribbons, but I now recognized that it was strands of her deep brown hair woven with the paler walnut-brown strands from Menessos and also some blond, which I would guess was Risqué's. Hair of a demon, or a half-demon, had to pack some power. . . . I was sure it was a means to help her control the power brimming inside her, but I couldn't help remembering the shabbubitu's words about Beverley being bound to the vampire. And Menessos *was* wearing a necklace of the same around his throat.

Eris announced she was going out for a smoke, and Lance accompanied her into the garage.

"I missed you so much," I whispered into Beverley's ear and squeezed her tighter, pulling her head under my chin. "And I was so worried about you."

She hugged me back. When she eased back into place, I saw her eyes were glassy with unshed tears. "What is it?" I asked.

"I'm just so scared . . . like my mom was. I'm scared of what I've become."

"Oh, honey." I smoothed her hair and kissed her

forehead. "All this Lustrata stuff scares me, too." I offered her my most reassuring smile. "But we will find a way. Together."

Minutes later, she slipped away from me and went to stand with Menessos. She slipped her hand into his and whispered something to him.

Movement on the other side of me caught my attention. Evan was slowly walking toward Johnny. Ares followed him. I got up and stepped to the doorway of the living room to watch. I'd been introduced to the boy, who was the spitting image of Johnny. He was polite, but there was an all-boy orneriness in his smile. Nana would probably have said he was full of piss and vinegar. But Ares clearly liked him, and that meant something to me.

Johnny wrapped his arm around the boy and gently pulled him closer. "Evan, did I tell you that Erik here is my very best friend?"

Evan shook his head. "No."

I noticed that Erik had proudly squared his shoulders. Beverley stepped up beside me and I felt Menessos at my back.

"Well, he is. We've been friends a long, long time. Who's your best friend?"

Nana and Toni quieted, both listening.

Evan shrugged. His voice sounded small and dejected as he said, "I dunno. Gramma said we were moving here. I won't get to see my friends anymore."

Johnny's smile diminished.

The joyful ambience of the room dropped into sadness.

"I'll be your friend," Beverley said, stepping into the living room.

Evan looked her up and down, and a slow smile came to his lips. "Really?"

In moments, they had decided to play. "Can I show him my room?" Beverley asked, facing me and Menessos.

"Yes," we said in unison.

The kids hurried up the stairs.

It was remarkable, and I was reminded that in youth, friendship really is that simple.

Johnny came to the doorway and extended his hand to Menessos as a lopsided smile rounded his cheek. "Thanks for comin', vamp."

"Your invitation was an unanticipated show of charity, wolf."

I grabbed their clasped hands in both of mine. I let them see in my eyes what this moment, what everyone together, but *especially* them, meant to me.

"It wasn't charity," he began, pausing briefly when we heard the garage door open and shut as Eris and Lance returned. "Sometimes blood and breeding aligns you with people you are glad to have in your life, and it's easy to honor those bonds. Sometimes it's the opposite."

"Sometimes Fate aligns you with people you don't want in your life," Menessos added, the obvious question conveyed in his tone.

Between my hands, I felt Johnny's grip tighten on Menessos.

"Sometimes we have to grow up and accept what Fate has in store for us, and put our faith in the alliances we are given."

Thinking on my recent experiences, I whispered, "All Hell is about to break loose. Are we ready for this?"

"We all now know"—Menessos paused to make a poignant glance at the people in the living room, and give a nod to indicate the kiddos upstairs—"precisely what we are fighting *for*." He added his free hand atop mine.

Johnny put his free hand atop Menessos's. With a wink at me, I knew he'd heard me earlier when his response was, "We will find a way. Together."

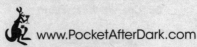

More bestselling
URBAN FANTASY
from Pocket Books!

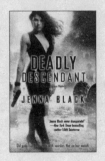